ROAR

VOLUME 9
RESISTANCE

Edited by Mary E. Lowd

Bad Dog Books

2018

ROAR Volume 9
First publication 2018

Edited by Mary E. Lowd

Cover by Kadath
Copyright © 2018

Published by Bad Dog Books
www . baddogbooks . com

BAD
DOG
BOOKS

TABLE OF CONTENTS

For the resistance.

FOREWORD

Resistance is personal. Resistance is exhausting (so take care of yourself). And the children shall lead. These are the themes that emerged to me from the stories you hold in your hands. There are a lot of ways to look at the resistance, a lot of different angles an author can take.

In this year's slush pile, I received—once again—a higher average quality of stories than I've received any previous year. Yes, the quality of writing in the furry fandom just keeps going up! Each year, the stories that I don't accept become better and better, and I'm always delighted to see them find homes in other furry anthologies. (So you should read other furry anthologies too!)

When I sat down to sift through all the submissions I'd read this year and find the anthology hidden within them, I realized I was going to be learning more about my own priorities and vision when it comes to resistance than anything else. Last year, the stories I received taught me about what paradise means. But this year, I had to choose from many perspectives on resistance and many exceptional stories in order to assemble the vision of resistance you will find here, expressed through the voices of fifteen amazing authors.

Here are the lessons I learned about resistance from editing this anthology—it is always personal, because each person will experience the slings and arrows of oppression personally, oftentimes internally; life goes on, and so you must care for yourself and find the gems of goodness that keep you going as you resist; and as we get older and more tired, more used to the injustices of the world and more weary of the possibility of ever changing them, there is hope in the children who haven't given up yet, for whom the unfairness of this world is still fresh, still changeable.

And yet, in spite of all that, at the end of the day, this is just a collection of stories, and I tried to pick stories I enjoyed, stories that I hope you, dear reader, will enjoy.

Take a break, take care of yourself, enjoy these stories, and when you're refreshed, continue to resist.

-Mary E. Lowd

Resistance begins with a surge of magic.

SAGUAROS

Watts Martin

When the walkway stones sang to announce Tamiisi's return, lanterns flaring to brighten the path ahead of her paws, the mansion's door barely had time to lift out of the way before Hanai marched onto the porch. The relief visible in her eyes yielded quickly to annoyance. "Tamiisi! Do you—"

"I'm sorry I'm late, Miss Hanai. The checkpoints are running slow tonight. Something must have happened." Even though the small sled she pulled floated frictionlessly behind her, her breath came quickly, shallow with nerves.

The coyote woman frowned, leaning down to lift the rabbit's right paw, to check the glowing strap encircling her wrist. In Hanai's presence, it pulsed a familiar warm color sequence. "This didn't let you right through?"

"Not tonight, ma'am. I'm very sorry."

She let go, straightening to her full, imposing height. "Nothing to apologize for on your part, and nothing to be done for it either way." She shook her head, motioning the maid to follow back inside. "Yes. Something's happened."

Nudging the sled along the walk, the rabbit circled the tall thorn-tree in the center of the yard, then made her way up into the house, guiding her floating payload away from the fragile vases decorating Hanai's foyer. "Do you know what?"

"Yes." She sounded tired. "And so do you."

"More Collapse? But it's not anywhere near *here*, is it? And it's not as if double- and triple-checking…" She trailed off as the coyote's ears went back.

15

"As if it helps?" Hanai kept her voice level.

"I mean no offense, ma'am. But I just don't see how it does."

"It's checking the magic, Tamiisi. And the Collapse is *very* near here. Just three blocks east."

"Oh."

"The Cultivation is—" She took a deep breath. "It's holding. But I've never heard of Collapse like this. Do you remember Toljee? His estate's across the park from the market with the beautiful fish you found just this summer. It's all...gone. Just gone."

She'd seen the guards closing the roads she used to travel down, but nothing beyond them. "What happened to Mister Toljee?"

"His son took him in. But he's lost everything."

"What about his servants?"

Hanai looked nonplussed, then disquietingly lost. "I don't know," she said softly.

Tamiisi nodded, biting her lip. "Have you...have you seen it? The Wild?"

"Only from as far away as possible." The coyote cocked her head, eyes narrowing as she looked down at the rabbit. "Have you had dreams?"

Tamiisi's voice didn't hide her puzzlement. "Dreams?"

"Of the Wild. Nightmares of the Horned."

"I..." She looked away, out the window. "Not since I was very young, ma'am."

"I have, little one. I have." She set her jaw, then lowered her voice to a confessional whisper. "I'm worried we're failing."

"Coyote magic is strong."

Hanai sighed, a thin hissing noise. "I wish I could be as sanguine as that. But yes. It is." She lifted an arm and brushed her paw through the air, claw tips leaving a trail of shimmering golden butterflies, then smiled, reassured. "Put the groceries away and start on dinner."

"Yes, ma'am."

***

Coyote magic is strong, coyote magic is strong. Hanai said it so often. Others said it so often. Even Tamiisi had said it, never struck before now by the sheen of desperate reassurance. But tonight, the words were just the butterflies that followed her into the kitchen: incongruous bright spots against plain stone and wood. Here, like her room in the servants' quarters, lanterns lit only when someone struck a match to a gas-soaked wick. (She was Hanai's sole servant now. When she tried to talk to the mistress about the butler who had vanished in the first nights of Collapse, she was nearly dismissed. Being left not just homeless but, given Hanai's connections, unemployable, terrified her as much as the Wild did. She suspected, though, that Hanai would never let her go: the coyote, widowed and childless, had her own terror: that of being truly alone.) Batting in irritation at a butterfly that hadn't yet dissipated, she maneuvered the sled toward the pantry and set to work.

She'd done this enough, prepared this very meal enough, that the motions had become automatic. But tonight, worry gnawed at her, tripping her paws, forcing her to pay closer attention. For tonight, Tamiisi had lied.

Each of the last three nights, she'd had nightmares. She had dreamt of monsters. *The* monsters, the Horned Ones. The creatures the coyotes had wrested part of the Wild from, keeping them at bay, casting light over darkness, wonder over fear. Hanai's people had given the timid rabbits safety, and homes, and purpose. They were under no illusion it was an equal bargain, but they had always believed—well, she had always believed—it was a fair one.

So why the dreams? Why now? When she awoke, she could barely remember the shape of the monsters, the shape of the wilderness. Tall beings with tall antlers, neither deer nor elk. Even taller cacti, proud and spiked, standing watch over the high desert. Uncultivated, yes—but dangerous? Wild? She couldn't remember. Had there been fire? Music? Dance? All she knew for sure was that she was just as unsettled as the coyote. *You should have told her*, she chided herself. But sharing the dreams with Hanai would only make her worried, or angry, or both.

After she had rubbed the spices deep into the tenderloin, spread the vegetables and meat across the comal, slid it into the earthen oven over the smoldering charcoal, Tamiisi washed her paws repeatedly. She used more soap than Hanai would approve of, too, but the mistress never noticed, and the cedar scent covered most of the meat-stink left in her fur.

As she rinsed off, she saw the wrist strap had stopped glowing.

No rabbit knew what the straps were made of, and no coyote would tell; Tamiisi doubted most of them knew, either. In lieu of the truth, rabbits shared whimsical, cynical theories amongst themselves: they were pure light, or enchanted water, or cold liquid glass—or coyote teeth that would bite off their paws if they misbehaved.

But now, for the first time, she saw a strap, her strap, without that beautiful, softly shifting glow. Now, it was just a strand of twine. Dirty, frayed twine, not even tied off very neatly.

She ran a finger across it. Before, it had been pliable, stretching over her paw to snug against her wrist when she let it go, soft yet unbreakable.

Now it felt like twine, too. Frowning, she tugged at it gently. It wouldn't go back over her wrist without untying it.

Panic began to rise in her chest. Instead of the strap the employed rabbits always wore, she just had a worthless, dirty string. This wasn't her fault! The enchantment, the magic, it had just—

Her breath caught. Not here. Yes, Hanai had said a mere three blocks away, but that was—that was downhill. That wasn't *this* neighborhood. No, no, it had to come back! She shook her wrist, flinging the ragged string about. "Glow," she whispered at it furiously. "Damn you, glow!"

Nothing happened. Squeezing her eyes shut, clenching her paws into fists, she shrieked. "*Glow!*" The shriek threatened to end in a sob, and she stood still, cradling her wrist, breath coming in gulps.

"Tamiisi?"

She jumped back, eyes flying open at Hanai's voice.

The coyote stood in the kitchen entrance, hands on her hips, expression balanced between irritation and concern. "Did you just scream? Are you all right?"

"I—I—" She looked down at the strap, and her eyes widened. It had returned to shimmering life, colors slipping and melting along its once again mysterious material. "I b-burned myself, ma'am. It's nothing serious, though. I didn't mean to startle you."

"Burned?" The coyote stepped forward, reaching out with a large paw. "Let me see if it needs a quick heal—"

"No, no, I think it's fine. I mean it will be. It j-just startled me. Thank you, ma'am."

Hanai frowned. "All right," she said shortly. "Do be careful."

The rabbit shifted on her paws uncomfortably. "I will, ma'am."

After Hanai had left, Tamiisi breathed out a long, silent sigh, then hesitantly touched a finger to the strap once more. It felt the way it should, but now she could see it no longer looked the same. The colors had shifted. It showed far more purple than before, almost the same shade as the rabbit's eyes. It was her favorite color, but she doubted it would get her through the right checkpoints. She'd have to work up the courage to ask the mistress to fix it.

But how? She couldn't tell her what had just happened. Not only would it worry her, if not enrage her, Tamiisi didn't *know* what had just happened. If it had been the first glimmer of Collapse reaching here, of the Wild threatening to overwhelm this sanctuary, it wouldn't have reverted to normal—yes, all right, close to normal—so quickly.

She remembered her earlier moment of doubt in coyote magic, and paused again. No, that wasn't merely foolish, it was absurd. She wasn't

18

a pipe the magic flowed through, a valve she could shut off like gas to a lantern. Even if coyote magic wasn't as strong as coyotes told themselves, a rabbit's bitter passing thought would hardly…

Her nose wiggled. The meat was done, maybe even a touch past the point Hanai liked it. Thankful for the distraction, Tamiisi hurried to finish preparing dinner.

After setting the mistress's customary place, filling her wine glass and bringing both steaming plates to the table, Tamiisi rang the summoning bell and started back to the kitchen to prepare leftover vegetables for her own meal.

However, when the coyote entered, she threw things into disarray once more just by speaking her name. "Tamiisi."

"Ma'am?"

"Stay with me a moment."

Hiding a nervous swallow, the rabbit nodded, moving to stand by the table as the coyote dropped into her chair. Seated, Hanai's ear tips just reached Tamiisi's eye level. "Can I help you with something else, ma'am?"

"I don't know. Perhaps." Hanai looked across the dining room, out through the glass wall. "Has anything…changed?"

Tamiisi stepped toward the wall. The neighborhood lanterns were first to meet her eyes, fixed lamps glittering from lawns and porches and thorn-trees, floating lamps trailing behind or in front of unseen travelers. As her eyes adjusted, she could trace the lines of sidewalks and carriageways, see the pennants atop the highest tents of the Great Market. Sky-fish flitted through the air, over and under the stone bridges, leaping to touch the rare flying sled. If she remained perfectly still, listened ever so closely, she could hear the clockwork birds twittering in faint harmonies as they returned to the park to roost for the night.

At length, she turned and shook her head. "It looks the same as ever."

The coyote stared past her searchingly for long seconds, then shook her own head, sighing. "Never mind." She waved her hand dismissively, then looked down at her plate, speaking more softly. "Go get your own meal."

"Thank you, ma'am."

As she walked past the table, Hanai caught her wrist.

Tamiisi looked back in surprise, then caught her breath. The coyote's gaze had locked onto the wrist band. "The colors."

"Ma'am?"

"They're wrong. The colors are wrong!" She looked up, horror in her eyes. "When did this happen?"

"I—"

At once she was on her paws, towering over the rabbit. "*When?*"

"I don't know!" Tamiisi squeaked. "I-I-It must have changed in the kitchen!"

Hanai turned back to the window, gaze darting among the lanterns, then whirled down on the rabbit. "Why didn't you tell me? You *know* you have to tell me!"

"I didn't see, ma'am! I didn't know something was wrong with the magic!"

Hanai snarled, yanking her hand away hard enough to knock the rabbit off balance. "*Nothing is wrong with the magic!*"

"I'm sorry!" Tamiisi stumbled back, covering her head with her paws, covering the horrid purple blotches across the strap. "I didn't mean—I know coyote—"

For a sharp, quick, dizzying moment the world spun around her. It spun into her dream, the figures and shapes now as clear as a cold full moon. As the vision faded, the words froze in her throat.

Hanai had her paws to her head. "The Controllers' Office. That's who to call. They'll know what do. They can fix this." She thrust a finger at the rabbit. "Stay right here. Don't twitch a whisker." She stepped back and waved her other hand, calling a shimmering window into being in midair.

In a few seconds, a coyote at the Controllers' Office would appear, and then—what? What would "fix" this? The strap wasn't broken. *She* was! She had to run—she had to—had to—

"No!" Tamiisi leapt up and pulled at the window, scrabbling with both hands. It tipped like a bowl set too close to the edge of a shelf, then fell to the ground, shattering into shards of foggy glass.

Hanai's muzzle dropped open. She shrank back a step, then another.

"I'm sorry!" The rabbit brought her hands up in front of her face. "I'm sorry, Miss Hanai—I—" Then she lowered her hands again slowly, staring at the wrist strap once more. It glowed solid purple. *Her* purple.

She touched it, thinking of a blue sky. The color changed to match. Another touch, and it returned to a shifting rainbow. Then she thought of the dream, of the horned figures dancing, holding out their paws to her. Back to purple, now as brilliant as a lantern flame.

"It's *not* coyote magic, is it?" Tamiisi whispered, looking up at the older woman's frightened eyes. "It never was."

"Stop being a fool." The coyote gathered herself up, pointing outside at the glittering panorama, leaning forward to loom over the rabbit. "It's all that protects you from what's out there!"

"No. What's out there is…us."

Hanai stiffened, dropping her arm, then opened her mouth to protest. "Before we—"

"No!" Suddenly Tamiisi felt rage boiling over, felt dizzy with anger, light-headed with pain. "No more stories! You're all so very good at stories."

The coyote's voice rose again, cracking in fear. "For all the stars' sake, Tamiisi, they aren't just stories!"

"Yes, Miss Hanai. They are." Tamiisi stared accusingly, then sagged, hit with one last realization she hadn't wanted. "You…don't know, do you? You've heard the stories so long that you believe them, too. But the stories are to protect *you*. Not us. You know the truth in your heart. The truth in the dreams."

"Nightmares!"

Tamiisi didn't answer. She turned to look outside.

Hanai turned, too, trembling. The lanterns had faded; the faint mechanical music had fallen silent. The light outside had become only the stars and moon. She let out a low whimper. "What are you doing, Tamiisi? Please. Stop."

"We are," she said softly.

The whimper became a frenzied snarl, and she leapt for the rabbit, claws forward, teeth bared and glittering. Tamiisi spun about just before Hanai slammed into her—

—and the coyote's eyes widened in abrupt, pained shock. She stared down at the sharp antlers impaling her shoulders, her side.

Tamiisi jerked back, her points pulling free, eyes as wide as the coyote's as she watched her mistress sink to the ground, gasping in pain, eyes squeezing shut against the gathering violet light.

When the coyote felt the smaller—was she still smaller?—woman's hand on her uninjured shoulder, she curled into a ball, barely hearing the last gently spoken words. "Find another story, Hanai. Find *your* story. This one has always been ours."

***

Hanai didn't uncurl until she felt an unfamiliar breeze through her fur. She lifted her head warily.

The shards from the broken window were gone. Her carved wooden furniture, her exquisite lanterns, her lovely intricate tiled floor, her colorful woven wall-hangings, all gone. Nothing remained to her but dirt and dry twigs and pebbles—and a strand of dirty twine.

Crawling forward, she moved toward the brightest light she saw, toward the wind, toward the distant sound of plaintive howls. She pulled herself out of the hole, a mere den scrabbled from the earth, then fell back against its side with a soft moan.

The landscape she'd known all her life remained, but nothing else did. No lanterns, only starlight. The shimmering, singing stone walkways had become only sandy paths. Where dazzling homes had sprawled, pathetic little piles of rock mounded in front of other sad dens. Where the magnificent, imposing thorn-trees had stood now rose dark, foreboding saguaros.

She put her hand to her shoulder, to the fur matted with blood. "Tamiisi," she called, barely above a whisper. Then, more loudly: "Tamiisi. Please."

Only the wind answered.

Hanai lifted up her hand, stretching out her arm. She spread her fingers apart, brushing them shakily through the air, again and again. Surely, the butterflies would come.

A nerdy cat delivering pizza has hopes for her future but is haunted by her past.

Ghosts

Searska GreyRaven

The street lights were just flicking on as I walked up the sidewalk toward a dimly lit industrial building. Well, dimly lit for a human. My feline eyes had no problem with it. I reached the entrance and hesitated, one paw clutching a thermal bag while the other hovered over a faintly glowing doorbell. I tried to take a slow, even breath. It came in ragged and left even worse. Damn it, I had it bad. Cats are supposed to be *aloof*.

I was anything but aloof.

You can do this, Cal. Breathe. Just ask her. The worst she can do is say no, right?

One hand-tossed anchovy and mushroom pizza, which is also how I like my pizza, and maybe sometime, if you're available and you, you know, swing my way, we could split one together?

Even in my head, that sounded lame.

"God, I'm bad at this," I muttered. My breath fogged the air, reminding me that the pizza in my arm wasn't getting any warmer and I needed to quit stalling.

I tapped the buzzer.

A speaker near the door flicked on. "Hello?"

My heart skipped a beat. It was *her.* I mean, I knew it was probably going to be her, but another guy, a human, would sometimes answer the bell. But there were always two pizzas when that happened. Just one pizza tonight.

"Fantasma Pizza delivery," I announced brightly.

"Oh awesome. I'll be right down." The speaker clicked off.

I waited a few minutes in silence, trying to slow my heart to a reasonable speed. My ears flattened anxiously and it was a struggle to get them to stand back upright. From the other side of the door came the stutter of footsteps and a sudden metallic clatter. The door knob twisted and suddenly, there she was. The most beautiful neko-form I'd ever seen. Sleek black fur covered her from head to toe, her whiskers were long and bowed, and her tail was long and tipped with only a small patch of white.

I stood straighter and held out the box I was carrying. A pair of green eyes studied me and my box for a moment, glittering hungrily. She took the box between her paws, claws scraping the cardboard, and grinned. Her lab coat fluttered as she shifted the box to one hand so she could reach into her pocket. *Her paw pads are pink. Perfect seashell pink.* They looked chafed, though. I wondered if it was just winter, or maybe whatever her current lab project was making her paw pads chap like that.

"That was really fast. You're quicker than the sub place!" she said, pulling a pen from her pocket as well as a few carefully folded bills.

Her lab coat rustled closed, sending a zephyr of scent across my nose. Gods, she smelled like coconut and honey and something else. Jojoba? I swallowed back the urge to inhale deeper. Not polite to flehman at customers, no matter how lovely they smell. My hands clenched as I resisted the urge to smooth my fur. There was nothing sleek or sinuous about me. I was all wiry limbs, scruffy pale fur, and mis-matched eyes. I barely passed as feminine most days. It didn't help that, as a neko-form, I lacked a few of the very obvious characteristics of a human female, like breasts. Don't ask me why. I'm a pizza delivery girl, not a geneticist.

Say something, Cal! She's talking to you!

"It, uhh, it was a slow night," I replied lamely. So lame. I am *so lame.*

"I didn't think pizza places had slow Friday nights," she said, sounding amused. That feline grin widened and I swallowed. My heart was making a fantastic effort to pound straight through my ribs.

"We, ahh, also prioritize regulars," I lied.

She laughed. She had a wonderful laugh. Jellicle cats, as a certain T. S. Eliot said, are merry and bright, and she was no exception. "I appreciate it. My experiments are at a critical stage, and I can't leave. And I can't leave Michael alone too long with my work. He's a good test-tube jockey, but he's no scientist."

She scribbled a signature on the receipt slip and handed it back to me, along with tip money. The scrawling signature was almost illegible, but I knew who she was. Deanne Novak, scientist, inventor, and, I suspected, half angel. No mere mortal had eyes like that. Even for a jellicle, she had striking eyes. "Michael? Fellow scientist?" I asked. "Intern? Boyfriend?" I mentally kicked myself. *Smooth, Cal, real smooth.*

She snorted. "Intern. Definitely professional only. Ugh, no, I couldn't stand to date him. I mean, I eat my share of junk food, but he seems to *thrive* on it. Disgusting. But as long as he keeps his chicken nuggets off my experiments, I can put up with him." She sighed, and her ebon tail flicked smartly, just once, behind her. "Just a little longer. His internship ends in a couple of weeks and I won't have to smell his greasy leftovers again."

"Just, uh, what do you study in there?" I asked, trying to peek around her and into the lab.

She blocked my view, arm bracing against the door frame and her ears backed. "It's really technical. I wouldn't expect—I mean, not that you're stupid, but—it's just very complicated and...umm, I'm sure you've got other deliveries to make."

For the first time since I'd first met her three weeks ago, I felt a crack in my hopelessly lovesick crush. I twisted my expression into something I hoped looked polite. "We can't all be scientists," I replied. "Or ghost hunters."

She blinked and frowned. "Wait, how do you know about—"

I gestured with my now-empty hot bag to the mailbox next to the door, where the latest *Ghost Hunting Monthly* was half-falling out.

"Just out of curiosity, if a ghost has unfinished business that can't be finished—"

"That isn't what we do here," she insisted defensively. "That's...that's not even *mine*, I swear. Michael and his juvenile obsession! It's not even real science. Definitely *not* real science."

I shrugged and tried to make it look nonchalant. But my tail was thrashing, my ears were backed, and I could feel the fur along my spine standing at full attention. "Sure. Whatever. I'm just a pizza delivery girl. What do I know about particle physics and alternate dimensions? Enjoy the pizza."

I left without another word. My heart had stopped racing and settled into my chest like a caged bird that had lost the will to sing. *Never crush on customers. It's a rule, and a damned good one. You're just a delivery girl, some rand-o chick. A means to an end, not the kind of person someone like her dates, even if she swung that way. Someone that perfect? Gotta be straight. Or maybe indifferent. You're growling down the wrong hole, Cal. Probably better you learn now rather than later.*

My rear-view mirror shivered, and it wasn't because the roads were rough. Through the static of my radio, I could hear a low chuckle.

I snarled and turned my radio off.

***

A week passed before Fantasma Pizzeria got another order from Ms. Novak. Sanchez, the owner, was in the kitchen, throwing pizza dough into the air and spinning it while Lilu took calls.

"Large anchovy and mushroom for You Know Who at You Know Where. Ross, you finished eating yet?" she asked. Her enamel bracelets clattered and jingled as she set the phone down on the counter. Pure human, with dark hair and darker eyes, she looked like a smaller version of her uncle, Sanchez. Well, smaller and female. Same solid, stocky build, same warm smile. She liked her pizza with hot peppers and sausage, with the crust so thin it was almost an afterthought. Part taco, part pizza, the best of both worlds, she'd said.

I sighed. "I got it. Ross will get lost. That complex is a maze."

"Rats are good at mazes!" Ross hollered from the break room down the hall. "And besides, I wanna meet the chick you been moonin' over."

"Shut it, Wormtail," I muttered. "I ain't moonin'. I'm over it." Ross had always been a bit of an asshole, but ever since he'd found out that I wasn't exactly straight, he'd become truly insufferable. But it was always this side of a firing offense, and Sanchez didn't have a backup driver, so Ross had stuck around. I wasn't exactly swimming in options either, so I hadn't left.

Besides, I was here first, damn it.

"Sure, sure," he said, coming into view and jamming a mouthful of olive and onion pizza into his maw. The crust was so floppy that he had to fold it over to eat it. He licked his greasy fingers, then smoothed the dishwater-colored fur on his head. "Maybe she's looking for a little one-on-one with a *real* man." He winked at me.

I scowled back at him.

"Don't cats *eat* mice?" Lilu commented.

Ross snickered. "If I'm lucky."

I glared at him. This was worse than usual. Then, I smelled it: the stale stink of alcohol on his breath. Either he was hung over or had a beer before his shift. With all the other scents in the pizzeria, Sanchez and Lilu wouldn't have noticed. I couldn't let him drive like this.

"I got it," I said. "I already know the way and Ross is still on break."

It was Ross's turn to scowl. "You're wasting your time, kitty cat."

I zipped up my jacket and reached for my keys. "Hope springs eternal. We've got the same taste in pizza, so that's something."

Ross's eyes narrowed. "That's assuming she's even your type," he snickered. "Poor Cal, falling in love with a straight girl."

"Shut. Up."

"Ross, you shut your hole, or I let her take you apart," Lilu warned.

"You know," he slurred, "I always wanted to ask, is it a cat thing or a lesbian thing, liking fish on a pie?"

Lilu and I stared at Ross, stunned.

Lilu recovered first. "Ross! Line, crossed. Apologize, *right now* or so help me—"

"Pfft, right. What's Caliban gonna do? Sic her ghosts on me?"

I didn't even realize I had moved. Ross was suddenly pinned to the wall in front of me, his faded Fantasma polo collar bunched between my fists, limp pizza splattered across the floor, and his naked tail writhing against my legs. The stink of alcohol gagged me, but I didn't let go.

"What did you say?" I snarled. Ross flailed, knocking the yellow-tinted glasses I wore to hide my odd-colored eyes off my face.

"God *damn it*, Cal, drop him. Ross, you apologize. Now!" Sanchez said, stepping out of the kitchen. I dropped Ross and he hit the floor with a thud.

"I'm sorry," Ross sneered, "that you're a freak."

"Sanchez, he's drunk," I said flatly. I wanted to find my glasses, but I'd heard them shatter. Wherever they were, they wouldn't be doing me any good now.

"You *lying* little b—"

Sanchez didn't give Ross a chance to finish. The grizzled pizzaiolo simply picked Ross up by his collar and threw him out the front door.

"I'm calling a cab, not because I give one tin shit what happens to you, but because I don't want you driving drunk and killing someone. You show your face here again, I take it off. We clear?" he said.

I don't know if Ross replied. The blood roaring in my ears was too loud. After a moment, I realized it wasn't just my blood pounding. I was growling.

Sanchez came back in, calm as ice, and shut the door quietly behind him. "Cal, are you alright? I'd've got out here sooner, but I was—never mind. I shoulda got out here sooner, dough be damned."

I swallowed and nodded. "I'm fine."

Sanchez narrowed his eyes. "You aren't, but I'm short a driver now. I'm sorry, *chica*. I hate to do this, but you're the only driver I got left tonight. You got this?"

I took a deep, shuddering breath and composed myself. "Yeah, I got this."

Sanchez nodded curtly and slipped back into the kitchen. He emerged a few minutes later with a hot bag and handed it to me.

I frowned. "She didn't order cinnamon sticks this time," I said.

"An extra," he replied with a smile. "The way to a girl's heart is through her stomach."

Lilu snorted. "Not just a girl's heart. Didn't Uncle Ray propose to you over a pan of lasagna?"

Sanchez laughed and shrugged. "*Sí*, but everyone proposes to me after eating my lasagna. Ray was the first one worthy of the honor."

I sighed. "Sanchez, this isn't going to work."

He shrugged. "Won't know until you try," he said. "*Chica*, I don't know who broke you, and I don't care. Sooner or later, you gotta pick up those pieces and turn it into something worth fighting for. You can't just drift through life like…a…"

"Like a ghost?" I prompted wryly. I tossed the shattered remains of my glasses in the trash.

Sanchez threw up his hands. "Just deliver the damn pizza."

I fled with the bag and didn't look back.

***

I half expected to see Ross leaning against my rust-bucket of a car, but the rat was nowhere to be found. Clearly, he'd taken Sanchez's warning to heart and vanished. Probably for the best. I would have smashed the pizza over his head. Terrible waste of a perfectly good pizza.

I looked up at the night sky, moonlight trickling through the dead claws of the October trees, and sighed. Everything looked different without my tinted lenses. Clearer. Sharper. I missed how my glasses turned the world into a study in sepia. My breath puffed across my muzzle before ghosting into the darkness.

Ghosting. Ghost.

I grimaced and laid the hot bag on the passenger seat before I buckled in. That hot bag was the only thing that had ever used the passenger seat.

I was so tired of being alone.

"I'm gonna do it," I said to the empty car. "I'm going to ask for her number."

But what about your—

I bared my teeth.

He won't be a problem, I vowed, finger pads slipping on the key in the ignition. I repeated that line to myself all the way to Deanne's lab.

Once again, I stood before Deanne's office door. But this time, I was armed with new courage and a box of cinnamon sticks. I took a deep breath, tapped the buzzer, and squared my shoulders. Even my wayward tail behaved, flicking only once or twice while I waited patiently.

Deanne answered the door a minute later. I could hear claws scrabbling with the lock on the other side, and then she was in front of me, eyes wide and whiskers spread.

She didn't look as perfect this time. Her fur was dusty along her nose, and her lab coat had greenish spatter on it. Instead of coconut, she smelled like ozone.

"Oh. Oh my goodness, I—I'm glad it's you. I wanted to say—I wanted to apologize for my unkind words last time. It was wrong of me and...um." She squinted at me. "You aren't wearing your usual glasses."

I shrugged. "They broke."

Deanne looked at me a moment longer, and I knew from her expression that she'd just noticed my eyes didn't match. I braced myself for the inevitable and waited. *Here it comes, the exclamation about my eyes being different as if I didn't already know, asking if I could really see ghosts. The sudden reluctance to meet my gaze, lest I steal their souls and keep them in jars or something.*

But she didn't say any of it. She met my gaze without fear and smiled. "You have lovely eyes," she said.

I blinked, nonplussed. "Uh, thanks?" *Real articulate, Cal.*

She cleared her throat and looked at the two boxes I pulled out of the hot bag. "I didn't order cinnamon sticks."

"No, but you do from time to time. It sounded like you were under a lot of stress so, uhh. Here," I said, handing the two boxes to her. *God, I'm such an idiot. Sanchez even gave me a perfect setup, and I can't do it.*

Deanne looked at the boxes like she didn't know what to do with them. "I...thank you. Hang on, I have something for you as well." She juggled the boxes for a moment and plucked something from the back pocket of her pants. A slip of paper.

A slip of paper with a series of numbers on it.

"Would you like to get coffee or something some time? I have tomorrow off, if that would work for you too."

I took the slip of paper from her hand and stared at it, utterly and completely dumbstruck. "I...yes. Yes! I have tomorrow off, too." I didn't, but Sanchez would give it to me if I asked. When I asked. I tore off a corner of the slip of paper and scrawled my own number on it, my paw shaking slightly.

What are you thinking? You're going to get her killed!

No, I thought, not this time. This time, it'll be different.

***

31

When I returned to Fantasma Pizzeria, Deanne's number in hand, Sanchez cheered and gestured to Lilu. Lilu rolled her eyes and sent a paper airplane into the kitchen. A paper airplane that looked a lot like a five dollar bill. Sanchez snatched it mid-air.

"Wait, you *took bets* on me? God, I work with a bunch of assholes," I said.

"About time you got your head out your ass," Lilu said. "So, where you gonna take your date?"

"Coffee," I said bluntly. "It's just coffee. Not a date."

"Coffee can be a date," Sanchez hollered from the kitchen.

"It's not a date! She might not even be interested in me *like that*. She might just want someone to talk to about…things. On a related note, Sanchez, I need tomorrow off," I said. "I know you don't have another driver, but—"

Sanchez's throaty laugh echoed from the kitchen.

"I got a nephew, though. He needs the cash and he just got his license. You got your night off, *chica*. Make the most of it!"

***

The next morning, I was a complete and total spaz and turned my tiny studio apartment into a disaster zone. I groomed my fur until it lay soft and sleek, then messed it up again because it just didn't look right. Every single article of clothing I owned was inspected, scrutinized, and discarded. Graphic tees, too nerdy. Plain tee shirts, too boring. Blue jeans, too casual. Cargo pants, too…no. Slacks were too formal, I didn't own a single pair of khakis, and I was *definitely* not showing up in one of my two skirts. An ex of mine had a thing for naughty schoolgirl roleplay and left them when we broke up. They were way too short for a first date. Hell, they were probably too short to wear in public. *Would she like to see me in a skirt, though? I mean, I hate them, but for her, I'd wear one on a date—*

It's not a date! It's just coffee. Everyone does coffee. Friends do coffee all the time.

I took a break and grabbed the snow globe off my desk. It was a cheap prop I'd bought ages ago at a yard sale, something you'd set out for Halloween. Unless you're weird, like me, and consider Halloween decorations a kind of permanent décor. With a flick of my wrist, I sent the black glitter inside swirling. "What do you think, Felix?" I asked the little cat in the globe. "Date, or coffee with a friend?" The cat didn't respond. He never did. Just stood on his little grave mound, mouth open in a hiss and back arched. I sighed, set it down on my desk again, and went back to the closet.

As I rummaged deeper, I heard a thump come from behind me, on my desk. I paused. There it was again, followed by a crash. I jumped back from my closet and skidded to a halt beside my bed.

Sitting in the middle of the floor were the shattered remains of the snow globe. The black cat stared up at me forlornly from the floor, tail and paws broken from the grave mound it once stood upon. Black glitter and fluid oozed across the floor and began to soak into the ragged rug next to my night stand.

"How the hell?" I murmured. Damn it, that had been my favorite snow globe. I'd deliberately set it far back on my desk so it wouldn't get knocked off and broken. How had it ended up over here?

The fur along my spine stood on end. There was no way that snow globe could have simply fallen off my desk. No *mundane* way. I lived alone in a tiny little studio, so there were no roommates to pull pranks on me. I'd never seen a mouse able to throw a snow globe many times its own weight, so it couldn't be that.

I shivered, running my paws across my upper arms, then froze.

No.

No, it's been quiet for weeks. It can't be that!

I whimpered and turned very slowly toward the mirror across from my bed. Panicked breath frosted the tips of my whiskers.

Caliban.

My name, written in blocky red letters, on the inside of the glass.

"Go away," I said, my voice cracking in terror. "You aren't welcome here. You're dead. You can't hurt me anymore!"

Sinful. Disgraceful. No kit of mine.

I shrieked and reached for something, anything to throw at the mirror. My paw landed on something cool and heavy. I gripped and threw, only belatedly realizing what I'd grabbed.

A snow globe. The one that was supposed to be in pieces on the floor. Only it wasn't. It never was.

The snow globe hit the mirror and shattered. The words smeared together like wet ink until they vanished below the edge of the mirror. All that remained were the broken pieces of the snow globe. The mirror was unscathed.

"Gaslighting me, even in death," I croaked. "I must have really pissed you off this time. Good." I bared my fangs at the mirror. "If you're angry, I must be doing something right."

When the mirror remained quiescent, I knew my father's ghost had run out of juice for the day. I cleaned up the mess, tossed the glass shards into the trash, and finished getting ready for my date.

Blue jeans, blue tank top with a Wonder Woman logo, and black Converse Chucks. The finishing touch was my backup pair of amber-tinted sunglasses with silver rims.

I looked at the mirror one last time. It rattled slightly. With a hiss, I fled my apartment.

***

Coffee was at a Rain Deer. There's one on every street corner these days, and I have yet to find a better place to get a sugary drink that in no way resembles real coffee. It's also considered a "safe" place for people like me. Non-human, non-straight, non-conforming, non-whatever. Thankfully, I'd come early enough that most of the tables were still unclaimed. A pair of corvine-forms occupied one table, talking in low voices. One had dyed the feathers along the center of her head bright blue. She looked at me, nodded, and went back to her conversation.

I ordered a blended concoction with coffee, caramel, mocha, and coconut before wandering to the end of the counter to wait. I was early; Deanne was nowhere to be seen. The barista (a lupine-form) finished my drink with a flourish of whipped cream and slid it towards me. I thanked him and found a table by a window.

What if she doesn't come? What if she stands you up?

Well, then Sanchez can find someone else to deliver pizzas to her address. I'll pick up a six pack of hard cider on the way back to my apartment, and by the time I finish it off, I'll be over it. Probably.

And so, I waited.

I finished my drink.

I ordered another one.

I waited some more.

I was halfway through the second one when Deanne arrived, looking flustered. For a moment, I didn't recognize her without her lab coat, but her laugh when the barista flirted with her gave her away. Deanne dug her wallet out of a shoulder bag covered in *Doctor Who*, *Supernatural*, and *Ghostbusters* pins, paid, and stepped to the end of the counter to await her drink. She peeked into her bag, rummaging around, and suddenly looked in my direction.

"Deanne?"

She looked at me blankly for a moment before her expression split into a relieved grin.

"Punctual, I like that," she said, setting her bag down.

"I deliver pizzas," I replied. "It's a hazard of the trade."

"Oh, right, sorry, I…" Her fur sleeked, suddenly making her look much smaller. Something in her bag vibrated loudly, and she swore.

"Stupid thing won't…stop…got it! Sorry, notification from the lab on one of my experiments. I'll just turn this thing off." The buzzing sound abruptly cut off.

I smiled. "It's fine."

"I'll…I'll be right back. I'll be less awkward after coffee, I swear," she said, and retreated back to the counter for her coffee.

She returned a few minutes later with a very large, very dark iced drink.

"Did I hear that right? Are there *six* shots of espresso in there?" I asked.

Deanne nodded. "It's basically a cardiac arrest in a cup. I'm a hopeless addict. So many late night experiments." She settled down into the chair across from me, her bag across her lap.

I gestured to the buttons on the bag. "I take it you're a fan?"

"Of which one?" she said with a laugh. "I stream episodes occasionally while I'm in the lab. So much of my work is the 'hurry up and wait' variety. I'm loving the new regeneration of the Doctor."

I grinned. "Me too," I replied. "The previous one was kind of annoying."

"Oh my goodness, you thought so too? Everyone else seemed so enamored with him. I thought he was such an ass."

We spent an hour just talking about geeky stuff. Not just favorite shows but books, comics, and movies. We nerded out over a mutual love of the new *Star Wars*, debated if Toothless could beat Smaug in a fight, and if Wonder Woman and Conan would be friends or rivals. Before I knew it, it was well after lunchtime.

"Oh crap, I need to head back to the lab. I can't believe we spent the whole morning here!" Deanne said.

"We should do it again sometime," I blurted.

"Any time," Deanne said. "Please. You have no idea. No one at work even knows who Drizzt is. They think I'm discharging static when I say his name."

***

Weeks passed, but I barely noticed. Funny how that happens when you're in love. We went to movies, tried out every sushi restaurant within easy driving distance, and spent one memorable weekend at a sci-fi/comic convention, nerding out in all the best ways.

I prodded Deanne now and again about what she did in her lab, why she had an entire bookcase of paranormal reference books on her shelves, and while Deanne didn't admit outright what she did, she eventually stopped denying it.

"Just don't go telling everyone I'm some kind of ghost buster," Deanne said to me. "Bad enough that paranormal phenomenon get derided as unscientific. I'll lose what little funding I have if there's so much as a whiff of pseudoscience to what I do."

Every time I came home after a date with her, things got worse. I'd walk in to find every cabinet door wide open, contents stacked in unwieldy pillars to the ceiling. Or my mirror smeared with black ichor. My stereo would randomly turn on at full blast with deranged yowling. It was as if the longer my relationship with Deanne went, the stronger and angrier the spectre of my father became.

Soulless. Spiritless. Hollow, sinful little stray, my mirror scrawled at me. The blocky letters faded away after a moment, but the after-image of them was etched in my mind.

I whimpered. What would happened if—when—I moved in with Deanne? Would this ghost follow me?

You have to tell her.

No, I don't. It'll go away. It has to. Sooner or later, my father's damned ghost will realize his unfinished business is never getting finished, and he'll move on.

Denial, thy name is Cal.

By Christmas, I had one harrowing haunting event a day, occasionally two, whether I went out with Deanne or not. I started finding excuses to not go back to my apartment, taking late night shifts or camping out in an internet café. Anything to get me away from that place. I was tempted to spend the night at Deanne's place, but I knew I'd never get any sleep. I'd be too terrified of what I'd wake up to.

"Cal! Order up!"

I startled. "Yes! Right! I heard you!"

"That's the third time I said it. You sure you're alright? You look like crap," Lilu said.

"I'm fine," I grunted. I shoved the pizzas in my hot bag.

"She's not hurting you, is she?" Sanchez asked, leaning over the counter. His usually bronze colored arms were coated in flour all the way to his elbows. Even his eyebrows, furrowed with concern, were dusted with white powder. It took much of the bite out of his threat when he looked like he'd just face-planted into a snow bank.

"No, not—not Deanne. Never Deanne," I said. "Just...having a lot of nightmares lately. Not sleeping well. Is that all for this round?"

Sanchez nodded and pushed back from the counter.

"Whatever's got your tail in a twist, *chica*, I hope it passes. If talking about it will help, you know my door's always open," he said.

I swallowed, and almost broke. I almost spilled the whole story, about the doors slamming, the lights burning out constantly, the way milk would spoil without explanation or the strange skittering noises I'd hear in the walls at night.

Right. Crazy Cal and her crazy ghost stories. Like they'd ever believe me. I'd learned the hard way that the fastest way to lose friends was to tell them the truth about what I saw. What haunted me.

But Deanne. Deanne might. She was still shifty as hell when I'd ask her about what she did in that lab or whenever the topic of the paranormal came up, but maybe...maybe.

"Thanks, Sanchez," I said, then grinned mischievously. "I would, but it's a girl thing and—"

He threw his hands up. "Say no more! I get it! Talk to that lovely lady friend of yours, and best of luck!"

Lilu spat something in Spanish that I didn't catch and finished in English. "My uncle, so brave until women things are involved!"

"It's why I have a boyfriend, *sobrina!*" Sanchez chuckled. Lilu threw a pen at him, and he retreated to the safety of his kitchen.

I finished my shift and spent the drive home doing some hard thinking. I woke up to the mirror in my bathroom iced over and every light bulb burned out. I replaced the bulbs and ignored the mirror.

I'd tell her. And if she didn't believe me, well, I tried. Better to know now, before things got any more serious.

***

I brooded into the evening and through the lovely dinner Deanne had made for us at her apartment. Finally, after half an hour of pushing my salmon listlessly around my plate, Deanne called me out on it.

"You keep scowling like that, and your face will stick that way." She said it gently, her ears backed in concern.

I sighed. "Sorry, just...thinking about things. Rent. Bills. Family things."

"You want to talk about it?" she asked. "It might help."

You need to do this. She deserves to know. I took a deep breath, exhaled, and began to speak. *I can do this. And if she throws me out or laughs, I can walk away knowing I tried.*

"My father was...he wasn't a good person," I began. "He had his moments, and I'm sure he loved me before—before he realized I wasn't like his other kittens. I was sick all the time and barely had the energy to walk, let alone play. But my parents did everything they could to keep me alive, because...because I had different colored eyes."

"Heterochromia," Deanne murmured, backing her ears briefly. "I'd heard that Angora purity cults try to 'breed' for it specifically. I'd... wondered, when I saw your eyes, but I didn't want to pry."

I nodded. "My father was no exception." I took a deep, shuddering breath and continued, "God, it makes me sick to even remember it. My father wanted me to marry a nice Angora neko-form, just like him. Salt-white fur, pale green eyes. He wanted to keep our bloodline pure. Thing is, I have no interest in males, and even less in kittens. As soon as he made it clear what he thought my future should be, I tried to resist. I tried to convince him that I didn't want that. He didn't listen. The fights we had were epic, but I didn't tell him *why* I wanted something else for a future until one day, I finally screamed at him I had no interest at all in toms *like that* and he—" I choked.

Soulless, spiritless, sinful little stray! No kit of mine. Get out! Get out! OUT! His voice howled in my mind, as loud as if he was right there, roaring it into my ear.

"He disowned you," Deanne finished. She came around the breakfast bar and wrapped her arms around me, purring softly.

"He threw me out," I said. "Wouldn't even let me get any of my stuff. I don't know if he thought I'd come crawling back or die in a gutter somewhere. I only knew I couldn't go back. I just...drifted from doorstep to doorstep for weeks. Months. Didn't go back to school, because there suddenly didn't seem to be a point to it. Graduation came and went, and I barely even noticed it. Sanchez found me digging through his dumpster for pizza crusts just as the trees were starting to turn and...I don't know. I don't know why, but he let me inside, let me clean up in the janitor's closet, and he asked questions. Not—not how I ended up like that, just if I could drive, if I knew the neighborhood. I didn't have a car, but I knew most of the major streets by then. He offered to rent me a car, gave me a job as a delivery girl. I got free pizza and a steady paycheck; he got reliable help. I guess he'd had a bad run on hiring drivers." I swiped at the damp under my eyes. I was *not* crying. I refused to. My father had stolen all the tears he ever would from me. "I didn't even know he'd...that my father had passed away until I got a note on Facebook from a high school acquaintance. I looked up the obituaries and there he was. I didn't even care. He's dead, and all I felt when I saw that obit was relief. And then…and then, shit, I felt sick because I *didn't* care, because I *should* care, because he was my father God damn it and…and…*fuck.*" I took a deep, shuddering breath and tried to compose myself. I pressed the back of my paw to my muzzle and squeezed my eyes shut, but it was too late. The tears came anyway. Ugly, wracking sobs that broke the dam I'd built to hold the pain back and left me shaking uncontrollably.

Deanne got up and hugged me. "How long ago was this?" she asked.

"Almost four years since he passed. Next Tuesday, it'll be four years," I said between sobs. "I shouldn't be upset. I shouldn't be so broken up about it. He was an asshole, and he treated me like crap because I wasn't what he wanted, but he was my father and I can't…I don't…it's all so confused. I tried to call my mom, but she never answered her phone." I had tried, several times a day, from the Fantasma landline and later from the cheap cell phone I could afford. After a week of nothing but voicemail, I took the hint. I don't know what I expected. It wasn't like she went looking for me after my father had thrown me out.

Deanne made a soft hushing sound and hugged me tighter. "I know it's only been a few months for us, but if you didn't want to be alone, you could stay here. I don't have a guest room, just a couch, and you'd have to share with The Holtz, but—"

"The what?" I blinked, rubbing the last of the tears from my eyes.

Deanna giggled. "My cat. Sorry, I know you haven't met her yet. She's so shy of new people. Let me see if I can coax her out from under my bed." She scurried off to the bedroom.

"You never told me you had a cat!" I called after her.

Deanne laughed, sheepish. "A lot of people think it's weird for a neko-form to have a cat for a pet. But she was a stray, and I couldn't just leave her out in the cold. Don't worry, she's had all her shots."

I sniffled and tried to groom my fur back into some semblance of order, but I knew it was a lost cause. Nothing short of a real shower was going to get the tear stains out of the white fur under my eyes.

I curled up on the couch, one pillow hugged to my chest, and I swore I'd only just closed my eyes when something soft and cool touched the tip of my nose. My whiskers twitched, and I opened one eye to find a very tiny black-and-white colored kitten in front of me, one paw raised and ready to bat my nose again.

I opened both eyes and looked at her. She looked back at me. Neither of us seemed to know what to do about the situation.

"Hello," I said softly. "You must be The Holtz that Deanne was talking about."

The kitten tilted her head to one side. Slowly, she closed both eyes and opened them again. I returned the gesture, which in Cat meant something like "I trust you, you can trust me." She made a happy *prurrow* and curled up on my shoulder, purring softly.

"Sorry Cal, I can't seem to find—oh, you found her."

"I can't move," I said. "It's the law. When a kitten falls asleep on you, you become the furniture until they wake up and move on."

"Wow, she must really like you. I've never seen her stay in the same room as anyone but me, let alone fall asleep on them."

"I can't believe you have an actual cat," I said. "And a *jellicle* cat at that. She's practically a cousin to you."

"It's not illegal, just weird. It's not even the weirdest thing about me," Deanne protested. "Also, you never told me you read Elliot."

I laughed, and the tiny kitten woke. She glared at me, then meowed plaintively at Deanne.

"Needy," she said, picking her up and plopping down on the floor near me.

"So what *is* the weirdest thing about you?" I asked.

Deanne sighed. "It's complicated. Besides, we were talking about you, not me. What do you want to do next Tuesday?"

"Do?"

"You need a distraction," Deanne said. "Something to take your mind off it. Movie? How about a movie. What do you say? Is it a date?"

"Yes! Yes, I'd like that."

"It's a date, then. I'll drop you off at your apartment on the way to work tomorrow morning."

"What? No, I can't…I'd be imposing, and I don't want to—"

Deanne hushed me. "Don't worry about it. I wouldn't have offered if I thought it was an imposition. You're safe and sound here." The corner of her lip quirked wryly. "No ghosts will haunt you here, I promise."

I relented, too tired to argue.

We said our goodnights, and while I was a little disappointed not to be sleeping in the same bed as Deanne, I was content to just be near her for the night. Even if she'd wanted to do more, I wasn't up for it. Too much on my mind to enjoy it. Our first time—if we had a first time—shouldn't come on the heels of me having an emotional breakdown.

God, and I *still* hadn't told her everything. She needed to know about the broken dishes and the light bulbs that kept burning out, and…but it would have to wait. Again.

I curled up, Holtz nestled under one arm, and closed my eyes. I was safe. I was sound. Nothing could get me here.

When I heard a cabinet rattle in her kitchen in the middle of the night, I didn't think anything of it. Deanne probably just got up for a midnight snack or something. It couldn't be anything else. Couldn't.

***

Before I knew it, Tuesday morning arrived. The hauntings got worse, but having something to look forward to made it easier to clean up after each episode. I even hummed to myself while restocking on light bulbs. I finished my shift at Fantasma and practically flew out of the parking lot toward my apartment to change. Sanchez and Lilu both cheered as I left, wishing me luck on my date.

I expected to walk in on an uncanny disaster, cabinets open and my mirror seeping black ichor. What I found was…nothing. My apartment looked exactly as I had left it, down to the last tin of Neko Chow tuna.

I didn't question it. *Maybe it's finally winding down. Maybe his ghost finally realized his business can't be finished and moved on.* I changed into jeans and a tee shirt as fast as I could and was back out the door, zooming toward Deanne's place.

I slid into the guest parking space and called her from my cell. "Dee? I'm here!"

"Be right down!" She made a kiss sound and hung up.

My heart fluttered and I grinned like an idiot. For the first time in what felt like my entire life, I was *happy*. I didn't think I could feel any better. But then Deanne was walking down the path toward my car, and… wow.

She wore a black long coat and a TARDIS-blue scarf, with a matching hat covering her ears. Deanne slipped into the passenger side and huffed, rubbing her paws up and down her arms. "Damn it, it's *freezing*. I don't usually see my breath this much unless I'm in my lab."

"With any luck, they'll have the heat in the theater cranked up," I said. "Wait, your lab is cold enough to see your breath?"

"Well, yes and no," Deanne replied, flustered. "It's not important."

"You *still* haven't told me exactly what you do in there."

"Science. Lots of science. With physics!"

"Paranormal science?"

Deanne gave me a look, and I grinned. My grin faded a moment later as a thought occurred to me.

"Alright, so a question about ghosts," I said. "Why do they haunt a place?"

"Or a person," Deanne said. "They can haunt people."

"So...why?"

Deanne sighed. "Look, this is all hypothetical, okay? No one has ever proved there are ghosts or even souls. But say they're real, and say people can leave pieces of themselves behind as they live, like fingerprints or hair, only spectral. Sometimes, that's all a ghost is: a walking memory. And sometimes, it's less like a fingerprint and more like a drop of blood smeared over the face of reality. Whatever it is that makes up a soul or a ghost, it lingers and it remembers much more than a moment in time. It remembers what it meant to be alive. Most of the time, they fade away in a few days, off to wherever souls go after their body stops supporting them. But sometimes they died so suddenly or violently that they don't know they're dead. Or they know that they're dead, but can't let go because they have unfinished business and can't rest until it's been settled."

The steering wheel creaked under my paws. "So...hypothetically, what if a ghost's unfinished business can't be completed?"

"That's when it gets complicated. They can't move on, they can't find peace. Most go mad. They become what is known as a poltergeist, and if they're really strong, they become demons."

"Wait, demons are real?"

"No! Of course not. There's no such thing as demons. Or ghosts." She didn't sound certain.

"So these imaginary ghosts with unfinished business, what do you do about them when they go mad?"

Deanne grimaced. "Not going to give up, are you?"

"Nope!"

She sighed. "You promise you won't call me insane or deluded?"

I held up three fingers in a salute. "Scout's honor."

"You were a girl scout?"

"Not for very long," I said. "Things are better now, but at the time, by troop wasn't very open-minded. They could tolerate a Neko, but a Neko who wasn't straight was too much for them."

"Smooth-skins can be so close-minded," Deanne muttered darkly.

"What, we're ghouls now?"

"Nah, real ghouls don't look like they're rotting apart. That's a zombie."

I pulled up to a red light and I turned to look at Deanne. She winked.

"You're yanking my tail," I said.

"Would I do such a thing to my own girlfriend?" she said with mock indignity.

"Wait, I'm your girlfriend?"

"Cal, you're slower than molasses in January. The light turned green."

"What? Oh! Damn it."

We made it to the theater with plenty of time to spare, but any time I tried to broach the topic of ghosts again, Deanne hushed me with a pointed look.

"Not here. I'll tell you more when we're alone, I promise."

***

"That was way better than I thought it would be," I said as we left the theater. I popped a few last pieces of popcorn into my mouth and tossed the empty bag in the trash by the exit.

"Eh. The book was better," said Deanne.

I laughed. "Isn't it always?"

I followed her out the back door and into the cold. Deanne took my hand, interlacing her fingers with mine and kissed me on the cheek. Snow fell gently all around us, dusting her black fur. I could barely see the fluffy flakes on my own pale pelt. Deanne licked a snowflake off my whisker, catching it on the tip of her tongue.

"Would you like to head back to my place? I have a bottle of spiced white wine we could share."

"I'd like that," I said.

The drive felt shorter, the walk up to her apartment shorter still. Deanne held my hand and I felt like the luckiest girl alive. She let go to get the wine and giggled.

She had a cute giggle.

Deanne returned and put a glass of wine in my hand. I frowned.

"Hot wine?"

Deanne smiled and nodded. "It's got mulling spices. It's supposed to be served warm," she said, sipping from her own glass.

I shrugged and took a sip. Sweet, spicy wine flowed across my tongue and down my throat, warming me to my core. *Ohh, this is nice.*

"I think she likes it, Mikey," Deanne giggled.

"I didn't take you for the wine type. Doesn't this kill brain cells or something?"

Deanne shrugged. "Probably. But after what I put up with all day, I need a vice of some kind or I'll go nuts."

I swirled the wine in my glass and took another sip. "So, what *do* you do all day in that lab?"

"You're going to think I'm insane," Deanne said, taking another sip. A droplet clung to one whisker, and I had to resist the urge to catch it on my tongue like Deanne had been catching snowflakes.

"You're dating me. I *already* think you're insane," I said.

Deanne sighed and sat down at the tiny table in her kitchen. "It's... complicated. And it's not considered sound science. We're trying to change that, but until we have a real breakthrough, people are going to think we're just wasting time and university resources."

"Ghosts," I ventured.

She nodded. "Ghosts. Physics has already postulated that there's more than one dimension. What we haven't figured out yet is why sometimes, those dimensions overlap and even mingle with our own. But they do, and something that should be dead reaches out across the gulf to touch our world. What we're trying to figure out is how it happens, and why."

"It sounds fascinating."

"Honestly, it's mostly boring. We haven't had a real breakthrough catching or even recording a real ghost. Not reliably. Something about them just shorts out electrical equipment, and we can't shield it without making it impossible to record. Old cameras with film sometimes work, but it's too easy to fake those. They can't be used as evidence."

"You can fake a digital picture too," I said.

Deanne sighed. "Yeah, that too. I have a few things I developed in the lab that are supposed to at least neutralize a ghost, but that hardly helps to catch one. Those I've been able to test. Of course, all the recordings just look like I'm shooting the darkness."

I laughed and took another sip of my wine. It warmed me right to the core and made everything feel really *good*.

"Do you need a partner?" I asked. I slapped a paw over my muzzle the instant it came out of my mouth.

Deanne laughed and looked at me. "Trying to get out of the pizza delivery business?"

I shrugged, blushing. "It pays the bills, but it's not what I'd call rewarding work."

Deanne swirled her wine in her glass before answering. "What can you do?"

"I, uhh, well. I know my way around electronics. Hardware and software. I'm pretty good with Linux and I can pretty much pick up whatever you throw at me."

Deanne made a sound of encouragement, so I kept going. "I'm a fast learner. I mean, I don't know particle physics or anything, but I'm willing to learn. Always was, just…no money for college, you know? But the library is free, and there are a few online courses I took when I could afford it."

She nodded. "Anything else?" she asked, twisting the stem of her wineglass between two fingers.

"I'm good with my paws."

I wanted to slap myself the minute the words were out of my mouth.

Deanne looked at me, one eyebrow arched upward. "Oh?"

I swallowed and nodded. Deanne set her glass on the table and leaned forward, her whiskers close, so close. I couldn't help it; I inhaled the scent of her. Wine and coconut and honey and popcorn from the theater and the sweet, spicy scent of just her.

Deanne nuzzled me gently, purring. She took off the tinted glasses I always wore and set them aside. "Just how good are you with your paws?"

"I can show you, if you'd like." It came out strained, my throat clenching as it tried to match Deanne's throaty purr.

"I would very much like that," she said and took my paws. She led me to her bedroom and, before I could do more than take in the pink walls or the black comforter or the dresser with an oval mirror, she kissed me.

God, I wish I had the words for it. My blood was already singing with the wine, but the touch of her lips made the song crescendo. The tip of her tongue teased along my lip, and I let her in, my paws sliding up her back. *No claws. No shredding her blouse*, I told myself.

Deanne pulled back, and I dove after her. We tumbled to the bed, a tangle of arms, legs, and tails. Her hands slid under my shirt, I slipped down the back of her pants. I wanted to touch her, every inch of her, to make her yowl and writhe until—

Something rattled next to me, and a sliver of warning pierced my awareness. It sounded…familiar. Like a mirror rattling against the wall.

Can't be. Not here. Can't happen here. Probably just the headboard against the—*oh God.* Deanne's tongue rasped across my bare belly, making me gasp and arch my back. She laughed, eyes gleaming in the half light from the door.

"You're beautiful, Cal," she murmured, kissing the curve of my hip.

"I've wanted to kiss you from the moment I saw you," I said.

"Was it everything you dreamed?"

I chuckled. "I don't know. Need to try it a few more times to be sure."

Deanne grinned and kissed me again, pressing her body against mine. She was warm, so warm, her black fur a few shades darker than the comforter we were laying on. She'd kicked off her shoes (I hadn't noticed when) and revealed lovely pink footpads on the bottoms of her feet.

It was adorable. I don't know why, but I found it adorable.

Deanne kissed me again and slid my shirt up. She hesitated, her paw resting on my chest.

"Cal, are those scars?"

Desire died. I scrambled backward, one arm over my chest, ears backed. "It...it's nothing. I, uh, I can leave my shirt on, if it bothers you."

I started to shove my shirt back down, but Deanne stopped me. She peeled my shirt completely off, revealing four long, shiny scars across my chest.

"Claws," she said.

"Yeah." I looked away.

"Who?" Deanne demanded. Her voice was low, cold. Furious.

"My father," I said. "From the day I left. They've mostly healed. They don't even hurt anymore."

Deanne hugged me, squeezing hard enough that my ribs creaked. "Ack! Air! Becoming an issue!"

"Sorry, sorry, I just...I can't wrap my head around why someone would hurt you, hurt *anyone* like this."

"My father was...complicated. He wasn't always like this. Or so my mother insisted. But if there were good times, I can't...I can't remember them. I was never his favorite, and when we had that last fight, he tried... well. He didn't succeed, and he can't now."

Deanne nodded and kissed me again. "I'm so sorry," she said, nuzzling my neck.

"I'm not," I said. "It brought me here. To you."

And this time, I kissed her first. I kissed her with all my heart and soul, no longer caring if this would be my only time with her. It didn't matter. She hadn't shied away from my quirks, from my scars, from any part of me.

Just this once, just for this one night, it'll be OK. Nothing will happen. I won't let it. I want to be happy just this once.

Deanne returned the kiss, one finger tracing the line of a scar. "Will you stay the night?" she asked.

"If you'll have me," I breathed.

"For every moment that you're awake," she replied. Her lips locked to mine, and for one beautiful, glorious moment, I was perfectly, deliriously happy.

And then that moment passed.

A snarl and a hiss came from the open door. Illuminated in the doorway was Deanne's cat, every inch of fur along her back raised and her ears flat against her skull. She hissed again, her gaze riveted to something on the far side of the room.

"Holtz? What wrong, sweetie?" Deanne said.

Holtz didn't answer. She hissed again, tail lashing, and clawed at the air but refused to step foot into the room.

Something rattled against the wall, and my blood froze in my veins. I turned to look at the mirror.

Have you ever looked into a mirror and seen something move out of the corner of your eye, but it vanished too quickly for you to see what it was? Something flickered at the edge of my vision, warping the surface of the mirror like a ripple just under the surface of a still pond. I stood and approached the mirror. My eyes, my mismatched eyes my father thought were so precious, stared back at me wide and stricken. I watched as the color bled out of them, watched at they filmed over as if in death.

"Deanne…"

My reflection leered, twisted. Something raked across the back of the image. *Like claws. Just like claws behind a sheet.* The mirror bowed outward, silvery surface bubbling with corrosion.

"Deanne, run!" I screamed.

The mirror shattered. I threw my hands up to shield my face from the shards of glass, my eyes clenched tight. Deanne yowled. I didn't see if she got away.

Something grabbed me, shook me like a kitten. "Useless. Soulless."

My father's voice rumbled like grinding gravel. I opened my eyes and looked my ghostly father in the face. Pale fur, white as salt, glowed in the dark. His eyes, once perfect sky blue, were filmed over with cataracts. His suit hung from his body in tatters, shredded and slick with rot.

"No daughter of mine will commit such blasphemy," he growled. He closed one paw around my throat and began to squeeze.

I'm not yours! You disowned me! I tried to scream, but I couldn't. His grip was too tight.

"Cal, close your eyes!" Deanne shouted.

I squinted my eyes shut, and suddenly felt a burst of heat along the side of my face. My father snarled and let go, dropping me to the floor. I lay, gasping for air and opened one eye.

Deanne stood in the doorway, a heavy contraption slung over one shoulder. She held what looked like a gun from a game of laser tag in her paws.

"What…the hell?" I coughed. "Is that…?" I couldn't think of the word.

"Nope. It's a spectral inverter. And it'll scorch your retinas if you look at it!"

The ghost of my father roared and flew at Deanne, who roared right back and hit him again with a beam of red-black energy. My father dodged and laughed.

"Sinner. Blasphemer. How dare you lay hands on my little kitten!"

"Over-protective assbag from beyond the grave!" Deanne snapped back. "Go back to where you came from!" She shot at him again, and missed again. My father ducked under the beam and grabbed Deanne's arm, twisting it viciously. Deanne shrieked and dropped the gun. With a cackle, my father lifted her and threw her against the wall. I heard something snap and screamed.

"Leave her alone!"

"Can't leave, Caliban. Come back to God, kitten. Come back, give up this sinful life. Can't let go until you do." He turned to me, blind eyes blank but his expression paternal. "Need to see you settled, need to see you taken care of, as God intended."

"I can't," I sobbed. "It doesn't work that way. I can't be what you want me to be. I never could. I never wanted a family, or even to be with a tom! I can *never* be happy like that! You have to let it go, let *me* go!"

"Never," he growled. "Never. My daughter. Mine. Children obey. You're mine, my own baby daughter, and you'll do as I say!"

"No," I said, shaking my head. I stood up straighter and looked him in his dead eyes. "I'm not your anything. You made that perfectly clear the last time I saw you alive." I touched the place on my chest where the scars of his claws lingered. "It's over. If that's your unfinished business, I'm sorry. It'll never be finished. I won't destroy myself in a life I never wanted, just so you can be happy! It's sick!"

My father went very still for a moment, his ghostly form wavering. "No. Can't move on. Must save. Save you. From this. Only way. My child. My sinful, soulless daughter." He tipped his head back and yowled, his pale fur growing even brighter. "Come to God, my daughter. It's the only way to save your soul. I see it now!" And he came at me again.

I ducked, slipping under his grip like I always had as a child. *Even in death, he underestimates how small I am.* Scrawny, wiry Cal, the runt of the litter, always head and shoulders smaller than my siblings. I skidded across the floor and reached for Deanne.

"Deanne!"

She groaned and shifted. "My arm. I think he broke it. Blaster needs two hands, too much recoil."

I picked up the blaster, aimed, and pulled the trigger. I blasted my father right in the chest, blowing a smoking hole in his ghostly body. He shrieked and drifted back from me.

"No more," I said, and shot him again. "Never again."

His form got more and more transparent. I shot him again, and he backed to the shattered remains of Deanne's mirror.

"Caliban. My daughter. My child." His voice was barely more than a whisper.

"No," I said. "No real father hurts their child the way you hurt me."

I pulled the trigger one final time, and my father's ghost dissipated into fine mist. Then, he was gone.

I dropped the blaster to the floor and sank down after it, tears matting the fur under my eyes. Everything after that was a blur. I remember getting back up, and I remember that I drove Deanne to the ER as soon as I stopped shaking. As soon as her arm was set and in a cast, I remember numbly driving her back home. We sat in my car outside her apartment for a moment, neither of us quite sure what to say.

Finally, an arm wrapped around me, soft and warm and alive. "I'm so sorry, Cal," Deanne said, finally breaking the silence.

"Yeah," I sniffled. "So am I."

"You know what this means, don't you?" Deanne looked at me.

"That my next three paychecks are going to go towards cleaning up that mess?" I ventured.

"Well, yes," she said, "but with my arm out of commission for at least a month, I can't hold my blaster, let alone a beaker. I'll need someone to help with my experiments, and Michael's internship ended yesterday."

I blinked. "W-what?"

Deanne grinned like the Cheshire Cat. "Would you like the job?"

***

"Cal, sweetheart, you gotta stop this. You're gettin' tears on the pies."

"Sorry, Sanchez. Just…yeah. I'm OK," I said. "I'm just really going to miss this place."

Lilu looked at me from her place by the counter. "Uncle, give her a break."

"Yeah, I know. But these pizzas won't deliver themselves, and my nephew is useless. Can't find his way out of a paper bag." He shook his head. "Gonna miss you, Cal. You're moving up in the world, but don't forget us, alright?"

I took the pizzas and shoved them into my hot bag. "I'll never get the smell of pizza out of the upholstery, Sanchez. And I never want to. Thanks, dude. For everything." I hugged him, and Lila, and I strode out into the cold. The snow had mostly melted, but even though winter had mostly ended, there was just enough frost in the air to nip at you.

Large anchovy and mushroom. And two orders of cinnamon sticks.

I put my car into gear and drove, hands numb on the steering wheel. I parked, pulled the boxes from the bag, and took a few deep breaths. Then I opened the door and walked up to the building.

I didn't even have a chance to press the buzzer before the door opened.

For a long moment, we both stood there, not saying anything. Deanne's lab coat was impeccable again, and her eyes sparkled. Her broken arm was snug against her chest in a sling, and she'd already somehow managed to draw a crooked TARDIS on the cast in bright blue ink.

"I, uhh. Reporting for duty. And I brought lunch," I said.

"Awesomesauce. Just in time, too. My experiment on ectoplasm's electrical resistance needs attention. Let's get you a lab coat and begin."

I nodded. The ghost of happiness uncurled in my chest, and stretched.

Let's raise the temperature slowly, easing ourselves into the boiling water of resistance by enjoying a nice, room temperature bath with a drunk frog.

FROGGY STEWS

A. Humphrey Lanham

The room was cold. The rain from outside soaked Uri's turtleneck. As a frog, he enjoyed water, but at the end of the day, he expected to be greeted by a warm house, not an icebox. He shivered. Well, not exactly shivered, as he didn't have an internal warming mechanism.

"Clyde," Uri called out. "You ungrateful behemoth of a jerkwad," he muttered to himself.

Opera music echoed down the stairs. Clyde was in the shower.

"Running hot water while he runs the A/C to 55," said Uri. His sea lion roommate was asking for trouble.

He dropped his bag, hopped up to the table below the thermostat, and cranked the dial from 55 to 80. Peeling off his grey turtleneck and $100 jeans, he stood on the central air grate in his briefs and felt the change in temperature shift from cold to comfortable. He would turn it down to the agreed 72 once he was warm.

If Clyde would hurry up and get out of the shower, Uri, too, could get warm and clean.

"I know what I'll do," he said. Leaving the warmth of the grate, he headed for the kitchen. He ignored his usual step stool and jumped up next to the sink. Clyde didn't like bare feet on the counter, but he could deal.

Uri picked up the rubber stopper by the sink, hopped down into the basin, and stoppered it. Back on the counter, he pushed the sink handle to on. Giving the basin time to fill, he crossed the counter to the stove. He pawed through the utensils sitting in a pitcher until he found the thermometer. He returned to the sink and climbed into the white ceramic basin, thermometer in tow.

He looked at the rubber ducky on the windowsill. It was fancy in a top hat and bow tie and hadn't been there before. It stared at him blankly.

"I know what you're thinking...uh...Steve," he said to his new friend. All friends needed names. "You're wondering why I have a thermometer in the bath with me. Well let me tell you. My grandmother ended up in a kitchen stew. Humans collected a whole bunch of my pond up, told us of a nice, warm bath, and turned up the heat. POW! It killed them all."

Steve continued to look at him. Blankly.

"Well...it makes for a better story after a few beers."

That reminded him. He had bought a six-pack yesterday. He glanced down at the thermometer resting in the sink of warm water. 83.

"That's plenty hot. And that's plenty of water," he said, pulling down on the lever. Leaving the thermometer in the sink, he returned to the counter, splashing water everywhere.

He hopped down off the counter and over to the fridge. It was a seal-sized, side-by-side fridge, but had been mechanized with a button that would open if pressed. Such was the life of a frog in the big ol' world. He could have lived in frog-designed housing across town, but it was a longer commute from work. If he had known how frustrated he would get living here, it might have been worth it in the long run. Even if most of the house had been made frog accessible.

He pressed the button, and the fridge swung open. He jumped up past the two drawers and landed on the bottom shelf. His six-pack was down to one bottle.

"Great. Another clear indication that my roommate has no regard for me or my things. Unless you're the one who drank my beer, Steve." He shifted back and looked at his new friend on the sill. If Steve was the culprit, he wasn't telling.

"Would you like some, Steve? Twelve ounces is a little much for me. I only weigh about five pounds." He hopped out of the fridge, gave the door a nudge, and stood back as the door clapped shut.

The bottom half of the freezer door was his, and luckily, the sea lion had left his frozen shot glasses alone. They were the perfect size drinking glass for him. Reaching out, he touched two with his wet hand. They instantly froze to his skin. One of the benefits of being a frog. You didn't have to worry about dropping your frozen beer glass as long as your skin was wet.

Holding the beer with his other hand, he half dragged, half carried his items across the floor. Instead of attempting to jump back up to the counter with all the extra weight, he made it up the four steps of the step stool and reached the sink.

He set down the beer bottle and reached his now free hand down into the warm water. Splashing some on the glasses, he flexed his fingers, and managed to release them from their icy grip. He dragged his beer over to a wall-mounted bottle opener, rested the pleated lid into the hole, and hopped on top of the bottle. The lip popped off and the bottle slammed into the counter. It didn't break, but it foamed and spilled everywhere.

"Easy peasy, lemon Stevie," he said, looking at the sill. Steve was not impressed by the new nickname or by the newly opened beer.

Uri walked back to the sink, poured two shot glasses full of beer, and set the bottle of beer down. Using a frog-sized hand towel, he picked up one of the frozen glasses and set it on the sill next to Steve. He stripped off his boxers, grabbed the other glass, and climbed into the bath of hot water. He double-checked the thermometer, which read 79 degrees, and relaxed.

"Cold beer, hot bath. This is the life," he said, reclining in the hot water. With his ear holes below water, he couldn't hear the operatic noise.

He lay in the water for several minutes, sitting up occasionally to take sips of beer. He filled the shot glass twice more. He quickly became a very drunk frog.

"This, Stevie, can I call you Stevie, Stevie? This, Stevie, is the life. Why aren't you in here with me? You're not afraid of a naked frog, are you? Get in here." He stood, dropping his empty shot glass into the water and grabbing his friend.

"And you haven't even drunk your first beer. What? Are you picky? Don't like IPAs? Heathen." He tossed the rubber duck over his shoulder into the sink. With his other hand, he picked up the shot glass and shot-gunned the remainder of the beer. He set it back on the sill and would have sat back down if he had not slipped and fallen below the water.

Uri panicked and flailed, unable to get footing on the slippery ceramic. Finally, he threw an arm around his buoyant friend, and pulled his head above water. Gasping, he pulled his friend tight. Steve screamed in terror, a long, deafening squeak as Uri again fell and pulled them both underwater.

Luckily, Steve was strong and determined and pulled them both up into the air. Uri held on but gave up trying to stand. He lay on his back, eyes closed, hugging Steve, head resting against the duck's rubber breast.

Uri was able to regain his breath and allow the panic to subside. He felt the calm of the bath return to him. He didn't die. He hadn't drowned Stevie. Everything was okay. His head was still spinning, but he would be okay. Uri opened his eyes.

Clyde was standing at the sink wrapped in a towel, staring at him.

"What are you doing naked in our sink?" asked Clyde, smiling. Sea lion teeth were large and sharp. Uri disliked seeing his friend's mouth open like that as a general rule.

"I was taking a bath and connecting with my friend, Stevie, here," slurred Uri. He didn't have to explain himself to this self-serving sea lion. Clyde had frozen the house and used most of the hot water with his shower. And filled the house with that god-awful opera. Who listens to Puccini while they bathe?

"Let me tell you," he said to his mammalian roommate, "I had a terrible day at the office. The special order of fliers were printed incorrectly and then got shipped to fifteen different locations without my go ahead. I got rained on, which was fine, but then I come home, and it was COLDER than it was outside. You know I can't regulate my own temperature like you. There's a reason I ask that the thermostat be kept at 72 degrees.

"And then. You go and decide to take a hot shower exactly when I usually come home. Meaning I can't take a nice warm shower in our bathroom to warm up, again. I find that you've drank practically all of my six pack. To top it all off, you're listening to La Bohème so loudly that I can feel it reverberate through my ear holes.

"So here I am doing my best to warm up and relax after a long, cold day at work. I'm drunk, and I'm just now warm enough to feel my toes. Although now I'm drunk enough I can't feel my toes. And it's all your fault!" cried Uri, breaking into sobs.

The poor fellow, being a frog, didn't have normal tear ducts, and so the sobbing was a little dryer than an average sob. Being in the water, however, helped balance out the wet factor. Although, the sink stopper was not as effective as it might have been, and by now, the frog was sitting in about an inch of cool water. His bath and day were both ruined. At least now he had a much lower chance of drowning with or without the support of Steve. Human infants were known to drown in an inch of water. Adult frogs not so much.

The sea lion stopped smiling. He went to the drawer next to the stove and pulled out a kitchen towel and offered it to the frog, who wrapped it around his green body and felt a little less naked.

"Does, uh...Steve also need a towel?" asked Clyde, looking at the rubber duck, who was naked save for the black bow tie and top hat.

Uri looked over at his yellow friend.

"I don't think so. His dignity hasn't been tarnished. He'll dry. Where did he come from anyway?"

"Oh, he was a decoration at a wedding I went to. You know the foxes, Warren and Linda? Apparently, they were going to serve duck at the wedding until they realized several of the guests were waterfowl. So they just put a bridal party rubber duck set on every table and served fish. I swiped one as a souvenir.

"But look. I can tell you've had a bad day. Why don't you hop to the living room and relax while I fry up some fish and flies and chips? I'll even clean up the mess you've made."

The frog nodded. Clyde offered up a flipper for Uri to climb onto. On a normal day, Uri would never allow himself to be carried around by a larger animal like that. Today, however, he didn't think he could successfully move from the sink to the couch without looking more ridiculous than he would in the arms of a sea lion.

He carefully placed Stevie on the flipper and then stepped aboard himself. Clyde moved slowly through the kitchen and into the living room and helped Uri and Steve settle into a blanket on the couch.

"I'm going to turn the heat back down to 72. Let me know if you want me to heat you a water bottle, k?" Clyde nodded and returned to the kitchen.

Uri lay in the blanket with his arm slung around Steve.

"I'm going to tell you a secret, but you have to promise not to tell Clyde, okay?" he whispered to Steve.

"I am thinking about moving out. We're clearly incompatible. I thought I could handle this oversized house, but the heating bill alone to keep it barely warm is ridiculous. Who needs 8100 cubic feet of space? No one. That's who. Well…unless you're large like our friend, Clyde."

Uri was getting annoyed at the inability of his rubber friend to connect and relate. Grabbing Steve's orange bill, he forced the head to bob up and down, causing Steve's rubber body to rasp slightly at the exertion.

"See? Was that so hard, Stevie?"

He forced the bill to shake his head no.

Warm in his blanket, drunk in his demeanor, the frog stewed himself to sleep.

***

The next morning was far brighter than a normal morning ought to be. Too bright. Uri squinted and blinked, adjusting to the sun-filled living room. He had fallen asleep on the couch and slept through his crepuscular evening and morning routines.

His headache vibrated in time with the opera music playing upstairs. Clyde was clearly awake.

The blankets were warmly tucked around him and…he looked at the rubber duck. What was his name, again?

It didn't matter.

He untangled from the blanket and realized he was still naked. Great. He looked around. No clothes to be found. He hopped to the hallway intending to head upstairs to find clothes, but the closer he got to the stairway, the louder the music got. He couldn't go upstairs to his room where the clothes were. His head would shatter.

So instead, he headed for the kitchen to find some AnphiProphen. Sitting on the counter was a plate of cold flies and fries. Clyde had even left a small flake of fish for him. Uri half smiled. His roommate tried, even if he didn't always get it right. He probably should apologize.

Uri found the AnphiProphen and filled a shot glass with water. Sipping, he stood on his stool, thinking hard about last night. He really had overreacted. And he really didn't need more than half a beer and still be a functioning frog. He wasn't a late stage tadpole anymore.

Heading upstairs, he hoped Clyde wouldn't notice his naked roommate pass by his door. With luck, Clyde was seated at his desk, swaying to the aria and oblivious to Uri's presence.

The frog grabbed his Saturday sweats, wrapped himself in his robe, and headed for a proper shower.

Feeling clean and refreshed by the shower, he headed back to his bedroom. Clyde was still sitting in his chair, but now the music was off and he was facing the hall.

"Good morning," Uri said.

"Hi, Uri. Feeling better?" asked Clyde.

"I guess. Headache, but that'll get better as the day wears on. Listen, I really wanted to apologize for last night. It wasn't called for, and I was downright mean, drunk, and inappropriate."

"It's okay. It's not the first time. Listen, I've been thinking about this for a while, and I think you should move out."

Uri looked at his mammalian friend, silently.

"But…I just apologized," he said.

"I know. And you always do. And I get that I can be frustrating, but I think we've tried this whole roommate thing for six months now, and it's not working."

"Look, I know we've had some issues, but it's nothing—"

"It's not nothing. I've looked up some housing options in your price range. There are some nice frog-quads a few miles from here, and I have a friend who can take over your lease. If you want, I can find my own place, but I think you would do better in a space that's more suited to your size, and I would do better with someone who is more temperature flexible."

Uri's face crumpled. He had never been kicked out before. This was what he wanted, but now it felt like a betrayal.

"And someone who likes opera," Uri said finally.

"Yes, and someone who likes opera would be nice."

This story is a beautiful tornado of emotions and world-building set in the same universe as Ellis Aen's "Puppets" in ROAR 7, but much earlier in the timeline.

Post-Isolation

Ellis Aen

Ben's whittling knife caught on a gnarled protrusion jutting out from the stick of driftwood he was cutting into. When he curled his fingers and pushed to get past it, the blade slipped free and bit into his thumb. He dropped the driftwood and hissed.

Gritted teeth transitioned into a frown as the raccoon lifted his paw for a look. It wasn't a bad cut; he had only nicked the surface of the pad, but it still hurt. He sighed, stuck the tip of his thumb into his mouth, folded his knife closed, and picked up the wooden would-be carving and set it aside.

Ben told himself he'd get better at it with more practice. That he just needed to relax and take it easy, that simple things like *cutting away from himself* would be much more obvious if he could focus. But with work at the law firm slow for the last few months, he found it harder and harder to relax.

Ben rocked in place on the porch-swing facing his home, one foot lazily supplying motion, while the other hung in the air, legs crossed with an ankle up on the knee. It was a hot spring morning at the end of the season, the sun warming the back of his neck and his forearms with the approach of summer, wet with recent rain. With the sleeves of his shirt rolled up, his fur ruffled with goosebumps, and his under-pelt dampening with the first signs of sweat, he sat in front of a small table stocked with iced tea and a smattering of pastries—which surely weren't going to help rid him of the fear of gaining any more weight. And with his wife busy inside baking an apple pie, promising to spoil him even further, the threat of an expanding midsection loomed even closer.

When the throbbing in his thumb faded, Ben pulled it out of his mouth and reached for his tea glass. He pressed the drink to the side of his muzzle and let it rest there a moment, soaking in the coolness of it. He was just about to touch his nose to the glass when he caught sight of movement in the reflection cast across the curvature. At first, he thought he had seen a robin landing on the railing behind him. He held his breath and watched the blurry little blob in the reflection, staying still as not to disturb it. It flitted here and there, behaving very much like a robin, until it did a funny little thing and drifted downward, bisecting itself with the railing.

Initially perplexed, Ben realized that the movement must have been from further out in the yard, and that it wasn't a robin. He lowered his drink down between his legs and reached for his glasses, pulling them out of the neck of his shirt. While he fumbled around with them and turned, he watched a creature with strangely alien movement hobble toward the house, its footing unsure.

"Mr. Forec?" the figure—female, and younger than he, by her voice—called out. "Have you seen Jaime?"

"Jaime?" Ben blinked a couple of times once he got his glasses on, stretching the muscles around his eyes and nose-bridge while adjusting their fit. "Jaime's at school."

One of the female's arms was spasming by her side, loosely twitching and jumping. When his eyes focused, Ben saw that she was another raccoon. Bipedal, like him. She was standing there, as if considering his answer. After an awkward pause, she said, "Oh no, it's okay, Mr. Forec. The college's afternoon classes were cancelled."

Ben furrowed his brows, confusion playing across his expression in deep lines. She must have seen it, because she went on to explain herself. "I was supposed to swing by earlier," she said, a squeak of something peculiar in her voice. Desperation? Sadness? "But I got caught up taking care of a few errands. We were going to head to the mall for a late lunch."

Ben stood up and his glass fell over. It hit the deck with a *thunk*, but did not break. Cold liquid ran down the inside of a pant leg and soaked into his fur. He hardly even noticed it. Suddenly, he was too hot, the morning was too bright, and he felt like his blood had been replaced with syrup, thick and slow-pumping. He stumbled down porch steps he didn't bother looking for and walked out of the shade. He had to raise a paw to block out the sun.

"Mr. Forec?" the other raccoon asked, when he did not respond right away. "Are you okay?"

When he met her on the mud-drowned lawn, it was in a coughing fit. With his mouth open, he had inhaled a few of the gnats crowding about. It took him a moment to recover, and to notice that his mouth had been hanging open in the first place.

Something was wrong. The other raccoon's nose was bleeding, and there was blood in the sclera of one of her eyes.

"Mr. Forec," she said, "you're scaring me."

"Marren?" Ben called back toward the house. It came out as a whisper. He swallowed and tried again. "Marren!"

The smaller raccoon tried to wipe at her muzzle with her paw. Ben caught her by the wrist before she could. "Don't," he said, with perhaps more force than he had meant to, as if now that he had raised the volume of his voice he could no longer find the knob to turn it down. He shook out one of his shirt sleeves and dabbed the loose end of it against the younger raccoon's snout. She didn't stop him or argue. All she did was stare at him. Into him.

A moment later, he heard his wife step onto the front porch. "What's wrong?" she called back, "Is everything—"

"Marren, call an ambulance." He said it flatly. His tongue felt numb.

Marren hesitated, fidgeting with her ringed tail. Her ears splayed, and she squinted into the sunlight, trying to peer around her husband's back. "Who's..?"

"Marren, get back in the house and call an ambulance. Right now."

The younger raccoon's pupils were wide. So very wide. She kept staring at Ben. She was crying, but her voice went unperturbed, as if she were unaware of the fact.

"What's going on?" the girl asked Ben. It was a simple question, but he couldn't think, let alone process an answer. "Did something happen to Jamie?"

Then the bees came. Thousands of them. They came from the ground, the walls of his home, from the vacant holes that had become the raccoon girl's eyes. They crawled free of her flesh and left her body, flipping up tiny little patches of fur like miniature trap doors. They swirled and swarmed until there were so many of them that they blotted out the sun and all Ben could see was screaming, buzzing darkness.

***

Laying in the dark on a bed of crunchy leaves, fur matted with sweat, Ben fumbled a paw haphazardly along the top of the bedside table, trying desperately to find an agitated, angrily-buzzing, rectangular beehive.

While he was slapping at it, he tried to piece together the puzzle emerging from the oozing muck of his rousing mind: why would a beehive ever be rectangular? Or why would he be trying to grab it, for that matter?

On the third swat he effectively did the opposite of what he intended to do: he knocked the thing off onto the floor. The dull thump of it touching down snapped the image in his head into a blurry focus, the post-dream world throbbing into the pulse of a hangover beating his skull from the inside like a building-sized courtroom-gavel on its block. It wasn't a beehive; it was his phone. He wasn't lying on a bed of leaves; he was lying on the bed in his apartment, and it was littered with dried wood shavings.

The phone continued buzzing around on the carpet, now muted but no less irritating. When a particularly valiant effort to disable it with his mind through the pillow over his head came up short, he let out a deep sigh—and nearly gagged immediately thereafter. The hot, dry smell of his alcohol-cottoned mouth saturating the fabric in front of his muzzle was not a pleasant one. He shoved the pillow aside and grabbed for the phone in the dark, momentarily thankful for his excellent low-light vision, if not his sense of smell.

He decided all senses were terrible forever, however, when a cursory check of the caller ID resulted in his staring into the face of a thousand pixel-y suns, one eye constricting while the other played catch-up.

"Forec, Attorney-At-Law," he groaned, covering his eyes. He rolled over onto his back. "Office hours are certainly not four-thirty in the morning."

"Ben, it's me, Connor," he heard an old friend say. "We've got another one."

Ben rubbed at his face. His eye sockets were sore, and he could swear he felt the bags under his eyes weighing down on them—little wheeled carry-ons full of lead weights. A matching set for each eye.

"Ben? You there?"

Ben pushed himself up and swung his legs over the edge of the bed. He felt his belly spread over the top of his thighs. So much for not getting fat.

"How bad is it?" he asked. His approach was cautious.

"I probably shouldn't say much over the phone. All I can say is that this one is different. You know I wouldn't be calling you, otherwise. Not after the Anderson incident."

Ben tried to ignore the twitching he felt on the side where he had nearly had a kidney extracted during said incident—with the fox's teeth. The fur still hadn't grown back in places.

Resting his elbows on his knees, Ben rubbed at his nose-bridge. Disturbed by his movements, motes of dust drifted in the room, flickering in and out of focus in his eyeshine. The bed was practically sporous with dead skin and fur.

It had been two years since the incident. Two years since he had last talked to his friend. He knew it must be important for the German Shepherd to be reaching out, now. They hadn't exactly parted on the best of terms.

"Alright," Ben said. "Give me a couple of hours."

"A couple of hours?"

"I was … out late. Don't worry about it. I'll call a cab."

***

The towering spikes of machine farms and high-rise buildings stood jutting up into overcast skies like black and white blades stabbing into a belly of pale-gray flesh. Layers of city skyline, great stacks of it, rose up to meet the early morning sun, each clambering over the last in the slow, cloying movements of decade after decade of construction. To Ben, the city of Great Root was not the great world-tree of stone and glass and metal it sought out to be; it was a zombie crawling up out of the grave of the old world, an abomination writhing in the muddied earth deep at the bottom of the hole dug into it.

Staring at his reflection in the window of the cab, several hundred miles beyond the perimeter of the crater the city was built over, the raccoon absentmindedly stroked over the half-finished wooden carving in the breast pocket of his suit coat. He drank black sludge—while feeling much like it—out of a paper cup. It was supposed to be coffee. The driver kept casting disapproving glances back at him through the rear-view mirror, as if an accidental spill could somehow make the mottled upholstery look any worse. And with what Ben could smell—the acrid, lingering scent of vomit coming up from the floor—he really doubted the cab's interior could get any worse.

The raccoon's eyes drifted over the signs of his aging, the wear and tear of the world framing his muzzle in gray. He noted a sullen similarity between his reflection and the gray skies outside, and how the pitter-patter of rain on the windshield, the muted *fwip, fwip, fwip* of the windshield wipers, and the bland music playing in the cab, all seemed to blend together, muffled and indistinct.

His phone sat in his lap. He hadn't bothered putting it away, yet. Connor might call again. He was almost sure that he would, if only to tell him never mind, that he was making a mistake. To remind him of when he went too far, when he pushed when he shouldn't have. The surrealness of the situation had him questioning himself, that he might've dreamed the whole thing, and that he'd be showing up just to embarrass himself and make things even worse.

The screen stared up at him, dim and half-obscured by the glare of refracted sunlight. A picture of his family hid behind meticulously organized icons. It was a photo he knew well. It was taken on Jaime's—his daughter's—eighth birthday, over at her grandparents' place on Marren's side of the family. In it, he stood behind Jaime, his paws affectionately gripping her shoulders with Marren beside him. Jaime was holding up a paw, making what looked like a peace sign. There was cake smeared over half of her muzzle, and she was grinning big.

He remembered that grin. Her grin had been so contagious.

***

Ben absentmindedly tipped the taxi driver and stepped out into the rain. It was falling much harder, now. He groused and jogged across the pavement, splashing through puddles in the cracks and potholes while struggling to button his suit coat. It was smaller than he remembered. That or his belly was getting even bigger.

Dr. Connor Able, his gangly old German Shepherd friend, met him at the gate with an umbrella, his tail wagging affably under the tail-flap of a heavy rain coat. Ben's anxiety over his weight flared up even more upon seeing the dog; while he would normally describe himself as "generously pudgy," when compared to the canine, he felt downright obese—even with the dog wearing the added bulk of a raincoat.

When Connor opened the umbrella and held it up over Ben, Ben nodded his head and thanked him for the cover. While walking up the long, beaten roadway leading up to the ward—a squat little building crouching for cover among barren trees and wet, fallen leaves—the two of them caught up with meaningless small-talk.

It was nothing like the conversations they used to have.

When Ben steered the conversation around the subject of his drinking, the dog was kind enough to play along, though concern did show in the wrinkles of his muzzle. Ben had cleaned up, but he imagined he looked about as bad as he felt. A suit could only do so much.

Connor dropped the umbrella into a bucket by the door once inside the building. He took a moment to shake out his raincoat and hang it up. "I called you in," he stated, "because I think we've got something here. Something we can use. But I can't risk another incident like with

Anderson. We're supposed to be helping people here, not agitating them. Is that clear?"

Ben pulled his suit jacket straight. "I understand," he said, resigned. He understood the reasons, but he still felt defensive.

Connor led Ben into his office. There were papers all over the desk, a photograph or two, and a work-history report. Ben recognized the ENGRAM logo immediately. He sat down across from the canine and set his half-empty coffee—he hadn't been able to stomach drinking the rest—on the edge of the desk. He picked up one of the photos and examined it. The vacant expression of a big, burly lion stared back at him.

"So, what have we got?" Ben asked.

Connor filled him on the details. The lion's name was Kent Lamont, and he had asked for Ben by name. It was a special case, and they weren't going to get another like it. And they weren't going to have much time.

So, they started working on a plan.

***

Ben tossed his keys onto the small table just inside the apartment door before elbowing it shut. He was back home, and it was late. The lights clicked on automatically as he moved from room to room, dimly in places, and coming on too late to matter in others. He pulled open the fridge in his tiny kitchen and surveyed his kingdom. Two cases of beer, several empty bottles, and some formless, fuzzy lump of leftovers in a single-use-repurposed-for-multiple-use plastic food container greeted him back. Like dying animals, they were wasting away on the glass plains of room-temperature shelving.

The refrigerator had failed. Again.

The taste of warm beer did not sound particularly appealing to the raccoon. The next couple of weeks were going to be rough: he needed to be sober. Both for his work, and for any hope of trying to repair his relationship with the old dog. He knew this, but it still took him a minute to close the door without taking a beer.

Instead, he grabbed the cleanest-looking glass he could find off of the counter next to the fridge and wandered down the hallway and into the bathroom. There, he opened the small folding-door closet for his supply of filtered water (the local groundwater had been contaminated now for close to a decade)—and discovered the remnants of what had apparently been an emergency supply of booze. He grabbed one of the water bottles from the pack, plunked the glass down on the sink countertop, and twisted the cap off to fill it. He went through two bottles of water before the disgust of staring at the empty beer bottles tucked away in the corner made him nudge the closet closed with a foot.

When he was done, Ben rinsed the glass out and rubbed it down with his fingers. He left it on the sink countertop and headed into the living room where he pulled the carving out of his breast pocket and shrugged out of his coat. He tossed the coat over the back of the battered old reclining chair in the middle of the room, then settled into it. Reaching down into the crevice of the chair where the seat met the back, he dug out the remote. It was next to a revolver and one of his spare whittling knives. The revolver had been Connor's suggestion, protection in case things ever got dicey. He doubted he could fire the thing without the kickback knocking out his teeth, but he had picked it up anyway, if only to ease the dog's mind.

Ben turned on the view-panel mounted on the wall. It was an old, aging unit that took a while to boot up. When it warmed up, a documentary in freeze-frame came up, suspended right where he last left off. The raccoon set the remote down on an armrest, fished out the spare knife under him, and then pressed the pause button with his elbow. He unfolded the knife and whittled on the carving while the documentary played in the background.

"...nd we are only now beginning to surpass Mankind's technological achievements, nearly four centuries later," the narrator said, while scenes from the earlier portions of the twenty-first century played across the screen. Men in business suits milled about in the busy streets of what was once New York. Images of cars and various computer electronics flashed by, progressively evolving in complexity, like a stop-motion animation of a growing, mutating mechanical monster; at first they were small changes, and then they flipped by rapidly and by leaps and bounds, shrinking and then growing again before being punctuated with the harsh exclamation point that was the Nevada Wake Incident and the plague that followed.

"In many ways," the narrator continued, over shots of the nearly perfectly half-spherical crater at the Incident's core, "we have only built upon the ideas and ideals of our creators. It can even be argued that we may be, in His absence, an extension—an evolution—of Man's ambitions, both in our genetics, manufactured as they are, and in inheriting His legacy through mimicking Him. It will certainly be interesting then, to see how we fare in this time of new, unventured frontiers. And with the advent of technologies like holoplastics, bio-mechanical augmentations, Subspace-Storage-and-Retrieval, and the investments we've made toward our very own reach for the stars—perhaps one day beyond even the furthest reaches of Man—our future is looking very bright indeed." The video began winding down for a commercial break, trailing off by showing footage of the Man-made space shuttle Apollo 11 as it was seen in 1969, rocketing high up into the atmosphere, aiming for the stars.

"Up next," the program announced, "we'll talk about the earlier phases of developing dae culture, pre- and post-Owner Abolition Act of twenty-three thir— ..."

***

Ben dreamed again. His sleep was restless.

In his dreams, Ben was back on campus, in his college days, straddling a concrete, curved bench in the courtyard and sitting across from a young Marren, not long after they had first met.

"Why study them?" he was asking, while eating the other half of an apple she had shared with him. There was snow on the ground as far as the eye could see. It had been a long time since he had seen it so white. It wasn't like being back with his parents, where it was gray and spattered from all the dirt and chemicals. Here, the sun could almost blind you with the reflections playing across its surface.

That's just the way it was: the closer you got to the city, the better everything seemed. Which made it that much harder to think about the people living beyond the city's reaches. Great Root was as wondrous as it was a momentous achievement, but it was rooted in the very world it sought to rise above. Many of those in the city thought of the people living in the poverty-stricken reaches beyond its boundaries as nothing more than the dirt necessary to nourish it.

"What, Humans?" Marren had a study-slate resting on her thighs. She was doing coursework while they ate lunch. A flybike zipped by overhead, the whirr of its engine distant and then fading. "I don't know, Ben. Why do you study law? They're just interesting to me." She put her paws on the bench by her butt and leaned back. She angled her head slightly to one side, resting her cheek on her shoulder. Ben admired the slenderness of her throat, the ruffle of her winter pelt and the way it played with the neckline of her sweater, the ebon-furred mask framing her earthy-brown eyes. He had no idea why she took a liking to him. She came from a family of money; for him, it had taken his parents giving everything they had just to pay a *portion* of his college tuition. His father, then unable to pay for his deteriorating health, had died for it. "We're probably the first culture able to analyze the actual, recorded history of their own creators," she said. "We're living in the wake of Mankind—we're living in the wake of His mythology. If we're to succeed Him and stand on His shoulders, shouldn't we know enough not to repeat His mistakes?"

It was a good question, one he thought about often.

When nothing else was said, and the silence dragged on, Ben realized that he was uncomfortable and had been for a while. His butt hurt from sitting on the bench. Only, now it wasn't a bench. It was a sparsely-padded metal chair, and he had been in it for hours—hours that felt like years. He pulled his eyes away from the snow and saw that he was staring at the speckled pattern of linoleum tiling. He wasn't outside any more. He was at the hospital. The chemical smells of cleaners and the lingering odors of the sick and the elderly were keeping him company—and they did, until it was time to drive Marren home. They were both older now, a few years past college.

On the way home, Marren cried. Neither of them said anything. Ben drove into the haze of smog, his heart heavy as the street lights blurred past, blotting out the stars in mottled oranges and decaying, plasticky yellows. He kept driving until he was in the graveyard, until the car was gone and the steering wheel had become a little box. There, surrounded by crumbling headstones of all shapes and sizes, stood another version of himself, three years his junior. He watched the doppelganger bury his own little box in the earth, and then he knelt and buried his alongside it. When he was done, he stood up, knocked the dirt from his knees, and stared at the moon while the sky slowly fell onto it. He thought nothing of the strangeness of this; he thought only of how this was now the second time he had buried a piece of himself, and how he felt all the more empty for it.

The falling sky collided with the moon, fusing with it and anchoring itself in place. It became a drop-tile ceiling when the moon bloomed into the light of a ceiling fixture in one of those tiles. He was in the basement back home—his old home, before the apartment. He was years older now, in his forties with a daughter. Finally, he and his wife had had a cub! He was a father and had been for nineteen wonderful years. But something was wrong. Rather than celebrating, he and his wife were fighting.

Marren slapped the top of the washing machine. The flimsy metal lid bowed in and popped back up. The laundry basket was on the floor, laundry scattered on cold stone. "No, Ben," she was saying, "you need to do something about it. Now. We're losing our baby, and I—" She choked mid-sentence; she was biting back tears, "—I can't lose another."

Ben tried to explain it to her. He wanted to do something. He really did. But if he took the case to court without concrete evidence, he ran the risk of a mistrial. Blow it now, and there would never be another chance.

"She's just slipping away, Ben," Marren would say, again and again as she did in those final days, "and you're letting it happen."

Connor was there when Marren wasn't. Ben found himself spending more and more time with the dog, proportionate to her absence. They were in a pub now, and it was falling apart. Plastic tubs were set out to collect the rainwater where it leaked through the roof. On the table, Ben was swimming in a glass of pale gold. He was tiny, already drowning, while the massive German Shepherd rambled on about some theory. Hebbian something, the dog was saying. Something about stimulating memories parallel to one another. They were making progress, he said. Ellen was opening up. She was starting to remember.

They were always making progress, Marren would yell at him, when he was back home. She didn't care about Ellen; she only cared about her baby. They were always making progress, but they didn't have any answers! It just made him drink more.

He aged, standing still in the doorway, through season after season of more of the same, until Marren stormed out and left him. When he looked down, he saw that he was holding yet another beer; when he looked at his left paw, he saw that his wedding band was missing.

In a panic, he found himself in an alleyway. It was a long tunnel with no light at the end, no sky above. He was smashed out of his mind, desperately searching. He had to have lost the ring at a bar. But which one? They all blurred together. He should have never taken it off. He kicked over a trash can and stumbled through a dying world as old and gray as he.

Despite all the trying, all the doctors' help, it just wasn't enough. Not enough for Marren. Ellen talked, but she didn't talk about the right things. She just told them what they already knew: Jaime had gone to college, and that she had met Ellen some time thereafter. She told them that Jaime had had financial trouble, that she didn't want to ask her daddy for money, that she thought that he deserved better than his father. The only thing she didn't tell them, the thing they wanted to hear the most, was why Jaime didn't come back home.

***

Construction in the room was almost finished when Connor delivered the bad news. Ben could hear workers drilling into the floor down the hallway. The smell of drying paint was giving him a headache.

"They're going to make the transfer tomorrow," Connor told him. "First thing in the morning."

The raccoon was in the makeshift office Connor had set up for him, poring over files scattered across the surface of the card table that served as his desk. He looked up over the rim of his glasses. He hadn't had a drink in almost three days now, but the urge to reverse that trend was quite strong at that particular moment. Temptation was practically tugging on his tail.

"I'm sorry, Ben," Connor said. "We had to get him on the books eventually. We've got to follow protocol here. You know the city has been trying to close us down for years. I just didn't think they'd find him this fast."

Ben checked his watch. Then he stood up and reached for his suit coat. "We've still got fifteen hours or so," he said, digging his heels in. He made for the door. "We'll have to improvise. Get everything together and call me when you're ready."

***

Ben was sitting outside, on a rusted old bench missing its back, the slats broken off and taped over for safety, when Connor came to get him. He was whittling again.

"You're getting pretty good at that," Connor said, lighting himself a cigarette. He shook out the match and took a few drags.

Ben screwed up his muzzle. He hated the smell of smoke, but he didn't say anything. The German Shepherd had let him be with his drinking; he could let the smoking go. Everyone had their coping mechanisms.

"It's something to do when I'm not working," he said, looking at his scarred thumb-pads. He hadn't always been good. "Work has been sparse."

Connor nodded. "It tends to be when you go sticking your nose in places others don't want you to. We've both been toeing the line for a while now, and you know that."

Ben drew himself up and closed his knife. "It's like you said," he said, "we're helping people. It's hard; no one else plays fair. But if you want to play, you have to play hard right back. Your heart has to be right, even if you lose your mind."

Connor nodded again, took another couple of drags, and snuffed out his cigarette. He tucked the remainder of it into his shirt pocket and studied the racoon.

"Why a lighthouse?" he asked, pointing at the carving.

"Jaime used to love them, growing up," the raccoon said, brushing loose shavings away. "My father took me to see one when I was younger. When she was around the same age, I did the same for her. It just seemed like the fatherly thing to do. It must've made an impression."

"C'mon," Connor said, something softening in the tone of his voice. He cocked his head back toward the building. "Had the boys go out and get us something. Let's grab a bite to eat before we get started."

***

Connor led Ben toward the guard sitting at the desk back at the entrance. The guard buzzed them in, and they passed through a set of bars into a sterile hallway.

"We'll have guys on the other side of the door, and he'll be in bonds," Connor said, "but if things go south, it'll take them a minute to get it under control." They cut down another hallway at the end of the first; it was just as bland. They passed by several rows of thick plexiglass doors on either side. At the end of the second hallway, they arrived at the solid, opaque door flanked by two panthers dressed in officer's uniforms. They both looked a little awkward in them. One of the panthers held up a paw to greet them.

Ben opened the door while Connor reviewed the panthers' roles with them. Before he could make it inside, the German Shepherd stopped him with a paw on his shoulder. The sudden touch surprised him.

"Just take it easy," the dog said. "Get him to talk. Guide him to the answers; don't demand them. We can't go having another incident on our paws. Not even for Jaime's sake. You know that, right?"

"I'll take it as easy as I can," the raccoon said. He thumped the manila folder in his paw against his thigh.

"I mean it, Ben. I know how much this means to you. But you don't get to give me a spiel about playing hard and then go on and pretend that I don't have skin in the game, too. You screw this up, and we lose everything. The research, the ability to help these people. Everything. Don't just play for yourself. Don't lose your mind, too."

The raccoon took a deep breath and closed his eyes. He nodded.

Connor squeezed his friend's shoulder. "We'll be bringing him down in a minute," he said, before patting the raccoon and slipping away.

The door clicked closed behind Ben, trapping him inside the room; there was no handle on the inside. In the center of the room sat a long, rectangular table, bolted down with chairs on either side; it occupied most of the floor space in the room. A large mirror affixed to the wall was oriented sideways. It still had a wooden frame around it. There was nothing behind the mirror. The walls, concrete and gray, still stunk of paint. A small electrical box with a red button stuck out from the wall behind the chair on the right. Ben walked up to the table and traced his finger-pads across the surface.

***

Ben wasn't one of Connor's patients. But over the years, the two had come to know one another well enough that he might as well have been.

It was awkward when they slept together. But Ben was lonely, and he had been for a long time. He used to think it was the booze making things easier, that he wouldn't have accepted the dog's advances otherwise. Sometimes he thought that it had only happened because of the attack, that Connor had only been taking pity on him.

It had been a wake-up call when the German Shepherd cut him off from the ward afterward. He hadn't realized how much the dog cared until that moment. He remembered it clearly, because that night, he had been sober.

He had been so singularly focused on Anderson that he hadn't been paying attention to the signs right in front of him. He was obsessed. He felt justified in being so, but that didn't mean it hadn't blindsided him any less.

Heavens knew there were times when he felt like he was losing his mind. Connor was right about that. All the stress, the loss of his father, his wife leaving him, his family falling apart. Right now, he felt like he was keeping it together. But how long would it last? How much more would it take to break him? Would he even know it when it happened? What if it had already happened?

**

The door handle rattled on the other side of the metal panel. Ben looked up. He had been stroking the carving in his breast pocket again.

One of the two officer fellows let himself in. Behind him, a lion almost twice again Ben's height walked in, wrists and ankles bound in chains. Behind him, the second guard followed. Behind the second guard, Connor lumbered in, carrying a heavy-looking case. The guards sat the lion down in the chair across from Ben. While they busied themselves with running chains through the loops on the table, tying the lion down, the canine unpacked camera equipment from the case in the corner. The lion took it all with a somber expression.

After double-checking the bonds, the two panthers backed out of the room. "You need anything, Mr. Forec, we'll be right outside," the latter assured him.

Ben nodded. "We'll be fine, I'm sure. We're just going to talk."

The door closed. Ben sat the manila folder down on the corner of the table before pulling the other chair out to take a seat himself. He folded his tail over his lap and opened the folder up. He pretended to study it for a moment. He knew the contents, but he still went through the motions. "Mr. Lamont?" he asked. "Kent Lamont?"

The lion looked up and sized him up from across the table. His eyes were distant and unfocused. After a minute, he said, "Yeah?" His voice was a little raspy. It sounded like he'd had one too many smokes.

Ben met the lion's eyes. "I've heard that you were wanting to make a confession?"

The lion scratched the front of his dingy white shirt. His chains rattled. He looked dubious, but his eyes were coming into focus. "Wait. *You're* Ben?"

"I am," Ben confirmed. "Ben Forec, Attorney-At-Law."

The lion laughed. It was a deep and bassy sound, like a bucket full of gravel shifting around. His laugh devolved into a cough. "You're kinda small, Ben," he said, when he caught his breath.

"I do seem to have been stunted in the growth department," Ben agreed, "but I can assure you that I stand quite tall in the eyes of the law." He tapped the open folder with a finger. "And I must say, I'm quite eager to handle your case."

The lion propped his forearms up on the table. "Why?" he asked. "I got mad and I stabbed my brother. I know I did wrong. And I'm sorry for it. That's what I wanna confess."

"And you need a lawyer for that?" The raccoon leaned back and idly drummed his fingers against the edge of the table. "Couldn't you have just had one of the officers take your confession? Why ask for me? It's not exactly standard procedure. There's more to the picture here, and that's got me curious."

The big guy shrugged. "Word's gone around that you fight for the little guy." He laugh-coughed again. "Sorry. It's just funny to me. Wasn't expecting you to be so little yourself."

"You're looking for a sympathy vote," the raccoon stated flatly. "Reduce your sentence, get you out a little earlier? Is that the idea?"

The lion wrung his paws together, knuckles popping. "You know how it is," he said. "It's like getting sick: you get sick, you don't get better. Prison time can be the end of a guy's life. Most of the time you go in, you don't come back out. That's just how the system works."

"It does seem that way, doesn't it?" Ben closed the folder. "All the money at the top, mega-corporations and private companies pulling the strings."

"Yeah," the lion said. "I knew it was a good idea to call you. You get it."

"We don't have much these days, Kent. But we do have each other. If we don't stick together, how's the little guy ever going to gain any ground?" Ben pushed up his glasses. "Shall we start then?"

Kent inclined his head in the affirmative.

Ben thumbed over his shoulder at the canine behind him. Connor had finished setting up the camera. "This is my friend, Dr. Able. Dr. Able is going to film our discussion for purposes related to emotional assessment and analysis. He's also going to be in control of the duration of our discussion. Any funny business and he's going to push that big red panic button behind me, and that's going to be the end of the discussion. Do you find these terms agreeable?"

"Doesn't bother me none," the lion conceded. "Whatever you think is best. You're the lawyer."

"Good, good." Ben rolled a finger in the air, signaling the canine. The red light on the camera came on. He turned back to the lion. "So, let's start at the beginning."

"You want the whole day? Or just at the argument?"

"The argument, please."

The lion straightened up and idly picked at the underside of his chin. "Alright. Well, we—me and my brother—we got into this fight: I'd quit my job at ENGRAM, and I guess he—my brother—wasn't all that pleased about it."

"We're all prone to disagreements, Mr. Lamont. But why stab your brother over an argument?"

The lion cupped the end of his muzzle into his palm. When he removed it a short while later, he said, "Because he was bein' a freeloader. Doesn't have a job, so he relies on me to feed him, keep a roof over his head. But then he has the nerve to bitch about me quitting mine? Like I'm responsible for him." He moved his paw away from his chin and looked at the back of his claw-slits, then put his arm back down. "I quit for a good reason. I didn't need his bullshit on top of an already difficult decision. Like I *hadn't* been thinking about the consequences."

"It's quite a leap to believe you stabbed him over that alone."

"I didn't. It was a bunch of things, all at once. See, I was in the kitchen, trying to make a sandwich, and he got up from watching one of those crime-scene-investigation shows he's always watching—whenever he ain't rotting his brain on that corporate-backed political news bullshit—and he comes in complaining about how we're gonna have bills come due soon and launches into some bit about how I'm a 'part of the problem'.

"And here I am, I just wanna eat, you know? I just lost my job. I've had a long day. And I keep thinking about how this guy has changed." He balled his paws up into fists. "Me and my brother, we used to be real close. He got this fancy tech job somewhere else. Moving up in the world, making it big, all that. Used to look up to him, even though he's younger than me. But then he loses the job and needs a place to stay. And we're family, and

I haven't seen him in a while, right? So I'm like, hey, my place is yours. But the guy that comes home isn't the same guy. He's not the guy I used to know. It's like someone flipped a switch inside of his head and made him *different*. He's testy, keeps trying to goad me into all this political crap. Talking all this shit about 'shaking up the system' while believing the people that've caused this whole mess are somehow gonna save us from it. That we need to break the 'status quo', when the status quo is what's keeping a lot of us from bein' homeless, in debt, or worse.

"I mean, at first I thought he was joking. So I called him out on it— because he's my brother, and there's just no way he's bein' serious. But no. He gets real upset. He *believes* all this shit. And he just keeps it up, constantly, as if I'm going to listen and give in and agree with his terrible opinions when he somehow manages to find the least offensive way to say them. Just because we're brothers! Like bein' family is somehow gonna bridge that gap and everything'll be just peachy.

"So yeah, when a guy who makes himself a vegetable in front of a view-screen all day comes in repeating crap he's heard on it while telling me *I'm* a terrible person for not supporting him hard enough, when I'm working a job I hate—that I had to take just to provide that support to begin with—I get real angry. Family or not, that kind of thing can get to you. You can only be the better half for so long before the pressure gets to you and you have to *do something.*"

The lion balled his fists tighter. "So I did. When he got all in my face about it, I told him to shove it. Pushed him away, and it escalated. We got into a scuffle, I grabbed the knife off the kitchen counter, and before I knew it, I put it in his throat. And lemme tell you: it's real damn hard to act like you're not the bad guy when you go and stab *your own brother*. I mean, hell."

"It sounds like a very frustrating situation to be in," Ben said. "The relationship stretched thin, tensions running high, and emotions coming into the picture. It's a recipe for disaster."

Kent just grunted. He unclenched his fists and pressed his paws to the table top, as if he could push the table down and away, and by extension the anchor holding him to the world, putting distance between himself and his memories of the encounter. His claws were out, but they receded after a moment. "Yeah," he said. "Don't make it right, but yeah."

Ben flipped open the folder again. He thumbed through a couple of pages. "Alright," he said. "Let's go back to your job. You mentioned that you quit for a good reason?" He looked up without changing the angle of his head. "Were you stressed from work? Why, exactly, did you quit?"

"That's your sympathy angle? That I was stressed out over work?" He laughed. "Shit, I thought you said you were good."

"One of the best," Ben said, "or so they tell me. You're going to have to trust me on this one, Mr. Lamont."

The lion grumbled. "I have a hard time believing 'one of the best' is gonna be working *pro bono*."

"You say that, and yet you still called me." The raccoon shrugged. "What can I say? I have a vested interest in your case. You stand only to benefit from that interest."

"Alright. Fine." The big cat rubbed at one of his eyes. "Yeah. I was stressed. Upset, even."

"Would you mind telling me why?" The raccoon tapped one of the pages in the folder. "I see here that you were working in PIR. Post-Isolation Recovery, is that right?"

"Yeah. One of the guys responsible for making sure clients under ENGRAM contract come back up out of it when it's over." He summarized loosely, waving a paw in the air. The chain attached to his wrist rattled as he went on. "We make sure the client is coherent, catch them up on anything relevant from when they were under—damages, breaches in contract, all that stuff—and generally make sure they're okay. Once we're done with all that, we pass them over to payroll so they can collect for their time."

The raccoon nodded. He waited for the lion to continue.

"Anyway, problems are real rare, you know? ENGRAM's got this whole thing down cold. Most of the problems that *do* exist are on the buyer's end. Some guy looking for labor, but he turns around and screws the contractor. You know, shit like that. They think we won't figure it out, but we do."

"Engaging in sexual activities without the contractor's consent would most certainly be a problem," Ben agreed.

"But it's not ENGRAM's problem, yeah?" The big cat widened his stance, spreading his feet on the floor. "No, that's between the contractor and the buyer. All those legal protections to make sure ENGRAM don't get involved. If the buyer screws up, he gets hit with the fees, rape charges. All that."

Ben adjusted the button on one of the cuffs of his suit jacket. "And that bothered you enough to quit?"

"No," the lion said. "No, that's fair. That's justice. The contractor knows what they're getting into when they make the contract; they know the risks. It's voluntary slavery. We ain't supposed to call it that, but that's what it is. The boys that put them under make sure as hell they know it, too."

"So what bothered you, then?" The raccoon let the folder fall closed again and focused his attention on the lion.

Kent brought his knuckles together. "A few months back, there was this doe," he started. "Comes into PIR, and I'm her recovery specialist. Beautiful gal with these big, beautiful, bright eyes. One of them blue, and the other green."

"Heterochromatic? That is a little unusual."

"Made her stick out," he acknowledged. "Anyway, she comes up, yeah? But she comes up a little different. Takes her longer to 'wake up' from bein' under. Sometimes there's hiccups like that. Usually it's nothing big. But this doe? She takes even longer than some of the longer ones." He started picking at the underside of his chin again. "I didn't think much of it at the time. She was coherent, knew where she was, who she was. All of that. It took longer, but she checked out. So we let her go."

"Go on." The raccoon gestured for him to continue.

"Right, so, a couple months later, this gal goes and plays in traffic. Has a complete mental breakdown, witnesses saying she was screaming her head off about someone else bein' in her body. And I know her, right? I know it's her. Because I see her on the TV, and she's got those same beautiful eyes."

"You're talking about the incident on 22nd and Harmony? Julia Rockheimer?"

He nodded. He winced as he recalled the details. "Gods, what a mess. She must've gotten dragged. Happened while some news crew was right around the corner doing an interview. So it was live, and they show it. You see all of it, right there on the screen. And her damn eyes are open. Those same different-colored eyes. Staring up at nothing."

Ben harrumphed. "It was covered for a good while longer than it should have been," he said. "In part, due to the lengthy discussion of whether or not the media had overstepped its bounds."

Kent waved dismissively. "Right, right. But forget about that for a minute. Let's go back to her eyes."

"Okay, so we'll go back to her eyes."

"See, I see them? I see them staring up at nothing." The lion pointed forward and up at a slight angle, looking in the same direction. "But I knew it, right then, that she wasn't staring up at nothing." He turned his chunky paw-digit around and tapped himself on the nose-bridge, between the eyes. "She wasn't looking out. Hah, no, this doe was looking *in*."

"I'm not sure I'm following you, Mr. Lamont. Would you mind elaborating?"

He cleared his throat. It sounded wet. Like he was getting sick. "We heard about this thing in PIR, this really rare condition. Something in the procedure goes wrong. Something about neurons firing off in close proximity to the isolated areas, after the fact. Activating them, bridging the gap or … something. I think one of the docs said it was like memory rehabilitation? But, you know, on accident."

"Which procedure is this again?"

"Memory-isolation. The one where they put the contractor under, flip the switch that turns off the memory portions of the brain. I don't know all the technical details—I just did recovery—but the point is, you *remember*."

"Why is that a problem, Mr. Lamont? They're just memories. I'm sure the contractor would be upset, but ENGRAM's legal team has covered their bases here. If she was released on a clean bill of health *and* self-confirmation, there really isn't much that can be done about it."

"Well, that's the thing. You remember. But the you that remembers isn't *you*. It's like a … a branching path." The lion spun his paw around in the air, as if trying to force his brain to produce the words necessary to explain himself. "You wake up, and you know you went under. But something's wrong. It's supposed to be blank. Let you pick up your life and move on. Collect your money for your time, you know? But you wake up, and it isn't blank. And this doe? This doe, she had fifteen *years* on her contract. Enough to get her ass retired."

Ben was about to reply when the lion suddenly stood up, sending his chair scraping backwards across the floor. He nearly fell over when his chains came up short, the table jerking in place. "And that got me thinking," he continued, putting his knuckles down on the table. "Fifteen years of memories. Fifteen years to think different. Fifteen *years* of your life learning things. New things. Things that are supposed to be gone when you wake up. But then they're not. And like, what if—and I know this is crazy— what if, for whatever reason, you don't want to give that up? What if you like the new you better than the old you? But the old you, well, the old you don't like that so much."

"You're implying the development of a split personality," the raccoon cut in.

"Yeah!" The lion pounded his fists against the table. It was loud and jarring.

Ben heard the door handle outside starting to turn. It was over. Connor had pushed the button. Ben felt his racing heart sink into his stomach. Only to feel it immediately leap back up into his throat when the dog addressed the panther who poked his head in.

"We've got it under control," Connor said. "Mr. Lamont is just getting a little excited, telling his story. He'll calm down. Won't you, Mr. Lamont?"

Kent settled back down into his chair and rubbed at his wrists, tucking fingers under the metal bands where they had chafed against flesh under fur. Satisfied, the panther nodded in affirmation and pulled back out of the room. Connor made eye contact with Ben, then nodded for the both of them to continue.

"Yeah, you're getting it," the lion repeated himself, his outburst subsided. He rubbed at the back of his neck, head down while he ran fingers through his mane. "I put it together after I heard what eyewitnesses were saying. When I saw those eyes. We just didn't know it at the time. We didn't know something went wrong with her procedure. Hell, how could we? It's not like we could see what she was thinking. She just took a while to come up, and then she did, and we sent her home. 'Contract's over, thank you ma'am, have a nice day.' "

Ben swept his tail out of his lap and leaned forward cautiously. "I can see where that might be bothersome," he stated, trying to talk around the pulse he could feel in his throat.

The lion's amber eyes glittered. He leaned in with Ben, his ears cocked back. "I don't think you *really* see it though," he said.

"Then why don't you tell me what I'm missing," Ben said.

"Just think about it: two of you. In the same body. Both of you say you're the real you. But which one really is the real you? I mean … shit, how do you know? Does the old you have any right to tell the new you to beat it? What about the other way around?"

"The mind is a surprisingly complex organic machine, Mr. Lamont. I'm sure these sorts of problems could be resolved with a psychiatrist and proper medical attention. She may have even worked it out on her own. She could have come up with some way to cope."

"She tried to headbutt a fucking *bus*, Ben. I don't think she figured out a way to cope."

The raccoon cleared his throat. He shifted nervously in his seat. "In her case, I would certainly concede the point."

The lion backed away and sat upright. His ears popped back up. "The worst part about it is, if no one knew, if no one knows—how many more are there? Maybe it's not as rare as we thought? Maybe it's not just some isolated incident. Maybe ENGRAM doesn't really know what it's doing. Hell, maybe they do, and they just don't *care*." He sank into his chair again. "I just couldn't work for a company like that. So, I quit."

After a moment of silence, Ben said, "I think that is as good a reason as any, Mr. Lamont. I do not know that I could work for a company like that either."

The raccoon adjusted his posture and reached into the back corner of the folder. He pulled a picture free from the paper clip holding it in place. He showed it to the camera and, by extension, Connor. He waited for the dog's assent. There wasn't going to be a better time than now. When

Connor signaled his agreement, he turned the picture around and held it out. "Going back to the assault for a moment," he said, "for the record: is this the person you stabbed, Mr. Lamont? Your brother, Jason Lamont?"

The picture was of a lion with a scar threaded across his throat vertically. It lead up to just under his jawline. It was a white, furless lump, still puckered up, mane shaved around it.

Kent took the picture and examined it. "Yeah," he said. "Yeah, that's him. Looks like it's healing up pretty good. Gods, I wish I hadn't done that." He rubbed at his muzzle and handed the picture back. "How's he doing, anyway?"

"He's very upset, understandably. According to the doctors, the few times he's been lucid, he just sobs uncontrollably while talking about you, and how he can't keep you out of his head." The raccoon slipped the picture back into the file. "Tell me, are you aware that Jason underwent an ENGRAM contract himself?"

"About six years ago," the lion confirmed. "Before I went to work there—after he lost his tech job. But he came up fine. No complications or anything that I'm aware of. Well, besides suddenly becoming a lazy ass and doing a whole lot of nothing, anyway."

"He had a two year contract, Mr. Lamont. I'd argue that he probably deserved at least some form of a break."

"For more than a year, though? The contract money wasn't going to hold us over forever. It was supposed to be a temporary solution, until he found another job. When he didn't, I had to come up with something better for the both of us. I never wanted to work there in the first place, but I didn't wanna be homeless, neither."

The raccoon gave a sympathetic smile. "I understand," he said. He took a breath, considering his words carefully. He needed to make ground, not follow the same pattern. "But before I go, Jason—"

"Kent," the lion said with a firmness like a sledgehammer cracking sidewalk. "My name is Kent." He started picking at the underside of his jawline again. He peeled off a small piece of loose scar tissue and flicked it away from a bald patch at the front of his throat.

Connor shuffled behind Ben. He knew the dog was going for the button this time. So Ben did the one and only thing he could do to stop it: he held up a paw to *ask* the dog to stop. He needed the German Shepherd's trust. To earn it, he would wait, not act. He wanted to move forward with every fiber of his being. He panged to the very core to push on. But he didn't. He stopped; he gave the decision to Connor, and he waited.

Ben could hear his heart pounding in his ears in the silence. It was a long and pregnant moment, but when it was over, no one else had come into the room.

"My apologies," the raccoon said. "It's just that you look so remarkably *similar*. Anyway, before I go, there's something I've been wanting to ask you."

"Yeah? What's that?"

"What happened to your neck?"

One of the blood vessels in the lion's left eye suddenly burst. It began bleeding into the white of the eye, expanding outward, toward the cornea. And then he paused.

It was not a momentary pause, but a full-body cessation. The lion just stopped moving.

Something danced behind the lion's eyes. There was something inside them, pawing around, scrabbling for purchase, struggling in their all-seeing vacancy. The amber rings of the lion's irises were like portholes to the soul. When that something inside reached the portholes and looked out, the amber rings framed the eyes of a sailor trapped on a ship sinking at sea. For one brief moment, that sailor was there, looking out from his doomed vessel. And then he was gone.

Ben had seen eyes like those, once before.

***

He didn't understand at the time. And by the time he did understand, it was already too late.

Jamie was still supposed to be at college, nearly finished with her second year. He found out later that she had only recently started her first.

She had gone to ENGRAM first. Then she had gone to college. She "met" Ellen not long after. Ben hadn't remembered who Ellen was until he found the picture.

It was after the divorce when he found it. He was packing up for a move. He couldn't live in the house any more. It wasn't the place it used to be. There was sadness in it. He could smell it on the walls, seeping into the floor. He could see it sucking the color out of the world, a sickness taking root.

He was digging through a box of old things, deciding what to throw out and what to keep, when something white and glossy slipped out and into his lap. It was a photograph taken on a midsummer weekend with an ancient camera Marren had been working on restoring as one of her Human-research projects.

Jaime was eight. It was her birthday. She was happy. He was happy. His wife was happy.

He had a family.

But there was someone he had missed. There was someone else in the family. She had been there all along. He just hadn't been paying attention.

He remembered it all when he turned the photograph over and read what he had written on the back.

"The Forec Family: Marren, Ben, Jaime (8; the big birthday girl!), and Ellen, over at Grandma's."

Ellen had been Jaime's best friend.

She was imaginary.

Jaime hadn't been making a peace sign.

She had been making rabbit-ears.

***

That's what he had been missing.

In Ben's mind, the state of the world was a phase, and he wanted the world to just grow up and out of it. Like a foolish father dismissing a little girl's imaginary friend, he was dismissing a part of that world, its troubles, its cares. In doing so, he was dismissing the people that lived in it. He was living for himself and not for others. He knew that now. And just like that, like someone flicking a switch in his head, he decided to change. To be different and to make a difference. Not just for himself, but for everyone.

"What's that got to do with anything?" Kent growled. Nearly two minutes had passed. The sound of the lion's voice brought Ben out of his thoughts and into focus with a startling sharpness; he could feel that sharpness like a blade wedged in his heart.

Kent's tail twitched agitatedly. His nose had started bleeding. It was minor. He wiped his paw across the end of his muzzle and looked down at it with not much more than annoyance. "I gave my statement," he said. "Are we done or what?"

Ben reached up and took off his glasses. He rubbed at his eye sockets. They were wet with tears. "Yes, we are done, Mr. Lamont," he said. "I believe we have everything we need."

"Good," the lion said, picking himself up. He wiped at his nose again. "Then I'm going back to bed. Another one of these damn headaches coming up on me."

"Headaches?" The compassion in his own voice surprised the raccoon. He almost laughed. How had he missed it for so long? He had been arrogant. Self-serving. Self-centered. "Do you want anything for it?"

The lion shook his head and waved a paw half-heartedly. "Sleep. Feel like I haven't been able to sleep for months."

"I know the feeling, my friend," Ben said. He leaned back and looked over his shoulder. Connor met his gaze and nodded sympathetically. Then he cut the camera off. They had what they needed. The dog patted him on the forearm as he slipped past to knock on the door and notify the orderlies that they were done.

The two panthers came in and undid the lion's bonds. They were leading him out of the door when he stopped suddenly.

"Hey Ben?" Kent asked, without turning around. He was dabbing his nose with a handkerchief one of the orderlies had given him.

"Yes, Mr. Lamont?"

"When you're done with this ... with me ... you should look into what's going on with ENGRAM. They might protect themselves from their clients, but if they don't know what they're doing, if they don't know what's going on? Or even worse, if they do, and they're still doing it? That's, that's ..."

"Medical malpractice? Corporate misconduct?"

"Yeah."

"I'll look into it, Kent. I promise."

***

The Diagnostic and Statistical Manual of Mental Disorders describes Dissociative Identity Disorder as a condition that is typically characterized by the presence of two or more distinct personality states that continually have or trade power over an individual's behavior. They are often subject to memory variations that fluctuate with the affected individual's personalities.

Symptoms of DID may include but are not limited to: headaches, amnesia, time loss, trances, self-persecution, self-sabotage, and even violence (both self-inflicted and outwardly directed). The afflicted, in their brief moments of lucidity, often describe this feeling as a sensation of being a passenger in their own body.

***

Kent Lamont was a coping mechanism of Jason Lamont's invention; his self-imprisonment was a scenario constructed from elements of oppression, introspection, and an over-exposure to crime-scene-investigation-style television programs. Jason Lamont was suffering from DID as a direct result of undergoing a faulty ENGRAM memory-isolation procedure. His case, the first of over two hundred confirmed cases of isolation failure, would be a landmark lawsuit that would set the precedent for a slew of subsequent litigation, ultimately resulting in the company's bankruptcy and the cessation of its practices.

Ben Forec, Esq., would head that lawsuit.

But before he'd do that, he'd go home and clean up his apartment. He'd take out the trash, sit on the steps in front of his apartment complex, and he'd finish the wooden lighthouse while watching the sun rise through the gaps between crumbling buildings, strangely aware of the lingering red of sun-bleached brick and the choking green of vines scaling it on either side. He'd remember the time when he took his daughter, then eleven, to see that lighthouse, a piece of the old Human world, before the rise of the metal and glass towers in its stead and the fall of the empire that built them. He'd remember when he told her what it was, standing there with her on the shoreline of ice reaching far off into the Pacific, and how she asked him what good it would do to guide boats if there was no water for them to be on. He'd remember how he told her that his father once told him that, sometimes, the boats were spirits sailing in the darkness, and that you couldn't always see them, but that they were in need of guidance all the same. He'd remember how she told him that she thought his father sounded like a good person, and that she was sad she'd never get to meet him. He'd told her that he was a good person, and that he hoped one day he'd find peace in the darkness. That they all would.

He'd encapsulate that memory in the wooden carving and send it off to a lonely little assisted-living cottage somewhere out in the red sands of Red Desert, Wyoming—far outside of ENGRAM's reach. With that carving would be a letter addressed to Ellen. In it, he would ask that Ellen wish Jaime a happy birthday for him, belated as it may be, and to tell her that her daddy wasn't upset that she hadn't had time to write him back— he knew that life could be hectic. He'd apologize for his gift running a little bit late, explaining that Daddy was just having things a little rough this year, and that things had been hectic for him too, but he was hoping they would get better soon. He'd tell her about how he was excited over a recent development in a case he was working on, and how he thought that, maybe, just maybe, things were already getting better—that there was someone out there leaving a lighthouse on for him.

And then Ben would finish that letter by doing something he should've done a long time ago: he'd wish them both well. He'd thank Ellen for taking the time to read his letters and deliver his messages over the years, and he'd tell her that, while he didn't have much of a family anymore, she was ever as much a part of it as Jaime was, and she should never, ever forget that.

Get your vaccinations.

RESISTANCE

David M Sula

The Lion wrinkled his nose pinching the pads of his paws over his offended nostrils. A squint eclipsed his yellow eyes. "Did you fart?"

Chase offered a meek half smile of apology. The lanky human's palms upturned in a gesture that Theo could only interpret as, "Not my fault," but that didn't stop the Lion from glaring anyways.

The couple lounged on their couch, Theo with a book in his paw and Chase tapping snarky tweets into his phone. The human had his back against the arm rest occupying two cushions by himself leaving his large Lion of a boyfriend with the last one. Theo had crossed his legs, leaning on the other armrest with his elbow. With his thick full mane catching the golden light of the lamp on the side table, he was the picture of poise and refinement until the noxious fumes encroached into his already limited territory.

"Jesus, Chase." He waved the book at the human, trying to waft away the tainted air. He leaned farther to the side, trying to get away without forfeiting his seat on the soft couch.

Chase rolled his eyes, trying to hide his embarrassment behind his phone. When Theo started to make gagging noises, Chase furrowed his brows. "Okay, it's not *that* bad."

"You don't have a predator's nose." Theo surrendered, moving to the arm chair on the other side of the living room. He opened his book again, this time squinting at the words in the dark corner.

"I've been having tummy troubles lately," Chase said in place of excusing himself.

"Maybe if you ate more, you wouldn't. You're as thin as my wrist." The Lion held up one of his thick muscular arms. Chase gave another eye roll at the exaggeration. He was skinny, but not *that* skinny.

The human snorted. "Well maybe if I wasn't on an all meat diet, this wouldn't be happening."

"I buy you vegetables," Theo argued.

The human sighed and shook his head. "You bring me home celery and brown lettuce. Leave it to a Lion to not know the qualifications of edible greens. Is that Rabbit still working there? What was his name? Cory! Talk to him, and let *him* pick out the produce for you."

"Brown fur? Floppy ears?"

"Yeah! That's him." Chase used to talk to him all the time when they shopped together. Theo had a habit of being really nit-picky with the butcher and would spend a half hour selecting the choicest meats. The Lion was worried about being scammed. During these endless negotiations, Cory and Chase would exchange pleasantries and recipes. The Holland Lop Rabbit was a friendly face for shopping trips. Chase missed that.

Theo closed his book. He leaned forwards and refused to make eye contact with the human. "He uh…I'm sorry, babe. He's dead."

Chase felt like his heart stopped. Everything froze. All senses became muffled from the news. The heat of the radiator faded. The clanks of the vents silenced. He stared at the feline with a slack jaw. "What happened?"

"The Butcher said it was a freak spinal accident. Hopped so hard he broke his own back after a car backfired outside his house."

"When were you going to tell me?" Chase accused. He was on his feet, phone clenched in a trembling hand.

"When it was relevant?" Theo guessed. Now it was his turn to bear an apologetic half smile. Chase could see the regret in his boyfriend's eyes, but that didn't cut through the fury he felt towards him.

"Why would you keep something like that from me?"

Theo set the book aside. "What good would it do to relay every tragedy that happens in the outside world? As it is, you spend all day reading all the bad news on your phone."

"What else am I supposed to do? I haven't left the apartment in three months, hon. My only connections to the outside are this stupid thing—" he squeezed the phone with a snarl— "and *you.*"

A slow delicate sigh wheezed out of the Lion's nose. Theo's face softened with guilt. Chase regretted instantly being so harsh; he hadn't meant to bring up how rough this situation had been, because he knew it bummed the Lion out. Theo was doing the best he could to keep up the illusion of normalcy. Neither of them wanted this to take a toll on their relationship, but every day was challenging for Chase, and some days were harder than others, especially with news stories growing even more grim as the weeks dragged on. Looking at the world pass by through a cell phone screen was making Chase more and more depressed. For the Lion's sake, he constantly tried to force a happy facade despite being trapped here, but he couldn't help but show how he really felt from time to time, especially times like now with this devastating revelation.

There was so much more he wanted to say, but Chase couldn't afford an argument, not with the only person he was allowed to see face to face. Everything he read on social media and online newspapers felt distant and foggy, but hearing about Cory shot a dose of reality into Chase that made him painfully aware of how much time was passing. He left the room, barely aware of his own body. His feet took him to his bedroom where he could lie down in the dark.

***

Theo opened the fridge and scanned its contents. There were lots of dairy products: milk, cheeses, yogurt, and three different types of coffee creamer. There were two loaves of bread—Chase insisted that refrigerating them would prevent mold. Then he opened the less-used produce drawers. The Lion pulled out the lettuce and sniffed it. He winced, a growl instinctively rumbling from his throat. It brought back a sickening memory of when he was eight and Kenny Hendricks dared him to bite into a lettuce head—or maybe it was a cabbage head—and he threw up. He wanted to make his boyfriend feel better though.

His ears fell flat into his mane as guilt rushed through him. Theo should have known better what constituted quality even with foods he couldn't stomach. He turned the lettuce over in his paw and spied what Chase had mentioned: a stain of dead brown coloration eating across the crispy leaves like rust. He tried to imagine Chase buying food for him that was this low in quality. Surely Theo could have done better. He had to fix this.

Theo put on a coat and grabbed his car keys and made his way to the front door. The door was obstructed by a phone-booth-sized box constructed from pvc pipe with soft plastic stretched around its frame. Gaffers tape adhered it to the wall and floor so that it was sealed all around the door frame. A zipper lined the side opposite the door. The zipper was still open from when Theo came home from work earlier. He opened the plastic flap and stepped into the box before zipping it closed. Then he opened the door and stepped out into the chilly autumn day and the lethal air.

He inhaled it through his nose. It was crisp and dry, no different from any of the other twenty seven autumns he'd experienced before. It even bore the same taste as before, but if Chase stepped into this atmosphere, it was almost certain that the human would catch the Chill. The disease came out of nowhere, a mutated flu virus that had evolved beyond the inconvenience this illness used to be. Anthros were immune, so immune that the virus couldn't even survive in their bodies, but humans were so much more susceptible to it. Every day the death toll rose, but the virus mutated too fast for vaccines to have any real impact. Some of the outdated vaccinations responded with mixed results, showing humans with increased ability to fight it off, but so many died later on that few people wanted to trust it. There was talk of some people building up a natural resistance to the Chill, but others said that those who became resistant eventually just fell prey to a stronger strain. As more news of the resistance spread, the populations of the world clung to hope, but even the resistance wasn't foolproof. It wasn't immunity. It just made it harder for the contagion to spread to them, and eventually enough outdoor exposure would contaminate them too, so almost no humans stepped outside anymore.

Theo watched the leaves fall as he walked to his parking spot. The painted ground of orange, yellow, and brown was a depressing omen. The world was full of a new death that just kept spreading. But at least Chase was safe in their apartment. The contagion had exploded in larger cities first, so a lot of small towns like theirs had only seen a few infections before every human household had equipped themselves with quarantine booths. Now plastic covered windows. Decontamination chambers were a must. Some entire businesses were put out of work because species liked to flock together. Diverse work forces were fine, but Theo's own office was struggling. Their boss was stuck at home as well as eight other workers. Thankfully they were still managing. Rent bills didn't stop coming in the face of catastrophe, and Chase still hadn't managed to find a job he could do from home. Clambering into their hybrid car, Theo turned the ignition and sped off towards the grocery store.

It was the same old store as before the Chill. The supermarket sprawled out with over a dozen aisles. The same old Crocodile manned the butcher counter. The same old Bluebird watered the flowers. The same old clumsy Hippo over-frosted birthday cakes, still unable to control how hard she squeezed the icing piper after all these years at this store. Theo waved a hello to the butcher and pressed onwards to the produce section. Carts of fruits and vegetables with fake wood-printed paper covering created the illusion of a farmer's market. Greens filled shelves while buzzing machines sprayed them continually with mist. There were Mice, Deer, Goats, and lots of other herbivores. No meat eaters to be seen. Immediately Theo felt self-conscious.

He had flashbacks to being a teen when he first discovered boys. He remembered being drawn to the romance novel aisle in the book store just to steal peeks at the covers of muscular shirtless male humans and Anthros. He always felt like an intruder or a pervert, like he was getting away with something. When the middle-aged women those books were actually targeted to stared at him, he would scamper away with ears flattened into his thickening mane. He wondered if it was fair to compare being an awkward gay teen to a Lion walking into a produce section. It seemed ludicrous to compare the two, but he still felt that same vibe: This isn't for you. He took a deep breath, trying to push those thoughts away, and approached a shelf.

The Lion paused in front of a wall of vegetables under a mister. Carrots, peppers, broccoli, and celery were all laid out before him. He picked up two carrots, one in each paw and compared them by weight. There were brown streaks around their shafts as well as little blemishes that resembled potato eyes. The only carrots he'd seen were in cartoons or the ones chopped into little finger shapes. What made them good?

"You lost?"

He turned his head, and he quickly dropped the produce as if he were afraid he'd just been caught with contraband. A small woman, a Rabbit who barely came up to his elbows, stood next to him. She was a smaller breed for sure. Short ears stood up straight and alert. Her fur was pure white, and her red eyes were a bit unnerving. The stare made Theo feel even less welcome, and he was about to turn tail and run back to the safety of a less polarized aisle, but then the woman smiled, showing off mismatched buck teeth.

The two-toothed grin made Theo relax a bit, and he laughed. "How can you tell?"

"Your tail is lashing like an anxious feral in a zoo. Don't worry. The carrots don't bite. But I'd keep an eye on those beets." She leaned in close and pointed at them conspiratorially, and Theo chuckled. "Shopping for someone particular?"

"My boyfriend. He's a human."

"Ah. Good for you."

Theo wasn't sure if she was congratulating him on having a boyfriend, being in an interspecies relationship, being willing to buy food for him, or just be so brazen about identifying his sexual preference in public. "I have no idea what I'm doing." He turned his attention back to the wall of produce. "How do I know what's good? Quality wise that is."

"Well it's not *that* hard." She laughed again. It was a sweet tinkling sound. She reached past the Lion for bundles of asparagus. She piled bundle after bundle into the cart and followed that up by clearing out the shelf of yellow and green bell peppers.

Theo snorted. "Go over to the butcher counter and pick out the best steak. I dare ya."

"Alright, point taken. Basically if it looks bright and crispy, it's good. If it's soft or pale, leave it for the dump." She then proceeded to plop plastic container after plastic container of fresh basil leaves into her cart.

Theo smirked. "A big feast?"

"Just h'ordeuvres."

"That's a lot of h'ordeuvres," the Lion remarked.

The Rabbit woman sighed and pushed her cart down a bit more to scoop more armfuls of greens on top of the peppers. "Yeah well, when you got eighty-six relatives flying in for the weekend, a lot only goes a short way." There was a certain stress to her voice like she was overwhelmed by the upcoming event. Theo could relate to that sort of pressure.

"Big party?"

"Funeral." She said the word like she was throwing it away, as casually as if she were announcing she was going for a fur grooming.

"I'm sorry."

"Thank you. It was quite a shock of course." Theo's face fell with sympathetic remorse. It didn't stop the visibility of the prying question in his furrowed eyes. The woman caught it and added, "It was my husband."

Theo tilted his head at her as she stared off into space towards another bin of vegetables. "Cory?" he guessed with a bit of hesitancy.

"You knew him?"

"My boyfriend did." Theo didn't know why it mattered who knew him. It didn't really change anything, but it seemed like it made the woman feel better. Theo wanted to offer more. "He…uh…my boyfriend that is said he could always trust Cory's opinions."

The woman smiled. Theo started plucking some of the red bell peppers from the bin, squeezing them gently to test for firmness. It felt like rubber and sounded like a child's drum when he tapped it. Shrugging, he put some into his basket and then grabbed some of the oranger thicker carrots. "I hope it's a lovely service," Theo offered.

"Thank you." She pushed her cart around him and started grabbing more greens.

"No carrots for the family?"

She laughed sarcastically. "Sure if I wanna give us all hypercalcemia."

As soon as he heard the unknown word that was unquestionably a serious ailment, Theo dropped the carrots back on the shelf like they were vipers. He flinched back. "I thought they were like good for eyesight. Oh my God, I'm gonna kill my boyfriend!" He buried his face in his paws, tail lashing even more.

The Rabbit set a paw on his arm. "Easy, kitten. Your *human* isn't gonna catch that from carrots; that's a Rabbit thing only. You give him anything on this shelf, and he'll be fine."

Theo huffed a sigh of relief. His shoulders trembled. He hadn't realized how stressed he'd become over this. "God. I'm so bad at this. I've been dating him for three years. I shouldn't have such a hard time taking care of him." Suddenly he had grown aware of just how useless he was for addressing the human's need. It was easy to just think the Lion way was good for all species. Just how hard had he been making it for Chase unintentionally? "Why is being in a relationship so hard?"

The Rabbit laughed that tinkling sound again. It was so real and genuine even as she was dealing with her current loss that it shocked the Lion. Theo raised an eyebrow at her. She wiped a tear from her eye. "Oh honey," she said with a shake of her head, "Relationships are *not* hard. I was married for sixteen years before Cory's accident. Being in the relationship is the *easy* part. The hard part is still being just you. I tell you it's so easy to dip into the comfort of pretending you're just half a person that the other 'completes.' And once you step into that comfort, you never want to leave. We want to pretend we're broken without the other to fill in those gaps that we really oughta be filling ourselves. We deny each other the rights to be our own individuals. Being yourself is the hardest thing you can do once you fall into that comfort. You gotta resist it though. Because..." her breath shuddered. "Some day you'll lose him, and then you don't know how to be your own whole." She broke down, tears pouring down her cheeks. She slumped against him. Theo turned towards her, wrapping her in his arms as she sobbed against his stomach. He didn't know what to do, if he should stay quiet or say something. He patted her back.

When the rabbit pulled away, she wiped her eyes and inhaled as if re-inflating her composure. "I'm sorry."

Theo stood there awkwardly, not sure how to respond, but oddly it was she who reassured *him*.

"Don't worry. You don't have to say anything. With how many relatives I have, I've already heard every cliché in the book. Just...take it from a young widow. Take care of your human. Because he's a whole person too who's probably worrying just as much."

Theo nodded. The thought was paralyzing but also comforting in a morbid sense. The Rabbit woman bid her farewell and moved on with her cart. The Lion turned back to the shelves of produce. She had given him a lot to think about.

***

Chase was slumped on the living room couch. He wasn't sure where Theo had run off to without a word. Usually Chase was the one who wanted distance after an argument. Though this wasn't really an argument…was it? It was hard to tell. But with the apartment to himself (a scenario he'd grown quite accustomed to over the past few months) he returned to the living room and flipped on the television. Watching the news was his usual ritual for the evening. Most of it was the usual stuff: incompetent congressional plans for budgeting the CDC, more school closures from the spread of the Chill in cities with high human populations, announcements for germ-proofing your home, all followed by a special interest piece about a Cat in Dayton who created a yoga class for people and their pets which seemed more like an excuse to bring puppies and kittens to their yoga classes than for anything practical. Even when the world fell apart, people could find ways to focus on nonsense.

After the segment ended, Chase called his mom. "How's Dad been?"

"Stir crazy as ever. It's not good for his news consumption."

"Let me guess. He's all, 'Ain't it weird how the Anthros aren't affected?'" Chase gruffed up his voice to imitate his father. He could practically hear the eye roll in his mom's response.

"Oh it's not *nearly* that subtle anymore. At least he stopped watching FOX News."

"Too much of a reminder?"

"Yup. So he's been scouring out more extreme confirmation bias on the internet."

Chase slumped back in the couch and sighed. "I hope he's remembering to wear his tin foil hat. Asshole."

"Now don't say that," she admonished. "He's still your father."

"Except I'm not his son anymore, remember?"

"You know he didn't mean that," she said with a sad insistence, as if she were trying to convince herself as much as her son.

"I'm sure his internet history would say otherwise. Theo's my other half. If he hates Theo, he hates half of me."

"Well by that logic I'm half asshole," she said pointedly.

"Oh come on, Mom. I—"

"I know it's hard, honey."

"It's not getting better though. It's getting worse. How many Christmases and Thanksgivings have we missed because of his—"

"Stubbornness?" she interjected.

Chase snorted. "I wasn't gonna say *that.*"

"I *know* you weren't."

Chase felt himself choke up. His throat was strangled by what he wanted to say next. "How many Christmases and Thanksgivings are even left?" He sniffled, and a tear rolled down his cheek.

He could hear the tearful tightness in his mother's reply. "Don't talk like that. We're all gonna be fine. You have to have faith that there will be a cure for us all."

His hands shook. He had to cradle the phone with both hands and hold it to his ear. He whispered, "I miss you, Mom." Chase never thought the Chill would happen. He always knew in the back of his mind that he wouldn't have his parents forever, but he never expected he'd be cut off from them so soon. Even when his father disowned him, the separation didn't wholly feel permanent. Now it was worse though. Chase felt like he was chained up, just out of reach while the clock ticked away, like when his grandma was dying of cancer. Any day a new strain could break out, something more easily passed that the quarantine doors couldn't hold back. Or Dad might do something stupid and get himself and Mom infected.

The last words his father spoke to him before the three-year silence echoed in Chase's mind again. "You're dead to me, Fur-faggot." Some day it could be more than words. He sighed into the phone. "Please be careful, Mom. I saw on the news that the heavier outbreaks were spreading upstate." They lived in Albany, only a hundred and fifty miles from one of the highest concentrations of the Chill in the country. Chase wished they could migrate elsewhere.

"Don't worry, Chase. We have our quarantine booths set up, and we get our groceries delivered."

"When was your last vaccine?"

"I got one last week."

Chase paused already knowing the answer but asked anyway. "And Dad?"

His mother tried to put as much confidence in her voice as possible, but the uncertainty of the future still leaked through. "I keep him inside." It was probably the best she could do. After a long pause where Chase could come up with nothing to say in response, his mother added, "We miss you too." He noticed how she said "we," but it still felt like it could only be an "I." Dad didn't miss him. His dad missed what he wanted Chase to be. He sighed. He heard the tromp of heavy footsteps coming down the hall. His neighbors were Gazelles and Hedgehogs, so he was pretty sure who it was.

"Theo just got home. I'll call you later?"

"Mhmm." They said their goodbyes, and Chase hung up as Theo walked in.

The Lion squeezed into the plastic booth and closed the door behind him. He dropped plastic bags at his feet and reached up to flip a switch at the top of the booth. A machine like a black leaf blower engine buzzed to life and pumped clouds of pale green gas into the booth. It was supposed to kill ninety nine point nine percent of germs and viruses. But that was only for now while the warm body of an Anthro still killed the microbes on contact. But every day the virus grew stronger. If it learned to survive in their bodies, a single kiss from his boyfriend could be Chase's doom. He tried not to worry about what-ifs though. There were already enough horrifying have-happeneds in the world.

Once the fog cleared, Theo unzipped the booth and stepped out with the bags. "I got you a surprise," the Lion announced. He beamed, but there was something in his visage that seemed plastic and fake. It made Chase suspicious.

"What?" He got off the couch and ventured across the room.

Theo pried open one of the bags. Chase peered inside and saw the pile of vegetables and fresh fruits. Yellow bananas, firm white onions, thick carrots, heads of lettuce as green and crisp as construction paper, and grape tomatoes like red glossy opals.

Chase looked up into the Lion's eyes with a leer of skepticism. "What's the occasion?"

Theo carried the bags to the kitchen and set them on the counter. "No occasion. Just thought we needed groceries. We were running low." The nonchalance did not fool the human one bit.

"Theo?"

The Lion slumped his shoulders. He didn't make eye contact. "I felt bad. I…I haven't been paying attention to your needs."

Chase rubbed the Lion's shoulders. He had to reach up to do so; the Lion was so much taller than him, but Theo leaned down into the human's touch. The boyfriends slumped against each other, arms wrapping around each other in a sideways hug. "I haven't been easy to deal with the past couple months," Chase conceded.

"I don't blame you though. You're not a Lion. That pride mentality is just a part of me. I expect people to cater to that, but it doesn't work for you. But I should be able to understand what a human needs at this point."

Chase snorted. "To be fair, most humans don't know what humans need."

The Lion laughed. His broad flat muscular stomach flapped in and out with the convulsions of his diaphragm, and then he purred. For that brief moment, Chase felt warm and safe with the Lion's strong arm around him, like a baby bird under a grown bird's wing. The vibrations of Theo's chest grounded him in the moment, and nothing else mattered. "I love you," Chase whispered. "*You're* what I need."

"I love you too." But as the words tumbled past Theo's lips on a desperate instinct, the Rabbit's words echoed in his mind, specifically the part about Chase being a whole person without Theo. And the Lion wondered if Chase *did* feel like a whole person on his own. Suddenly "You're what I need" didn't sound so much like a heartfelt sentiment as much as it did a cause for alarm.

***

Constantly consulting the recipes pulled up in swipeable tabs on his smart phone, Theo prepared dinner for them both. Whenever Chase poked his head in to offer help, the Lion waved a paw and told him to skedaddle. As Chase's insistence to assist increased, the Lion felt his mane fluffing up and his hackles raising with the ruffling of his ego. He may have been a dunce at the grocery store, but he was more than capable of following instructions as he sautéed vegetables in the pan, paying close attention to the colors as they cooked. The onions browned, which apparently was a good sign. The tomatoes softened, and he was cautious that they didn't get mushy. He pulled some scallops from the deep freezer too so the Lion would have something to pick out of the dish for himself. They sizzled on the pan, droplets of freezer burn vaporizing in the heat with the melted butter. In another pot the water boiled, and he added the rice. He felt pretty confident that his timing was going well. The stir-fried elements were nearly done, and the rice would cook quickly he hoped.

He made a sauce to top the dish and boiled some carrots for an appetizer. He kept thinking about that scary-sounding ailment that Rabbits could catch if they indulged in the vegetable, and he kept whispering under his breath, "Each species is different. Each species is different." His self-reassurance eventually slowed his pounding heart as he doused the flame under the frying pan with a crank of the stove dial. He laid out two plates for each of them and poured some red wine: Chase's favorite. Then he scooped the carrots onto Chase's plate and sprinkled some brown sugar on top. He read somewhere that would make the hot vegetables sweet and flavorful. He hoped he was right.

When Chase was finally permitted to enter the kitchen, he walked in nose first, sniffing the aromas with a broad hungry grin. Theo felt a rush of satisfied air huff out of his muzzle in relief. Some of the cooking smells had even tantalized the Lion, but others were off-putting, and he had been anxious as to whether that was a reflection of his cooking or his species. As Theo placed the big pot of stir fry and rice on pot holders he sat down and pushed the opposite chair out with his feet for his boyfriend. Chase seated himself and appraised the spread. "Wow. This all looks amazing, hon."

"Yeah?" Theo felt his chest swell with pride. "I wanted to give you some variety."

"I haven't had a good stir fry in forever."

"Me neither. Not since we went to that Japanese place that made me sick. Too much garlic."

Chase smiled. They both recalled the cramps that Theo endured afterwards. The massive feline had avoided the spice tonight, but the drooling appetite shining on Chase's face was more than enough validation for the Lion to be assured that was an okay choice. Chase dug in to the carrots first. He bit into the soft chopped chunk of brown-dusted orange and moaned. "Oh my God; this is so good."

"Not too much brown sugar?"

"Just enough. Try some." Chase stuck his fork into a few pieces and held them out to the Lion. Theo leaned back in his chair, twisting away from the orange veggies with a grimace. He clutched his stomach.

"Uhhhh."

"Oh don't be a baby," Chase teased. "Are you a Lion or a Mouse?"

"I guarantee you a Mouse would react the same way to *my* diet."

"Come on. I had a pet cat when I was a kid. We fed him carrots, and he lived to be seventeen."

"Oh really. That long? A whole ten years younger than me? Man, why didn't I jump on this sooner?"

Chase chuckled. He loved watching his big Lion pout. The way his black lips wrinkled in protest was adorable on his big fuzzy face. "You *know* that's over eighty five in Anthro years."

Theo huffed and crossed his arms. "Fine," he grumbled. Leaning over the table, he opened his maw and unrolled his rough tongue. Chase eased the fork onto the pink muscle, and the Lion closed his muzzle. Sharp teeth clinked on the metal of the fork. He pulled the food off it and chewed. His face was one of uncertainty.

"Well?"

Theo gulped. His pouting frown wrinkled. "It's good," he conceded.

To the Lion's disgruntlement, Chase tipped the big bowl of carrots and plopped a good portion onto the Lion's plate. He ate them disdainfully, a pettiness from being proved wrong. "Does this mean I'm expected to eat veggies too now?"

"Just the ones that won't make you sick. Don't worry. I can give you the whole list."

"Ugh. Fine. But they better not give me cramps or gas. I don't wanna pollute the living room like you did earlier."

Now it was Chase's turn to complain. "I need my roughage. Gimme a break."

"If this meal doesn't help, I'm buying you a cork."

After a fierce blush came and passed on Chase's cheeks, their conversation dwindled, and they enjoyed the meal. Theo helped himself to rice and most of the scallops, while Chase guzzled veggies like a little herbivore. Theo smiled. He liked watching his human eat. Perhaps it was the predator in him. He knew from nature documentaries that big cats hunted their prey while they ate, when they were distracted. There was something about that that translated through the genes of his Anthro body. He could just scoop up the little man in his arms and carry him away. He could kiss him softly. He could kiss him passionately. It wouldn't matter which. The human was a strange animal. They ate with their eyes on their plates. *They* could be so oblivious too, and it made Theo feel better about himself. As he scooped forkfuls of rice into his large muzzle, he watched Chase.

He was as sweet and innocent and attractive as the day they first met. Thin, fragile, easily broken. He was someone for Theo to take care of besides himself. He was someone to protect. It was the Lion's job to protect the pride. That's what his dad had always taught him. Chase was no cub though. He was a man in his own right, but with the world itself now an enemy to the human race, these walls were now Chase's whole world, and Theo was tasked with making that world safe. He could care for him. He could watch him. He could love and possess him. But Chase needed freedom, and Theo often forgot that. Humans were like avians in need of wings and cats in need of independence but also like canines in need of companionship and lizards in need of space. Just what were humans made of? Hairless flesh and contradictions. Humans baffled Theo as much as they fascinated him, and much like a natural predator would, he never grew tired of watching.

They continued to eat in silence, but they didn't mind that. In the silence they could hear every purr and sigh and breath. Sometimes, Theo could even hear the human's heartbeat across the room. He listened for it now, and it sounded faster than normal. It sounded like an anxious heartbeat, though Chase's expression was relaxed and calm. Human faces were so easily readable. Theo didn't have any reason to suspect anything pressing was weighing on Chase's mind, but he asked anyway. "You alright?"

Chase nodded with enthusiasm as he cut up his last scallop. "Mhmm. This is the best dinner you've ever made."

Again Theo grinned. He hadn't been searching for another compliment, but he accepted it all the same.

"You okay, Fuzzy? You're shaking the table."

Theo grumbled at that silly nickname and smoothed his mane. Then he became aware that he'd crossed his legs at some point. His foot paw shook so much that the wine swayed in their glasses. The Lion relaxed when the human's bare toes gently stroked his own. They both chuckled. A gentle blush warmed the Lion's golden cheeks.

"Just making sure you're enjoying everything."

"I am." He sipped his wine and then cleared his throat.

"Too dry? You like Merlot, right?"

Chase's brow furrowed. "It's good. I just cleared my throat. Are *you* okay? You seem a bit stressed."

"Of course." After a moment's pause, Theo pressed, "Want anything else?"

"Nah, nah. I'm full."

"You sure? Anything you want. You name it it's yours."

"Hon, you did enough. What's gotten into you. You've been acting weird since you got home."

"Nothing's wrong. I just want to make sure I can provide everything I can for you."

Chase's face fell. "Cuz I can't provide for myself." He laid his fork sideways across his plate.

Theo leaned forwards, grasping both of the human's hands in his paws. "No. No. That's not what I mean, babe. I just..."

"You pity me."

"I *love* you. And it's killing me to watch you cooped up in this apartment. I just want to make things better for you. I've realized I haven't been doing that."

He pulled his hands away from Theo's. "Well stop. It's like you're babying me, and I'm sorry that there's only so much I can do in a one-bedroom apartment besides send out job applications into a dystopian nightmare."

Theo bristled. "That doesn't bother me Chase. We're fine. It's just—"

"What?"

"You seem miserable."

"I *am* miserable. I can't work. I can't do *anything*. My stupid dad hasn't been vaccinated. And I haven't seen him in three years."

Theo's ears flattened. "Because of me."

"No! Not...it's because he's a piece of shit, but I kept hoping that with passing time he'd eventually stop being such a speciest prick, and we'd have a chance to start over, and I could have a relationship with him again, but time's passing by, and he's just becoming worse and worse. I can't...I can't do anything. I can't get through to him, and more than likely I never will."

"Chase."

"It's so hard!" Tears welled in the human's eyes. It ripped Theo apart to see. He wished he could do something. Now the double-edged sword of that pride mentality cut him deeply, but there was nothing he could do. He couldn't fix Chase's relationship with his father, or assure his or his parents' safety. He couldn't even provide the human a breath of fresh air. The Lion shook his head. He'd stupidly thought this dinner would make things better. Like a meal would change the fact that the whole world was falling apart for an entire species.

"I'm sorry," Chase cried. He wiped his eyes on his napkin. "I know you're trying to make things better, but—"

"I can't. I know I can't. I wish I could." Theo knew that he wasn't enough, not for this. He did everything right today for his man, but it wasn't enough. The Rabbit was right. Being in a relationship was easy. Being himself, being a whole was hard. "What do you need?"

"To not be a human." He threw the suggestion away casually, sarcastically, and painfully like a bee sting. It came out so easily but it pulled out the rest of him with it.

"I *like* that you're a human. I know that's not what you want to hear, and it may sound horrible to say, but you wouldn't be the same if you were anything else. I don't care what anyone else says. You complete me. You fill the holes in me." And in his despair, Theo understood. He needed his boyfriend. He wouldn't know who to be or how to be without him. To be by himself, to be himself and *only* himself? It would be hell. Theo could never live like that. He stood and walked around the table.

Chase looked so small with his shoulders hunched, his head low, his hands drooping between his legs. The human refused to look up, and Theo wouldn't accept that. He curled a blond knuckle under Chase's chin and lifted it, forcing eye contact. "No matter what it takes, if you can't step out into the world, I will bring it to you."

Chase stood and threw his arms around the Lion's midriff. He buried his face in Theo's shirt and sobbed. "I'm sorry, Theo. I'm sorry. I'm just *so* scared."

Theo rubbed his back. "Shhh. I know. But we're in this together."

Theo walked his boyfriend to the living room. They sat on the couch and just held each other. Arms clung around backs. Fingers massaged scalps. Noses sniffed necks. Theo's heart thumped a slow steady pace against the human's small panicked one. Pound pound pound. There were no words. Just breath and life.

After a while though, Chase pulled away and clutched his stomach. It ached. He winced.

"You okay?"

Chase shook his head. It was like something in his guts was twisting.

"Probably ate too many veggies," Theo teased, trying to lighten the mood any way he could. He poked his boyfriend's stomach and winked. "I told you meat is the only real way to go."

Chase stood up arching his back. Perhaps if he could achieve the perfect posture, the cramps would go away, but they got worse.

"I swear if you fart, you're sleeping on the couch tonight."

Chase winced. He normally would have laughed at that, but instead he contorted in pain. He felt nauseated. A pressure built in his throat like a fist working up his esophagus. His Adam's apple felt stretched. Something bubbled inside him, and his lungs heaved. He coughed once then twice, and on the third cough he felt the rush of food coming back up. He covered his mouth and ran as fast as he could to the bathroom. Theo watched with wide eyes.

Chase made it just in time to collapse before the toilet. He hurled into the porcelain bowl. The nasty taste of bile burned his tongue. Mushy food splashed into the water, splattering onto the toilet seat. Some dribbled down his chin. Theo tentatively strode over to him, standing just outside the bathroom door. "You okay, hon?"

Chase wanted to say "yes," but he also wanted to say "no." In the end, he had to settle for dipping his head back into the bowl to puke again. His whole body shuddered with the convulsions of his upset digestive tract. Chase fell back on his bottom. He placed one hand on the rim of the toilet seat to support himself as he wobbled back and forth. The wooziness took everything out of him, and every organ itched with the self-disgust of his innards emptying themselves out. His lungs squeezed, and the stomach acid burned his throat. He coughed into his other fist. His whole torso clenched. He coughed again and again until he doubled over, hacking violently.

Theo pushed into the small tiled room and knelt in front of Chase. He laid a massive paw on the human's shoulder staring with concern. His first thought was one of self-deprecation. His cooking wasn't as good as it had seemed. He didn't cook the scallops all the way through. There was something wrong with the sauce. Chase had an allergy neither of them were aware of.

Then Chase lifted his head, pain in his eyes. When Chase tried to catch his breath, it was a wheeze. His hand was stained red with blood.

***

They came in yellow hazmat suits, Anthros only. They bustled around the apartment, swabbing everything in sight, checking the windows for leaks, taping everything up. Theo sat on the couch, paws folded between his legs. A Raven in a suit swabbed the inside of the Lion's cheek. It felt invasive. Chase was in the other room, being tested. They didn't want to risk bringing him outside unless they absolutely needed to. Theo's foot thumped continuously on the carpet. His heart pounded. He could still smell the human blood. It was salty and full of that awful wet metal stench. He tried to distract himself by guessing the species of the medics by the lumpy jaundice-colored silhouettes. Finally a Tiger came into the room, gloved paws folded. He stood before Theo and looked down. His eyes were expressionless behind the narrow glass eye shield. His muzzle was hidden from view behind the breathing apparatus.

"Can I see him now?" Theo asked. He wasn't sure if it had been minutes or hours. Either way it felt like days.

The Tiger ignored the question. "The tests are conclusive. I'm afraid that it's the Chill." The medic's voice was muffled through the apparatus. It vibrated like air through a fan. It sounded unnatural and devoid of that spark that made Anthros different from ferals.

Theo started to whimper, his face scrunching in agony. "But…h-how? We use th-the booth. We do everything right. W-we…we we we." His words caught in his throat.

"The strain has evolved. Anthros can carry it now."

Theo uttered a series of hiccupping sobs, trying to force out words, but he couldn't manage anything. Every word was trapped in his squeezing lungs. Tears poured down his cheeks.

"I'm sorry."

"I'm c-carrying it?"

"The saliva tested positive. Still immune, but a carrier all the same."

"When did this happen?" His voice squeaked and cracked. He thought his own face might split under the pressure of the sadness in his own leaking eyes.

"Your boyfriend has been infected for about a week now. He had the resistance, but...the virus won out."

"I want to see him. I...I n-need to see him, can I see him now? I need to see him!" he roared. He pushed himself onto wobbling feet that could barely support his weight. The Tiger in the yellow suit sidestepped to block his path, his eyes finally showed a tinge of emotion: pity. He looked like he was about to say something, but then two other yellow blobs rounded the corner. They pushed a gurney upon which rested the black zippered body bag.

Theo felt something in him shatter. His chest caved in as he watched one of them pull apart the quarantine booth so they could push the gurney out of the door. Tears ran in rivers through his fur as he moaned. Theo struggled to fill his grief-crushed lungs. He tried to push past the Tiger, but his limbs were weak and useless. They disassociated from his brain and barely responded to his wants to push forwards. Theo slumped against the other feline and outstretched a paw to the wrapped-up body. The Tiger held him up and held him back. Then Theo roared. "Nooooo! No no no no! Nooooo!" He pulled free of the Tiger and fell to the ground, eyes on the gurney as it was wheeled through the front door and out of sight. He moaned and sobbed and screamed. His eyes clenched shut as tears flooded his vision. He buried his face in his paws. Claws extended and ripped through his mane.

The Tiger crouched and offered a paw. "Sir, I need you to come with me. We're evacuating the whole building and quarantining it. The CDC is on their way. Sir, please, I need you to get up."

Theo blindly batted away the Tiger's paw. He sniffled and could still smell Chase's scent in the carpet, in the air. It was everywhere. It was still strong and fresh and alive. He couldn't leave this room. He could never leave this room. "Leave me alone!" he roared. "Get out! Get out!"

The Tiger sighed. The largest medics of the team surrounded him. Thick arms, perhaps an Elephant's or a Rhinoceros's, scooped under his armpits. The yellow suits were cold and indifferent, like the way rubber blocks an electric charge. They didn't feel alive. It was like the Anthros were just calloused machines as they dragged him squirming and screaming out of his apartment. Theo hated them. He hated them. He hated Anthros. He hated himself. He hated the Chill. He hated everything with a heartbeat, because they were luckier than Chase. He tried to tear himself free, tried to run off. His heels dragged on the carpet. He dug claws into their sleeves but

106

the suits were too thick to puncture. What were these stupid suits made of that kept these soulless medics safe? And what were humans made of that made them so weak?

END

This is a tiny, gemstone of a story, but inside its facets you'll find one of the most epic tales of reincarnation and transformation.

THE HARD WAY

Val E Ford

"Come with me..." Liam's voice was scratchy from the tubes that had been sustaining him during the last bout of pneumonia and worsening health. He fumbled to unzip his fleece jacket with the hand that wasn't holding hers.

An image burned itself into Katy's being. She knew truth when she saw it; it was one of her gifts, to see the in-between spaces, and this was one, this was for her a liminal moment. She had to walk off this bridge alive today.

"Not this time, Love." Katy stared wide-eyed down at the roiling floodwaters, hooked her knees through the space between the metal railings and moved her grip on him from a hand hold to a wrist hold. "You come back home and do it the hard way."

"Katy...I can't...I'm burning. It's time. We have to go." His voice extended into the realms beyond her ear's ability to hear, and the essence of his elemental fire gift burned through their connection as he sent the command she'd been dreading ever since they'd realized he'd be living disabled for the rest of his life after the car accident. "I can't live this way." He sat on the balustrade, and his free hand pulled up on the orthopedic brace to lift his leg over the rail as she tugged at him to prevent the move. Even ill he was a great beast of a man and beyond her physical control.

He had taken it as his job over their several lifetimes, the killing of them both, so they could be together again. But Katy never remembered it being like this. Never such a choice. But maybe it had been; memories of other lives came on slowly, mostly after they found each other again. This time was different, maybe it was just that her attitude was different.

"I love you, Katy. We have to go." His elemental fire was licking along his outline, breaking through into the air around him.

She fought his blazing command, bringing up the blessed coolness of the earth and binding the heat, sending it through her body and out her pores to meld with the wind and let it be carried away. "I'm not going. I'm not ready. You get back down here before you pull my arm off." She started fighting his fire for him too.

"Katy! We. Are. Doing. This." He swung his other long leg over the railing. "It's just a step, Love." He smiled and took it.

Katy tried to pull him back over the edge, but his mass only took a second to lift her off her heels; her knees around the rails were the only thing keeping her out of the air. And by the moment she stopped trying to save him and instead save herself, his grip on her arm was winning. So, she breathed in the power of her connection with the spaces *between* and sent it flowing down the shining fluid pathway that anchored their souls together, down into the spaces between the cells of his heart muscle, and by the time she was done, so was he.

"Goodbye, Love," she told her soulmate as his dying fingers slipped from their grip on her arm. He finished his long falling step into the flooded river alone. "We'll find each other again," she whispered as her tears followed him into the encompassing water below. She braced herself against the moment when their connection blazed and disappeared, and then she sat on the cold concrete for a long time taking in what it meant to be alone.

Over the next few weeks, Katy took to wandering the streets at odd hours on foot and in her car. She was unsettled, lonely, not sleeping, going long stretches between eating until a smell awoke her hunger and then she couldn't stop. At first, she cried at silly things, sometimes everything, but after a while numbness crawled out of the crater inside her soul, and she started a new routine. She'd walk at first light to the bridge and cross, following the path along the shore until her feet didn't want to go any further, and then she'd stop for a while, breathing in the sea air before walking back.

And then one day, like sun through a break in the clouds, she felt the moment he returned. And she cried because they were off kilter. A soulmate in diapers wasn't an easy thought. But the crater inside her eased, and she slept well again.

And so, she started living again too. She started seeing clients once more, telling them the truths she saw in the spaces between their current selves and the ones they would become. She sketched for them their liminal scene, the one that might change them, the image that burned in her mind as she sat with them. And before they left, she gave them the picture along with whatever words seemed right. Often no words were needed; sometimes it was just a hug.

She was finishing a session with a client who had come because she was feeling upset with her marriage, and yes, she needed a hug. The picture had been of the client's next-door neighbor opening the door to a motel room, and familiar shoes were sitting beside the bed. That hug went on a while, and when the woman steadied enough to step into her new life, Katy opened the door.

A squeal sounded under the woman's foot as she walked out. A fluffy black and white Mountain Dog puppy cried on Katy's doorstep, and when she picked it up, she knew.

"Hello, Liam." A vision of herself and the slightly older puppy at obedience school with a chain collar and a leash filled her head. And she smiled, perhaps a little too long.

And so, Katy had a dozen years of friends and gardening and working and good doggie companionship, until the day Liam the dog started flaming and his wide muzzle and sharp teeth gripped deep into her lower leg, piercing the skin as he tried to pull her over the edge of the riverbank.

As she fought him, a vision filled her mind, she saw a huge set of balancing scales in a spotlight on a table. On one side a mess of her long hair and longer skirts showed the pile of bodies to be herself as she had been the five times Liam had drowned her. On the other side of the scales, she saw Liam lying pale and sprawled in his unzipped fleece jacket, seaweed in his dark hair as a spotted dog was lowered beside him. The scale barely righted.

"Fuck you, Liam! I am not dying today!" Her leg was on fire, and anger churned through her as she fell over the bank. They both rolled through the dried grass and blackberry vines and into the water. She hugged the big beloved dog, and with a practiced breath, she stopped his heart and watched him flop into the shallows.

When she got back home alone that night with stiches and burns on her calf, her tears were back, and she swore off pets.

When she woke up on Saturday morning, Katy took her graying head to the hairdresser and her sore knees to the gym, and she opened all the windows and burned sage in their house and pounded on her drum and let her towels and sheets dry in the sunshine. Then she vacuumed dog hair off the couch and out of the corners and smiled as she made lasagna and savored their favorite meal alone.

Three months later a fuzzy black and white kitten crawled out of a stroller that a couple little girls were pushing toward her down the sidewalk. His littermates cried, their faces popping over the edge to see where he had gone. Katy picked him up, kissed him and ran to catch back up with the girls. "Enjoy this one, Love," she whispered to the kitten. Katy scratched his ears and gave him to the youngest child. Liam the kitten yowled and bit the child. The little girl dropped him looking heartbroken.

Katy grabbed the kitten as he dashed around her legs, thumped his nose with her fingernail, and swaddled him tightly in a dolly blanket before handing him back to the child. "He'll be better now I bet," she told her. "He told me his name is Liam, and he loves tuna."

Liam the cat was her constant companion as she worked in the garden and sat on the porch. But she never let him inside their house, and she never fed him. He attacked everyone who came to the house, even the UPS deliverywoman. At midnight every night for a month, he scratched and yowled until the screens were shredded.

When summer was heating up and Katy couldn't take the hot air anymore, she took down all the screens to have them remade with scratch proof materials and reinforced with grating. She was opening the back of her car, parked on the busy street in front of the screen shop, when she was struck in the shoulder by a flying twenty-pound black and white and burning fuzzball.

She stumbled and flung the cat away and nearly fell in front of a bus that slammed on its brakes. "That is IT, Liam! You want war?" she said, looking around and patting out the places where her shirt was scorched.

Then she felt the connection snap, and she was alone again in this world as the bus rolled away from a squished black, white, and red form.

The next morning, Katy woke up with mosquito bites layered over yesterday's burns and scratches, so she made a special trip to the store for bug spray and let off a great blast before going to work.

Her first client of the day was Doris, who really just wanted to know somebody loved her. Katy's talents failed her. The only image in her head was of Liam choking and burning, so she put Doris's plate of cookies into a sandwich bag and reassured her that children leaving home for college was a good thing as she walked her to her car. Then Katy quickly drove back home and opened all the doors and windows.

She found Liam hiding under the couch and let him spend the next day on her arm, drinking and dying as mosquitos do. And when he was gone, slow salty paths traced her cheeks as the drops of her tears fell beside him and upon him. She buried his tiny insect body beneath their favorite rose bush and sat on her knees remembering when they had planted it.

She longed for solace, for a full life with him, the children they had never had and the feel of his arms around her. She reached her essence deep into the soil and let the energy that lives *between* flow upward into her being. She brought the power up into her heart and let the imbalance of betweenness affect her, let the spaces between cells and molecules disrupt, and felt her death nearing as the gentle rhythm broke.

And then the earth beneath her feet became hot and heavy, and a drop of fire fell from the thorn of a rose and broke her concentration.

"Thank you, Liam," she whispered and cried a while, but didn't attempt it again. She sat out in the cold night air feeling the beauty of being alive fill and restore her.

At midwinter, their connection renewed as he entered the world again. And when the image came, she could barely believe the beauty of it. Liam had chosen a new way. He was a preemie whose head was misshapen, and his heart was barely clinging to life. So, she moved 100 miles and went to the hospital and volunteered to do some cuddling.

272 long days after Liam came into the world as a teenage addict's infant son, Katy held him as he took his last painfilled natural breath. And then she held the now sober mother, their once great, great, grandchild and helped wield the shovels and sing the prayers as the baby, Liam, met with the earth. And a few days later, she brought the girl home with her.

When she felt Liam enter the world again at midwinter, she felt expectation as the days grew longer and spring once more filled her garden. And then one afternoon at the end of a nap as she rocked on her porch, a vision of the scales appeared again, nearly evenly balanced.

She started walking again, saying her goodbyes to everything she loved, wandering pets, laughing children, the woman girl who was growing in her own ways. She walked often over the bridge and down nearly to the ocean, and eventually she started seeing a great sight, a black and white seal swimming along with her as she walked. And one day when Katy was ready, she took off her shoes, her knobby tender old feet exposed to the rocks as she waded into the cold water, and they went diving. And with her last breath she also took his.

The hardest person to resist against is yourself.

Coyote Magic

Ryan Campbell

The guidestone didn't look like anything special: a smooth globe of dark grey rock about three feet in diameter. It looked out of place sitting there in the middle of the lush room. Pel squirmed uncomfortably on the couch next to his mother. He tried to pay attention to the counselor, but couldn't help stealing glances at the stone now and then.

"Pel!" His mother nudged him in the ribs. "Pay attention. He's talking about your future." He didn't know why she'd made everyone dress up for this. It wasn't like anyone but the counselor was going to see them, and his blazer and tie would be uncomfortable if he ended up running around in the woods, or clambering through a volcano. He considered kicking off his dress shoes before touching the stone.

The counselor chuckled. He looked pretty old, even for a counselor, with wiry eyebrows and spotted skin, but he had a comfortable, unworried manner that put Pel at ease. He leaned back in his chair and interlaced his fingers. "It's all right. I haven't seen many boys or girls his age who could sit still before a joining. You must be pretty anxious, eh, Pel?"

"Yeah," he started to say, but his mother spoke over him. "He's the youngest in his grade. All his other classmates have their guides already, and he's been getting left behind. I really wish we could have done this sooner."

"A lot of parents feel that way, but it's good you waited until he turned sixteen. The earlier the joining, the more likely to be complications."

"But there aren't going to be any, right?" Pel asked, feeling anxious.

The counselor crossed his leg over his knee, his purple robe exposing a bit of spindly old-man leg. "Naturally, we can't make any guarantees. The magic does what it chooses, and anyone who claims to know its purpose is a charlatan. That said, in all my time as a counselor, not once has one of my initiates been vacant."

Pel smiled to show he was reassured, but he really wasn't. Any chance at all was frightening. He'd had dreams for weeks now of touching the guidestone and ending up in a white, empty expanse, where no guide came to meet him, and he'd had to tell all his friends and family he had no guide, no magical ability at all, and his friends all laughed at him, and his parents told him how it'd been his fault for something he'd done. He'd awoken from those dreams covered in sweat, wrestling with reality and the relief that it had been only a dream after all.

He'd seen vacants going about in public with their special white bracelets that marked them as unable to use magic, and had watched them with curiosity until his father told him that it was rude to stare. Everyone was always very gentle and careful with them, of course. It was polite to help a vacant if asked, but never to assume they needed help. He wondered what it would be like to go through all of life like that, with no future—never able to get more than a bottom-level job, never able to marry anyone other than another vacant. Thinking about it now made his stomach feel even more uneasy.

"Listen," the counselor said. "The important thing is not to worry about it. Your guide, whatever it is, will be personal to you. Special. It will be whatever makes you happiest."

Pel nodded again. "Okay."

"All right, then. Are you ready to get started?"

He wasn't. "Yes, sir."

"Good. Come on over and stand next to the guidestone."

Pel hopped off the seat. "Can I take my shoes off?"

"Pel!" He winced at his mother's voice.

The counselor chuckled. "Whatever makes you comfortable."

He toed the shiny shoes from his feet without untying them, a habit he knew annoyed his mother. Up close, the guidestone appeared even more ordinary than before, its surface dull and waxy-looking. He wondered if they ever cleaned it, or if it was caked up with the oil and dirt from millions of fingers.

"Now, I'm going to use my magic to light the guidestone," the counselor said. "When I tell you, go ahead and press both your palms to it. Once you do, you'll be in your guide's home. It could be any number of places, and some of them might seem scary, but don't worry. You can't be harmed there.

You'll have only a few minutes to meet your guide, and then you'll be back with us, and you'll have magic of your very own. Are you ready?"

"Yes."

"All right. When I say." The counselor closed his eyes and touched the stone. The light of his magic flowed from his fingertips, gold and silver, running over the surface of the guidestone like mercury. As his magic lit, his guide appeared, an iguana that clung to his shoulder. It regarded Pel with one disinterested eye and licked at the empty air as though catching an invisible fly. The magic coated the guidestone and then stilled, shimmering, a silver bubble webbed with veins of gold.

"Now," said the counselor.

Before fear could deter Pel, he lifted his hands and pressed them firmly to the guidestone, closing his eyes. The magic was cool like water on his hands. Then it disappeared.

A breeze ruffled his hair. He smelled plants and recent rain. He opened his eyes to rolling, yellow-grassed hills covered with scraggly bushes and low trees. A little bit prairie, a little bit forest. That was disappointing— the really powerful guides preferred to appear in wondrous settings—but only a little. Places like this could be home to strong guides like buffalo, elk, or mountain lions. He searched the grass, turning. Everything looked as real as real life, so much that he almost wondered if he'd simply been transported elsewhere. But no birds sung, no gnats swarmed in the air. The only sounds were the wind and his heartbeat. Where was his guide?

Ears perked in the grass. A grey lump that he'd only just looked past moved. It stood up on two feet. At first Pel thought it was a dog, but it had a slight, rangy frame and a pointed snout. It waved one paw and said, "Hello, Pel." It grinned and wagged its tail vigorously.

He stared, struggling to understand. "What are you?"

The creature tilted its head, lowering its ears slightly. "What do you mean, Pel? I'm your guide. Don't you know me?"

"You're a coyote."

It nodded, perking its ears again. "Yes. You're coyote-kin, Pel."

He shook his head, dazed. "No. No, I'm not," he mumbled. "Go away. Go away and send something else."

The coyote's tail stopped wagging. It took a step forward. "What do you mean? There is no one else. We're joined. I belong to you. You're my life."

He felt sick hearing the words. "No. No, there must be something else. Coyotes are—are all thieves and—and vagabonds and street people."

"We are?"

"So you can't be my guide. You understand? There was some kind of mistake. I don't accept you."

The coyote gave a hesitant grin. "You're joking, yes? Coyotes are jokers sometimes. But this is kind of mean."

"It's meaner to me. You're ruining my life."

The grin fell. Looking frightened, the coyote hurried toward him. Pel didn't want to look at it and turned away. Guides looked different to their owners, people said—to everyone else they were just your animal, but to you, they would be something else: half animal, half you. If he saw himself in that thing, everything would be real somehow. He groaned into his hands. "What am I going to do?"

"Pel. Pel." Its slender-fingered paws tugged at his shirt. Its voice broke when it spoke. "I guess I understand how—how I could be a disappointment." He hated that it even sounded a little like him. "But just try me. You'll see. Give me a name, and we can do magic. It will feel amazing, I promise. Don't you want to know what your magic feels like?"

"No. Not if it comes from you. I'll never name you."

"But that's not how it works, it—"

There was a sound like the rustle of wind, and then they were back in the guidestone chamber. Pel kept his hands at his face, hoping that somehow the coyote had not come with him. Maybe this happened sometimes, and no one talked about it. Maybe they could send him in again, and he'd find something better.

"Pel?" His mother's voice was sharp and frightened. "Pel, is something wrong?"

He lowered his hands and saw the coyote standing next to him, looking up at him with ears half-raised and a hopeful smile. So his life was over. Coyote-kin were the scum of the city. None of them worked for a living. They waited outside transit centers, playing music or casting dream-spells, begging for money. Most were just outright crooks. *I'd sooner trust a coyote* was a common saying.

He looked around at his parents, his mother's mouth pursed below her pointed nose. "Well, go on, son," the counselor said. "Tell us what you saw."

The coyote gave a slow wag.

He sighed, miserable. The lie was the only way out. "Nothing. I saw nothing."

Disbelief crossed his mother's brow. "What do you mean, you saw nothing?"

"Pel?" The coyote tugged at his pants. It sounded frightened now. Good. "Pel, what are you doing?"

He felt more confident in the lie, now. It was terrible, and his life would be a dull and meaningless one, but at least he wouldn't be hated. "It was just a white, empty space." He teared up at the words, letting them fill him with despair. "I'm a vacant."

***

The journey home was miserable. He sat in the back seat and stared out the window, listening to his mother leaving a message for his father, and then crying softly into her hand. Any time he looked over, he saw the coyote sitting in the opposite seat, hunched down and staring at him with an expression of confusion. So he kept his gaze out the window and toyed with the new white bracelet around his wrist, the one that marked him as a vacant, someone who would always need assistance. The bracelet could be loaded up with spells that would let him open locked doors, make purchases, and do the other normal, everyday things that magicked adults could do.

When they got home, he shut the car door before the coyote could get out, and followed his mother to the house. When he looked back, it was pressed up against the glass window, watching him bewilderedly. He closed the front door behind him. His mother asked if he wanted anything, and when he said no, she went off to go drink wine by herself in the living room.

Pel knew how disappointed and sad she was, but it was nothing compared to what he was feeling. His mother had her ermine, Valla, and his father was so proud of his great Pericles the gryphon. They had their great lives. He was the only bad thing in it. And at least he wouldn't be coyote-kin. He climbed the stairs to his room and almost cried when he entered. There, on the wall opposite his bed, was the smaller space his father had nearly completed for the guide: a wall nook with a bed and a hardened clay floor for practicing magic. Pel wouldn't need them now. He flopped onto his bed.

"Is that for me?" The coyote had somehow appeared inside, and was looking at the unfinished niche. There was no pillow or cushion there. A lizard or snake might have required a warm spot, a salamander a shallow tank. Pel and his father had planned to go to Guide Comforts after the joining.

"No. It was supposed to be for my guide. Stay out of it."

The coyote hunched lower and nodded. It curled up on the floor near his bed.

"Don't lie so close to me. Move over there." He pointed to the wall by the closet. He closed his eyes and wished it were yesterday, and he still had not touched the guidestone. He wouldn't cry, though. He wouldn't shame himself in front of the coyote.

"You can't just ignore me forever," it said after a while.

"Yes I can."

"You're supposed to give me a name." Its voice pleaded. "You're the only one who can. Please, won't you name me?"

He pulled the pillow over his head.

"You'll change your mind if you just feel your magic." Even with the muffling of the pillow, he heard its claws ticking against the wooden floor as it approached. It sounded a little hopeful, now. "Just try a little. Feel?"

Its awful fingers slid against his, rough and soft at once, and where they touched, he felt something inside him push to get out. There was a giddy flip in his stomach and a sense of anticipation, like when the train hung for just a second at the top of a roller coaster. His fingertips tickled, and he opened his eyes to see a rich indigo light, glossy and slick like oil, pooling around them. Frightened, he squeezed his hands into fists and pushed the coyote away with one arm, sending it sprawling onto the floor. When he opened his fingers, the magic was gone.

"No!" he shouted at the coyote. "Don't you understand? I can never do magic now. It's illegal to wear this bracelet if you're not a vacant. I'm not ever going to use your stupid magic. And I'm not ever going to name you, either. I don't want anything to do with you. Don't you ever do that again."

It flinched as though he'd hit it. "But Pel, this is the only life I get. And it's yours, too. You were supposed to be amazed with me. We're supposed to be so happy right now."

"I know. Sucks, doesn't it?"

***

He didn't go back to his regular school. There would have been another year of education in general magic, and then he'd have been split into his specialty classes based on his tests and performance evaluations. By law, the school was required to provide classes for every kin, but coyotes tended to drop out or get expelled. And that was if they went to school at all. Since Pel was a vacant now, there was no point in magical education. His mother had to drive him across the city to a special school for vacants. She said hardly anything the whole way, and her jaw was set forward like she was angry.

The school was sterile and white, like the designers thought seeing bright colors might remind the students that they had no magic. Pel followed his mother to the head counselor's office and tried not to look at the coyote, who stalked behind them with its nose wrinkled, muttering to itself.

The head advisor gave him a speech that was probably supposed to be encouraging, about how the important thing was to remember that life wasn't over, and how he had a choice and could either give up on life or try to do the best he could with what he had been given, but it was obvious she'd said it so many times that she was bored by it. He nodded and said, "Yes, Ma'am" in all the right places and was shown to his new class.

He shuffled in and said hi to everyone, and they all said hi back. They seemed overly normal, somehow. In his old school, if someone new came into class, some people would say hi, but others would make jokes to each other, or talk, or sleep. Here, everyone was sitting up and being polite. The teacher was a heavyset woman wearing some kind of elaborate wrap, like she was from another country. She gave him a warm smile and directed him to his desk. All the desks were set close to each other. In a normal class, each desk would have a smooth platform attached to each side so that joined students would have somewhere for their guides to sit. No need for that here. He squeezed himself into his seat.

"Where am I supposed to sit?" the coyote demanded, standing in the aisle.

He gave it a little shrug and then pointedly ignored it.

"Fine." It threw itself dramatically down into the aisle, wedged between seats, and folded its arms.

The teacher was talking about jobs that didn't require magic. A lot of vacants were excellent with mathematics or organizational systems, she said, and could often get very high-paying jobs. That sounded awful to Pel; he'd never been good with math at all.

"Ugh, boring," the coyote remarked.

He felt a flash of annoyance at sharing anything in common with it. "Shut up," he whispered at it.

"Why? We shouldn't be here. We should be out learning magic. Having fun."

"Be quiet!"

The coyote scowled at him. "Or what? You won't learn how to live without me? You're coyote-kin! It's what you are! You can't hide from it." Pel flushed at the word "coyote-kin," and the creature gave him a wicked grin. "Coyote-kin!" it shouted. "Coyote-kin, coyote-kin, coyote-kin!"

He couldn't hear anything the teacher was saying; the coyote was so loud and shrill that he put his hands over his ears. It got to its feet and stood right next to him, shouting into his ear over and over, barely stopping for breath. His ears rang with the sound. He squeezed his eyes shut and waited for it to stop, but it didn't; it just kept shouting "Coyote-kin" endlessly, as minute after agonizing minute ticked by on the clock, until finally he screamed back at it, "Shut up, shut up, shut up!" He beat at it with both arms, and it dodged deftly out of range, making him lose his balance and spill out of his chair onto the floor.

"Pel?" The teacher hurried over to him and knelt next to him. "Are you all right? Do you need me to call your mother?"

***

His mother never came. He took a bus home. He hadn't had fare for the bus, but the driver, his hands glowing amber, his bumblebee sitting on one shoulder, had glanced at Pel's bracelet with a look of pity, and said, "Go on back, kid." Pel deliberately waited until the doors closed behind him before stepping all the way in, keeping the coyote outside, but after he took his seat, he looked over to see the coyote in the aisle next to him, glaring furiously.

It was thirteen blocks from the bus stop to his home. A group of boys by a convenience store called, "Hey there *shell*, why you walking all alone?" and laughed to each other.

His mother was sitting on the living room couch. Crimson light spooled from her fingers into an open book, etching calligraphic lines on the page. Valla's white head poked up from behind the sofa, and she snapped her teeth at him.

"You were supposed to come and get me." He spotted the mostly empty bottle of wine on the coffee table and added, "But I guess I'm glad you didn't drive."

His mother didn't turn to look at him, focused on her work. He wondered if being drunk affected it at all, but he guessed not. Some people said alcohol made magic easier. "It's not my fault you got sent home early. I'd have been fine to pick you up if you were let out on time. Screaming in your classroom, telling the teacher to shut up? I thought you knew better."

What could he say? "I'm sorry."

"You know this isn't what we wanted for you. This isn't our fault, what happened. No one in my family was ever a vacant. Nor your father's."

Until you. He hunched down, his ears burning.

Her face was hard and cold. "I guess you think you're the only one this affects. You have to leave your school, with all your little friends. But guess what. This is disappointing for us, too. You never had magic. You won't know what you're missing. We do. And what are we going to say to Grandma? And our friends? You had promise, Pel. And now it's gone. All gone."

He wanted to shout at her, to say that he hated this more than anything in the world, that it was his life that was ruined, not hers. He wanted to tell her how selfish she was being. But shouting never helped. Anger never helped. It would just make her more angry, for longer. Apologizing was the only way to make this go away.

He shuffled forward, and the red light of her magic vanished with Valla. "Mom, I'm real sorry. I guess I didn't think about how hard on you it would be."

"I have to drive across town every day now," she reminded him, but he heard the anger easing out of her voice.

"You don't have to. I can take the bus sometimes. Maybe when it's raining or snowing you could drive me? I'll try to make this easy on you." He felt instantly better, having made the offer. It was only right. It was his stupid coyote magic that was the reason he had to go to that school at all. "I'm so, so sorry, Mom."

She looked back at him and smiled. Her eyes shone with tears. "My sweet boy," she said, and she pulled his head down to kiss his hair. He relaxed. Everything was easier when he apologized. It felt wrong, somehow, deep inside, but not as bad as the anger. He looked back at the coyote, who was still glaring at him. Whatever. It didn't matter.

When he got up the stairs to his room, he slammed the door on it, and it fizzled out of existence like a candle blowing out, only to reappear a few feet away. "Coward," it growled.

"Useless piece of shit," he said back. He hated it. He hated it more than anything. He spent a good hour spreading everything he owned across the floor so it would have nowhere comfortable to sleep.

***

It was a sunny day, so he walked home from school. Two months in, and still most of the studies eluded him. It wasn't that they were difficult; they were just so boring and useless that he couldn't pay attention to them. The coyote slunk behind him. It hunched toward the ground all the time now, and had grown thinner over the days. He tried to ignore it, but on almost a daily basis it would beg him to do magic. It would go quiet if he yelled at it to shut up a few times, though.

He tensed as he walked by the convenience store. The guys who were always hanging out there eyed him. They enjoyed harassing him as he passed. Usually they didn't come over, but today they did, all swagger and grins.

"Hey there, shell," one of them said. He was seventeen at the oldest, and shorter than Pel, but he looked wiry and mean. "What you doin', comin' through here every day?"

"I'm not doing anything," Pel said, keeping his head down. "Just walking home."

"Yeah, that's right. You're not doing anything. And you never will, will you? You leech."

"I'm going to school to learn a trade!" He heard the words come out of his mouth before he could stop them. "That's more than you're doing."

The guy's face darkened. "Yeah, well I don't have to learn a trade, shell, because I have magic. I'm a damn wolf-kin."

That explains the pack, thought Pel, eyeing the two much larger guys standing over his shoulders, grinning at each other. Wolf-kin could be dangerous. "I'm sorry," he said, hunching down.

"Yeah, I bet you're sorry," the guy said. "For what?"

"For—for coming through your neighborhood?"

He knew from the guy's scowl that not only was that not the right answer, but that there *was* no right answer. "How about sorry for taking food off my family's table?"

"I—what?"

"You kinless, you go to the government with your hands out, and everyone has to bend over backward to take care of you. And what do you contribute? Nothing. So the rest of us all have to pay to coddle you and give you special treatment. I figure you owe us something back, huh?"

"I don't have anything," Pel said. The lie fell easily from his tongue. He'd gotten used to lying, these last few months. "Vacants buy stuff with the bracelet. It won't work on you," he added hastily.

The guy spat. "Too bad. You're gonna pay up one way or the other." He grinned to his friends. "Whaddya say we make this kinless skinless?" Light crackled at his fingertips, bright white veined with cobalt.

Pel didn't wait to see what would happen next. He ran. His backpack was heavy, and again he cursed the vacant school, using only heavy paper books that didn't have to be magic-activated.

He thought about dropping the backpack, but it was no good; the three had already caught up and flanked him, their feet quickened with blue-veined light, a great white wolf running just behind him and snapping at his heels. Shouldering him and leaning into his path, they forced him to veer and run down an alley full of leaves and trash. There was no way out. He ran up against a link fence and could go no farther. The chain link sang against the weight of his body.

He turned, and the three guys were right there, the wolf and magic light gone for the moment. Down the alley, the coyote watched, its ears perked, legs splayed as though about to bolt. Good, he thought. Run away and don't come back.

The wolf-kin pulled a thin knife out of his pocket. "Come on. Nothing you can do, shell. You should know that. Give me your wrist."

He held out his left arm, knowing he had no choice, and watched as the wolf-kin cut the charmed bracelet from his arm with a deft twist of the knife. That would be hard to replace.

"Now give us the backpack."

"That's got my books. You wanted me to be a productive member of society. Don't take my schoolbooks."

The wolf-kin's arm was a blur, and Pel cringed, thinking he was about to be struck, but no blow came. Something tickled at his cheek, and he put his hand to it. His fingers were dabbed in blood. A sharp pain ate into his face.

"I said give us the bag, shell!"

Something was coming out of him and he couldn't stop it. It rose up through his heart and lungs and went down his arms, welling at his fingertips. It felt good. It felt right.

"Shit," said one of the other guys, one of the big ones. "He's got magic! He's a phony!"

"Where's his guide?" the wolf-kin growled, and the white light appeared around his hands as his wolf flickered into view.

It was too late. Ribbons of indigo light crawled out of Pel's fingers and dipped toward the guys' heads. He felt his magic tickle at their minds, making them forget it was there. He could feel the parts of them that hungered, that dreamed, that wanted to believe the wonderful, the marvelous, and with just a touch, he made them light up like stars. "Congratulations," he told them. "For years, I've been cursed by a raven-kin, all my magic locked away. My parents put out a huge reward—seventy-five thousand—to anyone who could break the curse, and you've done it. I don't know how, maybe by making me so scared. I'm so happy now, I don't even care that you hurt me. You cured me. Go to the police. Take my bracelet and tell them what you've done. They'll give you the reward right away."

It felt so easy, so natural, to lie to them, to coax them into believing. He felt like he was hunting mice, toying with them, watching them scurry back and forth as he loped around them, heading them where he wished them to go. He was almost sad when the light winked out.

"Man," said one of the bigger guys, "obviously there's no reward. That's a load."

"Yeah, obviously." The wolf-kin snorted. "But it's seventy-five thousand. What if he's not lying?"

Pel gave them a wide-eyed shrug. "I'm not! You saw my magic, didn't you? How could I have done that if I were lying?"

"I guess it doesn't hurt to check," the wolf-kin decided. "But if you are lying, you better not show your face around here again, or we'll cut it off of you."

The throb of pain in Pel's cheek was all the convincing he needed. "I got it. This is your territory." He stayed against the fence as the three walked off, not daring to move for several minutes.

The coyote ran up, his tail wagging. "Did you see what we did? Did you see it? We finally worked our magic. Now you know what you can do. You know how it feels!"

"Why did you make me do that?" Pel shouted at him. "Why? I could have replaced the books."

The coyote's ears lowered. "I didn't make you, Pel. You wanted to. You had to. He was hurting you!"

"Now he'll go to the police. He'll tell them I did magic, and they'll know it was me because he has my freaking bracelet." He rubbed at his cheek and his hand came away red.

"So what? You don't have to pretend you're a vacant anymore. You know how the magic feels. Didn't it feel good, Pel? Didn't it feel right?"

"It felt horrible." He didn't know what made him lie; he just knew he wanted to hurt the coyote more than anything. "It was evil and wrong. I never want to do it again."

He had never seen anything so satisfying as the stricken look on that stupid coyote's face.

***

Pel hid in the arched doorway of a duplex until the bus went by. There. Now he could say he'd missed it. He didn't want to go home yet, not with his report card. The ink from the D's and C's smudged with the sweat from his palm, staining his fingers. Today would be just another disappointment. He wondered how long his mother would be angry. Weeks, probably. His father would just look at him with that weary expression, and say nothing. That was worse. He'd given up on Pel by now. And Pel had to admit, he'd kind of given up, too. Being a vacant was supposed to be easier, not harder. But he couldn't even get passing grades in most of his classes. He wouldn't just end up stuck in a vacant job. He'd end up stuck in a *shitty* vacant job.

He scowled at the coyote, which barely moved anymore, but lay in a heap of bones and fur and stared at nothing. It was very thin, now. It would probably be dead, but a guide couldn't die, not until you did. So it just lay with its tail over its nose. It didn't get up and walk around anymore, but still Pel couldn't be rid of it. Once he got far enough away, he'd feel a little tug at something deep inside him, and then the coyote would appear close by. Sometimes it would look at him for a second and then give a deep sigh and look away again. Each time, it drove Pel crazy.

He'd preferred the angry coyote to this. Sad coyote made him feel deeply frustrated, like all of this was his fault somehow. He couldn't relax with the frustration always there. It was like trying to go to sleep with the light on. It made him hate the coyote even more. He hated it with everything he had, so intensely and persistently that it burned away all his other feelings. He couldn't focus on his studies. He couldn't play, or go biking, or read. He didn't even enjoy food. His mother had commented that he looked thin, and urged him to eat, but he couldn't make himself eat. All he could do was hate that damned thing that he was stuck with for the rest of his life.

Maybe once a day, sometimes less often, it would lift its head, and ask in a numb, weary voice, "Why won't you use your magic?" Most times he ignored it. He had grown exhausted of telling it how much he hated it. Even hurting it no longer gave him that surge of miserable and vicious satisfaction.

Today, though, it got to its feet and shuffled over. Its fur had begun to fall out. Patches of grey skin showed here and there. Once he would have been pleased, but now he didn't care. It looked at the report card, ears and tail drooping. "Not good at being a vacant," it observed. "Because you're coyote-kin."

"No, I'm not."

It spread its padded palms. "What's so bad about me, Pel? Why do you hate me so much? How can anything in our magic be worse than this? You're killing us, you know that? And I don't even understand why. Don't you owe me that much?"

He snorted. "I don't owe you anything." He watched it begin to droop again, and snapped, "Fine. You wanna see what you'd make me into? Let's

127

go." He got to his feet and turned down the street, not watching to see if the coyote followed.

He wasn't sure exactly where he was going, but he knew that coyote-kin often hung out downtown, around train stations and tourist centers, at least until the police came along and shooed them away. He'd seen them there, when he was a kid, flipping cards, juggling, telling stories with images that floated in the air in a haze of entrancing magic. He'd been curious, and wandered closer, but his mother had called him back sharply. "You stay away from those people," she'd said in a hoarse whisper. "They're not good. They'll rob you blind. Or kidnap you, until I paid them to get you back."

"Why don't we put them in jail?" he'd asked.

"Because they always get up in front of a jury. And coyote-kin are very, very good at tricking juries. They use their magic and make everyone think they're good and innocent."

He'd stared back at them. They'd seemed dirty, sure, but harmless, even charming. That must have been more of their tricks, working on him even. And since then, he'd stayed as far away as he could.

It didn't take him long to find one, in one of the parks near city hall. She looked old, but was probably much younger, her skin weathered by the sun, her black and grey hair bound up in several brightly colored rings. She'd set up a little table made out of milk cartons, covered it with a clean-looking purple cloth, and had charm cards spread out on it, animated with the pale green magic that spilled from her fingertips. On the ground, she'd set a top hat with several coins in it, and beside it, her coyote performed a sly little four-legged dance, grinning up at Pel, tail giving a slow wag.

"Tell your fortune, young vacant? Even an unmagicked future may hold great wealth and power." She grinned, and Pel was disgusted to see that most of her teeth were missing, the few that remained yellowed and cracked.

"See what you would make me?" he whispered to his coyote.

"You don't have to be like her," the coyote said, but he backed up to hide behind Pel's legs.

The coyote-kin frowned. "What's that, boy?" She beckoned to him with fingers heavy with rings jammed around swollen knuckles. "Come here." When he hesitated, she spat to one side. "What, you afraid of a helpless old woman?"

"You're not old," he said, keeping an eye on the dancing streams of magic. "And you're not helpless. You're coyote-kin."

"Just a name, boy, just a name. Not a fate. Not even the cards can tell that. They can only hint. Take one," she urged him, spreading her fingers, and for a moment it seemed that the cards shuffled themselves around on her table. But none of them truly moved; Pel could tell that it was only the symbols that moved, printed by magic over blank cards.

He pushed the cards across her makeshift table. "There's no point. You can't trick me. There's nothing on them. You're just a con artist, like every other coyote."

"Now how would you know that?" Her eyes, a bright green, peered at him keenly from beneath lashes clumpy with mascara. The light of her magic went out, and her hand shot out and snatched his wrist, fingers tight and surprisingly strong.

"Let me go!" He tugged at his arm.

She stared into his eyes, and her own widened. "You're no vacant," she whispered. "You're like me."

"I'm nothing like you!" He twisted fiercely at his arm, yanking it away. "You disgusting old thief. I don't have any magic."

"What?" She spat again. "You think you're better than me? Because you got nice clothes and a roof to keep the rain off you? I see what you're doing. You're lying to everyone, ain't you, boy? You've got 'em all fooled. With your pretty little bracelet. Playing dumb. Playing cripple."

"You don't know what you're talking about. I'm a vacant, a—a shell."

"No, I know, I see it. Just an ordinary vacant. Just need a little extra help here and there. A little sympathy. People let their guards down. Kid, you've got a con going that would make any coyote blush. Me, I just lift rings and wallets. You, you're stealing their pity. Their mercy. And they don't even know they've been robbed, do they? You just live off 'em. Boy, you're the greatest coyote I ever met. I bet you don't even use magic."

"Shut up!" he screamed at her, not caring now if he was making a scene. They'd just see an old thief hassling a poor vacant anyway. They'd be on his side. "I'm not stealing anything. This was my life all along. Coyote stole it from me!" He pointed at the coyote behind him as he said it, and felt his magic trying to flow to his fingers. He squeezed his hands into fists, cutting it off, forcing the magic back down inside him again. He would never let it out again, not ever.

"Coyote stole it from me," she said back in a mocking voice. "Who you think you're talking to? You should be proud."

He looked behind him. Passersby had stopped. They were watching, talking to each other quietly. "I shoulda known not to talk to a coyote," he shouted loudly, and then turned and walked away as briskly as he could without looking like he was running.

"You ain't no better than me!" she called after him. "You're the same! You're just the same!"

***

He stormed into the house and slammed the door behind him. It didn't wake his mother, who was asleep on the sofa, an empty wine glass in her fingers. In his room he sat down on the floor and buried his face in his hands. He didn't have to look to know that the coyote blinked into the room next to him. He was quiet for a minute, and then on an impulse yanked the bracelet off his arm and threw it against the wall.

"Why'd it have to be you?" he asked the coyote, who sat and stared dully at the floor.

"Same reason it had to be you, I guess." The coyote looked pretty emaciated, his breaths shallow and painful-looking. "I don't understand. You were supposed to love me beyond anything else. We were supposed to have fun together for our whole lives. I don't get why you'd take that away from me. I don't get why you'd rather have nothing than me."

"Well, I do. I hate you. I don't know why you can't just go away. Go away forever and leave me alone."

"Why don't you go away forever and leave me alone?" the coyote snapped. "You think I enjoy getting dragged everywhere with you treating me like dirt? Why do you do this to yourself? Why?"

"I'm not doing anything to myself. I'm doing it to you."

The coyote got to its feet, its lips curled back from its teeth. It leaned forward and shouted, "I *am* you, you idiot!"

He stared at it. Then his memory fractured. He couldn't remember who had yelled the words, him, or the coyote. Or maybe they'd shouted it together. He felt as though he had lost his balance at the edge of a terrible cliff, and scrambled to hold onto it. "That's not true," were the words that took him to safer ground, and he spoke them like a lifeline. "That's not true."

The coyote stared at him despairingly, and then sank to the floor. It looked up at him with miserable brown eyes, reaching out its paws to him. "Just give me a name," it pleaded. "That's all I want from you anymore. Just a name."

He half-ignored it, but then an idea occurred to him: one last thing he could do to it to punish it for shoving its way into his life and ruining it forever. He didn't have to give it a nice name. "You want a name?"

The coyote half-lifted its ears and gave a slow nod.

"Fine," Pel said in his nastiest tone. "Then I name you Shame. That's what you are to me, everywhere I go. That's what you mean to me. You're my Shame."

His coyote's eyes widened. "Yours," he whispered to Pel. He burst into tears. "Thank you. Thank you so much."

Pel stared back at the coyote's eyes, round and grateful. They looked just like his own. A surge of something powerful rose inside him, something so insistent and irresistible that he felt it would burst him open. The magic tingled at his fingertips, and then it flowed out of him in brilliant indigo streams, painting the room with the deep blue light, and in the depths of it, white specks glittered like stars. The magic poured out and out of him and would not stop.

We can resist the passage of time, but it will march on, slowly changing our world anyway.

The Last Roundup

Amy Fontaine

Russ Clifford stands in a dusty sunbeam at the center of the ruined stable. His paw rests on the horn of a forgotten, moldy saddle. He smells leather, faint traces of manure, and abandoned memories. The Australian cattle dog's big ears, which poke through the holes in the top of his wide-brimmed cowdog hat, twitch to and fro, listening to mice scuttling along the floor. The mice have been eating through the leather tack and other artifacts that were left in piles in this stable: saddles, bridles, reins, lassos.

Soon enough, there will be nothing left.

But Russ remembers a time when this rotting corpse of a building throbbed with life: when there weren't any gaping holes in the ceiling, when the loudest sound was the neighing of horses, not the rustling of mice.

Russ hears the distant murmur of the ocean beyond the stable's walls. He closes his eyes, gliding his paw along the slope of the saddle.

Remembering.

***

It was dark that morning, as it was every morning for cowdogs. "Dark-thirty," they jokingly called the early hour when they rose to start work. Dark-thirty, when even your strong canine eyes couldn't see the wet, glistening nose at the end of your muzzle. Russ had been a pup back then, but on that special morning he was finally old enough to help the cowdogs. He had felt a thrill of excitement as he put on his chaps and boots and hat and then bounded across the yard from the ranch house to the stable.

From the yard, he could smell and hear and just barely see the foamy white caps of the waves, just a few yards down the slope to the east of the ranch. A dock jutted out into the sea in that direction, the dock where the ferry would be waiting in a few hours.

As Russ entered the stable, the cowdogs greeted him with crisp nods and wagging tails. There were ten adult males that season, including a border collie named Phil who was sharp as a tack; a German shepherd named Chris who would give you his coat in a rainstorm if you didn't have one of your own; an old English sheepdog named Joe whose card tricks delighted Russ and his sisters—they always wondered how he pulled off such impressive sleight-of-hand with that curtain of hair over his eyes. And, of course, there was Russ's cattle dog father, Bryce Clifford, the owner of Clifford Ranch. Russ looked up to his father with all his heart.

During the working season on the island—the summer months—the ranch hands stayed in a bunkhouse near the stable. But Russ's family lived in the ranch house, and they stayed on the island year-round.

The cowdogs saddled up their horses in silence, working swiftly in the dark stable. Russ's heart pounded as he readied his own horse, his tail wagging wildly. His father handed him some jerky, which he gratefully wolfed down.

Then, it was time to ride.

Vaperro Island has an area of about 84 square miles, and at that time, all of it belonged to Clifford Ranch. Cattle roamed all over the island, grazing on the scrubby grass that grew on the rolling hills and windswept dunes. The cowdogs howled to each other to stay in touch as they rode across the island, scouring crags and glens, slowly gathering the scattered cows.

To young Russ, rounding up the cattle felt like a fun game: a scavenger hunt, perhaps, or hide-and-seek. Would there be a cluster of cows around the next bend, drinking from the artificial pond in the valley between two hills? Or would he find them dancing along the edge of a bluff that faced the sea, flirting with death like mountain goats? Every mile Russ rode across the island led to a new discovery, and his heart swelled with pride, knowing that all of it—every wild, beautiful mile, every cove and cliff and hidden cave, every cow and calf and bull—would belong to him when he grew up.

By the time dawn peeked shyly over the horizon to the east, Russ and the ten adult cowdogs were together again by the dock. Guiding their horses gracefully, as if each cowdog and his horse were one animal—indeed, as if the entire pack of them was one huge animal—the cowdogs rushed the herd they had gathered, driving them down the dock onto the ferry that was waiting there now, the ferry bound for the mainland twenty-five miles across the sea. Russ watched from his horse, panting triumphantly, as the ferry embarked into the sunrise, cattle in tow. Bryce reached across the chasm between their two horses and patted his son's head.

"So, son, ready to make this your life?"

Russ nodded, his tongue lolling from his mouth, his tail wagging furiously. He was the newest cowdog on Vaperro Island, and the happiest pup alive.

***

The Dalmatian came to the island thirty years later. The ranch had been struggling for the past five years. Water was always a logistical problem. So was getting goods and products from the mainland. Worse, industrial farms on the mainland were making family operations like Clifford Ranch obsolete. The Cliffords needed a miracle.

Russ was sitting down to breakfast with his wife and their five pups in the ranch house when Robert cried, "Daddy, look, a boat!" The pup pointed out the window. Russ squinted at the dim shape on the horizon. He stood from his chair and licked Maria on the cheek, saying, "I'll be right back." Then he left the house and walked down the hill and out to the end of the dock. And he waited.

The sailboat was a sleek, fancy new model. As it drew closer, Russ spotted the bright display of a newfangled GPS navigation system through the windows of the cockpit. The boat had polished, fake oak siding with silver and chrome accents, fresh white paint, and an engine that rumbled like a dragon. It sliced through the water toward the dock like an arrow.

Russ narrowed his eyes as the boat pulled up beside the dock, squinting into the sun. He hadn't been expecting any visitors today. Relatives and friends sometimes came over from the mainland to visit during cattle season in the summers, and the entire Clifford family came to the island in December for Christmas. But this was fall, part of the off-season. Plus, none of the dogs Russ knew ever showed up in an expensive boat like this one. He found a growl rumbling softly in the bottom of his throat and the hackles on his neck rising.

A female Dalmatian emerged from the cockpit of the boat and waved to Russ from the deck, a bright smile on her face. "Hi there! Can you help me tie up, please?"

Russ's expression softened as he realized she was the only dog on the boat. He helped the Dalmatian tie the boat to the dock. Stepping onto the dock, she looked Russ up and down, the bright smile never leaving her face.

"Greetings, sir! Are you Russell Clifford?"

Russ nodded silently. The Dalmatian's tail wagged.

"Great! You're just the dog I'm looking for! I'm Megan Walsh from the National Park Service." She tapped the name tag and badge pinned to her crisp khaki uniform, then stuck out her paw for a pawshake. Russ stared at her clean, spotted paw for a moment before shaking it slowly in his own calloused, dirt-crusted tan paw.

Russ studied Megan's speckled face. She still beamed at him, the naive grin of someone who had gone to college in the city, someone who had no idea where her jerky came from.

"I have business to discuss with you and your family. Well, *prospective* business," she added, with a flick of her folded ears. "Shall we take a walk?" She gestured up the slope, towards the yard where the stable, the ranch house, the bunkhouse, and the cattle pens overlooked the sea.

The sailboat bobbed on choppy waves. A gull mewled overhead. Russ stared at the young Dalmatian. He didn't like the familiar way she had gestured to his home. As if she already knew what awaited her there. As if it were already hers.

"We just made breakfast," Russ said warily. "If you want some. We have coffee, too."

Megan clapped her paws together, her tail wagging harder. "That would be grand! Thanks!"

Turning on his heel, Russ walked briskly across the dock. Megan hurried along beside him.

"Mr. Clifford," the Dalmatian said, "it has come to the attention of the National Park Service that Vaperro Island possesses very special natural resources. Through surveys conducted on and around the island, we've discovered all kinds of incredible things. Marine mammals once thought to be extinct. Peculiar geological formations. Entirely new genera of perennial flowers. Diverse, thriving coral reef ecosystems. A unique endemic species of island vole."

Russ stopped in his tracks, narrowing his eyes at the Dalmatian. "Are you saying you've been surveying my island and nobody told me?"

Megan's eyes widened. "My apologies, Mr. Clifford!" Megan said, sounding sincerely horrified. "We thought you were informed!"

Russ shook his head. "Crossed wires, I guess," he muttered, the edge of a growl in his gruff voice. The warm sand shifted beneath his paws as he climbed the path up the hill toward the house, the Dalmatian following behind him.

"The National Park Service would like to preserve this island's resources for the enjoyment of the public," Megan went on. "We would like to purchase Vaperro Island and make it into a new national park, Vaperro Island National Park."

Russ whirled around, gaping at Megan as if she had bitten him. For a moment, he couldn't speak.

"What?" he said finally. Stupidly.

Megan held up her paws, almost defensively. "We will still allow the Clifford Ranch to operate, of course! This is your home, and we don't want to take it from you. We just want to share the natural beauty of this island with every American who would like to enjoy it and keep it intact for generations to come. We want to teach them all about this place. About the land."

Russ found the hackles on his neck rising again. He laughed bitterly.

"Teach them about the land? Miss Walsh, no one knows Vaperro Island better than I do. I've ridden every mile from Finger Cove to Phoenix Point. This island is my home. My life."

Megan nodded as if she understood. But she didn't understand a damn thing. Russ's lip curled upwards, exposing his teeth.

"I know how much this place must mean to you," Megan said. "And I also know that Clifford Ranch has been struggling for the past few years. We will pay you generously for the land if you sell. And aside from us building a few new facilities and allowing park guests on the island in the summers, your way of life will continue as it always has." The Dalmatian reached out and gripped his shoulder. "We're on your side, Mr. Clifford."

Russ shrugged her away. But he saw her warm smile and her wagging tail, and he knew she really meant it. He sighed. "How much will you pay?"

Megan told him. She was right: it was generous, more than enough to get Clifford Ranch back in the black. Before Russ had finished his eggs, bacon, coffee, and toast that morning, he had signed away his ownership of Vaperro Island to the National Park Service.

Less than a month later, a construction crew arrived from the mainland. The burly dogs built a visitor center a stone's throw from the buildings of Clifford Ranch. They turned the main riding trails into wider, more accessible public hiking trails, complete with benches, trash cans, and interpretive signage. They renovated the crumbling dock, turning it into a larger, more modern structure.

When summer came and the cattle season began, a swarm of park visitors arrived with the bewildered handful of ranch hands from the mainland. Many of the park guests wore Hawaiian shirts, shorts, sunglasses, and cameras dangling from their necks. Most of them belonged to non-herding breeds. Mothers pushed wailing puppies in strollers, and daughters and sons pushed elderly dogs in wheelchairs. Russ found it all rather overwhelming.

But just like the Dalmatian had promised, Russ's life went on as it always had, at least for a while. The cowdogs sang to the stars around the fire every night. The sun shone just as brightly as ever on the golden hills when Russ rode from one end of the island to the other. The cattle continued to graze, and Russ and his children still visited their hidden coves and secret caves, places the public didn't know about yet. At dark-thirty, when he was howling and galloping through the darkness with the other cowdogs, the island was his again.

Russ should have known it wouldn't last.

***

Twelve years after the Dalmatian had arrived on Vaperro Island, Russ sat in a stuffy Santa Barbara courtroom, shifting uncomfortably in his seat. He wore a stiff black suit, the only suit he owned. It had belonged to his father, Bryce Clifford—and before that, to Bryce's father, Russ's grandfather. Russ was quietly grateful that his father and grandfather hadn't lived to see this day.

Russ was one of the defendants in this case, and his very way of life was on trial. His accuser, a prim Maltese, glared at him from the bench across the aisle. The judge, a stately Rottweiler, coughed from his bench at the front of the room.

"Will the plaintiff's attorney please give her closing statement?" said the judge.

The Maltese's attorney, a perky Akita, sashayed to the front of the room.

"Your Honor, as you know, my client, Frederick Smith of the nonprofit Earth4Dogs, is suing the National Park Service and the Clifford family for improper management of the unique wildlife habitats on Vaperro Island National Park. The National Park Service has a mission to protect natural habitats for the enjoyment of the public and the benefit of wildlife. By continuing to allow the Clifford family's negligent grazing on Vaperro Island, the Park Service is failing in this mission."

The Akita paced behind the witness stand, her tail swishing behind her.

"Cattle degrade habitats. They pollute the water, posing a risk to native wildlife. They eat endangered plants and erode the soil. In short, they have no place in a national park. Thank you."

The judge nodded at the Akita, dismissing her to her seat with a wave of his paw.

"Now it is time for the closing statements of the defendants. We will begin with Russell Clifford, member of the Clifford family and manager of Clifford Ranch. Mr. Clifford, please come forward."

Russ slowly made his way to the front of the courtroom. He felt the eyes of all the other dogs in the room staring at his back. His fur stood on end. He desperately wished he had been able to afford an attorney. He wasn't sure if he would even have the nerve to speak again.

After reaching the witness stand and taking a deep breath, Russ turned and faced the courtroom.

"Your Honor," Russ said, "Vaperro Island is my home. It was my father's home, and my grandfather's, and my great-grandfather's before that." The cattle dog looked down at the floor, his forepaws folded behind his back.

"The Clifford family has never meant to hurt the land. We've taken care of it the best we could, in the only ways we know. The National Park Service is devoted to preserving the cultural heritage of this country as well as its rich natural history. And ranching is an important part of our cultural heritage."

The judge nodded. "Thank you, Mr. Clifford. You may be seated."

Russ opened his mouth to say something more, but he choked on his words. What could he possibly say? The blood of generations of cattle dogs coursed through his veins, and he could never explain to these crisp city dogs how much that inheritance meant to him. What it felt like to herd cattle onto the dock at dark-thirty in the morning. To sit around the fire with the other cowdogs, laughing and singing to the stars. He could not describe to them the supple feel of leather reins in his paws. They would never smell the sea on the wind as it whipped past his face, as he galloped his horse all the way to the top of Phoenix Point and then, panting, tired but happy, turned his horse around, surveying the whole sweep of the wild, golden island behind him. Vaperro Island. His home.

Russ just nodded at the judge and stepped down from the stand.

Before the end of the hour, his world came crashing down.

***

The National Park Service gave the Cliffords one month to leave Vaperro Island, one month to gather the pieces of a shattered life. The cattle were loaded onto a ferry and shipped to the mainland for the last time. The horses refused to step onto a boat. After some debate, the Park Service decided to turn them loose on the island after the Cliffords left and allow them to live out their lives there. Russ and Maria Clifford and their pups went to live with Russ's cousin Skip in Napa Valley until Russ could figure out what to do next.

But Russ returned to the island one last time. Standing on the beach in front of the dock on that warm summer day, he watched visitors pour from a huge ship, barking excitedly to one another. A cute Australian cattle dog puppy clutching a purple pony plush pointed eagerly to the ridge above the crumbling Clifford Ranch buildings, tugging her mother's sleeve with her teeth.

"Mama, look! Horsies!"

Russ's chest tightened as he looked up at the ridge, at the horses that stood watching the passengers get off the boat. Horses that no longer belonged to him. He stared at the young cattle dog, a cattle dog who would probably never get to see a real cattle drive.

The pup's mother walked past Russ without noticing him, starting down the path toward the visitor center. As the pup turned to follow her, Russ stepped in front of her. He knelt and looked into her eyes, placing his paw on her shoulder.

"Kid," Russ said, "see those horses up there?" He nodded at the ridge.

The pup nodded brightly. "Yeah! They're pretty!"

Russ cracked a smile.

"Those horses belonged to the Clifford family. They rode them all over the island, before other dogs ever set foot here. Long before you were even born. This island was their magical kingdom. Their home."

The pup squealed with delight. "Really?" she gasped. "That's so cool!"

Russ laughed warmly, patting her shoulder.

"*Really.* You remember my story, okay? Remember that there were cattle dogs like you on this island once. Cattle dogs who worked the land, and sang to the stars, and took good care of those horses." Russ's eyes shone with tears. "Cowdogs who loved this place more than anything."

The little pup nodded in a serious way. "Okay. I'll remember." She hugged her pony tightly to her chest.

"Anna!" called the pup's mother, whistling for her like a cowdog, waving a paw at her from halfway up the path to the visitor center. After one last look at Russ, and then one last look at the horses, Anna scampered up the path towards her mother.

Just then, Russ felt a paw on his shoulder. He heard the Dalmatian's voice behind him as if from the other side of a tunnel.

"Russell," said Megan. "Russ, are you okay?"

Russ stood up, surveying the Dalmatian in her khaki uniform. Though Russ had been suspicious of the park ranger when they first met, she had become a close family friend over the years. She had even gone riding with the cowdogs a couple times. Megan smiled pleasantly at Russ, but a lot of other feelings showed in her dark brown eyes. Sadness, pity, guilt, sympathy. A thousand unspeakable things.

"Are you ready to go, Russ?" asked Megan.

Russ shuffled from one paw to the other. "I'm going to go up to the ranch one last time."

Megan nodded. Before Russ started up the path to his old house, Megan gripped him by the shoulders and looked into his eyes.

"I'm sorry, Russ," said Megan softly.

Russ nodded. "I know." Brushing past the Dalmatian, he walked up the hill towards the ranch without looking back.

***

Now, Russ opens his eyes, looking around once more at the neglected stable. He has been wandering through the crumbling buildings like a ghost for a while, but he knows that the ferry won't wait. He wipes his tears on the back of his paw. He looks at the place where he carved his name into a beam as a pup with a pocket knife. He looks at his first riding saddle. He sifts through all the memories gathering dust in his mind.

Russ leaves the stable and walks back down to the dock.

Megan is waiting for him by the ferry that will take him to the mainland. "I'm sorry, Russ," she says again. She envelops him in a hug. He hugs her back, not sure what to say.

"We will talk about the Clifford Ranch on every guided tour," Megan says. "I'm glad you liked that new display about the Cliffords in the visitor center. I hope we can create many more displays like that, exhibits that capture the ranching history of the island for park visitors. We will do our best to keep your legacy alive."

Russ smiles sadly and shakes his head. "I appreciate that. But that ranching history you speak of, we didn't know it as history. We knew it as a living, breathing thing, not some sign in the corner of a visitor center. It was our way of life. But it's gone now. And we'll never get it back."

Megan sighs. Her eyes are wet. For a moment, she is speechless, looking out across the water.

"Change is hard," Megan says. "I know. As a teenager, I watched the forest I played in as a kid become a strip mall. I knew then that I wanted to join the Park Service. To…" Megan chokes on her words. Her voice falls to a whisper. "To help protect beautiful things, before they slip away."

Russ nods stiffly, looking up at the wide, blue sky. Megan puts a paw on his trembling shoulder.

"I know it will never be the same here. But we'll do our best to keep the history alive. If you'd like, you could come back and give talks at the visitor center sometime. Tell your story in your own words. I'm sure it would mean a lot to our visitors."

Russ nods. "I'd like that," he says, through the lump in his throat. But he knows in his heart that he'll never come back.

Russ looks back along the length of the dock, the dock down which lines of cattle once marched into the sea. Taking a deep breath, he steps onto the ferry.

From the top of the golden hill, the last horses of Clifford Ranch watch the ferry sail away.

Let us all be pangolins together.

SAFE MODE

John Giezentanner

The power was out. Devices and implants wouldn't connect to the network, which had never happened before. Jonah realized after a period of bemusement and then steadily increasing frustration over failed attempts to interact with everything electronic in his apartment that he didn't even know what time it was. Restless and wondering if it was just him, he went outside and immediately saw that it was not. Traffic was stopped, making the city street oddly quiet. Some of the cars had grumpy looking occupants but others were empty, and people with forlorn expressions were wandering in all directions.

He hurried to a small gathering at the end of the block to see what they were looking at—a drone had landed in the street, LEDs all blinking yellow. The screen that would normally display the drone's face showed the words SAFE MODE. He stared at it curiously, listening to the confused conversations around him until he gathered that this drone wasn't the only reason traffic was stopped. The screens in all the cars were showing the same message. He didn't know what it meant, but he felt the air being sucked out of him. He needed to get home, back inside. He rushed in, breathing heavily and made it as far as his bedroom before collapsing, curled up tight on the floor just shy of his bed.

Jonah was not completely a pangolin. He had thumbs and teeth and didn't eat thousands of live ants every day, but the aesthetic of the peculiar scaly mammal had always appealed to him. He started adopting pangolin traits early in life and while most people with animal augments stopped at the level of fashionable fur colors, tails, and facial features, he became a

145

short, roughly human-sized animal. He still walked bipedally, but so did some pangolins. He liked having an unusual phenotype and the literal armor it gave him against—anything, hypothetically.

But the reflexive curling up that happened sometimes when he was startled or feeling overwhelmed seemed to be a side effect. When it happened there wasn't much he could do but wait it out as a rounded fortress of broad, loosely shingled scales. The big ones along his back and tail projected slightly from the curvature of his body; his long muzzled face was shielded by his foot claws and his long tail curled all the way around him, over the top of his head and neck and pressed against his back.

***

A few months ago his friend and roommate Nekoda had convinced him to go out and meet up with their friends at a popular club. It wasn't their normal scene, but she was trying to get him to socialize more with the whole group and thought it might be a good change of pace. *Sera Tonic* was located on a pedestrian mall, and various people were hurrying through the nighttime winter air to one or another bar, club or café. Some looked like humans always had while others bore obvious genetic or cybernetic modification, or both. Nekoda was a red panda, rounded to the point of androgyny by an extremely fluffy coat she'd recently modded to cause the normally red areas to grow out green instead (a shift that had coincided with her changing to female pronouns.) He hoped to find her waiting for him outside the place but avoided eye contact with everyone he passed.

He had always been shy, a trait the AIs had apparently not yet gotten around to weeding out of the gene pool as they had with more serious conditions. So he didn't go directly into the bar when he didn't find his friends outside. He paused, studying the venue through the windows, trying to map the place—the size and layout, the number and character of clientele, the décor and atmosphere—before committing to entry. The lower level was styled like a traditional tavern, dimly lit with lots of dark wood and brick. It was crowded, and he could already tell from the noise emanating that the music inside was too loud.

He sighed and walked to the end of the block and back again, hoping Nekoda would show up. He wondered if the vanilla humans or anyone else inside would stare at him; he didn't want to go in alone. He knew it wouldn't be a big deal in any case, but there was also a doorman he'd have to pass. He couldn't understand why someone would be willing to sit at the door and greet people for hours on end when that work could be so easily automated. But there he was, an enormous modded human with a chiseled, angelic physique that probably stood a meter above average height when he got up from his chair by the door.

The prospect of that little interaction was another deterrent. Jonah would rather have a cold but predictable interaction with a machine than a short but unpredictable interaction with a stranger any day. Facing a person, his mind would go into overdrive trying to imagine everything the other person might say so that he could plan his own responses in turn, and playing out scenario after scenario in his head became exhausting.

He circled the block, and circled it again. Each time he came near the door he veered away as if from magnetic repulsion. Maybe he didn't really want to go in. It was getting cold. His scales did not insulate him as well as other people's fur; he wore a heavy coat, hat, scarf, and long woolen sleeve over his tail to keep it from freezing, and he feared that all the extra clothing made him look like a cartoon character. If he had wanted to be noticed, he could have gotten genetic programming for every scale on his body so that they would grow in different colors to spell words or create pixel-style art. He could glow in the dark. But he chose his phenotype for himself; he had normal, light brown pangolin scales because he didn't want others to notice.

Maybe this place wouldn't have anything he liked to drink. With all the effort it would take to get through the door, he had to consider whether it would be worth it. He felt overly conspicuous as he passed by again and hoped the doorman somehow hadn't noticed him and wasn't thinking that he was some kind of weirdo. But if he had, and if he were, then Jonah really ought to just go home before he made it any worse. He plodded once more toward *Sera Tonic.*

Just go in, he told himself. *It'll be fine. Just go in.*

He skimmed by like a spaceship on a too-shallow trajectory, failing to make reentry and skipping off the atmosphere. He was starting to shiver, and his nose was freezing. His friends were in there, and he wanted to go in. But how could he be *sure* that he wanted to go in? Something told him he wasn't allowed to, a primitive, inarticulate warning of danger. He knew the alarm was false, but the fear was real. He tarried, pacing in a circle, no longer trying to go in but composing his excuse.

Just message them and say you can't make it tonight after all. What should he say, exactly? How to word it?

"Excuse me."

He startled and hunched over, barely resisting the urge to curl up. He turned to see a drone hovering behind him.

"Excuse me," it repeated in the clear, unaccented tones common to its kind. Its iconic face appeared pensive. "May I help you?"

Jonah blinked. "No…"

"Are you sure? It's cold and your behavior does not appear recreational. You have been studying this establishment closely for some time. Do you plan on going in?" Its face remained the same and its voice just as clear, but the question felt accusatory.

The discomfort of remaining on the street suddenly exceeded the discomfort of going inside. "Yes. I'm…I'm going in right now." He backed away from the drone which remained stationary and quickly headed to the door.

"Hello! How's it going?" Despite his size, the door person had a welcoming voice.

"Hi." Jonah offered his left wrist, where his ID was embedded in an off-colored scale.

"Was that thing hassling you?" The door person swiped a scanner over Jonah's wrist.

Jonah felt a little embarrassed. "I think it thought I was going to steal something."

The doorperson laughed. "I swear, that one is getting more paranoid every day."

***

Jonah lost track of time, drifting through a mix of memory, analysis, and daydream with his eyes closed tight inside his scale fort; he may have nodded off. The front door opening and closing startled him alert, and he retightened his curl. His shoulder had fallen asleep from pressing against the floor, but there was no help for it. He could hear Nekoda's familiar muttering to herself as she sloughed off some carried items and came inside. He kept his eyes covered and closed, willing the darkness to be his own creation that would be dispelled with good news she might bring. He heard her slowly padding forward, a sound he'd never noticed before—her foot paws were soft, the carpet was soft, and the floor didn't creak—her footfalls should have been drowned out by the drone of traffic outside and the apartment's ever present hum of electrified modernity.

"Jonah?" Nekoda called softly. "Jonah? Oh, no!"

He felt the slight deformations of the floor as she rushed over. He braced himself for the inevitable hug.

She knelt and hugged him, resting her head on his side. "You're all artichoked. Are you okay?"

***

Part of Jonah secretly longed for these moments of *deus ex amicus*. Often times a kind word and gentle touch from a friend was enough to break him out of his internalizing and save him from himself. When he had hurried inside *Sera Tonic*, feeling off balance from the strange interaction with the drone, he'd swung his tail around to pull the sleeve off, and it felt stiff. Some of his scales had frosted together. That weird feeling of scales being stuck together and then breaking apart when he curled his tail was actually a relief, a normal fact of winter.

He weaved through the crowd on the noisy lower level until, not seeing a familiar face, he was compelled to ascend to the even more crowded and painfully loud upper level. There he saw his friends passively watching the band that was playing and went to them as to a lifeboat. There was Keros, who on a dare had traded in his gray fox phenotype for a vanilla human physique that did nothing to diminish his roguish smirk; Jeremy, a slouching white tailed deer with his inexplicable hoodie, his antlers nicely regrown since the scary camping incident the previous year; and Terah. She had gone the feral route, like Jonah. Extensively modded, she was a person-sized theropod dinosaur, as near as one could be invented, with pretty iridescent feathers. She was graceful and imposing, but taciturn and occasionally socially awkward, and Jonah couldn't help a slight crush on her, never mind that she was in a few relationships already and didn't prefer males. He exchanged hugs with them all, but it was too loud to hold a conversation; he excused himself to get a drink and retreated to the lower level.

He waited in the mass of supplicants who had congealed around the bar, studying the taps. There was still no word from Nekoda, for whom being tardy was an art form. He let more assertive folks go ahead of him; deciding what to drink was a new ordeal. He wondered how people always seemed to know so quickly and decisively what they wanted when there were so many possible wrong choices. After a few minutes of hemming and hawing he walked away, frustrated and feeling more isolated and oppressed by the crush of strangers and noise than he would have in an empty, quiet room. The others might decide soon enough that they didn't like the band or the crowd and head out to a different place. He awaited them curled up in a dark corner.

"Hey!"

He glanced up to see Nekoda standing over him with a colorful mixed drink in each hand.

"People are going to start tossing their coats on you."

He smirked. "That might muffle the noise a bit."

"You don't like the music?"

"It's okay. Just too loud. Where have you been?"

Nekoda's whiskers drooped. "I kind of crashed after work. And fell asleep. And overslept." She raised one of her drinks in a weary imitation of the rest of the group. "*That's our Koda!*"

Jonah chuckled. "Since you came late, can I leave early?"

She lowered the drinks to him. "These are for you."

He was skeptical. "Both of them?"

"Both of them."

***

If nothing else, the need to appear all right in front of others would usually compel him to uncurl when they asked if he was all right. Not today.

"What's going on?" Jonah muttered.

"I don't know. It happened right after I got to work—everything just died. We couldn't have classes, obviously, we had to wait for all the parents to *walk* down and get their kid so I was just babysitting all day. It was crazy."

Nekoda was still hugging him. Actually, she was kind of lying on him. Jonah knew she must be much more exhausted than him. He ought to be the one hugging her, but it was all he could do to open an eye. There was a soft red glow from the computer sheet Nekoda had used to light her way. It would be fine for months without a charge, so they wouldn't be completely without light, at least.

Nekoda sighed heavily. Jonah wondered if she was falling asleep, and he wanted to let her. He felt like asking more questions would only confirm more fears, but he was too confused to leave it at that. "So…no internet at all? No drones came and delivered a message or anything?"

Her jaw pressed against him as she spoke without raising her head. "Nope. It was really weird."

The feeling in Jonah's stomach escalated to something like nausea. "So it's like this everywhere, then."

"What do you mean?"

"The school's a pretty important place. Don't you think someone would send word if they could, so you could tell the kids everything is going to be okay?"

Nekoda shifted uncomfortably on top of him, curling a bit herself. "It seems like the whole city's down. They must be focused on fixing whatever it is."

"What if it's not just the city?" He heard his voice taking on a desperate, whiny tone that annoyed him, but he couldn't help it. "What if it's everywhere?"

"It can't be everywhere."

"Why not?"

"Because…" Nekoda obviously didn't want to think about it. "That doesn't make any sense."

"Who says the end of the world has to make sense?"

Nekoda sat up and glanced at her sheet to see if anything had changed in the last few seconds. "I'm sure this has happened somewhere before."

"Before. Before the world was run by artificial hyper intelligences that anticipate every issue and solve it before it becomes a problem, that make sure nothing ever breaks. Nekoda, I don't think anything did break. The cars slowed to a stop, the drones landed. All the infrastructure, the machines, everything is fine. There's just no one controlling it."

Nekoda shook her head. "That's impossible. The AIs don't get old or sick, and no human could hurt them, even if they wanted to. They can't be gone."

Jonah managed a slight shrug. "We don't get old and sick anymore either, but most people still decide to self-terminate eventually. Maybe they ended themselves."

"No. No, they wouldn't do that to us," Nekoda shook her head more emphatically. "Their whole existence is based around how much we need them. Even if they wanted to, there's no way they'd do that without warning us first."

Jonah argued from behind the safety of his scales. "Maybe they were secretly depressed. Maybe they couldn't stand the thought of all the drama it would cause to announce it. Maybe they stopped caring."

Nekoda frowned. "All of them, though? All at once?"

"All at once to us. Their qubit god-brains experience time a lot differently than we do."

"You've gotten all wound around inside yourself thinking about the worst that can happen." She put a hand on his shoulder and shook him gently. "You do this, you know. You need to get out of your head and relax. Let's get some snacks and pretend we're…"

"Camping?"

"Don't—don't even say that word." Nekoda sighed. "Let's just pretend that we're eating cold food in the dark at home, but on purpose for some reason."

Jonah snickered, though he remained curled up. "Sounds great."

***

"Oh, I like this one!" Terah's feathery crest stood up as the song changed. "Let's go!"

She pulled Nekoda out toward the dance floor, and Nekoda, empowered by a nap and a few drinks, joined her.

Jonah perceived an odd effect when he hung out with more than one or two friends at once. He found himself watching conversations unfold as if from behind a two-way mirror. He could hear everything that was said, but it was out of context and he struggled to keep up. Most people equated his quietness to good listening, but they didn't know about the other conversation he was having, not with the person in front of him but with a simulacrum of them in his mind—he strained to keep ahead of the conversation, to figure out what they *would* say and what he ought to say in response, or, when that became too taxing (or if the conversation failed to hold his interest in the first place) daydreaming about something completely unrelated. When he wanted to feel like a part of the group it made him feel separate, like a weird drone that could only observe and not interact.

Sometimes, alcohol could help with that. The wall between him and the environment dissolved, and he wasn't thinking about the right thing to say—he was listening to what his friends were saying, in that moment, actually listening and replying honestly, off the cuff. It felt good.

He knew he could get medicine for his anxieties, or even a genetic mod, but somehow the idea of medically changing his behavior felt more *invasive* than mere changes to appearance, and he had always shied away from it. For now, Nekoda's prescription made him feel like he was actually connected to the people around him and that he might even enjoy the music.

"Gentlemen!" Keros slapped an empty bottle down on the little table they'd huddled around. "My good talking coat racks and leaf piles: as you know, I don't have a tail anymore. Do I miss it? Yes. Did it help me dance better? Yes. But damn if I will stand here idly by and be upstaged by a frolicking dino and Koda's fluffiest-tail-this-side-of-the-Mississippi." He clinched his fists with a rhetorical flourish. "Now, then, what say you?"

Jonah laughed.

Jeremy shrugged. "I guess it's dancing time?"

Keros pointed down at the table for some reason. "Yes."

He twirled and strode out to the dance floor.

They laughed at him; then Jeremy sighed. "Well, I guess this is happening. Are you good?"

Jonah nodded and watched him go. His friends all having fun together was a familiar sight. They could be so open and playful, so *silly* with each other. He wanted that too. He finished his drink and helped himself to what the others had left behind. Sometimes he felt like there was a second pangolin curled up inside of him. It got upset when he moved; it always warned him, "It's too dangerous! Stay still!" But it was quiet at the moment.

I don't get drunk, Jonah thought. *It does.* And when it did he could sneak past it and have fun for a while.

I'll join them, he decided. Low key, just work his way out there, just be dancing—ninety percent of what everyone was doing was simple bouncing with the beat anyway; it didn't require any skill. He'd sneak up and join the perimeter of their dance circle, and they'd notice him one by one, and it would be like he'd been there all along, and Terah would be impressed, no big deal. Dancing time.

He slipped off his bar stool and made his way to the edge of the crowd where nodding heads, tapping feet, and wagging tails gave way to more active movements. He took a few deep breaths, copying the head bobs around him, and continued forward, trying to be unobtrusive. He was immediately aware that he was not dancing yet. He paused, trying to get a feel for the beat, to saunter his shoulders along with it—someone tripped over his tail.

"Sorry!" he yelped. His tail wasn't hurt and whoever had tripped was already gone, but he curled his tail around himself and crossed his arms in front of it for safety. He needed to find his friends so he wouldn't be a lone weirdo holding his tail. He wandered forward and around the crowd until he got a bearing on them and ran to meet them.

"JONAH!" He was noticed all at once, his arrival announced by Keros. "Get in here!"

They pulled him in. In the wash of shifting party lights and extremely loud dance music, suddenly, the inexorable flow of time in the universe went around a bend and left him washed up, cold and covered with kelp. He was in the middle of the circle, expected to dance. His friends were all staring at him, or it felt like they were. People moved their bodies intentionally. They were trying to get him to do the same. This song had moves. Specific moves. Keros was demonstrating and now handing it off to him. He was supposed to move his body.

Right now.

In an intentional, decorative, enthusiastic way.

For everyone to see.

The floor was hard and cold. He covered his ears with his feet, his eyes with his tail.

"Maybe if I just take a few breaths and get centered..." said the voice in his head that either did not or would not see the utter disaster unfolding.

Various clawed hands caressed his scales. "AW! Hey, buddy, what's wrong? Are you okay?" various friendly voices said.

Tell them you're okay, he thought. *Tell them you just need a break. Laugh it off.*

"Jonah?" That was Keros. "Guys, I think I broke the pangolin."

Oh, no. Not sympathy. Too late now, can't pretend to be normal. Okay, okay, just—just—just—

"Give him some space!" It took Jonah a second to recognize Nekoda's voice with such volume and authority as her students probably feared but which her friends hardly knew existed. Even the music sounded reprimanded.

"Are you breathing?" she asked. "Remember to breathe, okay?"

Say 'okay.' Say something. Nod, just nod, then.

But he didn't. His body was like a fawn in tall grass, believing its only chance of survival to be stillness and silence.

Come on, he pleaded. *Do* something *before they get scared and call for help. You're ruining the night! They'll say it's fine; they'll hug me and apologize* to *me, but I'm the one who's messing it up.*

The other pangolin, the one that kept his stomach clenched and warned him to stay away from the dance floor in the first place, uncurled and glared at him.

"Get up!" it snapped. It bared fangs and snarled. "You stupid pinecone! Artichoke! Say something, Leaf Pile! ANYTHING! What is *wrong* with you? They're going to fly in medics. They're going to evacuate the club because of *you,* Shingles. You're going to make them roll you out of here like a spare tire, aren't you? Damn it, you gross pile of finger nails. Why are you like this?"

The other pangolin hates me, Jonah thought.

It only wants me to curl up forever but also hates me for curling up. And I can't beat it. Why is the worst, meanest, most broken part of me also the strongest, best equipped, most resourceful part?

Jonah felt a surprising detachment from his panic as he thought this and meditated on it. But thinking it did nothing to help his predicament in the middle of the dance floor.

***

"What if you're right?"

Nekoda sat on a pillow across from Jonah, nibbling on graham crackers. The paper-like computer sheet lay between them, glowing softly.

"If they're gone, if they're…dead…" She held a half-eaten cracker with both hands.

"No, you're probably right." Jonah returned from the fog of memory with watery eyes. Nekoda's snacks had not been enough to entice him out of his curl. "I'm just thinking the worst thing, freaking out like I do. I'm sorry."

"No, I'm not the most practical thinker," Nekoda admitted. "I hope this goes away. I hope the lights come on and everything's normal in the morning. But…this seems pretty bad."

Jonah drew a deep breath, shivery with nerves. "Yeah."

Nekoda's voice suddenly rose, surprisingly loud in the quiet. "How am I supposed to know how everyone else is doing! How did people get by before they were connected all the time?"

She looked down at the computer sheet, its functionality so reduced by lack of connectivity that it wasn't much more than a candle. She pawed at it for the simple comfort of touching a screen. "What if there's no food? Drones bring food from wherever the farms are. What do we do when the pantry's empty? What'll all my kids do when their parents run out of food?"

"I don't know," Jonah whispered.

"This is so stupid!" Nekoda jabbed her fingers at the computer sheet as if performing CPR compressions on the internet. "Come on!"

Her whiskers would droop to the floor if they could. "Can I just curl up with you?"

This I can manage. "Of course."

She pulled a blanket off his bed and covered them both with it. Jonah enjoyed the added warmth in all the parts of his body that weren't numb from lying in place too long. He and Nekoda didn't speak for a while.

She turned toward him, her computer sheet partly crumpled beneath her but still illuminating their little tent.

"What if there's politics," she said. "What if people go back to being the way they used to be. What if there's wars—people killing people—" Her eyes immediately teared up.

His arm darted out and pulled her toward him.

"Whoa! Hey, you moved!"

"I'm as surprised as you," he said. "It won't, though."

"Won't what?"

"It won't be that bad. We'll be okay, even if AIs are dead."

"How do you know?"

Jonah hated that he remembered the worst parts of things first. That horrible night in the club. His mind was so quick to recall the mistake, the humiliation, the awful self-punishment. It was easy, automatic even, to dwell on those things. It took more effort to remember how things had turned out afterward. He lay there, paralyzed and hating himself, bullied into a corner of his mind by the other pangolin. The music continued to play, but the crowd was quieter.

"They're staring at you," it said. "You're making everyone feel awkward and uncomfortable and embarrassed for you."

He was curled so tight it hurt his back. He saw prickling red behind his eyelids. He wanted to grab one of his big shoulder scales and rip it out. He wanted to rip a scale out because of how terribly it would hurt. The acute, bleeding sting would bleach the wrong thoughts from his mind and atone for how he had wronged his friends.

He sobbed but slowly became aware of his breathing, slowly calmed under Nekoda's soft hands while she cradled him, petted him, whispered to him. He was disoriented when he dared to open an eye—the dance floor was different all right, but not empty.

They were all curled up.

His friends and not just his friends. Everyone. A hundred strangers. He wasn't singled out; most of them probably didn't even know why they were doing it or for whom. It was just a thing that had spread from his friends outward. Pure solidarity. Jonah poked his head up, looked at Nekoda, blinked.

She hugged him. "Better?"

He sat up, feeling dazed and silly, no other pangolin to be seen, but a lot of people pretending to be one. *I'm a silly person,* he thought. *But it's all right, I guess?*

"We're in safe mode," he said in the present, to Nekoda, under the blanket, "Like the drones."

He didn't know if it was generations of AI-driven, species-wide eugenics or something that was already in human nature, but when he freaked out in the club a bunch of strangers had helped to heal him by *becoming him,* as much as they were able.

"There won't be politics and wars," he said. "We'll figure it out together."

"I can't be a farmer, Jonah." Nekoda's ears flattened with an edge of panic. "I don't know how plants work. If I have to be a farmer I'll starve."

He smiled. "I'm pretty sure you can keep being a teacher. It's not like we'll have any less need for those."

He took a deep breath. "But if the drones stay in safe mode, we might have to...not."

"You mean...uncurl?"

"Yeah. I mean, eventually." The sudden prospect of action made him dizzy. "Maybe not right away. We could probably wait until morning, at least. Right?"

Nekoda nodded. "I'm sure that would be fine."

He swallowed. "I am hungry, though. I could. I think I could."

Nekoda smirked. "Well, if we've got all night to be in safe mode, you could come scrounge in the kitchen with me."

He nodded lightly. "Sounds good."

"You ready?"

He took a steadying breath and released it slowly. He started to speak, panicked, closed his eyes and held his breath. Then he opened them and breathed again.

"Ready."

Duncan is a dhole torn between honoring his heritage, fitting in with his band, and truly being himself, but maybe he can find a way to bring those aspects of his life together.

Laotian Rhapsody

Al Song

The pleather-clad dhole stomped his buckle-lined boot on the polished planks of the stage to the heartbeat of the bass drum produced by the water buffalo in the back. The smooth licks of the lead guitar from the punk doe beside him flowed with the warm harmonic chords of the keyboard by the tiger. The elephant's nimble plucking of her bass guitar and the dhole's own rhythmic strumming on his six-string flowed through his veins as he howled a final string of notes from the F major scale and let a final B flat major chord ring into the crowd.

Duncan opened his eyes to a few scattered golf claps and a mostly empty bar. A couple wolves were talking as they ate nachos, and a few vixens pointed to the stage and started giggling.

An arctic fox glowered at the dhole from near the bar and shook his head.

"Woo, Seattle, we love you!" the punk clad dhole shouted into the microphone with a fist stuck up in the air. "We are *Southeast Ambrosia!*"

A stout badger walked onto the stage with a mic in his paw and slid in front of the dhole. "Thank you, *Ambrosia.* That was… interesting. Okay, up next is karaoke so get your song selections ready folks," the emcee said as the curtain closed behind him.

"That was great, guys!" Duncan said, raising his paw for a high five as his bandmates either glared at him or averted their gazes away from the singer.

"What was that?" the arctic fox yelled from behind the dhole.

"What do you mean?" Duncan asked with a genuine smile.

"The first couple of songs you played were good, those cover songs. Then you started laying some hipster indie nonsense on the stage," the fox growled with crossed arms. "I don't pay you to drive away customers. Lenny convinced me to give you a chance, but we no longer need your services. Please leave."

"Okay, we're sorry for letting you down," Duncan said with a grimace.

"Speak for yourself," the spotted deer scolded.

The band quickly stored their instruments in their cases, packed up their equipment, and then left the bar.

"So, finance manager, how much did we make?" the dhole asked the deer.

"Duncan, we really should have stuck with the covers," she said sternly.

"So, how much is that?" he asked with a hopeful smile.

"We can now afford feta in our gyros," she said, her annoyance showing.

"Oh." He stopped in his tracks.

"We don't want to break your heart, but the music you write is... okay," Elizabeth the elephant said as tactfully as she could, resting a hand on the dhole's shoulder. "These past few gigs haven't gone very well, and the rest of us really don't want to burn bridges."

"I thought you guys liked my songs," Duncan said, defeatedly looking at the ground. "They're about immigration, and fighting xenophobia and homophobia."

"Your songs have a lot of important themes," the tiger agreed, "but like Elizabeth and Marie said, it's probably a good idea to stick with the covers."

"The problem is that they're just okay," the deer said with a sigh. "There's no wow factor to them."

The young musicians loaded their equipment and instruments into their van and then hopped aboard. Duncan remained quiet throughout the ride, watching downtown Seattle pass by as they headed up north.

***

Duncan woke up in the late morning, smacked the blaring alarm clock on his nightstand, and groaned at the sensation of the sun assaulting his eyes.

Another week of rude and idiotic customers, he thought to himself as he got ready for work.

The dhole put on a pair of black slacks and a navy blue polo shirt. He went to the mirror and plucked out his ear and brow piercings. Lastly he removed his septum piercing from his dark brown muzzle.

He ate breakfast, which consisted of some leftover gyro filled with falafel, and then took the bus to his parent's restaurant. During the commute he listened to a few alternative songs on his phone as he wrote in a small notebook filled with tabs, chord progressions, and song lyric ideas. The bus dropped him off at a park where a couple people practiced tai chi in unison and a few others flew box kites.

A few blocks later the dhole reached a Thai restaurant called 'King of Siam' and entered the side door in the alley.

"Duncan, you were almost late!" his father yelled at him when he entered the kitchen.

"Dad, chill out. I got here ten minutes early, plus there was extra traffic," Duncan explained to the older dhole.

"Then you should have taken an earlier bus," his father said sternly.

"Put on an apron. You're doing dishes today," his mom said and tossed a piece of folded cloth to him.

"Why am I on dish duty?" he whined.

"Jim called off." His mom placed a ticket on the order wheel.

"Why does he always get to call off?"

"Because his mom is in the hospital," his dad replied with disgust coating his tone.

Duncan held his hands up defensively and said, "Sorry, I didn't know."

Well at least dishes don't yell at me, he thought to himself and headed to the back corner of the kitchen.

He filled the left sink with hot soapy water, the center sink acted as the scrap and soap drain, and the right sink he added a disinfecting solution to. The dhole plugged his ears and started up a playlist of his favorite indie songs. He was in the groove clearing off each plate, soaking them, scrubbing them, and then rinsing them until they were spotless. The instrumental section of 'Systemic Recession' played as Duncan got out his trusty air guitar and started shredding in front of the sink.

"Stop goofing around!" his dad scolded as he ripped out an earbud. "Get back to work! We need clean dishes, and you're working too slow."

Duncan sighed and cleared off a half-eaten plate of pad thai.

The dhole's parents were from Laos, but their restaurant served Thai food. Duncan's father said that Americans are more familiar with Thai food than Lao cuisine, so of course they had to Americanize the meals.

His father told him when he was a cub that if people serve the actual authentic stuff then it turns off the American customers, because it's not what they're used to. People who have Thai food on a regular basis don't go to Thai restaurants very much, since they can get it from their family or they could make it themselves.

Duncan pondered this as he washed off a plate coated with curry sauce and then turned up the music on his phone.

The dhole ate some tofu pad thai during his lunchbreak in the back office and saw his dad marching up to him with a stern gaze that made the smaller dhole avert his eyes.

"Eating my food again?" his father sighed.

"I asked Joel to make this for me," Duncan said confused. "I didn't know he made a plate for you too."

"That's not what I meant," his dad said switching to Lao. "Who buys the ingredients? Who pays Joel to cook? Who keeps this restaurant running so you can keep eating?"

"Sorry, I understand," he said and turned his gaze downward. 'To understand' was an interesting verb in Lao, literally translated into English it was 'to enter one's heart,' but at this moment it seemed like the only thing that was going to enter his heart was a sharp object.

His father's stare ranged from icy cold to something so finely pointed that it could pierce the delicate skin under his sun-kissed russet fur.

"When will you find a job?" the older dhole asked, ending the silence.

"What? Do you want me to quit working here and then work at some other Thai restaurant? Do you want to replace me?" Duncan asked worried.

"If you work at a different restaurant, then you can pay for your student loans yourself, and I don't have to give you money to indirectly pay for them."

"I'm still tutoring, and the band makes some money."

"You're wasting everyone's time!" he said through gritted, sharp teeth. "How much do you make from teaching people math?"

"Well..." the younger dhole stuttered.

"I pay you more," his father quickly interrupted. "What about when you play music?"

"I think you know the answer," Duncan said quietly.

"It was a mistake to let you study abroad," the older dhole said and shook his head. "I had to take such a big loan out of that greedy bank for you, and you still haven't paid me back fully."

Did he regret going on the 'Semester on the Pacific' program? Absolutely not. Did he enjoy being in extra debt? That was a definitive 'no.'

"You didn't need to go on a boat to learn math," his father said.

"I know," he said defeated.

The pacific was where he had met his boyfriend, where he had learned about cultures that he never would have studied, and there had been some of the most beautiful views he had ever seen. It inspired him to take a gamelan class when he got back to the University of the Pacific Northwest.

He had still been acquiring his 'sea legs' and stood on the deck staring out at the ornate orange and milky cobalt melting into one another during an astounding sunset. He remembered looking over at a tall, plump river otter sinking into the railing, admiring the toasted tie-dye of the horizon where the sky and sea embraced one another.

The otter was an engineering student and the two had an abstract linear algebra class together. Duncan had mustered all the courage he had in his gut and walked up to the handsome otter and started chatting with him about Jordan canonical forms. That was how it had all started for the two of them.

Eventually Duncan's father left him alone, and he finished his meal.

A couple hours later Duncan rode the bus back home and changed into a dress shirt with a plain tie and khakis. He looked into the mirror, smiled, and then let out an audible sigh as he grimaced. He grabbed his old backpack, a few math materials from his desk, and placed them in his bag.

He walked a few blocks to the library near his house. He always wondered when they would actually renovate this branch of the library. The ones at the university were always being remodeled, and the ones in the rich neighborhoods had updated furniture. When he entered the iron barred gate over the front door, the dhole waved to the attendant behind the help desk, and the young ewe waved back at him. He informed her that he'd reserved a study room for the next hour, and she told him room five was available.

Duncan pulled out a few sheets of blank paper and a sheet of formulas typically used in an 'algebra one' class. He organized everything, sat down, and waited.

Where's Jesse? he thought to himself, tapping his claws on the desk. He then took his phone out to play a quick puzzle game. When he was in high school the dhole definitely knew people who weren't always the most punctual, but he also knew that Jesse's mom always dropped him off, and they were usually ten to fifteen minutes early so the boy could look at a few novels.

The phone suddenly vibrated in his paw, and he dropped it on the wooden table. He fumbled for the phone and answered it as his thumb stabbed the 'accept' button.

On the other line was Jesse's mom.

"I'm sorry I'm calling so late, but I think we have to cancel the tutoring sessions," she said in a blasé tone.

"Wait, but why? What's going on?" he asked, feeling his heart lurch up into his throat.

"Oh, I think Jessie's still having a tough time with algebra, and his test scores aren't improving," she said with the same aloofness in her voice. "I don't want to hurt your feelings, but this might be for the best."

"Alright, well I wish him the best of luck," the dhole said, trying to be as diplomatic as possible.

"Thank you, I wish you the best too, buh-bye!"

He knew at that point he would need to start putting up more ads online and maybe walk around with a staple gun and stack of flyers.

He walked home disheartened and practiced his guitar until the numbness went away, which was about the time that he started to head to band practice at Fredrick's house.

The dhole put on his leather jacket and threaded his face with his piercings again, and then he walked to the water buffalo's home in the dimming light of the evening.

The group of five set up and tuned together and then practiced a couple cover songs.

In the middle of their practice session they took a little break, and the dhole said, "For Friday's show how about we do half cover songs and half original ones?"

"How about we stick with covers?" the doe said with a glare. "You know, because that's what the crowds actually want from us."

"Okay, how about we sneak in two original songs?" the dhole suggested.

"Fine, you get one, and we put it in the middle!" Elizabeth said and crossed her arms.

"Yes! Thank you," Duncan said gleefully.

"It better be a good one." The spotted deer glowered.

"Alright everyone, how about 'International Generation?'" he asked.

The rest of the band shrugged, and they practiced his song.

Duncan looked over at the water buffalo. He had known Fredrick Sucharitakul ever since they were in middle school and met in band class. The dhole played the clarinet, and the buffalo was a percussionist. The drummer's parents were from Thailand, and their parents got to know each other pretty well. When Duncan came out to Frederick he was cool with it and was always there for the dhole when he needed it. The buffalo was like a brother to him. He acted as the manager since he was always organized, responsible, and good with paperwork that most of the band didn't want to deal with. He also studied business administration when he went to UPNw. It was disappointing for Duncan to see his best friend not stand up for him, but he knew that the other four were united in their opinion, and he also knew that Fred always wanted to stay out of drama.

The dhole looked over at the miffed deer. Elizabeth de Rama and Duncan had met in the LGBTQ center at UPNw. She'd been dating Marie, the bassist elephant at the time. The deer was probably the toughest person Duncan knew and had the ability to stand up for herself along with the people she cared about. Her parents were from the Philippines and owned a small pan-Asian supermarket in downtown Seattle. She studied accounting and was the band's financial officer.

Duncan turned to the Marie Tep, who was wearing her rhinestone, heart-shaped sunglasses as she kept the bassline moving. The elephant was always so kind, and outgoing. She was always up-to-date on all the latest trends. She was usually on her phone and always had a large following on all her social media apps and sites. Duncan had met Marie through Elizabeth and recognized her from her internet presence. Marie had studied marketing and acted as the band's social media director. Her parents were from Cambodia and worked with various online services to translate websites into Khmer.

The dhole listened to the fluid notes of the keyboard created by the tiger behind him. Louis Dang was the quietest one of the group. He had studied computer engineering and was a big fan of cars. Duncan had met Louis when they had a music technology class together. He worked with Marie to set up a little app for the band, and he always drove his van around to pick up the rest of the musicians and got them to their venues. Since he didn't drink he was always the one they counted on to get them home safe. His parents were from Vietnam and worked as automotive sales representatives.

Duncan knew he was the front man, but he also knew that dictating what the band should do wasn't his job and that listening to them was important too. Internally he sulked and cringed as he sang the lyrics to a cheesy rock cover of a pop song about how a guy can't get the girl of his dreams.

***

Parnassus was their venue that Friday. It was a decent sized bar that served food for a place near the downtown core of Seattle. The employees wore laurels, and the walls were adorned with murals of ancient Greek ruins with lush mountains behind them. The floor tiles were made of graying squares of white stone. The tables were large slabs of marble, and the chairs surrounding them had little wave patterns running across their backs.

Their sound check was early in the afternoon, and Duncan had to beg his dad to leave his shift early. It seemed like performing never was the most difficult part about being a musician for the dhole.

The bar already had a good crowd of patrons mingling within as servers in togas rushed around them. On each side of the stage stood a large plastic column with fake ivy spiraling down, and the stage curtains were black and an orange shade of bronze depicting three smiling vixens. One spun a thread, the second measured it, and the third held the end in one paw and a pair of sheers in the other.

In the chaos of the back stage, Elizabeth said to Duncan, "Stick to the set list."

"Don't worry about me," he said with a nervous smile.

From behind the drum set, Frederick asked, "Duncan, are you okay?"

"Yeah, I'm fine. Let's do this."

"Alright, this is gonna be sweet," Marie said with a grin.

"How's everyone doing tonight?" the dhole shouted as the curtain opened and the crowd cheered back. "We are *Southeast Ambrosia*."

The group started off with a rock cover of a fast paced pop song called 'Birthday Cake,' by DJ Cotton Kandy. The crowd danced and sang along to the electronic beats emanating from Louis' keyboard and the dhole's strong yet silky, tenor voice. Repeating 'birthday cake' and 'tastes great' a couple dozen times mostly annoyed the dhole, but he kept up the charade.

Halfway through the show, Duncan shouted, "Alright everyone, here's a new original song from us for you!"

Fredrick counted them down, and the dhole started singing as he strummed a few basic chord progressions. The crowd started clapping with confused faces. Some of the diners sat back down at the tables and started eating. Duncan's heart started racing as he saw people ignoring him, and he heard someone booing from the audience. He felt his own strand of fate snapping like a guitar string with the audience members holding warped scissors and knives, jeering at him with twisted grins on their muzzles.

More members of the audience started booing, and then someone in the front yelled, "Play something else!"

Duncan looked over at Elizabeth, and she gave him a stern look. The dhole brought his paw into the air and closed it to signal the rest of the band, and then they went to the last phrase of the song as a wave of derisions crashed into him.

"Here's 'Pop Rockz!'" he said, and Fredrick counted them down smacking his drum sticks in the air.

The crowd started cheering again, and Duncan tried his hardest to not let his queasy smile falter.

***

The next day Duncan took a bus to the UPNw campus. He walked past a series of buildings with large, worn columns lining their exteriors as he headed toward a group of decaying blue and white dormitories. 'Athena

Hall' was carved into the cement façade of one of the graduate student dorms in an antiquated typeface. He climbed a few sets of stairs and knocked firmly on a peeling door. A large river otter opened the door, and the two embraced.

"Brent!" the dhole squealed as they squeezed one another tightly.

The tall, chubby otter rubbed the dhole's back. "How're you doing, hon?"

"Amazing now that I'm here with you," Duncan said as he nuzzled the large otter's chest.

"I'm sorry that I haven't been able to keep up with you."

"It's totally fine!" The dhole gleamed up at his boyfriend. "I know you're busy."

The otter sighed with relief. "I'm just so glad that midterms are finally over."

"I do miss school sometimes, but I definitely don't miss the tests and stress."

"The stress increases exponentially, at least for me. It's like playing something on new game plus."

When they entered Brent's little living quarters, they kissed, and the dhole breathed in the the scent of his lover contained in the space. He looked at the instant pictures of them fastened to the mini-fridge in the tiny kitchen. Then the two sat cross-legged together on the cushy bed.

The river otter opened his laptop and placed it on his nightstand. He put on the latest episode of *The Deliberative*, a fictional, historical comedy set in ancient Greece. The two cuddled as they stared at the screen and laughed at the classically antiquated antics. They loved that the show had LGBTQ characters as well as a diverse cast showing how much of a nexus for trade and travel the setting was.

Duncan felt warmth emanate from his chest when he watched a shy, gay jackal meet the ram of his dreams. The jackal kept fumbling his words as well as the parcels and scrolls he carried. Duncan and Brent were excited to see this new storyline for the jackal who had been there since the beginning of the show. Near the end of the episode, after the priest-king gave a heartfelt speech about how they managed to work together despite their differences, Duncan let out a deep sigh.

Brent hit the space bar, pausing the show, and then hugged the dejected dhole closer.

"What's wrong, bud?" He kissed his boyfriend on the top of his head.

"Is it that obvious?" Duncan asked glumly with a slight smirk at the corner of his muzzle.

"I'm your boyfriend. Of course I know when you're sad," he said and kissed the dhole on this forehead.

"It hasn't been the easiest week," he sighed.

"What happened?" the otter asked cocking his head.

"Well, my dad got mad at me again for not having a 'real job' and mooching off of him."

"Dang, I'm sorry that he's being such a pill. Have you had more shows booked or any new students to tutor?"

"That's where I also have some issues," the dhole sighed. "Another student cancelled lessons with me, and the rest of the band's upset at me too."

"They're your friends. Why would they be mad at you?"

"They're mad because I want to play the music that I've written during performances."

"I'm sorry, bud," he said and hugged the dhole tightly.

"It sucks because I double majored in math and music, but I can't teach math, and I can't write music. So what was the point of me wasting all of my parent's money on stuff I can't use?"

"Hey, you didn't waste your time and money. You studied music intensely, and your band has a gig almost every week. That's really good, right?"

"I guess," Duncan sulked, "but I don't want to just cover pop songs all the time, especially with the radio music that's out today. They're all just boring love songs and break up songs that keep repeating the same things over and over again. I want to perform songs with depth, but the band wants to do what gets us gigs, and I can't blame them. I really don't want to be the reason why the band breaks up, and I especially don't want them to kick me out or replace me."

"That's definitely understandable."

"We've all got parents from Southeast Asia, and I wanted to write about my experiences being Asian American and what my parents went through to get to America and about Lao culture, but the audiences watching us don't care about that, and mainstream media almost never shows stuff about that."

"Maybe you just need to find the right audience. Throughout high school there were so many people who I knew who hated math and science, and then when I went to UPNw I met you and a lot of people who found the beauty and wonder in math and science."

"But they're already into math and science. How do I get new people to become interested in something so many people know nothing about, like Lao culture or linear algebra?"

"Well, you were taking advanced math classes to fulfill quantitative logic credits, right?"

"Yeah," the dhole said with a little nod.

"You told me that a professor on the 'Semester on the Pacific' trip convinced you to major in math rather than just minoring in it, and you said that he persuaded an undecided undergrad student to pursue math, right?"

"That's true too."

"So it can't be impossible to help people learn about new things and teach them about what it's like to be Lao American and gay at the same time."

"I guess," he sighed. "I really want to change the world and make things better! But I don't know if I can, and a part of me is starting to doubt if art can actually do anything to improve the world," the dhole said as he put his head into his paws.

The otter next to him held him tightly and said, "Art has influenced so much of the world around us. People say that life imitates art, and it's important that there are creators and performers like you out there."

"If science is my religion and math is the language of science, then I'm doing a bad job at spreading the word."

"Aw, Duncan," the otter said gently. "Don't be so hard on yourself. You're one of the most diligent people I know. You work in a restaurant, you tutor, and you perform in clubs. I don't know how you juggle three jobs and still manage to be one of the sweetest people I know."

"That's the other thing. When do people find the time to do all of this with full time jobs? I work two jobs, and I'm struggling to find time to perform, practice, write, and sleep. Will it be worth it?"

"If it's what you want. You have the stability to keep pursuing music."

"What if it doesn't work out?"

"You still have students, and maybe if you get a teaching certificate you could teach in a school," the otter suggested and rubbed the dhole's back.

"You're lucky," Duncan said.

"What do you mean?" Brent asked and raised his brow line.

"You majored in engineering, like how every parent wants their child to study. Now you're getting your master's."

"Well, it's not like I'm guaranteed a job after this. That's the scary part."

"That's true. I'm sorry," the dhole said feeling guilt rise in him. "I know you'll find something. You always find a way to make things work."

"It's okay. Hopefully after I graduate, I can get out of this dorm and we can live together in an apartment."

"That'll be amazing."

The two smiled at each other and finished watching the rest of the show.

***

Duncan took a deep breath, stood from the keyboard, and stared at the ceiling. His dark brown eyes turned toward a poster of one of his favorite indie artists called *A Band You Probably Haven't Heard Of* or *ABYPHHO*, pronounced 'Abby Foe.' The band lived the indie dream, and he loved their sound despite their absurd, hipster antics. He then looked at a khene hung up on his wall, sandwiched between a picture of his parents and extended family at Wat Xiengthong and of them at Wat Aham, each in a golden frame. The dholes looked so happy and serene at the temples with kind monks, enormous trees, and a clear sky behind them.

He plopped down on the black, rectangular cushion and played around with various chord progressions as he tried to figure out a string of notes to create a melody that would complement them. Maybe something basic and simple? Possibly in the key of C major? Maybe using a jazz scale could be unique or helpful? Nothing sounded right. It was so frustrating.

What about lyrics? He thought about the time someone called him a weird coyote, and when he said he was a dhole, they kept calling him a coyote. The thought connected to the time someone had cast red foxes from England to play dholes in a Hollywood film with a scene in Bangkok. Then he thought of the time he saw a real 'No Fats, Femmes, or Asians' sign outside of a new gay bar that had opened up downtown. Last but not least, he thought of the time he was told to speak 'American' when he was talking to an elderly relative in the hospital. He tensed his finger muscles and banged on the keyboard to create an exasperated cacophony of discordance.

It felt impossible to string together some notes to make a few measures, which would then create a couple phrases, which would then synthesize into a song. A lot of people had done it, so why couldn't he? He had majored in music performance which meant he took classes in music theory and even a few in composition, and he took a intro poetry class to try to figure out how to write lyrics. It all seemed completely useless.

The dhole hopped onto his bed and stared at the poster on his ceiling again. He reached for his phone on his desk and plugged his ears with his earbuds. He listened to 'Thirteenth Labor' by *ABYPHHO*. He closed his eyes and exhaled as the snare and bass drum set the scene, followed by a smooth, hypnotic riff from the bass guitar caressing his ears. They kept the beat and created a foundation; suddenly an anguished tenor voice and an electric guitar lick cut through the mellow background. It was like eating spoonful after spoonful of custard and then biting into a bright, juicy slice of lemon.

He looked at the mini Parthenon on his desk. The grand structure had the golden ratio, a spiral that made it beautiful. Music also had the golden ratio in it since there were triads containing the Fibonacci sequence. If only there were a formula for writing music that people actually wanted to listen to.

He put his face in his paws and groaned, "Why can't I do anything right?"

***

He stood in the kitchen eating veggie fried rice from a takeout box and staring at the fridge.

On the refrigerator was a picture of his cousin, Jeremy, who studied medicine and went to Columbia University. There was a magnet of the wolf statue of liberty holding up the photo. On the other side of the fridge was his other cousin, Jordan, who studied law at Harvard and had a vixen lady justice magnet keeping his photo upright.

Duncan's uncle and aunt always talked about how successful their children were, and his parents always made him feel bad for not pursuing those career routes. He kept eating his meal, glaring at the two of them. Duncan was always unsure of why his parents never put up pictures of their immediate family on the fridge.

No one wants to be my student, no one wants to be my parent, and no one wants to listen to my music, he thought to himself and reduced the pace of his chewing.

Moments later Duncan's father walked into the kitchen and opened up the freezer, took out a few ice cubes, tossed them into a glass, and filled it with water, as Duncan averted his gaze.

"So, I applied to work at the music store," Duncan said out of the blue.

"Good, you'll get to work with music," his dad replied in Lao.

"Dad, I'm sorry I'm such a disappointment. I thought getting good grades was enough to be successful, but I guess there's more to it than that," he blurted, frustrated. "You and mom came to America as refugees with nothing, and now you guys own a successful restaurant, and I was born here, and I have a degree, and I still can't do anything right. I'm sorry. You achieved your dreams, and I'll never do that, because I'm not good enough. I'm sorry I can't be like Jeremy and Jordan, and I can't be a great musician or mathematician. I want to play music that talks about important stuff like immigration and what it means to be Lao, but people don't want to listen to that. They don't care about some country with a long and painful history. I want to tell your story and the story of our people."

"Get your guitar," his dad said quickly. "Come with me."

Duncan grabbed his guitar from his room and saw his father walk into the master bedroom. The larger dhole pulled a record player from his closet and took out a vinyl. He lifted the needle, set the record down, and played the song. A fuzzy static flooded the room as smooth flutes, majestic reedy woodwinds, and jolly percussion instruments performed. A smooth, melodic voice and shrill strings joined along.

"Listen to the lyrics," his dad calmly commanded.

"I don't understand them all," Duncan admitted.

"The song is about how Lao and Thai people used to be one. The Mekong divided the countries physically, but everyone acted like brothers and sisters, and now they're two different countries, but there's still a yearning for and an acknowledgement of the past."

"That's definitely cool, and this song's pretty good."

"It's Khap Thum, which is a northern Lao form of Mo-Lam," his father explained. The older dhole had lived in the countryside in the north of Laos, and his mother was from the south. They met as teenagers in Vientiane. "Can you play a rendition of this on your guitar?"

"I think so," Duncan said and messed around on the fret board. He played the melody and copied a few of the string and woodwind sections.

"Not bad," his father said. "Khap Thum and Mo-Lam have songs about love, but also about hardships. They talk about the history and what was important to Lao and Isan people. These days people make pop music out of these traditional songs, so maybe you can make a rock song."

"It shouldn't be too hard, but I don't know if people want to listen to Lao music, and I don't think they'll understand me if I sing in Lao."

"I was going to ask if you want to perform at the restaurant," his father said after taking a sip of water.

"What? Really?" Duncan asked stunned at the statement.

"We can move tables and chairs and make a stage. This might be a way to get more customers."

"Okay, that sounds great. Thank you, Dad."

***

Duncan set up the equipment on the small make-shift stage in the corner of the restaurant with a couple diners gawking and smiling in anticipation. The band quickly tuned when they all got to the stage and were ready.

"Looks like you got your wish," Elizabeth said with a smirk, and then Frederick counted them down.

The song was quieter and slower than most of their other performances, mostly because the venue was smaller and Duncan's father had added some regulations to what was allowed. The guitarist composed the songs to resemble rock and metal from the eighties. The lights dimmed as he sang the traditional Lao lyrics.

Duncan saw a couple older diners mouthing the lyrics excitedly while a few people clapped along. There were people at the window of the restaurant curiously looking in.

When the song finished a grand cheer rose from the diners and the large line in the waiting area.

Duncan knew that the people who wanted to listen to the music were mostly of Southeast Asian descent, but it was definitely a start. He let the applause envelop him in joy and validity as he strummed into the next song.

Set in the same universe as Bill Kieffer's collection, Cold Blood: Fatal Fables, *from Jaffa Books, this story shows a Gator and a Cat in love, struggling to resist in their own ways, based on their very different backgrounds and life experiences, while still trying to fit together.*

QIBLA

Bill Kieffer

It was almost a perfectly lazy Sunday. After a dinner of seven fishes (literally, in the Alligator's case; 14 Sushi pieces in the Cat's) and the brushing of Jinx's coat as they watched the cartoons of Cecil's youth (strictly forbidden in the Cat's Darwin upbringing) the phone rang, summoning Cecil to a police station on the other side of the county.

Jinx frowned comically. "We were supposed to have all day together."

The Tonk ignored the 'Gator's elegant gesture to the night sky and continued to express his disappointment. Cecil knew that as long as Jinx was talking, he wasn't terribly mad. Since the last election, calls for work from the police departments had become less frequent. Like most conversations with the Cat, Jinx argued both sides, knowing exactly what Cecil would say – if the Gator could keep up with his chatter.

"I'll come with you," Jinx volunteered and then settled into a silence that gave the large man pause.

Cecil nodded and said, "OK," although he knew that he should have said no the second that Jinx started bouncing about with glee. "I'm going to translate," he warned. "You'll have to stay quiet."

Jinx nodded and then proceeded to list all the times that he'd been quiet; which was true enough. When the Tonk had come back into his life last year, he'd been so uncommunicative that Cecil had worried that Jinx had been terminally ill. Instead, the young Feline had been sick with guilt and shame. He'd mostly recovered from his excommunication from the community that he'd grown up in.

175

Cecil mugged a dubious look, knowing that Jinx could read his stiff face well enough to pick up on it.

Jinx slammed his lips together and used an invisible key to lock his jaw in place. He threw the key over his shoulder. It was a gesture he'd learned from the new-to-him cartoons.

Cecil shook his head and hands in silent Rept laughter as he waddled up to the display case where he kept his religious articles. He attached the tzitzits to his chest quickly as his lover watched raptly. The Cat's tail twitched about, knocking unlit candles over.

Still amused, Cecil attached the last one and met the Cat's eyes. "Did you want to touch them?"

Unable to resist the invitation, Jinx stepped closer and reached out his furry right hand. With a gentle stroke, the black fingertip touched the first badge with reverence. "This celebrates the band of green," Jinx said as his furry ears brushed the underside of Cecil's jaw. Surprised and caught off guard, the Alligator pictured the Everglades, as he imagined them in his head. The warm finger moved across his chest to the other green knotwork badges, and the Tonk evoked their images and meanings. His parents' faces came to him, but instead of the near dead walking corpses that he saw last, Jinx's soft voice triggered an image of them here in the house, drinking tea at the colorful low table.

"Your name was Sea Isle Pine," Jinx told him, and Cecil couldn't help but picture the rap star who inspired him to speak up, to fight the status quo. Before Jinx could go further, Cecil grabbed both his arms and gently pushed him back until he could look down his snout into the Cat's eyes.

"What?"

Cecil opened his mouth, but nothing came out. He had so many mixed feelings about the symbols of his former faith that he didn't know where to begin. He didn't normally wear the little knotwork badges. They did, however, put Chromatic victims at ease. The woman on the end of the phone had made it clear it was a White Band Chromatic who had been beaten. Instead of explaining, he mimed zipping his mouth shut and then locking it with an invisible key. He shook the invisible key in front of Jinx until the Cat's tail curled with amusement. Only then did he toss the key over his own dark green shoulder.

Jinx blushed in his ears and smiled in casual defeat. "I'll bring my book," he said agreeably.

***

"Professor? Hi! Take a seat over there. I'll let the Captain know you're here." The Ursine clerk pointed to a row of plastic and metal seats on the far wall, just behind the two vending machines.

Jinx gave Cecil a curious look at the title but said nothing. The Alligator made a gesture that meant "later" and walked to the vending machines, and then stopped the Cat there. He caught their image in the large round mirror that allowed the clerk to see who was sitting in those chairs (on the off chance someone in this sleepy riverside town might be waiting for a cop to pop out of the squad room). They were both dressed in similar business suits, at Cecil's insistence. It had meant dressing down a bit for the 'Gator. It meant dressing for a wedding to Jinx. The suit covered the religious symbols, but he would unbutton it before seeing the client.

On the trip to the Twin Mills Police Station, Jinx had chatted about whatever came into his fuzzy head, which had delighted Cecil. The truth was, acting as a translator often meant a lot of hurrying up and waiting. It would be nice to have a distraction for the waiting parts.

He hoped the Cat had gotten the chattiness out of his system, but you could never be too sure. Worst case scenario, he'd have to make the Tonk go sit outside in the van. So far he was doing very well, despite the frown from Jinx when he caught Cecil looking at a few strands of fur on his otherwise immaculate shoulder.

To distract the Cat from his obsessiveness, Cecil whispered some insider information. "The acoustics here are so bad," he said softly. Cecil then pointed to the benches and then made an arc in the air with his thick, gnarled finger to the open transom that separated the squad-room from the waiting room. "You can hear anything in the hallway behind that door from those chairs. And vice versa."

Jinx nodded solemnly. The Cat threw away another invisible key.

Cecil smiled and nodded, satisfied that his young Cat had gotten the point. Being alone was no guarantee of privacy. He tongued the Cat's little itty-bitty lavender nose affectionately and then they walked over to the chairs. The large green man leaned against a wall, letting his thick tail take most of the weight.

Jinx grabbed his own thin tail and dropped into a seat without a second thought. It took a moment for it to sink in that the Alligator wasn't taking a seat. "Aren't you going to sit down? Or do you think he'll be right out?"

Cecil shook his head. Then he gestured at the row of seats. They were all rigid fiberglass/plastic models atop metal rails broken up by steel rods that acted as armrests of a sort. None of the public chairs made any allowances for thick tails like Cecil's. The Alligator made another gesture with hands that waved it all away. *Don't get me started*, he mimed.

Jinx took on a thoughtful frown, as if not sure if he should be angry for Cecil's sake.

Cecil caught his attention after a moment and pointed to the hooks in the far wall about four feet off the floor. The wall below the row of steel hooks was pretty well gouged with deep scratches and had obviously been painted over several times. Jinx got up to look closely at the wall and its hooks. They seemed too thick and too strong to be mere coat hooks.

The Cat and 'Gator fell into a silent communication between themselves, gesturing expletives and promises to talk on it later. Jinx took photos of the hooks and scratches with his cell phone, but didn't post them as Cecil waved him off. They practiced their signs, the only other language Jinx was interested in learning.

It was almost twenty minutes later when Captain Fisher met Cecil. The Crane's Avi head took them both in before turning one eye towards the Alligator with penetrating avian attention. He gently shook the large green man's proffered hand. "I'll be right with you, Professor." The white and brown head bobbed and then moved to focus the other eye on the Cat in a softer, curious regard.

"Sir," the police captain spoke brightly then, almost as if Jinx was a friend he'd not seen for a while, and he did not want Jinx to realize he'd forgotten his name. "Can I help you?"

Jinx was taken aback a bit, but in typical Tonk fashion, he felt compelled to verbally respond. "Actually, he was here first. That is to say, I'm with the professor here." He might have babbled on a bit longer, except the Avi's long beak spun to point in Cecil's direction, only to turn slightly down as the intense one eye stare re-engaged.

"Captain Fisher, this is my new partner, Jinx Tonka. He's here to observe."

The Avi nodded and looked at the Cat. "You speak Chromatic, too?"

Jinx almost responded that Chromatic wasn't a language, but a subtle hand gesture from Cecil stopped him. "I'm more of a expert on Heartland languages." Cecil rolled his eyes for this was true enough in the sense that Jinx could order off an Ethiopian menu almost like a native speaker. Or so the Lion waitress who flirted with the Tonk assured them both.

With a surprising display of will, Jinx fell silent as Captain Fisher accepted that with a nod.

"On the phone, you said you needed me to translate for a Chromatic victim?" Cecil saw no reason to push Jinx's restraint much further than need be.

"And, now, potential suspect," Fisher added with a snap of his bill on every pause, the soothing voice he used on Jinx now gone. "He had a knife hidden on him, and the only reason he's not under arrest just yet is that I got a bunch of drunken yahoos that keep changing their stories, hogging my cells until County gets here."

Cecil nodded and pulled a paperback-sized clip board from his inside pocket. He had the captain sign the standard forms, even as the Crane said that they could do the paperwork later. Cecil nodded agreeably, pretending that he'd not been stiffed before. "Do we know our victim's name, Captain?"

The Avi nodded as he buzzed the door to be let back into the squad-room. "As near as we can make out, it's Zinn Kiki, but don't ask me how to spell it."

Cecil nodded, his curiosity peaking a little higher as the Crane led them past the mostly empty desks in the squad-room. The door into the interview room was "normal" sized, so that made it one of the nicer rooms to sit in. His respect for the Crane went up a little bit. Cecil had to unbutton his suit jacket to bend down low enough to look through the thick wire-reinforced plate glass set into the door.

His respect for the Avi dropped back several points as he saw the blood-spattered figure sitting behind the door. The blood wasn't too surprising since Cecil had been warned on the phone about the injuries. The small sand-colored Fox with his head uncovered did surprise him. He straightened up and turned his snout up to the ceiling as he re-buttoned his jacket, hiding his annoyance until he could get it under control. He did not want to antagonize the Crane.

At least I do not have to worry if he can see my merit badges.

"Your suspect appears to be a Fennec. His name is probably Something Singh Khikhi. Was he wearing a turban when he came in?"

The Crane nodded. "Sure, that's how we knew he was a Chromatic. He was wearing all white, so we figured he was once of your White circle believers." He looked at Jinx, as if for approval.

"I believe you mean the White Band," Jinx said slowly, looking the Avi in the eye turned toward him. "They do often wear shades of white and pearl, but as Cecil pointed out, Fennecs aren't Chromatics. At least not usually, and not if they are wearing turbans. At least not usually."

They both looked up at the 'Gator. "So, you don't think he's talking Chromatic?" The Crane asked, and Cecil almost sighed, but that Warm affectation hadn't grown on him quite that much. He simply spun the air in his lungs a bit slower, in the fashion of his people. In one nostril and out the other.

"He probably speaks Punjabi," Jinx suggested before Cecil could say anything. "Cecil speaks Punjabi."

The Crane's head feathers moved a fraction into what could be categorized as a smile. "Good, then, let's get to it, Cecil."

The Alligator wasn't sure who to glare at first, so he fell back on the calm game. "Fennec carry five articles of faith on them all the time. He's going to ask for them back as soon as I introduce myself." Demand would probably be a better word, but Cecil did not want to risk the Crane becoming spiteful.

"I expect you're going to tell me the knife is a holy object of some sort." The Crane somehow managed to give a respectable growl for such a narrow throat.

Cecil mugged a Warm smile and shrug. Even though Captain Fisher wasn't a Fur, Avi tended to react to "normal" emotional cues better. Jinx jumped in before the 'Gator could give the policeman some insight.

"Yes," the Cat jumped in. "The knife's a kirpin; it's just supposed to be self-defense. There should also be a wooden comb, a bracelet, a special kind of underwear... and head covering."

Cecil held his breath, but the Crane looked at the Cat and nodded. "Well, we certainly haven't touched his panties. I can give him his comb, his bracelet, and his turban... but not the pins that held it together. He can collect that... and his pretty little blade *if* he plays nice *and* I decide to let him out the front door."

Cecil knew better than to press further. He wasn't the man's lawyer, just an advisor and translator. He nodded and went over the rules for the translation, as much for Jinx's benefit as for the cop's. The Crane nodded and then rapped on the glass with a talon that rivalled the Alligator's own clawed fingers.

***

"Are you mad at me?" Jinx asked after a note-worthy pause in his stream of conscious monologue.

Cecil concentrated on the road ahead, unsure how to answer his young partner. *"You can be such a Fur, sometimes,"* seemed too mean and an unproductive opening gambit to the conversation that they needed to have. Yet, the growing silence in the car was equally bothersome, too (although he was sure the silence ate at the Tonk more than it did him). "I was surprised that you know a lot about Fennec and Chromatics."

"I've been reading," Jinx boasted. "Books and religious blogs. Been following a lot of experts on Owo-Book and Shouter, too. I spent most of my life with the Darwin echo chamber, as you know. I didn't know half the things I really should have."

Cecil nodded and made a silent production of checking his speed on the dial directly over the windshield. Jinx getting kicked out of his family and his cultish religion had thrown them back together. Jinx had been just another John their first time around, but neither one had realized their age difference. As good as Cecil was with the Warms, he had known the Cat was younger and spry... but not that Jinx was still in high school when they'd begun to hook up. Jinx began to lie as soon as he realized the 'Gator was twice his age. That lead to some ugliness and a breakup.

Since then, the young tom had matured considerably. But he was still a Cat, ignorant of many things that made up the unpleasant world of a Rept trying to live his life in a Warm world.

"But you are mad at me," Jinx said after a suitable pause, maybe a block or so.

"I am angry, Jinxie, but not with you." Cecil fiddled with the controls in the steering wheel by touch and adjusted the temperature in his seat warmer down a few degrees. "Well, *not you* exactly."

The Cat purred a harrumph, which was something Cecil had never heard before. The Alligator spared a glance to see Jinx's ears and tail weren't exactly laughing at him. He had to be careful; with a snout so large, any cop could see if he was paying attention to the road or not. It didn't take much for a Rept to get pulled over, even for a split second of checking on his passenger. Especially big 'Gators whose mere existence seemed to threaten well-armed, Furry Cops into questionable weapons discharge issues.

"I'm angry with... the cops," Cecil said lamely.

"Uh-huh. Because they almost locked up Mr. Khikhi for not speaking Aenglish?"

"They almost locked him up because they thought he was Chroma, Jinx." Cecil made a fist to underscore the anger that barely colored his voice. "I mean, he should be grateful they didn't call ICE instead of me...or American Soil Security. Which is what they might have done if he was a Rept. I don't know, Fisher can go either way."

"Captain Fisher said he thought you were very well spoken." Jinx offered soothingly, but the Pforde's brakes squealed in protest. Luckily, this was a back road with no traffic.

Cecil pulled over to the side of the road and then threw the van into park. His tail thumped three times before he turned his toothy snout to Jinx. "Well Spoken?" he asked. "Well Spoken?" he repeated the question when Jinx remained uncharacteristically silent. His fur had fluffed out, and his ears went back, but other than a quick double blink and a nod, the Cat seemed at a loss for how to respond.

"I speak five more languages than anyone at that police station." Cecil growled. "Six if you count the XenoVox slang I picked up from the street when I was a kid. I can go to over a dozen countries in Homeland and Heartland and speak like a native, and that... *that bird* says that I'm *well spoken?*"

His dark green fists pounded twice on the steering wheel's outer edge, careful to avoid all the additional, expensive ADA controls that allow a short limbed species like Alligators to drive a car designed around "*normal*" people. *Furry people.*

His tail thumped several times as he sat frozen. Jinx reached over and rubbed his shoulder. More than talking, the Cat liked touching things. Cecil was comforted a little, not just because of his lover's touch, but because their first go-around Jinx would have started arguing back immediately. He wasn't sure if that was a Cat thing, a Darwinist thing, or just a Jinx thing. He didn't know too many Cats, which was one of the reasons he hadn't realized just how much younger his Tonk was.

He mugged a sigh, just to let Jinx know the anger was released. He watched without moving his head much as Jinx relaxed a little. His wide tail thumped lightly once more on the floorboard behind his seat, not as convinced. Jinx cocked an eyebrow, and Cecil remembered that this Feline was not his enemy. Far from it.

"Did you notice how Fisher and the Detective kept referring to you and not me?"

Jinx thought about that for barely a second. "Well, yeah, but that's the rule you set out; once you sit down, you translate everything they say to the suspect, but you don't translate 'crosstalk.' You're supposed to be invisible, more or less."

"Even after the interview, they kept referring to you. I'm not supposed to stay invisible."

"Well, you never brought a partner with you before, right? I'm sure it was just the novelty factor. Do they know you're gay? I wasn't sure. I never thought to ask. I just concentrated on not giving too much away."

"That's true, and they probably do, but they wouldn't want their 'faces rubbed' in my queerness." Cecil's tailed thumped as Jinx opened his mouth, and the 'Gator's long head swayed back and forth in a slight expression of impatience. "What really annoyed me was the way they talked to you. Like an equal. Right out of the gate. Not 'cop equal,' of course, but they accepted your humanity right off. They didn't question your qualifications."

"Good thing, too," Jinx interjected. "I'm a fraud. I'm sorry I talked so much. Just when he started talking to me, I couldn't just ignore him."

"No, you handled yourself fine, as far as that goes." Cecil had been rightly annoyed when Jinx had stepped on him in the Cat's eagerness to show off what he knew about Fennec and their holy symbols, but in the end, it was his smooth management of the Crane and the Dog that got Mr. Khikhi released that night without needing a lawyer. Jinx had impressed him and the police who weren't known for their patience.

"Do you know why they call me Professor?"

Jinx shook his head but brightened almost immediately. "Because you're smarter than them?"

Cecil blinked his eyes, too quickly for it to count as his version of the Feline nonvocal, *I love you.* "They call me Professor because I'm a *'reptile that went to college.'*"

Jinx's face curdled as Cecil parsed out the honorifics of capitalized nouns that modern Aenglish used. Dropping a honorific wasn't just rude. It was insulting. Technically, all Repts were reptiles; cold-blooded creatures. Repts were as evolved and as human as any Mammal or Avi. To call a Rept a mere reptile was to imply that Repts were more animal than people. "When did they call you a reptile?" Jinx looked properly scandalized at the specism, yet the 'Gator caught himself.

Just a moment ago I called Fisher a bird.

Cecil felt his anger dissipate on that thought. Unlike most Mammals, most Repts had a hard time holding onto anger and fury. "They didn't call me that... not directly, and certainly not today... not within my hearing... but it's... implicit... in their tone when they talk to me... as opposed to say how they talk to another Warm." The Alligator pointed his snout in the Cat's direction. "Like how they talked to you tonight."

Jinx smiled and squinted slowly. "Would you like it better if they called you a Cunning Linguist?"

The 'Gator's hands left the wheel to touch his throat and left cheek with a blush gesture. "Don't make jokes about this, Jinxie."

"But it's just an... endearment. They like you. I can hear it in their voices."

Cecil nodded. "But, I've asked them to call me Mr. Kanëhtaikhö, or Mr. Green, or even just plain Cecil. But it never takes." He looked ahead at all of the quiet houses on this road. Blue and grey television shadows danced in the windows of most of them. No one was looking out the window in fear of who might be parked randomly on their street. These houses were probably full of Avi and Mammals, because a strange car parked on a Rept street could be trouble. "Yes, they do like me. Yes, it's an endearment. It is... but I am endeared to them because I am *their* Rept. I work for them; I do what they tell them, and I know my place... if they call me Professor, they can stop thinking about how strong my jaws are or how many bullets it's going to take to stop me."

"Wow... that went dark fast."

Cecil gave his Cat a look. "Welcome to my world."

Jinx unbuckled his seat belt and crawled into Cecil's lap, pausing only to move the steering wheel out of the way. Even then, the space was tight, and Jinx ended up wiggling his mass under the steering wheel, between Cecil's legs. The 'Gator was too surprised by Jinx's constantly moving tongue to protest more than warning him to be careful not to flood the engine. He knew he was being "managed," but the street was dark and the spot they'd parked was darker still. Their first romance had been exclusively in this vehicle.

He was fine with being managed at the moment.

Before Jinx could unzip Cecil's trousers, dancing blue and red lights filled the street.

Both Jinx and the police siren wailed in the same key, as soon as the Alligator muttered the word, "Police."

***

Strobing lights, a steady stream of walkers, moving down the steps.

The smell of so many Mammals afraid. There were all afraid. Few had seen the jet hit the first of the Global Village Towers, but they'd all seen the aftermath. Moments before, many of them had stood against the glass walls, staring at the fire and smoke meters away, until they began forcing themselves to turn away.

Most on the observation deck had lined up in an orderly fashion to take the elevators down.

But then they stopped coming back up.

Then someone with a radio announced that two other jets had crashed into other targets.

Not buildings... but other targets... and the real exodus had begun.

***

Cecil awoke alone, but that was not an issue.

Jinx typically slept in three or four hour shifts, whereas the Alligator usually slept like a log. The Tonk would catch a "cat nap" just before dinner. His Darwinist heritage meant that he'd come from a long line of Cats that had been bred to be especially Feline. Human Husbandry didn't sit well with Cecil, but he felt he shouldn't judge. It was no worse than their poly-cannibalism.

184

As an Alligator, Cecil had his own morning ritual to attend to. He could hear Jinx puttering downstairs and talking on the phone, going by his pauses. He decided not to ask the Cat to join him in his shower. Alone, he walked again on all fours. He'd get up on his proper legs once he got some heat into him.

One shower and a good oiling later, Cecil walked down the stairs as gracefully as his short legs allowed him to. The tip of his tail tapped every other step clumsily.

Jinx wasn't downstairs, but there was evidence that he'd been there. Half the kitchen floor had been swept clean of the fur that the Cat seemed to constantly leave behind, and the little pillowcase lined barrel that Jinx kept his excess fur in was smack dab between the kitchen and the dining room. Once a week, a "shed woman" came to collect his silver-blue offerings, for reasons that were both about recycling and Darwinistic, but also thrifty. His pedigree coloring netted a few extra dollars a month.

My parents would have approved... but they'd also have been somewhat appalled.

A good Chromatic house must always be clean. Cecil did not know how the warm-blooded Chromatics wives managed to keep a clean house with the entire household shedding left and right.

Not my problem, he thought, *I'm no longer a Chromatic. I can let this house get as messy as I want it to.*

Still, it bothered him to see the before and after scenes of a good sweeping. He forced himself not to finish the job that his lover had started.

In the kitchen, he found a five pound box of lox that the milkman had brought. He set aside a pound of it for Jinx's breakfast and lunch in the refrigerator where it belonged, and brought the rest over to the sink so that he could easily wash the pink "crumbs" down the garbage disposal. He cleaned out his mouth with a few cubes of frozen coffee. The Creator had granted the Alligator with several feet of effective flexible lips, but he had been less than generous with cheeks. The stereotypes of Alligators being messy eaters were true; if one wasn't careful. Cecil was raised to be careful so that they could eat in public.

When he was done rinsing out the sink, Cecil realized that he heard the printer going. The Alligator poked his head into his office, but the Cat wasn't there. The existence of a wireless connect to a printer still surprised him from time to time. He peeked at the printouts and saw that Jinx was on a research kick. Mostly about Skinks and the law; the articles were a mix of legitimate news sites and a few Cold Power websites so left wing it made the Alligator mug a frown even though there was no one else in the room.

He found Jinx on the back deck, staring at his lap top, Oh-My-Godding in hushed tones. His ears were wide with shock, and Cecil wondered for a long dark moment if Shattered Shards had dropped a jet on another building. The Cat looked up at him with wide black eyes and seemed almost at a loss for words.

Being a Tonk, Jinx quickly recovered.

"I found out what the hooks are for." He managed to take his voice somewhere between a whisper and a yowl. "Oh My God."

Incredibly relieved, Cecil barked a laugh that sent two of his coffee cubes into the backyard. He shut his own mouth when the Cat somehow managed to look even more irate.

"Did you know that they bag Skink suspects in nets and hang them on those hooks?"

The Alligator nodded solemnly and swallowed the rest of his coffee cubes so he could talk. His stomach would complain later. "Sometimes Skink witnesses, too." It was a terrible injustice, but it was old news to a Rept who'd grown up seeing such things.

Jinx looked almost comical as he glanced back to the computer screen. He shook his head and swore to a heaven that Cecil wasn't sure the Cat actually believed in. The Alligator came around the table and peeked over Jinx's shoulder. It was a video clip of a reality crime show that Cecil recognized by type rather than by name. A tan-uniformed Mutt Dog held up a medicine ball-sized prisoner. He loosened the clamp on the rope of netting, which changed the bundle of Rept flesh from a ball shape to a tear drop. The Skink immediately started thrashing about in the bag he was trapped in. With a straight face, the police officer forcibly returned the clasp to its original position. To keep his tail, limbs, and snout from getting crushed, the Skink balled up again. It was a smooth, jerky process, but Skinks were small and weak, and only dangerous in numbers. This Dog's lone prisoner didn't have a chance to resist. He (or she, because you never could tell with a Skink) could only glare at the Dog from the net with Cold indignity.

Jinx looked up at him. "Can they breathe like that?"

Cecil gave a short nod. "Shallowly. If they're smart, they try to relax and..." The Alligator wanted to say hibernate, but he wasn't sure that his Furry lover would understand. "Sleep it off." But those words sounded lame to him.

"Most Skinks are too small for prison cells. You can't handcuff them; their wrists are too small. And even if you could, you can't put them in the general population, Skinks would be stomped to death by most of the

Mammals behind bars within hours. Plus, guards react badly to prisoners clinging to the ceiling. They are safer on those hooks, believe me."

As awful as Cecil felt for defending the treatment of Skinks, Jinx seemed to take it worse. "How can you say that? You of all people?"

Cecil felt slapped, but he'd always expected to hear something like this from Jinx. You know a Furry long enough and you always do. "What do you mean, me 'of all people?'"

Dark hands gestured up and down at the Alligator's body. "Look at you. Short limbs, long torso, long tail... you're practically a giant Skink yourself."

Cecil's glare lessened a bit; enough for him to realize that he had been glaring. He'd never been compared to a Skink before, at least not to his face. His own distaste at the comparison surprised him as much as anything. "I've worked with the police for 20 years, Jinxie. Skinks are a lot harder to catch than Alligators. Do you know what happens when you chase a Skink for twenty minutes? He gets away. Do you know what happens when you chase an Alligator for twenty minutes? He dies. The lactic acid and fatigue poisons build up in a 'Gator's system, and he dies a horrible death of agony and pain, often paralyzed and unable to speak... thrown into a jail cell until he's ready to talk. Which he cannot do. So forgive me if I am not overly sympathetic."

Jinx's mouth fell open. Cecil went back in the house before he could say anything else. He felt the strangest need to slam the sliding glass door, but he couldn't get his tail out of the way fast enough.

***

"What's the matter, Cecil? Cat got your tongue?"

Cecil was startled; although only those who knew him or his Species well would have recognized the eye movement and shoulder twitching as the Alligator's version of "startlement." It even took him a moment to focus on the Bear's face in front of him and recall that he had been speaking to the national director of public relations for the Queer Resistance Network.

"You could say that." He eyed his office door, which was closed. "I'm feeling like I had my first fight with Jinx... since he moved in, at least. But it wasn't really a fight... I just sort of corrected him."

Ted Shahd raised his eyebrows and leaned back in a big easy chair only the nearly tailless could be comfortable in. He smiled in a way that was both non-judgmental and suggestive. "Did you now?"

The Alligator rolled his eyes and let himself smile a little. He and Ted had shared the back of the Pforde three or four times. It had never gotten much further than curiosity and "stress-relief" after speaking events, but they remained good friends with a mutual interest in LGBT activism.

"No." Cecil thought about it. "Maybe... Jinx just discovered Skink-bags. He was up all morning on the Internet printing out articles to read later... he even logged onto my Electro-Nexus account to print out research."

"He hacked your account?"

Cecil shook his head reluctantly. "No, I gave him my password last week so he could research Monster-Sow."

"Oh. So... are you still so Green band that you're annoyed by all that wasted paper?" Ted was also a Chromatic, more casual than actually lapsed. He liked to tease Cecil about his supposed cheapness. Just as the Alligator teased him about the Golden band's openness and sartorial boldness. The Ursine businessman wore a relatively mild pumpkin colored suit with light brown piping today. Next to the rainbow hair extensions that he wore as a beard, it was hardly worth mentioning.

"No... I wish it was. Then I could just apologize or something." Cecil's tail scraped along the table leg of his desk, too confused to actually thump in annoyance. "It's just that he came with me to the police station to translate for a victim, and he was surprised that they confused a Fennec with a Chromatic. Then he was *surprised* that I had an issue with the nickname the cops gave me. Then he was *surprised* when a cop pulled us over for parking on a public street. *And then he was surprised* by finding out *what the hooks in the police station were for.*"

Ted made him back up a bit and then quizzed him on details. They went back and forth, and Cecil had to wonder if he'd picked up some of Jinx's bad verbal habits. Luckily, Ted kept bringing him back to the subject.

"So, you're not upset that Jinx is something of a drama queen?" Ted gestured with a Rept's circling hand gesture that often meant *all this and more.*

Cecil shook his head. "His passion is one of the things I love about him. I'm not built to be so... expressive. It's like he gives me a voice I've never had with anyone before. I don't even have to mug my face into a fake Warm smile. He can so read me."

"I like your fake Warm smile."

Cecil ignored the tease. He was too busy trying to get a grip on his own emotional reasoning.

"Why is he always surprised?" In true Rept fashion, the tension suddenly left his hands, neck, and tail as reached the core of the issue. "Everything out in the real world just surprises the hell out of him."

The Bear nodded. "Well, until a while back, your Jinx lived a very sheltered life. A very privileged, *Darwinistic* life. It's strict, yes, but they've an equally rigorous merit system that bends over backwards to create good works. They were performing same sex marriages a hundred years before anyone else... not that any of them would have held up in court... But, my point is that until Jinx got himself excommunicated, I don't think he actually lived in the same real world that we do."

Cecil had known all this and had been patient with Jinx's little ignorances and assumptions, but it wasn't merely that. He wished they'd been drinking tea, so he could hide the sudden twitch of his fingers behind his bowl of tea. "Actually, Ted... we don't both live in the 'same' real world. I know you're totally behind us Repts and totally sympathetic to our issues... but it's not like you have to worry about any of this directly. You're a Warm-Blood living in an Warm-Blood's World. And now that, you... you know..."

"Married a straight female Bear?" The Bear's face was as still as Cecil's. "I'm a bisexual, Cecil. I fought for years for the right to marry who I wanted to. So, I married Yasmin. Whom I love with all my heart. I still am attracted to men of many breeds... but I didn't fall in love with one of them. I fell in love with *her*. So I married *her*."

Cecil fervently wished that he had the ability to blush. Instead, Cecil had to grip the sides of his head as if to close his mouth shut. There'd been a short but vocal effort to oust Ted from QRN because certain people kept insisting that the Bear had stopped being gay. It was as if they'd all forgotten that Bisexuals put the B in LGBT. It was one of the uglier confrontations, as brief as it was, because these certain people had honestly felt betrayed by Ted's marriage.

Just as Ted probably felt betrayed now. Bi-erasure was as legitimate a problem as any other Queer issue they currently faced. He'd just walked right into i,t and he fell silent as he took a moment to work up an appropriate apology.

Instead, the Bear seemed to relax, and he spoke before Cecil could. "You know, it was about this time last year you accused me of being blind to my own Warm Privilege. And you were probably right. Still, I do know you. I love you like a cousin. I chose you to be part of my family, and I would choose you again. That said, I have to ask you... as Fam... do you think some of your irritation might be because Fall is almost here?"

Cecil blinked and realized that he had been holding still too long. "I don't have Seasonal Affective Disorder. I know a lot of Repts seem to have that these days, but—"

"No, Sea Isle Pine, who is both friend and family, you must know that tomorrow is the first of September," Ted interrupted in his almost rusty Arabic. Cecil was startled into silence, because of the sudden formality that

Arabic meant and because the Bear had used his first chosen name, as if Ted were an older and wiser cousin with a right to school him.

Summer had flown by so swiftly with Jinx back under his roof, this time as a lover. He was doubly surprised to realize how much faster time goes the older one gets. Cecil held still, indecisive, because there was a prickle of irritation that felt like Ted might be right. The Bear stood and reached out, laying his warm palms on the back of each of Cecil's hands which hadn't moved away from his jaws after his mugged blush.

"In less than two weeks, it will be the anniversary of The Falling. The anniversary of the death of your parents. This has always been a bad time for you."

Cecil's mouth fell open a bit as he blinked, surprised to feel his tail thumping against his desk and then his desk stool. He looked at his calendar as if to put a lie to Ted's words, but the Bear was right. This was the last day of August.

The Eleventh was right around the corner.

His parents had sent him ahead, to help a legless woman down the final flights of stairs. Some Warm-blooded stockbroker named Ester who sent him two cards. A "Thank You" card and a "Condolences" card a week after that, presumably after she somehow learned that his parents had died in the Towers. He'd nearly died himself, but for the Herp Hospital nurses who recognized the unique needs of an exhausted Alligator.

Ted let him stare into the past for several minutes. He had to claw his way back to the present. Cecil tried to let go of how betrayed he had felt by not only fate, but by his father. And by his own people.

For the Scattered Shards were Chromatic extremists.

"You know..." Ted put his phone away, as if Cecil had just emerged from a trance. It must seem that way to the always kinetic warm-blooded. In a way, it was true. For a moment, he had been back in New Amsterdam. The Alligator latched onto the Bear's words as if they were an anchor to the present. "Jinx has called me a few times to talk about Chroma. He had some questions."

Cecil's long snout bobbed up. "Jinx..." Belatedly, he remembered that his Cat had always liked older men and the dating pool of available men in Stone Harbor wasn't that great. Of course Jinx would have Ted's number. He dismissed the small flare of jealously with a slight but conscious effort. Ted was very definitely off the market. He quickly chose a different tack. "He could have asked me."

The Bear nodded and scratched at his arm. "My understanding is that he has asked you. But mostly he called me because he wanted to talk to a practicing Chromatic, I think."

190

Cecil nodded and got off his stool. "He has asked..." Without conscious thought, his long snout pointed to Qibla, and his body eventually followed. One of the advantages of living in the house he grew up in, he always knew which way to face for the Heart of the Homelands. Although he could not see it, he knew that he faced the mihrab with its rugs and display case. It was where a silent and broken Jinx had found the Green family tzitzits over a year ago.

Those little pieces of green knotwork had appealed to the Cat, and Jinx wanted to touch them so badly, but he refrained because he could tell they were special. Cecil gave him permission and the Tonk, opened up, explaining why he'd been excommunicated from the Darwinists. The attraction was still there, between them, but Cecil had resisted. The pedigree Cat had been a rescue, living with the Alligator to avoid living on the street when his family disowned him. Cecil couldn't allow himself to be "with" Jinx until the young Cat was back on his feet and living elsewhere.

That took a few months.

The Cat came back with a vengeance once he made up his mind that he wanted to be with the Rept. Cecil had also missed his chatty friend and, by then, he was ready to risk his heart. They dated for awhile, a novelty for Cecil who grew up in a time of quick hookups with "Johns and Tricks." Jinx moved in a few months later when the Alligator realized that the quietude that he had always sought was not the cold comfort he needed.

Cecil blinked and then turned away from Mecca to face the Bear again.

"He has been reading a lot of books lately. I really never looked at the titles." Cecil moved his snout out of the way so he could slap at his own forehead. His arm barely reached. "I just assumed he was reading... fluff."

"Because he's a Cat?"

"No. Because he's Jinx. If it was interesting, he would have mentioned it. You know him; he's your basic Tonkinese Cat."

The Bear smiled as if Cecil had said something cute. "Jinx is a lot deeper than you credit him with. I mean, he's not, you know, YOU. But the important stuff, you've got to reach deep inside him and pull it out."

Cecil blinked and looked at his short arms. "I don't know if my arms are long enough for that."

Ted laughed at that harder than he probably ought to have. Cecil was better at translating jokes than actually making them. The 'Gator wondered if Ted had been about to make the same joke.

***

Jinx was toweling dry his pelt when Cecil poked his long green head into the Cat's bedroom. Although they often slept together, the Tonk's nocturnal habits didn't allow him to remain in one place all night long. In lieu of spending money on rent since moving in, Jinx had spent a small fortune on recreating the gaming and media systems he'd left behind when his family had kicked him out. Cecil didn't mind; the mortgage was long since paid off. Plus, he usually slept through most of the smack-talk Jinx sometimes engaged in

Cecil said, "Hey," and picked up the brush on the edge of the Cat's bed as he climbed up onto the mattress.

Jinx wasn't surprised as he turned his head toward the 'Gator. A hopeful smile lit his blue-point face, a slow blink that meant all the world to the older Rept. "I hope you're not mad at me any more."

"Nope," the Alligator gave a slight shake of his head. A larger gesture might have bashed the elegant feline head as he walked on his knees to press Jinx into his soft belly. The damp fur was pleasantly cool against his quilted, yellow belly. The dark pointed ears tickled his throat as Cecil tossed the wet towel across the floor.

"I mean, you're an activist. I just thought that would be something you'd be interested in. Something that you'd want to do something about."

Cecil said nothing but began brushing Jinx's back where the Cat could never reach on his own. It had taken awhile to learn the proper amount of pressure to apply so that he wouldn't be pulling out the hairs from the roots and yet would still be effective enough to prevent the worst of the shedding. (You could never really stop the shed completely, he had learned to his dismay). Cecil was proud of how good he had gotten, considering that brushing was a chore that he himself had never needed. Although, he did sometimes need a good scraping to shed loose scale, it was hardly the same.

Jinx didn't start purring, Cecil realized. The 'Gator decided that he needed to actually answer his lover's question. "Yes, I'm an activist, pretty kitty, but I'm a Translator first. I do need an income. My work is very important to me. Then I'm a gay rights activist. That work is very important to me, too. I do a lot of needed work —"

"Queer rights," Jinx corrected with all the fervor of the young.

"Queer rights," Cecil agreed with the correction, pleasantly enough. Old habits died hard. "But you know the work I do. I take in young queers to help get them off the streets. Kids that aren't good fits for the shelters or aren't ready yet. That's a lot of one-on-one work. It doesn't leave time for much else."

"You haven't taken in anyone in months."

Cecil pressed his wedge of head into Jinx's left cheek. His tongue flicked the Cat's whiskers playfully. "Not since you moved in, no. I want us to get all settled in, and I wasn't sure if you were ready to play counselor-in-residence. It's not for everyone."

"Oh, good. I was worried that you were afraid that I'd sleep with the next hot mess you brought home."

Cecil stopped moving for a moment, as his mind showed him images of Jinx's furry body twisted, intertwined with the dark mud-colored Xolo that used to be the Cat's flatmate and then Ted's bare bear body pressing Jinx's limber form against a shower's wall. Jinx caught that stillness and stopped the purr that had only just started to form softly. "I was not worried about that. You were one of those hot messes once. You can control yourself... but don't think I'm above jealousy."

"Good, I wouldn't want you to be taking me for granted."

Cecil chuckled and continued to brush the Cat, moving on to the places that Jinx could easily reach, stopping every few moments to pull a clump of silvery fur from the brush and drop it absentmindedly into a growing pile in the middle of the bed. His cool eyes noticed belated that there were two pillow cases full of fur behind the bedroom door.

"What's with the bags? Your shed woman sick?"

Jinx shook his head, his ears turning with a bemused slant. "Isidore discovered that I'm exiled. It wasn't unexpected, you know. I'll find another."

Cecil nodded and debated on turning this brushing into foreplay. He tried to mimic Jinx's purring but it came out as a bit of a growl. Jinx's head twisted easily around with a limberness that surprised the 'Gator. "I'll find another," Jinx repeated firmly.

OK, he's not feeling too playful himself, Cecil thought as Jinx turned away.

He pulled a few gentle strokes on the Cat's back, and then moved to the slight rise of Jinx's head fur before he realized that he had gotten so used to the Tonk's overt emotive displays, that he had forgotten that Jinx might have other feelings beyond the ones he let others see.

Like a Rept, Cecil thought.

Almost immediately the Alligator realized what he had forgotten to do.

He pulled the slightly less damp body against his own and wrapped his short arms across the silver-blue chest of his lover. "I'm sorry I snapped at you, pretty kitty." The Cat melted against him, releasing the last of his tension. Cecil had overlooked it until it was gone. "I don't ever want you to doubt me or believe that I think of you as anything less than my equal. I...

The anniversary of my parents' death is coming up soon. It's a hard time for me. I mean that's not an excuse, but –"

"You're talking too much, Mr. Green," Jinx teased and spun his body around so that they were stomach to stomach. In a moment, he twisted again and took Cecil with him so quickly that his large corrugated tail ripped the bedsheets as it joined them atop the mattress. Cool fur and a patch of warm flesh against a cool, quilted hide. Cecil was pleased to discover their shared eloquence in mutual physical apology.

***

In the stairwell, the Alligator who'd begun life as Boy Green, and had spent much of his rebellious teen years as Sea Isle Pine, tried not to panic. Unlike the Skinks that raced up and down the walls and ceiling, an Alligator was not full of boundless energy. Alligators were shackled with amazing speed and a surprising grace, but it all came at the high cost of constant energy management, more so perhaps than any other Rept.

He looked back at his parents. They were both more than a foot larger and thicker than himself. They'd done the math, and he could see it in their eyes. They should have stopped long before now. But as they got closer to the bottom, the line got thicker, and the exodus slowed. It was getting worse. A five minute break might cost you ten or twenty minutes. They gestured that he needed to keep moving.

Within the hour, he was going to be an orphan.

***

Cecil snapped awake, his back surprisingly hot and awkward with a humanoid ball of fur impossibly glued to his thorny spine. Even with his fur padding, Cecil was surprised that Jinx could sleep atop his armored and serrated back. The stereotype was proving true, at least as far as Jinx was concerned. This Cat could sleep anywhere!

Cecil raised up on all fours carefully and inspected the bed linens in the dim green light of Jinx's digital alarm clock. They weren't completely ruined, but then they weren't made to handle an Alligator's threshing. He hoped they weren't of sentimental value to his Cat. In his old life, Jinx's linens were made from threads spun from the fur of other Darwinists, mostly relatives. He had never slept on wool until he'd come to stay with Cecil. He cherished his first set of jeans and most of the outfits that Cecil had bought for him (but not all; the generation gap still poked it's head in every once in awhile).

The rocking movement dislodged Jinx eventually from his backside. A cool breeze from the open window brushed across his back, lifting a few pieces of discarded fur, but leaving most behind. Before Cecil could make his escape back to his own room, Jinx crawled under him with a purr.

"Jinx?" But the Cat was asleep again, with the larger man uncertain what to do about the wonderful ball of warmth across his stomach. At least, the Cat's breathing sounded as if he were asleep. The tiny hairs brushed against his tender quilted skin in seductive waves. Not quite a tickling sensation, but then Alligators weren't known for being ticklish. This was as close as he might get.

Cecil lifted his left hand and rubbed the sensitive nerves in his jawline, pondering how – with all the terrible things going on in the world with the Beast – this was what was keeping him up at night. He chuckled and decided that he could always roll to the left and use his boyfriend as a plush doll to hold over his heart if Jinx protested his weight.

Before Cecil could roll over, however, he noticed several books on the night stand in the strange green light.

I wonder which of my father's books he's been reading?

He reached out for them, but the best he could do with his short arm was move the books enough to read the titles on the spines in the dim electronic light.

Cecil blinked so hard his bulging eyes ducked back into his skull, making his inner eye lids bounce. *Facing Qibla, A Warmer Rainbow*, and *Mosaic Speaks to Mammals*. None of these were books from his father's library. Or his. These were brand new books for Warms, like Jinx.

Ted must have loaned him these books.

Cecil gingerly moved forward to better examine the books, flinching as he heard the sheets tear at his weight. The 'Gator's eyes were better equipped to read in the dark than Jinx would have believed, especially by the clock's emerald light. Ted tended to fold corners and highlight pages with pencil marks. These books were practically virgins, with only either yellow or orange highlighter underscoring a passage here and there. The Bear hated highlighters.

These were the books of a student looking to convert.

These are Jinx's books. He bought them.

Cecil felt a draft blow across his cooling back, and against all reason, his logical mind denied the feelings it brought with it.

With the utmost care, Cecil crawled off the bed and then walked silently on all fours out of his sleeping Cat's room.

***

The sound of the jet hitting this tower isn't a sound at all in his nightmare. Some people run back, as if to check. To deny. To be heroes or witnesses. Everglade Keys almost turns back the way they had come. His father's large but gentle hand on his chest. Their eyes meet. He can see the pain in his father's eyes; the way the older man's pale inner lids kept trying to protect his eyes from the damage the steps were doing to his body.

Everglade turned away and kept walking, down and down, trying to stay calm and pace himself. It only took a few minutes for those with AM radios to confirm the second jet, but the Alligators paid them no mind. Step after step, they did their best to not hold up those behind them. Everglade worried the stairwell would fill with flaming jet fuel, but that never happened, except in some of the crueler nightmares.

Walkers to the right; catch your breath on the left.

The walls squirm with Skinks, more than he'll ever recall in the light of day. The Repts that can cling to walls pass the stream of Furry commuters at full accelerated speed. Everglade doesn't see the Geckos or the others. To see them is to accept jealousy into his heart, because the Creator did not make him that way. No one is jealous of the little Skinks; no one wants to be little cold blooded rats, even if they have a seemingly endless supply of energy to tap into.

The Alligators have to be satisfied with attempting to out-walk death.

In a few moments, the Creator was going to press his finger down firmly on the first tower.

***

Jinx made breakfast for them both. Not that Cecil's needed much prep. Open the lox and drop a few pounds of it into a bowl. Maybe a spoonful of non-dairy sour cream and chives. A bowl of coffee ice cubes or a liter of fish broth with a caffeine boost to get him going. The Cat had learned all the little things that Cecil liked.

"Good morning, Honey," Jinx said cheerfully as the Alligator waddled into the kitchen. Reading Cecil's unenthusiastic pose correctly, he softened his tone. "Did you not sleep well?"

Cecil shook his head. "No. No, I did not."

"Nightmares?"

Against his better judgment, the Alligator nodded. "I get them a lot this time of year."

The Tonk's ears went back a little. "I wish there was something I can do to help."

You could stop reading about Chromatics.

196

You could stop talking about Skink rights.

You could stop... just stop trying to make me happy.

Stop trying to be perfect.

Jinx stopped and looked at him with a cock of his head that was startlingly more Dog-like than Cat-like. After a moment, he wrapped his warm fingers around Cecil's cold fists. "It looked like you were going to say something, Cecil."

There is no God of Love.

"No, I'm just not very... well, not much of anything this morning. Sorry."

Jinx nodded with an understanding smile, although his tail stopped swaying a little. "That's OK, but if you don't have any appointments today, maybe you should try a nap."

For a moment, Cecil thought Jinx was poking him with a joke about his age. Then he realized that, of course, a Cat was going to suggest a nap.

Well, now who's stereotyping?

"Maybe I should." Cecil put some apology into his voice, although he wasn't sure why he felt compelled to. Jinx, at least, did seem to appreciate it. He leaned over to rub his nose on the tip of the 'Gator's snout. The Cat's eyes closed slowly in the feline signal of "I love you."

Cecil returned the gesture by winking his inner eye lids.

It took the silver-blue Cat aback for a moment. "Take a nap, Babe." The Tonk kissed the edge of the grumpy green snout. "I've got to get to work."

***

They came to the Dog in the wheelchair on the 8th floor.

In the nightmare, the echoing noises of the stairwell blended into the ghastly ambient murmuring one heard at the gates of hell in a movie. Everyone was too exhausted. The Canine and her co-workers had started out on the 22nd floor. They had struggled to get her and her mechanical chair down more than a dozen flights, resting on most landings for a few moments. Her escorts had left here there, just moments ago, to see if they could get the firemen to come up with a stretcher.

His parents paused at her side, to rest. To give comfort.

Father held her hand. Mother leaned against the wall, allowing the Skinks to cross across her body as if she was a mere tree trunk. He rested, too. It only made him more aware of his own pain and fatigue.

"Miss," his father said, with scholarly detachment, "My son is going to carry you downstairs. He's going to get on all fours, and you're going to have to hold onto his back. It's the only way."

Everglade shook his head 'no.' The young Rept opened his mouth to protest, but his father reached out and shut his snout with embarrassing ease. Their eyes would have met then, except the elder's eyes were covered with the milky white inner eyelids. In the dream, their eyes were opaque and saw nothing.

***

By the time Jinx got off the bus, Cecil was wrapping some dishes in foil to keep them warm. He felt strangely excited to see Jinx walking down the street. The Tonk's blue-point tail was ou,t and Cecil was pleased to see it wave and curl a bit more with each step closer to home.

He met the Cat at the door with a smooch. He apologized, and Jinx accepted it by reassuring the Rept that people get cranky. A weight was lifted off his green shoulders, but Cecil still steered his young man into the formal dining room. Cecil hadn't used it for a meal since his parents' wake. Jinx seemed impressed by the spread the 'Gator had laid out. "I'll be eating leftovers all week!" the Cat joked after a moment of speechlessness.

They hugged, and Cecil relaxed, happy that his bleak mood was eased, at least for now. That they could talk without his growling, but with any luck, Jinx would do all the speaking with Cecil providing knowing nods and reassuring smiles on cue. Sooner or later, Cecil was confident he'd find an opening to talk about Jinx's new religious obsession.

And it might have gone that way, if Cecil hadn't let Jinx go up to his room.

The Cat who came back down brought an unruly and jerky tail behind him.

"What did you do with the bags of shed I left in my room?"

Before Jinx even finished the sentence, the Alligator realized his mistake. He had done the one thing Jinx had asked him not to do. "Ummmm," he said, trying to think on his feet.. "I... found a shed woman. Teddy recommended her."

Jinx's hackles went up so much that even his head fur bunched forward.

Before Cecil realized what was happening, they were arguing. Never mind that Jinx was no longer a Darwinist, he had grown up with that strange need to do things with hide and hair. Some habits were harder to break. Luckily, Jinx got angry enough to go silent for much of their meal. Long enough for Cecil to explain that the matronly woman was at Teddy's house when Cecil had called to talk about something else. He just sent her over.

"I wasn't thinking when I agreed. I thought I was doing you a favor," Cecil apologized lamely, although he was smoothing over the truth a bit. He'd been more than a bit cranky. "But she does spin all the fur into yarn and thread, Jinx. Really, she does. She's just not a Darwin approved vendor."

In a few moments, Jinx's fur flattened, and his tail stilled. "OK, I get that... you just have to stop treating me like a child."

Cecil began to protest, and then stopped and stared at the dinner table. He wasn't a Mammal, he just knew what he'd seen on television. Yes, it looked like the dinner spread any number of TV husbands had come home to.

But it also looked like the kind of dinner spread a school boy might come home to.

Cecil spent much of the evening kicking himself for being a jerk.

By desert, catnip and mint in aspic, Jinx seemed back to his normal self. As if they'd never had a fight at all.

As they cleared away the table, Cecil wasn't sure that he could trust this good mood. Jinx wasn't just what he saw on the surface. The weeks of his stoic monk-like silence when he'd been rejected by his family and expelled from the Darwins was an extreme, but legitimate, reaction. Day to day moods were bound to be less extreme... and more subtle.

Cecil loaded up the dishwasher as Jinx wrapped up the food for storage, thriftily reusing the sheets of foil the 'Gator had used to to keep things warm. Cecil resisted the urge to tell the blue-point to be careful about getting fur into the food.

Jinx kept his usual running monologue. Cecil was too happy listening to interrupt.

"That was nice, thank you," Jinx said as they went into the living room. "It was a nice change from eating at the tea table." The Cat nodded at the closer to the ground table just outside of the kitchen. The color tiles represented a rainbow of diversity, and it had seemed most appropriate to share meals there. It had been way too small for the spread that Cecil had decided to make.

"I wanted to do something nice for you, especially after being grouchy and snapping at you this morning."

Jinx stopped and faced the taller man. "You're allowed to be grouchy. You're allowed to have moods. You're allowed to mourn for your parents. I do not want you to think that you have to walk on tiptoes around me. I'm not that fragile. Thanks to you."

Cecil was touched and a little bit guilty. "Have I really been treating you like a child?" he asked softly.

Jinx's tail drooped, and his ears rocked back with guilt. "You are trying so hard to take care of me. I love that about you, but I want us to be more like partners... and I feel bad that I have so little to bring to this relationship. I'm trying to catch up with where you are... but you're a cheater. You got such a big head start." Jinx laughed at his own joke. "And I feel like I'll never be as smart as you, or as organized, or as randy as you are."

Cecil made a pose of embarrassed modesty, his hands touching his cheeks. "That's more biology. Let's just say I'm always 'ready.' You might as well complain that you'll never have as many teeth as I have."

"Point," Jinx conceded with another chuckle and pulled Cecil to the couch. "I love all these things about you. Even the teeth. Maybe even especially the teeth, but when we got back together, I was starting over from scratch. You saved me, gave me a direction. I needed all of that. But when we moved in together, you said it was because you were ready to see me as an equal."

Cecil nodded, feeling schooled, but marveling from the center part of his brain at how well this young tom was handling this lesson. "You are always finding new ways to impress me."

Jinx smiled. "Good to know." He snuggled into the 'Gator's lap and unbuttoned the now food-stained shirt. The Cat caressed the little piercing scars on the yellow chest with a reverence no one else ever had. The Tonk was deep into a food induced coma a moment later. Trapped by the Cat, Cecil could barely reach his flip phone. He texted Ted, one letter at a time, still awkward with his "outdated" phone. Ted responded promptly. The new shed woman did make yarn and thread that he could buy back.

***

His father began to pull the Dog from her chair. She was only half-willing, stuck between desperation and hopelessness. "Everglade... get down on all fours."

"This... will kill me. You're asking me to kill myself for a complete stranger."

Gray eyes met his again in a somber regard that was as disturbing and as chilling as anything he had ever witnessed in his entire life, including the flames and smoke coming from the tower next door.

"It is what the Creator asks of us. It is what Mosaic would ask of us."

Then, suddenly, the Skinks swarmed, screaming, "OUT! OUT! OUT!"

***

Cecil snapped awake and glanced at his clock. 1am.

Huh, not too long ago, I'd be out partying, especially at this time of year. Anything to avoid thinking about the deaths of my family. Anything to fill the ache in my heart; as long as I didn't actually get too close.

Now, look at me... sharing a bed with a Kitty Boi, nearly half my age, with my belly up and unprotected half the night.

Part of him missed taking the van out and the anonymous hook ups, he realized. There was a strange safety in keeping lovers at a distance.

He knew that safety was just an illusion. That there was no love without vulnerability. How many clients had he told that? How many youths had he sheltered here, only to convince them that hiding was not a good long term plan?

He stroked a dark claw through his Cat's fur. "Physician, heal thyself," he whispered to himself.

"Or Professor," the Cat purred with a half opened eye. "As the case may be."

***

"Remember what we were talking about last night?"

Cecil downed a huge chunk of salmon in one smooth motion, one of the advantages of his physiology: when you were in a rush, chewing was optional. "You mean how I begged you not to call me Professor?"

"P'shaw." Jinx waved a black palm dismissively as if the matter had been decided and not necessarily in Cecil's favor. "About us being equal partners."

A bunch of warning bells went off in Cecil's wedge shaped head. The hardest to silence was the idea that this was a typical Warm move. That Jinx was uncomfortable that a Rept had more power than he did. Warm Privilege. So, very carefully, and as neutrally as possible, he said, "Yes."

Jinx seemed to catch the formality behind his reply, but kept his smile. "Not about your business. I could barely pick up sign language, and that was a required course for Darwinists. Taking me in as a partner there would be more an act of charity than a good business decision. Not that I'm opposed to taking charity, obviously."

Cecil felt his body relax. He nodded, making a smile gesture with his left hand. The rest of the salmon disappeared while Cecil considered his response. "You don't still feel like a guest, do you?"

Jinx shook his head. "The separate bedrooms felt odd at first. You know, it felt like when I could only be with you in the Pforde van. No, you were right. Our sleep patterns are so different. It makes sense. Plus, the separate bedroom lets me play video games or read with the lights on when I feel nocturnal. I've been your guest; this doesn't feel like that at all. "

Cecil wanted to pounce on the reading thing, but he checked his instincts. There was a bigger picture to worry about. "But does it feel like home?"

Jinx nodded, and he moved forward to kiss Cecil on the tip of his snout. "Mostly, it does."

"Mostly is a good thing," Cecil said, "But what's missing?"

"To me," Jinx said after a pause, "Home has always had a spiritual component. When I got kicked out, it wasn't just being spurned by my family... I lost my moral compass. I lost my faith. But you took me in, you gave me direction and time to find my own path. That path is with you."

Cecil pushed down the fear and checked his tail from slapping the ground. "I think so, too." He hated the way his voice choked on those words.

"But the path may have many forks in it." Jinx reached out and laid his hands on Cecil's right fist. "I want to help choosing which way we go."

"That seems fair." It felt weird not to have full control of his voice, especially when speaking was so much of what he did for a living. Why should translating the heart be so much harder than other languages? Was it merely because he thought Jinx was going to bring up converting to Chromaticism? He'd been looking for the chance to bring it up ever since reading the titles of the books on Jinx's nightstand. He couldn't make heads or tails of how he actually felt at that moment. "Can we talk about that when you get home from work? We both have to get out the door, or we'll be late."

Jinx smiled, yet looked Cecil up and down like he was measuring every little thing about the 'Gator. He might well be, for no one had known him so well as this pretty young man who had embraced his rough ugliness. There was more than a smidgen of ownership in that glance, and the hunger that came with Warm youth in bloom. He felt vulnerable in the Cat's regard. This both scared and delighted him. "OK," Jinx agreed. "But you have time to walk me to the bus stop."

Cecil checked his phone for the time and could not argue.

***

By dusk, Cecil was more interested in listening to the weather report than really thinking about where he was driving. The days had been unseasonably warm, but nights were paying attention to the calendar. The announcer reminded his listeners to make sure they were wearing their electric hoodies and to stay alert. This station never reminded any of their

Bill Kieffer

listeners to "stay warm." It catered to the Urban Rept crowd, and they saved the word, "Warm," for their editorial and news shows. They did not use it in a nice way.

The buttons on the steering wheel allowed him to switch to a local jazz station. The DJ here might well be a MP3 player set to "random." Which was fine. Whatever horror story was passing for normal at the White House today could wait for later.

He was having a bit of trouble with letting go of his day at the Twin Mills courthouse. The drive was supposed to be for thinking about what he was going to say to Jinx. If Jinx caught the early bus, he'd be home before Cecil got there. The 'Gator felt totally unprepared for the conversation that they needed to have.

Cecil and the prosecutor had both wanted to be elsewhere by the end of the day. As was often the case, they were more professional than the victim. With patience, they were able to cover all the facts, yet Mr. Khikhi was so combative that it tainted the whole proceeding. He looked like the hothead the bullies claimed he was (once they sobered up). Finally, the prosecutor announced that he was going to just get suspects to plea to disorderly conduct. Cecil hesitated, but he used the same tone when translating. That was his job. Although he'd rather they'd bump this to county as a hate crime, Mr. Khikhi's own prejudices were proving obvious.

The Fennec agreed. He was halfway to withdrawing his complaint because Americans had no idea how to deal with wrong-doers.

Cecil did not translate that last bit of sour grapes.

The truth was, he was tired of being the voice of reason.

When the judge asked the Fox if he was OK with their plea as there were injuries, Cecil translated his answer: "That is good. But what would be better is if I never see these men again." The judge was kind enough to take that into consideration and added assault charges to the conviction and a restraining order for each for the next year. The assault charges would be held in abeyance, unless the dependents violated their restraining orders. For now, they simply had to pay a fine.

Cecil was floored by that. The Dogs who had beaten on the shorter Fox readily agreed. They were getting off cheap, they realized. There were several Repts who had gone ahead of them. The Rept defendants had been treated much more shoddily than those Dogs, and the judge had never asked the Rept victims if they were OK with the punishment their abusers were getting. Not that there were all that many Rept victims in court, he realized belatedly. Twin Mills was almost 25% Cold. There just should have been more.

The red and blue lights flashing in his rear-view mirror broke Cecil out of his reverie. Instantly, he lifted his thumb off the accelerator dial and checked his speed above the windshield. 40. County road 172 had a speed limit of 45. He should be good. There was a nice wide shoulder, and the setting sun gave them enough light, but a chill touched his spine as he realized what town he was in.

Cecil kept his hands on the steering wheel as he watched a familiar looking Coati get out of the patrol car.

He sighed without mugging and was mildly amused that he had picked up the Mammalism. It made him feel less alone and vulnerable to think there was a little bit of Jinx with him.

This might even go smoother without Jinx here to work the cop up. Cecil thought, *I'll just comply and accept this as the cost of Driving While Cold. He won't even remember me, I bet.*

A glance in the side mirror checked the positive energy the 'Gator was trying to work up. The Coati's tie was loosened, the top button undone, and his long ringed tail bounced out behind him against standard dress codes. This did not bode well.

He hit the Bluebeard button on the wheel and turned the speaker volume down. He took a risk and moved his hand off the wheel and stabbed a claw at flipping open his cellphone. Redial was the easiest button to hit. He heard a soft ping and some ringing. Odds were he was going to get Ted or Jinx. Didn't matter. They couldn't rescue him... voice mail would be best, in case anything happened. He could laugh it off later. He turned the speaker off completely as the cop came to his window.

"Hello, Officer..." Cecil said as he brought the window down. The Coati's name-tag wasn't on his shirt, but Cecil's memory did not fail him. "Tikal, wasn't it? What can I do for you?"

That earned him a dark look over a white muzzle, but the officer merely asked for his license, insurance, and registration in a near robotic tone. Cecil kept those handy in the dashboard slot. He moved slowly and kept his hands in plain view just the same. The robotic voice thanked him and then asked him to keep his hands on the wheel as he "checked these out." The flat, almost neutral, voice concerned Cecil. It might simply mean the angry cop had taken one too many downers; however, he couldn't think of any legit reason behind being stopped. Cecil was afraid that this was the calm before the storm. Cecil wished he had waited to pull over in a place with witnesses.

But I have a witness, he thought with a glance at the phone partially hidden between the front seats. *I hope.*

"I've been stopped by Officer Tikal on County Road 172, in a wooded area south of the Twin Mills border, north of Winslet River Road. He's partially out of uniform and is acting... detached? Drugged? I don't know... I don't smell alcohol on his breath... he took my ID cards... I'm just waiting to see what bullshit excuse he has for pulling me over. He pulled me and Jinx over a few weeks ago, found us parked on the side of the road and made me get out and kneel on the ground. Tried to make me put my hands behind my head... but my arms just do not bend that way. So far, I've gotten to stay in the car. This road is too busy to get on my stomach and play Simon Says to satisfy him."

He glanced to see what the Coati was doing. He could see the officer on the radio reading off his info to his dispatcher. For a Chromatic, this was always the worrisome part. Even a former Chromatic like himself had many monikers; the police were famous for 'accidentally' confusing aliases if they were similar enough. Being a Rept that didn't fit the standardized descriptions that were still weighted towards the Warm species didn't help either. Alligators named Cecil Kanëhtaikhö were rare, but Repts named Green were as common as Mammals named Smith or Pforde.

If the cop wanted to really mess with him, he could find something.

"I just have to hope that he only just wants to jerk my chain," Cecil told the air. "I don't want to spend the anniversary of my parent's death in jail."

The Coati came back to his window, paying more attention to his clip board than where he was going. "Mister Kanie Hatch Ko, here are your papers back." The black furred hand stopped outside of the car and released the papers just as green, leathery hands reached for them. They fluttered into the street as a van passed. Cecil had to check himself from jumping out of the car.

"Can I please get of my car to get my paperwork, sir? You've dropped them into street."

"We're not done here, Cold boy. You are a boy, aren't you? Please forgive, but it's hard for a Mammal like me to tell."

"Yes, sir, I'm a male, but I really need those cards you dropped."

"I'm sorry, *boy*. I didn't catch that." A little emotion seemed to slip back into the cop's voice. Cecil didn't like where that might go.

"Yes, sir... I'm a boy. May I please, *Sir*, step out of my vehicle and get my paperwork before it blows away."

The Coati shook his head. "We are not done here yet." Several cars passed in both directions then, and Cecil saw his red labeled registration float up in the cross-breeze and turbulence in their wake. His stomach knotted, but he remained still. It was the best trick his Alligator body knew.

He called in my information. He can't write me a ticket for driving without my license now, can he? Cecil knew he was just going to have to let the cop lead this little dance if he was going to get out of this before the temperature dropped with the sun.

After a moment, the robotic voice asked, "I suppose you know why I pulled you over."

"No, Sir. Now that you mention it, I'm afraid that I do not know why you pulled me over."

"Are you aware that you have a broken tail light?"

Before he could stop himself, Cecil said, "No, Sir, I do not have a broken tail light."

Dammit, I should have said, "I was not aware that I had a broken tail light."

Yet, Cecil could not bring himself to voice the correction in the second that he had to fix everything.

Suddenly, the edge of the clipboard was slammed against his snout. The Coati had known exactly where to hit him, right on the line of little black dots on his jawline that Jinx had teasingly called his forward sensor array. Integumentary sensory organs were unique to Alligators, and unless Cecil was underwater, he forgot about them. Spots swam in front of the Alligator's eyes, and he felt he was suddenly deep underwater. His inner lids slammed shut as the taste of lactic acid and blood spilled on his tongue. He forced his grip to stay on the steering wheel; he wasn't underwater. His throbbing jaw telegraphed boats above him and bodies sinking beneath him.

He held his body still, ignored the impulse to thrash and rise to the surface.

I'm not underwater.

He forced himself to let air into his lungs. He managed to stay as still as a statue, except for the gray membranes over his eyes that he was having trouble pulling back.

He was able to open them at the sound of the officer's clipboard slamming into the Pforde's driver side tail light. The Coati smiled little rodent teeth, and Cecil could not stop his tail from tapping the floor of the van in anger. "No, it's broken."

"I see," Cecil said. He did see. Someone had shown him how to handle an Alligator. It made his chest tighten with anxiety. Trapped in the van with only his snout exposed, Cecil was defenseless unless the Coati was willing to risk loosing a few fingers. If it got that far, he saw no good way for this night to end. No matter how many times the cop struck his jaw line in that spot, he wasn't going to leave a bruise. At least, not a visible bruise.

"I'll get that fixed right away, sir. Thank you, for letting me know."

"Just doing my job." The Coati frowned. "Are you sure you're a Boy? I just want to be sure."

Cecil nodded and concentrated on keeping his tail from slamming against the floorboards. "*Yes, sir,* I'm a boy."

"I'll take your word for it."

Then the Coati was distracted by a car that had pulled in behind his patrol car. He held a furry finger up to Cecil, as if he was a cashier who had to stop processing a check-out order in order to tell another customer where the bathroom was.

Cecil's stomach knotted tighter.

"Excuse me, Sir," the Coati called out in a polite and civil voice that was still obviously an order. "Please stay right there. I'll be right over."

"I don't think so. Why are you interfering with an officer of the court?"

The Coati snarled, emotion coming back into his voice with volume. Civility was pro forma now. "Stay behind my car, Sir."

Cecil recognized the Avi's voice, and he looked in the side mirror to see Captain Fisher exposing his badge as he walked pass the local cruiser. "I think not, Officer Takhi. Are you OK, Professor?"

Cecil was never so happy to see Fisher in his life. Right at this moment, he was thrilled to be somebody's Rept. "He just pulled me over for a broken tail light."

Fisher stopped where he was and looked at the broken pieces of red plastic under his feet. "I see," he said as he bobbed his head.

The Coati unsnapped his holstered weapon casually. "Sir, I'm going to only ask you once more to step behind my vehicle and wait until I finish with this gentleman."

"I'm afraid that you're confused about where exactly your jurisdiction is." This was a pretty ballsy statement as Twins Mills had a large sign a mile up the road asking drivers to come back again. "You're in Twins Mills, and the Professor there is obviously a victim of an act of vandalism that happened in my town."

"Please, step back." The Coati stepped toward the Avi with his hand on his weapon. He snarled.

Fisher placed his hands over his white head as he began to back up. His business suit opened enough to expose his shoulder holster. "Officer, you'd better think about how you want this fuck-up to end. Stand down and holster your weapon."

A ripple went through the Coati's tail as he reached for the flapping epaulet on his left shoulder with his left hand. His microphone wasn't there, and it startled him. The weapon hadn't cleared his holster as far as

Cecil could tell, but he could see the hackles rise on the back of the Coati's neck.

"Don't they teach you people to do anything except escalate the violence in cop school?" Cecil shouted before he knew he was going to. The Coati gave him a sour look for a split second, and the Mammal's anger just infuriated the 'Gator further. "Honestly, do you think you can outdraw an Avi? Did you not see any Westerns as a child?"

It was a terrible stereotype, but Cecil felt no qualms throwing it in the Mammal's face. Nature had given the Avi tribes all kinds of advantages with firearms. While there were a few Mammals and Repts who could outdraw the average Avian Human, there wasn't a Species on Aerth that could match the average Avi in deadly accuracy.

The Coati hesitated although he wasn't as good at holding still at an Alligator was.

"Please," Cecil nudged in a softer voice. "I don't want anyone to die today."

Not to mention, if there's a shoot out, we all know which one of us is going to die in a hale of gunfire.

Cecil heard the snap of Takhi's gun being strapped down.

Cecil relaxed as Takhi began walking towards the captain. His heart silently reminded him that he was getting too old for this. Once the two policemen got to talking, Cecil snatched up his phone and checked to see if Ted or Jinx was on the other line. The screen popped up to a number he didn't know. He turned the volume up, and he heard Captain Fischer's voice dressing down the patrolman.

Suddenly, there was a bang and what sounded like the tinkling of glass. Cecil jerked up and saw Fisher in the rearview mirror pecking at the patrol car's break lights. The Coati held still as the Crane gave him a demonstration of how fast an Avi could move. He clearly did not appreciate the demonstration, but Cecil could hear Tahki agree to go home and sleep off whatever the hell he was on. Cecil wanted to argue that bigotry wasn't something you "slept off," but he was content with getting out of there with his life, if not his dignity.

Without saying much more, the Coati got back in his patrol car and peeled away with his lights blazing. Cecil let his jaw drop to the steering wheel, feeling his stomach melting from a tight hard rock to its normal softly demanding self. He prayed his thanks to the Creator, not caring if he was pointing to Heart of Homeland or not. God was everywhere.

After a few moments, Fisher was tapping on his shoulder. Cecil opened his eyes and saw that the Avi had collected his paperwork for him. The laminate on his license was a little worse for wear; it looked like it had gone up against a cheese grater. The insurance and registration cards had clear tire tracks on them, but everything was readable.

"Thank you," Cecil whispered and hiccupped as he put the cards away in their holder.

Fisher was leaning against his window, obviously wanting to say something. Cecil didn't want to be lectured, but he felt he owed it to the captain to give him an attentive listen. "What?"

The Crane seemed to smile behind his long narrow beak. "Cop school?"

Cecil snorted and then hiccupped. As he dropped his jaw back to the steering wheel, his whole body began to shake. He had no idea if he was laughing or crying, but he knew it was going to be awhile before he was going to be able to drive the rest of the way home.

***

Fisher followed him home and walked him inside. The police captain didn't bat an eye at the large home or meeting Jinx just home from work.

The captain explained everything simply. Cecil had been spooked by a cop who thought it'd be fun to pick on an "intellectual." Luckily, Fisher had been heading to Stone Harbor to drop off the signed paperwork that the Alligator had left behind. He'd been only a few minutes behind Cecil. He would have passed the scene about the same time even if Cecil hadn't called him. The Crane played everything down, but then maybe the Avi couldn't read the Alligator's body as well. Jinx didn't need more than a glance at his 'Gator to know it was more complicated than that. Cecil gestured that they'd talk about it later, before the Cat could dig.

Fisher left with a handshake and a pat on Cecil's head. Jinx gave the Avi a hug and walked him out so that "his old man" could get some rest.

As it turned out, "later" turned out to be just long enough to make tea for each of them.

Cecil told him about his horrible day in court. He had taken the county road to avoid traffic. The Coati who had pulled them over before had acted. Cecil imitated the flat scary voice with only a little exaggeration. "Takhi threw my paperwork into traffic. He dared me to make something of it. Then the bastard bigot made me declare that I was 'a boy.'"

Cecil paused, deciding to leave out the part about getting whacked by the edge of the clipboard. There was no way someone who wasn't an Alligator was going to understand what that had felt like, not even his sweet empathic Kitty. Jinx's eyes were already as large as saucers.

"You're lucky Fisher got there." The Cat poured some more tea, and Cecil wished he had something stronger in the house.

"I hit the last call button, thinking that I was going to get either you or Ted, but I must have missed Captain Fisher's call. Thank the Creator I got him."

He watched a series of emotions play out on his Cat's face and with his tail. Jinx's eyes glittered when Cecil mentioned the Creator. "Fischer spooked the Coati so much that he'd drawn his weapon to try to chase Fisher off. But the Crane had seen my broken tail light pieces on the road right there. It was obvious what happened. He ripped the Coati a new tail hole in a very thorough dressing down. I nearly pissed my pants."

Cecil had, in fact, released a little urine into his cloaca, but he had no intention of mentioning that. He wanted to put this behind him. The lactic acid buildup had fully receded, and the Alligator was ready to digest the whole thing as a good story he'd be able to tell in the future.

We'll laugh about this tomorrow.

"I reported Takhi after that first stop," Jinx declared, his arms folded across his slim chest. His tail twitched its annoyance as Cecil blinked up at him from his father's couch. A look of growing horror began dancing in Cecil's eyes, and his own tail nearly threw him off the couch as it tried to slap at the floor.

"You did what?"

Jinx grabbed the folding tray and the tea kettle as Cecil's struggles to get up nearly knocked them over. "I said, I reported Takhi."

Cecil got to his full height and fought to close his mouth. He shook his head until he felt his massive jaw begin to work. "How could you do such a moronic thing!?" Cecil screamed and slammed his tail into the sturdy couch. It had been designed to withstand adolescent Alligators. But he was an adult Alligator, and he was furious, so it moved with a satisfying scrape.

Jinx was not impressed and his fur barely fluffed out at the display. "He was a bad cop and an obvious bigot. You shouldn't have to drive 10 to 20 minutes out of your way to avoid Little Podunk on the off-chance this Nazi was driving around looking for minorities to torment on his little power trips. So, I found his social media pages, and I sent them to his commanding officer, along with an email detailing what happened to us in August."

Cecil's claws raked at his snout as he processed Jinx's words. "I... I could only shake this off... because... because I thought I got Takhi on a bad day. That he was having a bad day, and I was just the first Rept he saw. That he had to let off steam."

Jinx nodded with satisfaction and reached out to touch his mate's chest. "That's no excuse. Don't make..."

Cecil slapped the delicate hand away. "No! I told you to let this drop. But you couldn't, and now your Warm Liberal Guilt has set an anti-herp cop's sights on me. When its a random event, it's annoying, but when it's over, it's over. What are the odds of it happening again, right? Oh, but thanks to you I'm on that prick's short list!"

Jinx's face fell, and his tail went flat.

"You outed him as a Warm Supremacist to his captain. You probably caused him a little annoyance with HR. Maybe he had to write on the blackboard, "I won't be a bad cop," a hundred times... but more likely he just had to delete a few posts to make everything better. Now he's going to remember my name and my van! Every time he has a bad day, my name is going to be on his list."

Jinx was horrified into silence as Cecil's tail thrashed in anger behind him. An ottoman went flying across the room.

The Alligator shoved his jaws at the young Cat. "Oh, and I know Fisher is going to talk to the tailhole's captain tomorrow. So, if we're lucky, they might suspend Takhi for a few days with pay. Maybe he might even get fired. Either way, he'll know where we live and have plenty of time to find a way to show his appreciation."

Jinx covered his face, and his tail drooped as Cecil ranted a bit longer. As progressive as the area was, police forces still tended to attract people like Takhi. Dollars to doughnuts, he was going to share his list with others and turn as many cops against them as possible. Eventually, he might turn enough police against him to impact his translation business.

He was merciless in yelling at his Cat and didn't let up until Jinx was mewling snot out of his nose. Something bent in him then. He tasted more lactic acid in his mouth in his sudden horror at himself. The anger would not shut off like it usually did. The unwelcome energy would not disperse. Forcing himself to turn away, he stomped upstairs. This time his movement wasn't stealthy, and the whole house reverberated when he slammed the door.

"But it isn't right," Jinx wailed between sobs.

Behind his closed door, Cecil growled. "That's just the way it is."

***

Alone and cold in his bed, Cecil faced his father in the stairwell of the second tower.

"This... will kill me. You're asking me to kill myself for a complete stranger."

Gray lidded eyes met his in a somber regard that was as disturbing and as chilling as anything he had ever witnessed in his entire life, including the flames and smoke coming from the tower next door. Worms moved behind those eyes, although there would be nothing left of his father's body to bury when all this was over. Crushed, torn, ripped, shredded, ground meat and bones inseparable from the brick and mortar debris soon to fall upon him.

"It is what the Creator asks of us. It is what Mosaic would ask of us" the zombie says with devastating authority. Everglade accepts it for the death sentence that it is. He slips off his shoes and bemoans the paths of the world that he's never set foot on. All the miles he'll never walk in sunshine.

To give one's life was the greatest gift. Still, as the young 'Gator put his hands on the landing floor, he felt cheated and confused. He prayed softly to the Creator, unsure in this windowless room if his body was lined up for Qibla correctly. In his twisting descent, he was sure to face the Heart of Homeland several times. Mosaic, blessed be his name, would forgive him for that.

***

Cecil snapped awake, startled that he'd survived the stairwell.

Of course, that wasn't quite true, the young Alligator he'd been, Everglade Keys, had died in that tower when his father sent him to die to save a stranger.

The orphan who came home to an empty house no longer put his faith in any god. That Rept called himself by the nice "normal" name of Cecil. It's what his Warm school friends had called the younger Sea Isle. Kanëhtaikhö was an old Seneca word for Green, his legal surname, and it sounded like the least Chromatic name he could think of.

Waking up alone; it was a life long habit that had only been recently breaking.

Tonight, the Warm bundle of flesh that was Jinx was sorely missed. Shame dappled his face, and his eyes felt wet. He got off his bed and forced himself upright before he left his bedroom. His tail dragging behind him. Jinx's door was unlocked. A chill breeze danced out into the doorway from the open window overlooking his Cat's empty bed.

He checked the urge to call out for Jinx. He was afraid that Jinx wouldn't answer. He was afraid that he was alone again in this big house. Not that he could blame Jinx if he had abandoned him after his torrent of rage and blame. What a monster he must have seemed with his chainsaw mouth opened wide enough to swallow the Cat whole. He deserved to be abandoned. Still, Cecil didn't want to believe that Jinx was gone.

Feeling at turns selfish and hopeless, Cecil checked the other rooms on the second floor before heading downstairs, because Jinx liked to read in out of the way places. Like Cecil, his lover did not need much light to read by.

He found the Cat downstairs at the Mosaic tea table, behind a laptop with a pot of cooling tea and a debris field of used tissues covering the tiled surface, leaving only a few specks of color popping out from beneath. Jinx had piled all the seat pillows onto the one side and had made a bed out of them. The Tonk wasn't asleep at the moment, and he stopped typing to meet Cecil's eyes over the computer.

Cecil squatted just within arm's reach, and for a moment, he wished his chatty kitty could fill the room with words and make everything instantly better. This time, the older man knew, he had to do the heavy lifting. Different words and phrases battled to be let out, however. He had to take a moment to find the best... but that was impossible. He chose, instead, to go with simple honesty.

"I'm sorry, Jinxie," he whispered. "I'm so sorry I was mean... mean to you."

"It's ok, Cecil..." The cat reached a sleek arm out and stroked the Alligator's muzzle.

Cecil flinched.

"What...?" Suddenly, hesitation and concern danced in the Cat's eyes.

"That cop... hit me here. Not like punched me... that wouldn't have been so bad... but he hit me with a clipboard exactly on my ISO strip. It was like kicking me in the groin."

"With a clipboard?"

"Like getting hit with the edge of the ruler. Trust me, it really hurt and... it was very disconcerting. I forgot where I was."

"I believe you." Suddenly, Cecil's huge wedge shaped head was wrapped in warm, soft fur, and the 'Gator couldn't stop himself from sobbing in relief and frustration. The hiccupping sound filled his body with shame.

"I was so... He was trying to provoke me, Jinx. He was trying provoke me, and I was so scared... and I didn't dare let him see it. I was so scared. He wanted to get me to be... *uppity*. So he could arrest me or shoot me... so he could teach me my place."

"You felt like a Skink, trapped in a net," Jinx added softly. Cecil's whole body flinched at that. He deserved that, and he had no idea what to say to get past that. A big creature like him not allowed to fight back. At least he wasn't going to be hung on a hook like a trophy. The thought did not ease his pain.

Jinx fingered his tender jawline. "It does feel swollen, Cecil." He gently flicked a kiss on the injured area. He was touched that the Cat knew his every inch. That he could see past his thick ugly hide. "I'm so sorry," his love continued. "I'm so sorry that you have to deal with this every day. That you have to think about how to avoid trouble every day."

"It's alright, Jinxie. I wish I didn't have to, but I do have to think about this every day. I just can't..." Cecil paused, surprised by this urgent need to confess. "I can only fight so many battles. I have to pick my fights. I have to pick which banner to fly. I can't fight for equality in everything. I chose gay rights over everything, because the gay community has always been more accepting of Repts than any other group."

"Queer community," Jinx softly corrected.

Cecil barked a surprised laugh. "Give me a break, I'm an old man. But, yes, yes, the Queer Community, the LGBT Community, the QUILTBAG Community..."

"Enough." Jinx gently licked at the edge of Cecil's snout. "You can't use my jokes to change the subject."

Cecil thought about that for a moment. "I don't want to talk about how scared I was any more."

Jinx nodded and moved his head deeper into the 'Gator's embrace. "It's ok."

For long moments, they simply embraced. Then Jinx pulled away. "I want to show you something that might make you feel better."

Cecil forced a smile gesture. "They announced Amendment 25?"

Jinx smiled, his ears perking forward. "I said *might*." He reached back to his laptop and turned it so that the taller man could see the screen.

Grateful for the change of subject, Cecil pulled a pillow from the pile Jinx had made and fell on it. On the screen was a female Canine in a brown pants suit. She wore a light colored hijab that covered her headfur, but not her ears. From her white fur, pointed ears, and curled tail, Cecil suspected that she might be a Spitz. He wasn't good with all the Dog Breeds. Either way, he didn't recognize her, and he said as much.

"This is the woman you rescued."

Cecil shook his head. "The Dog I rescued was legless, wheelchair bound."

Jinx smiled. "That's Ester Finsk-Spets. After you rescued her, she vowed never to be helpless again. She exercised, lost a lot of weight, got some prosthetic legs, and started running. After the Falling, she saw what happened to you. The press turning on you, right? Calling you a traitor, accusing you of being some 'inside man.'"

"That was Everglade Keys," Cecil said softly, surprised that Jinx knew about any of that. It was a lifetime ago. Almost literally in the Cat's case.

Jinx squeezed his hand and pulled on it, not letting the 'Gator go completely still. "It wasn't just you, you know. Chromatics all over the country suffered. No one probably suffered in New Amsterdam more than modest Chroma women. Bullies just seemed to find them easy targets. So, this woman started wearing a hijab, daring bigots to come at her. She became an activist. She researched Chromaticism and converted about a decade ago. She became Bark Pointer of the Brown Band."

Jinx picked up a printout. "According to her social media, she is considering renaming herself Social Justice Warrior. But I'm not sure if she's joking."

Cecil found his eyes stinging and his inner eyelids twitching. His hands twitched.

"Why are you showing me this?"

Jinx paused and looked the 'Gator in the eyes, letting the silence hang over them for a long moment. He could see the Cat was tired, but his Feline eyes were glittering with excitement. "Before I tell you, I want to tell you something. I'm Tonkinese. The greatest trick my Breed knows is talking. We're all chatty. We can yak about anything and nothing for hours." The Tonk paused long enough for Cecil to mug a smirk. "But... It's something of a trap. A self defeating trick, if we aren't careful... we can get all caught up in things. You're my rock. My stone. You keep me centered... and at the same time, you show me a whole new world. The real world outside of Darwin's Circle."

Cecil was touched. He went to say as much, but Jinx stopped him with a delicate dark finger on his snout. "I'm not done. It occurred to me that you Alligators have your own great trick. Stillness. Heck, you can go so still, I swear you're not even breathing."

"We don't inhale and exhale like you do," Cecil told him.

"I know, you breathe like birds." Jinx smiled at his words. "Like Avi, I should say. But they sorta skipped over that in comparative biology. But never mind that. The point is... that stillness can also be a trap."

Cecil nodded and found himself going still. He couldn't help himself. Jinx saw this and smiled with tender tolerance. "Bark Pointer is an alderman in New Amsterdam. She's also a marriage officiant. She is one of a dozen that can perform marriages in One Global Village. I want her to marry us this time next year."

The Alligator's jaws opened.

Jinx waited patiently for a sound to come out, amused by Cecil's reaction.

Slowly, Cecil's tail curled about him until it finally pushed him up a few inches by bunching up under him.

"I have a lot of mixed feelings about going back there, Jinxie."

"We will have a whole year to sort them out, Cecil."

The Alligator nodded and pulled his Kitty Boi closer. A moment later, Cecil allowed Jinx, a third his weight, to drag him upstairs back to bed.

Life isn't always easy to label; sometimes we need to expand our definitions, open the boxes we live in.

DEAR SIS

Matt Doyle

Dear Sis,

I hope you're doing okay. How's Granddad? Does he still smoke that awful smelling herbal mix that he used to put in his pipe? I bet they hate that up that way. Mom and Dad are the same foxes as ever. Dad still bosses everyone about like he's on the building site, and Mom still ignores him when he gets too silly. They're good though. It was their anniversary this week. I made them a collage; lots of photos of all of us together, all pointy ears and bushy tails. They really liked that. It's hanging over the fireplace now.

Oh, and Auntie Sally came to stay for a few days. She'd had a bit of a fall and caught herself on a bollard. When she came to us, her eyes were still a little swollen, and she was having trouble tracking movement. You know how the Reds in our family are, especially the older ones. Not being able to track us like that meant she was near enough blind for a while. She seemed much better when she left though, so that's good.

Things have been tough since you left.

School was going well for a while. It still is, I guess. In studies, I mean. I'm passing most of my classes, and once we get through the next year, I'll be looking at colleges. Mom's really excited about that, Dad not so much. He worries a lot. That's kinda my fault though.

I stuck by what you said for a long while. Some days, I wore boxers, other times, bra and panties. As long as I always wore the male uniform and stuck to boxers on the days we were doing sports, it was all good. You were right too, light coloured bikini tops showed up a lot less. I'm just glad that the school shirts were thick enough for most people not to notice the fancier underwear.

A couple of months back, the school installed Trans toilets. That made me happy. Sure, it was essentially an extension on the disabled toilets, but it was a good first step. It gave me hope, because everyone just sorta accepted it. The one time we had a problem was when a parent defaced the door to them. A parent. Can you believe that? The school dealt with it really quickly though. I think they even got the police involved in the end.

So anyway, when I saw how well everyone was taking the toilets, I took the next step and borrowed one of the girl's uniforms from the lost and found. I wasn't really ready to tell Mom and Dad yet, so I just left it in my locker and changed into it when I felt like it. At first, I spent days like that kinda hiding myself away. It sounds stupid, but I felt ready to dress how I felt each day, but not to show everyone. Looking back on it, I think I was just trying to find my bearings. So, on femme days, I looked out for empty classrooms, or just went to the toilets for a bit. Pretty lame, right? There I was, trying to free myself by getting all cramped up in a cubicle. It was fine though. I was happy. I was even considering telling a few people who I was close to.

The problems started when one of the boys from the year below, Steve Gall, saw me coming out of the toilets. He didn't recognise me from behind and came on over to try hitting on me. Get this, he actually told me that I may be silver, but he thought that my body was golden. It was a real struggle not to laugh. When he realised who I was though ... honestly, I've never seen a Dalmatian go so wide eyed. I swear, the colour drained right out of his spots. He got all freaked out and went to Mr. Peterson.

Long story short, Mom and Dad now know. As does most of the school.

It's been weird. Some are trying to understand it, and they're mostly cool with me, but a lot either think I'm a freak, or that I'm doing it in protest of Trans rights. It's stupid. The worst part is that if I stop now, things won't get any easier, because everyone will just think this isn't really part of me, and it'll look like I really was protesting. If I keep going though, I'll keep getting all the dirty looks and the insults. I can't win, and I hate that I've put myself in this position.

Mr. Peterson was honest about the whole thing and said he doesn't really understand where I'm coming from. He's been great though, really supportive. Between him and Mom and Dad – I guess you were right about their reaction too – I *do* have support. They all think it will blow over when people adjust. I'm not so sure. My social life has pretty much bottomed out too. Oh, and I've started using the toilets when everyone else has gone to registration. It means I'm late a lot, but the teachers know what's going on, so they don't really do anything about it. But hey, at least I get to wear whatever feels right around the school without hiding it now.

Home got better though. Mom and Dad aren't entirely sure how to react, their faces give that away. Whenever I come in dressed differently than the day before, Mom does that thing where she crinkles her snout up and the edges of her mouth twitch. Dad ruffles my ears a bit, like he used to with you when he thought you were sneaking out with that wolf from across the street. Sorry, I forgot his name. They're trying though, and that's what matters. Being able to just be me around them is good. It's more than I ever expected.

I got a part time job too. Bet you thought that day would never come. No social life equals plenty of free time to earn cash, right? If it weren't for Mom and Dad, and the way they've been, I wouldn't have had the confidence to even try.

The old café on Main Street, Redwood's? It's there. Or, it was. Miss Redwood, the old bear who used to arrange the carol service every year still runs it. I don't think she'll be bringing the carollers to our door this year though. I actually only met her there twice, once at the interview, and once again today. The job started out well. I liked waiting on the tables, and the uniform is pretty much the same for either gender, so it wasn't too hard to cut loose. The other staff were really friendly, and I got on well with my direct manager. The shifts were good too, two hours after school and five hours on Saturdays.

The last two weeks, I've been switching quite a bit though. On femme days, I'd been doing my lashes and painting my claws. I was careful and kept the colours close to my natural shades, all really subtle stuff, but apparently someone noticed. So, today, Miss Redwood turned up in the morning and called me into her office. She's a scary woman at the best of times, even at her age. Today was really bad though. I could see how it was going to go the moment that she said there were certain *expectations* I hadn't been meeting.

She was casually waving her spectacles as though her words were nothing more than a simple statement of fact, and *not* something designed to cut. They were meant to hurt me though. I could tell by her tone. The old bear doesn't get it. She didn't even want to try. She just glared at me and said that if I couldn't follow a simple dress code, then she didn't see how she could continue to employ me.

That was when I cried. I hate when I do that. My nose runs, and the tears all drip down my muzzle and into my mouth, you know? And when I cry, I cry *a lot*. It was the same when I first told you, too. It's like I know how to turn the taps on full force, but I don't know how to turn them off again. Oh, and the worst of it? The only thing I could think to do was apologise. I just sat there, hiding behind my tail and whining about how sorry I was for something I can't even control.

By the time I'd finished, you wouldn't know I had any Red DNA in me at all, because my tail fur was so weighed down from the tears that it lost all of its bushiness. I must have looked pretty pathetic. What she said next summed up how life is for me right now, at least outside home.

"We are not so behind the times that we can't make allowances. If you simply felt that your body is *wrong*, then there are certainly things you can do. We could even have supported you if you'd told us. I understand from some of the customers that this isn't the case with you though. This switching back and forth between one look and the other? It confuses the customers, not to mention your peers. I dread to think what it's doing to your colleagues. No, I am sorry, but this has been going on quite long enough, and it is simply too much of a disruption."

And that was that.

I left my badge on her desk and came straight here. Technically, there's another couple of hours of my shift left, so Mom and Dad aren't going to expect me home just yet. Miss Redwood won't tell them either. Honestly, I think she'll likely be gone before Dad has a chance to march down there and bark up a storm. That's good. That he'll probably stand up for me, that she'll be gone, and that I've got time. I need this right now.

It's stupid, but you're really the only one that … I mean, you never made me feel bad about it. Mom and Dad don't now, but they used to, when they'd tell those jokes. *You* were the one who was always there. You were the first person who I told about how I felt, because I *knew* you'd support me. You never once let me down on that, you know that, right?

But yeah, like I said, it's been hard a lot lately. And Miss Redwood wasn't really wrong. If it was just that my body wasn't right, then I could have done something about it. That's a hard path to take. A long one too. And I'm not even saying things are perfect for people when they reach the light at the end of the tunnel. I *know* how hard they have to keep fighting, even after all that. I get that. I do. But at least there *is* a light at the end of the tunnel for them. I admire everyone who has the strength to do what they need to to be the person they are. But I'm envious too.

And it's not like I haven't thought about it. After you left us, I thought about it a lot. You wouldn't believe how many nights I just lay there in bed telling myself that I should have been born a vixen. I told myself that it's not too late. Go to the doctor, start getting things moving, and in a few years, everything will be fine. I really wanted to believe that. And you know, some nights, I did. There are times that it *would* make things right. There are times that I can sit there, look in the mirror, and say yes, I *am* a girl, *this* is how I want to be.

But it doesn't last.

It never does, because some days, I'm happy in myself. I'm not ... what do they call it? CISGendered? I'm not that, not really, but there are times when I feel close to it. But that's the problem. Even if I *am* spending more time as a vixen now, there are still times when I feel male. Or mostly male at least. If I transitioned, what would that do in the end? It would leave me in exactly the same position, but with the opposite body, and a lifetime of medication to take. And then there's the body trauma of the operation itself. I meant what I said. I admire people who have the strength to go through each and every struggle that they need to, and I truly hope it makes them happy, but it's ... it's not me.

Anyway, I'm sorry it's taken so long to write to you. There was a good reason though.

Do remember what you told me when Granddad died? I was really upset, and you told me, if there was something I still wanted to say to him, I should write him a letter. When I wasn't sure what to say, you said I should tell him what the best thing he left me with was. We sat there on your bed, and we both remembered the story he told us about Dad getting into a fight with Mr. Fendle when he was a kid. Dad, the big, strong fox who lugs steel girders around the building site getting KO'd by a skunk who works as a massage therapist. We always loved that one. That was what he left me with. The smile I get whenever I remember one of his stories. I'm smiling now, just writing this.

When I'd finished the letter, we took it out to his grave and burnt it. You told me if I did that then, wherever his spirit is, he'd get it. I never did figure out whether you really believed that, or if you were just trying to make me feel better.

That's why it's taken so long to write to you though. I wanted you to know what the best thing that *you* left me with was. At first, even trying to think about it was hard. When we lost you, I lost more than a sister. I lost my best friend. And my refuge. Then, once I stopped crying every night, I just couldn't figure out what the biggest thing you did for me was. You did so much.

Today, I figured it out.

Everything that's happened lately has been hard. But, every time I start to feel like I should just go back to being what everyone expects, I remember what you told me that night when I broke down and just spilled everything to you.

"I won't lie to you; a lot of people aren't going to get it. That doesn't matter though. *You* get it. *You* know who you are. And now, so do I. Tod or vixen, it doesn't matter, even if that changes every day of the week. Just be *you*, and you'll always be my little buddy."

You were right that a lot of people don't get it. Honestly, I don't think most of them had even heard the term Gender-Fluid before all of this. And, if I'm being honest, there are times that I wish I didn't feel this way. It would be so much easier if I could just take that side of me, lock it up somewhere, and walk away, even if doing so was a lie. But I don't do that, no matter how much it hurts to keep being who I am.

I can resist the urges to lock that part of myself away because of you. That's what you gave me, Sis. The strength to be me, even when things get *really* bad. And that is a far bigger thing than you could ever have known. For that, I will never be able to thank you enough. The best I can do is keep living my life and promise to try to make the next letter a bit more positive.

I miss you Sis, and I love you.

Your little buddy.

A gray fox with an unusually bushy tail gathers up a pile of papers and stuffs them back into their bag. They smile at the letter they've written, fold it, and give it a kiss before pulling out a lighter and setting it alight. They watch the paper burn to ashes on the grave of a loved one, and the tears start to fall again. By the time the breeze has taken the ashes to the sky, the tears have run dry for another day.

The fox gets to their feet and starts to walk home. They know now what's important. Tomorrow is another day, and sometimes, it's the memories of others that give you the strength to resist the darkness and keep fighting to be who you are. No matter what gives you strength though, the message is simple:

Be you. Nobody should ever expect anything else.

A touch of magic. And a whole lot of cats.

EVERY LAST PAW

Blake Hutchins

Once there lived a kitten who had a coat of inky-black fur with white paws. Her humans called her Mittens, because humans are stupid like that. They didn't notice how her pale-green eyes caught the moonlight just so while they slept, or how diligently she warded the house against mice and spiders. But they fed her and made room for her on their beds. The grown humans made room on their laps for her and the children stroked her with gentle hands. She loved them all, and felt loved in turn.

But one day the humans put out things the size of cat treats that were wrapped in crinkly skins, and smelled funny, like they weren't quite food. The children covered their faces with other faces that smelled of plastic and paint. Finally, the humans set out hollow vegetables on their porch with little fires burning inside. It was all very odd. Mittens sensed a stillness in the air, as if something bad were coming, like the world was holding its breath. The humans, naturally, detected nothing, because humans are blind and deaf to most of what the world reveals to cats. So she stood guard at the window that night as the moon rose almost full through the black clouds.

She was just starting to nod off when a rangy cat with a patchwork coat sprang onto the roof outside, startling her. She jumped back, fur raised, ears back.

"Hey kid." The cat peered in, yellow eyes narrowed. His tail twitched half amusement, half contempt.

Mittens pounced at him, for all kittens are born fearless. "Get away! My humans! My house!" She thumped harmlessly against the window glass and collapsed in a heap.

"Tch." The cat studied his forepaw as she picked herself up. "You got game, kid, I gotta say. That's worth a lot. So...wanna see something cool?"

Curiosity, the humans say, kills the cat. In this they are actually right about something. A great desire to know what this cat was offering came over Mittens, growing in strength until she could not stop her little body from bouncing back and forth.

"What? What? See what?"

"It's Ratfight Night. We gotta go." The cat glanced at her, shrugged. "Well, maybe not a good idea, after all. You're kinda tiny. No offense."

"But I want to go!" Mittens nuzzled the cold glass.

"C'mon then." The cat turned to go.

"Wait!"

He looked over his shoulder. "What?"

She bipped her paw against the window. "Can't."

He grinned. "That all?" He breathed against the glass. The fog of his breath left the glass rippling like the water in Mittens's water dish.

Tentatively, she put out a paw. It slipped through, the crisp night air chilling her footpads. Being a kitten, she sprang through at once. On the wooden shingles, the strange cat seemed much bigger.

"What was that?" she asked.

"A little cat magic," he said.

"How do I get back in?"

"Dumb question. Just meow at the door."

"Won't my humans wonder how I got out?"

"Nah. They'll figure they left a door open. They're clueless that way." He gave her a yellow-eyed wink and sprang onto a nearby tree branch. She happily threw herself after him.

***

They followed the secret paths only cats know. The almost-full moon floated in the gloom in the shape of a cat's eye to light their way. Mittens' companion introduced himself as Riptop. He was rough but kind, and smelled of soot and old scars. As they traveled, Mittens sensed other cats running alongside them like a shadowy army, more than she had ever imagined in her fiercest kitten dreams.

"It's like this, squirt," Riptop explained. "This night every year, a door opens between the spirit world and our world. Mostly not a problem, but humans' worst dreams and desires beckon like tender meat to some things. The stronger ones try to dig into the humans' heads, sickening their souls." His tail made a jaunty flip. "That's where cats come in. We see those critters, and hunt them down. But the worst of them, the very worst, is the Greed Rat."

"What's that?" Mittens asked. They ducked behind a streetlamp next to a wide stretch of water and slipped betwixt and between spaces, emerging into a weed-strewn alley leagues away. The place stank of urine and despair, and Mittens wrinkled her nose at the stink, but soon they were leaping between again, on a long shadow trail that unfurled before them like an endless ribbon. When they took a brief rest in a place of tall houses that towered over them and cradled the moon's image in their glass faces, the two cats had to shake frost crystals off their whiskers. Mittens asked her question again.

"The Greed Rat is the worst of the very bad things," Riptop explained. "Because humans have a special weakness to it. Once it crawls inside them…" He shivered. "The world suffers."

They resumed their journey along the secret paths. Until at last they stopped, at a place that smelled of oil and metal, with great canyons formed by towering corpses of the loud, rubber-pawed road-beasts Mittens had watched her humans climb inside and ride sometimes. The air fell deadly silent as the host of cats gathered.

"Anytime now, kid. Stick close," Riptop muttered. "We're gonna make the Yondercat."

"OK," said Mittens, pretending to be brave, but staying right by Riptop's side. "What's a Yondercat?"

"A big cat magic. Shh."

From the steel cliffs came a rustling, and the bloated shape of a rat grew, fed by smaller rat shapes jumping into it, until it towered over the wreckage. Its eyes burned like blood. The Greed Rat cackled, its toothy maw an echo of its eyes.

The cats yowled in answer, then began to merge in the moonlight, forming a gigantic cat.

"This is it!" hissed Riptop. "Let's go!"

But Mittens, curious, peered into the red eye of the Great Greed Rat, and fear froze her kitten heart for the very first time.

Riptop nudged her, then sighed mournfully. "On second thought, you should sit this one out, find a place to hide. You're just too small. I made a mistake bringing you. Now scoot!" He tapped her gently with his paw, and then joined the rest of the cats as they surged together.

A huge tabby striped with nightdark and starlight turned lightning-blue eyes toward the Rat and roared a battle-cry. Shaken from her trance, Mittens ran away to hide in the shadow of a fallen tire, quaking.

The two giants crashed together with only Mittens and the moon to witness. Metal creaked and groaned around them as they fought. The Yondercat's great claws tore at shadow sinew and slashed at the enemy's barbed, poisonous tail. The Rat's sharp teeth chomped on star-furred flank and snapped at the Yondercat's flashing eyes. As the fight escalated, the two great spirit-beasts battered and tore the canyons apart, hurling torn chunks of metal flesh into the air, accompanied by torn rubber tires and shards of broken glass.

Dodging the pieces of metal and glass that smashed into the ground around her, Mittens found shelter beneath a pile of tangled rubber and metal guts. She couldn't follow the battle blow for blow, but saw the Rat slash open the great cat's side at last, then heave its bulk to pin its opponent amid a pile of shredded metal beast bodies. The Yondercat struggled to free itself as the rat opened its huge red mouth for the killing bite.

At that moment, Mittens caught its eye again, and her eyes watered with horrible visions: humans fighting, smoke in the skies, the earth itself gutted, fat humans with rat-like eyes grinning in triumph while her own family of humans cowered, their house stolen, their spirits broken.

No... Her humans! Her house! But what could a mere kitten do? Nothing, but...*something*. She had to try. At the least, she could try,

Shaking, she took a step, one tremulous paw, then another, and then she was running, heart athunder. She knew, in that instant, what she had to do. As if in answer, a pair of rats dripped from the Great Rat's body and scuttled toward her, beady eyes hungry. She sped for the Yondercat, hurdling oily puddles and skirting jagged spars of glass. Pushing aside the last of her fear, she uttered a defiant mew as the rats grasped for her, their black claws a whisker's width from her neck.

Since the dawn of time, everyone underestimates how fast a determined kitten can go. And so it happened here. Mittens leaped; the rats missed. Yet they still might have seized her, had not the great tail of the Yondercat flicked across the battlefield to meet her in mid-leap, and so she joined with the others.

Mittens moved through the Yondercat's great form like a mote of light flashing across swift water, past the spirits of cats struggling with rage and pain and death. As her furious spirit flickered by, their will sparked and tailed hers, pushing her to the very tip of the first toeclaw, which unsheathed in a sickle of brilliant silver lightning as the Yondercat twisted and stretched up to pierce that contemptuous red eye through and through.

The Rat screamed like a passing rail-beast and arched to free itself, whereupon the Yondercat took the opening and tore out its throat. The Rat crumbled into hundreds of rat bodies. Many lay where they fell. The rest scattered.

The Yondercat uttered a victorious yowl before exploding into a mass of angry cats. These sprang after the fleeing rats, eyes hot with excitement.

Mittens picked her way past wounded and fallen cats and the twitching forms of dying rats. Echoes of rage still scratched at her heart. Her kitten body was tired; she wanted nothing more than to curl up atop her humans in the snug, safe bed.

"Hey, kid!" A cat licking a blood-clotted flank turned yellow eyes toward her. It was Riptop. "You did good there, at the end. I was wrong. Everyone matters. Even the smallest paw."

"I know." She sat by him and stared wide-eyed at his flank. "Are you going to die?"

"Pfft. I still got a few more lives banked up. I'll be stiff for a few days, but I'll mend." He cocked his head. "You're not a kitten anymore, though. You met your fear and clawed the spit out of it. A proper cat's deed deserves a proper cat's name."

She twitched her ears in muted excitement.

After a moment's thought, he stood and drew a deep breath. "Yo, everyone! Three yowls for *Ratblinder*! The cat that beat the Rat!"

As the acclaim of a thousand cats split the night, Mittens—now Ratblinder to her tribe—washed her face and wondered what her humans would put out for breakfast.

A young raccoon on a faraway planet simply wants to buy a few honeyed dates, but instead, he gets swept into an entirely new life.

Mixed Blessings

Kittara Foxworthy

Tony, a raccoon boy from the supply ship the *Dark Matter*, was in the middle of having several dozen packages for sickbay sent to the shipdock when he heard the comm crackle to life. "Tony are you there?" He glanced at his chrono to make sure he hadn't missed a check in, but it read that he still had a half a chron before he had to report again.

Confused, he politely excused himself and stepped a meter or so from the shopkeeper to answer. "Yeah, I'm here. What's up?" His black and white ringed tail flicked from side to side, showing his concern.

"Return to the ship immediately. Captain's orders." Vanessa the comm officer said, "We've had a change of plans." There was worry in the otter's voice.

"Sure thing, I'm about finished here anyway." He clicked the comm off and was about to return to the shopkeeper to finish his transaction when he spotted a small coin dangling from a string of beads, like the ones he wore in his fur, mixed into a display with some other jewelry.

Glancing at his chrono, he licked his black lips thinking about honeyed dates and how the other kits on the ship would treat him like a hero if he could bring some back. Surely the captain wouldn't mind if he picked up a few dozen of the delectable treats before he headed back to the ship. After all it took at least a half chron to fire up the engines and do the proper safety checks before takeoff.

Making sure there were no other customers in the shop, he turned back to the shopkeeper. "Been doing much stargazing lately?" he asked in a bland tone.

233

The shopkeeper gave him a once over tilting his head to the right and responded, "Been watching a particular nebula." Then he nervously glanced around the shop to see if anyone was listening.

Tony grinned as the shopkeeper realized there was no one inside but the two of them. "Nebulas are nice enough, but I prefer a *Black Hole* myself." He rested his paw on the counter with some of his personal credit chits in his outstretched palm. The mention of the Independent Colony had the shopkeeper's eyes widening, and he took a step back nervously.

"Alright raccoon, what do you want?" The shopkeeper licked his lips nervously, his tail flicking wildly behind him.

"I recently found out that you have honeyed dates for sale. I'd like to purchase some." He tried to sound more sure of himself than he actually was.

The shopkeeper frowned, then nodded slowly. "If it'll get you out of my shop. How many do you want?"

Tony shook the chits in his paw. "How many will a hundred get me?"

The shopkeeper, now switching to bargaining, rubbed his muzzle, before offhandedly offering, "Twenty."

Tony relaxed into the familiar role of haggler. "Twenty? That's highway robbery." The phrasing was old, handed down through the generations, some said it came from the Makers themselves. No one really knew what a highway was or why you'd want to steal one, but the words were a traditional part of the bargaining process.

"Fine, twenty-five. But you're taking food right out of my children's mouths." The shopkeeper delivered the correct line, but his attention was on the door and not on the bargaining ritual. Tony knew people back on the *Black Hole* that could bring tears to your eyes with their inflections and tone while delivering that same line.

"How about thirty, and I don't tell anyone where I got them from?" Tony held out his paw in the traditional gesture to seal a deal of this sort.

Five cens later, after completing the medical transaction, with his dates in his paws, Tony stepped out of the shop and turned toward the spaceport. It was a bright sunny day, and there was a light breeze that ruffled his fur as he walked back through the city. To his ship bred senses, the breeze might as well have been a strong wind; it was leaving all kinds of dust and other detritus in his fur along with some of the local insect life. He was going to have spend a half chron in decon when he got back just to feel clean again.

He was ambling along nibbling on one of the sweet fruits when his comm buzzed once more. "I'm on the way back," he said as the channel opened.

"How far out are you?" Vanessa asked, she sounded a bit rushed, like there was something else on her mind.

"He glanced at the display on the comm unit before he replied. "About three kilometers away. Why?" He picked up his pace, dodging around several slower moving hybrids that were also walking along the roadway.

There was silence for a mil; then a new voice came over the comm. "Tony," The captain's voice sounded sad and angry all at the same time. "You have to hurry. We haven't much time. Vanessa just found out that the ship whose ident we are using was decommissioned six cycles ago. We have to leave. You have about ten cens before we make a break for it."

Tony's heart skipped a beat, and he started to run. "On my way, Sir!" He dodged in and out of the foot traffic, trying to recall the fastest route back to the spaceport. Ten cens meant they were cold starting the engine; they had likely already started the process when they first called him since the process took fifteen. He silently cursed the Makers that he hadn't left then.

A group of rabbits was blocking the path up ahead; it looked like a crèche outing, with only a few adults but what seemed like hundreds of kits. "Out of the way!" he yelled as he came up on them fast. The little ones scattered, letting out high pitched shrieks and falling over each other in their efforts to avoid being run over. If he had to guess, he'd say these were primary crèche kits. They didn't look to be old enough to be in secondary, and they were far too young to be in tertiary like he was.

As Tony ran between two small bodies, one of the adults reached out to grab him but missed and instead caught the bag holding his honeyed dates. The small, individually packaged, dried fruits erupted from the bag spilling over the ground and the kits alike, but Tony didn't stop. He just dropped the now empty bag and kept running, a panicky feeling urging him to move faster.

The comm unit buzzed. Tony glanced at the screen to see that he was no more than ten meters from the spaceport and the ship. As he was about to respond, the screen flickered, and he saw the face of the captain in miniature. The whitetail buck looked haggard, like he hadn't slept in a week or more. His ears were dropped to the sides, leaving little doubt in Tony's mind that the situation had gotten worse. "Tony, I'm sorry, son."

The words hit him like a punch to the gut, and he stumbled, losing his footing and sprawling face first on the roadway. His fingers loosened, and the comm unit went flying from his paw. He tried to grab for it, but he fumbled, only managing to spin it further out of reach as the underside of his muzzle crashed into the hard surface of the roadway. He blinked away the dizziness to see the comm unit lying a quarter meter from his outstretched paw, broken into three pieces.

He whimpered and looked up as the familiar whine of the *Dark Matter's* engines passed by overhead.

"There he is! That's the one!" someone shouted behind him.

Turning he saw several hybrids in uniform hurrying toward him with one of the adult rabbits in the lead. "Stop, Pirate Scum!" Tony scrambled to his feet, grabbing the pieces of his comm and shoving them into pockets in his ship suit. "I said stop!"

Tony scanned the area ahead of him. Where was the entryway to the spaceport? Behind him the Peacekeepers and the rabbits were closing in fast. He bolted down the nearest corridor, scanning the sides for any possible escape routes.

The lightweight sandals he was wearing were not meant for this kind of punishment. The strap over the toes on the right foot gave way, and he ran right out of the sandal. He stumbled and grabbed the wall so he wouldn't fall. His paw felt a texture that wasn't the same as the rest of the wall. Looking closely he realized it was an opening to the ventilation system. Without pausing to think, he pulled the cover off and dropped it to the ground. It looked big enough for him but too small for a full adult to follow.

That was enough to make up his mind. He reached inside and pulled himself head first into the shaft. His left sandal fell off as he used his toe claws to find purchase against the wall and shove himself the rest of the way into the shaft. Once there he used his fingers and toes to pull himself along the slick surface until he found a junction. Behind him he could hear the Peacekeepers yelling and scrabbling at the opening to the ventilation shaft.

One side of the juncture lead back toward the city, the other into the spaceport. He was most familiar with the port, so he headed further into the maze of conduits sliding forward, always choosing the path that would take him to the landing pad the *Dark Matter* had used.

If his spatial sense was correct, and years of crawling around inside the guts of the *Dark Matter* meant it usually was, the empty landing pad he could see through the grate to his right was the one that he was looking for. He pressed his muzzle up against it and peered around, taking in the situation.

There were about a dozen armed Port Authority uniforms poking into several stacks of goods. Tony recognized many of the insignia on the goods as ones that he'd had transported to the ship. A brown weasel standing against the wall under Tony was talking to a white rat about what was happening.

"Pirate Scum! Just like them to use our ident codes to steal goods from honest working folk."

"Myers says all the stuff piled up here was paid for."

"Yeah with stolen ship credentials."

"No, with galactic credits. They only used the ident to land on the planet. Everything they bought was legitimate."

The weasel snorted. "Doesn't mean they didn't steal the credits from some other unsuspecting planet. Or have other stuff sent in first that was on the contraband list."

"Why do you always think the wors—"

Their conversation was cut off when the Peacekeepers and an adult rabbit burst into the landing pad. The large bulldog who seemed to be in charge of the Peacekeepers looked around at all the Port Authority uniforms and barked out, "Who's in charge here?"

A soft voice answered him from behind a stack of crates where Tony couldn't see. "That would be me." The individual moved into Tony's view, and he gasped softly. Mink were a rare sight on the Independent Colony. They'd only ever had five if he remembered his history correctly. All male and all refugees from one planet or another. This one was so blindingly white that even with the green of his uniform to break up his fur, Tony still had to blink several times before his eyes were used to the sight.

The mink was followed on either side by large black dogs, sleek and athletic looking, like whippets or Greyhounds. They towered over him, like two hulking shadows.

"Is there something we can help you with?"

Tony tuned out their conversation, figuring the mink wouldn't let the Peacekeeper get involved in his case. He was right; a few cens later, the only personnel in the bay were the Port Authority people.

The mink spoke again; this time the growl was more pronounced. "Find him! I don't care if you have to tear this place to the ground. You find that pirate and bring him to me! Someone is going to answer for this fiasco, and if it isn't him, then it will be your hides!" He flicked his tail angrily from side to side as he stalked out in the same direction as the Peacekeepers.

Tony jerked back further from the grate, trying to stifle a whimper and calm his racing heart. There had been such rage in that voice, and all of it was directed at him!

"You heard the lady—get a squad of mice in here to scour the vents! In the meantime move all these crates to impound until we figure out what to do with them?" black dog number one said while number two followed the (female? hard to tell at this distance) mink into the corridor.

Tony saw his chances of escaping this situation fading quickly. Mice were small enough that they could come in after him. If he didn't get out of here soon, they would find him, and he didn't like the thoughts that the minks last words were putting into his head.

More concerned about escaping, he moved closer to the vent to peer out into the landing bay. Several of the uniformed figures were beginning to pile the various crates onto a platform connected to a ground vehicle of some sort. The rest were standing in places where they could see all three of the exits from the landing bay. It looked hopeless.

As Tony watched the people scanning and stacking the crates, he noticed something he hadn't before. Some of the crates were oddly shaped and couldn't be stacked easily. These were being left to the side, presumably to be placed on top of the finished stack where they wouldn't overbalance the rest of the crates. If he was right, that would leave a space at the top where he could, if he was very lucky, slip into and get low enough that they wouldn't see him. It wasn't a great plan, but it was the only one he had. Of course it all depended on him being close enough to get onto the top of the stacked crates in the first place.

"Creators save us from the depredations of Pirates!" the weasel said, then spat to the side.

"You kiss your mother with that mouth Johnson?" The rat sounded disgusted.

The weasel snorted. "Just think of it like a heartfelt prayer if that suits you better Hikomi."

"It would suit me better if I didn't have to listen to your bigotry."

"Bigotry? You telling me you'd take that pirate's side over that of honest citizens?"

There was silence for a mil before the rat responded. "Not necessarily, but you can't deny that he's being hunted purely on circumstantial evidence."

Tony tuned them out. From his vantage point, there were only three exits: one led into the corridors of the port building, one went into the maintenance section, and one wasn't clearly marked. The unmarked exit was the only one that had a ventilation grate over it, which pretty much made up his mind. Glancing at the crates, he realized he only had a few cens or he was going to miss his chance altogether.

Determined now to put his plan into action, Tony moved down the conduit searching for a juncture that would lead him back toward the unmarked exit. His spatial acuity led him around the landing bay until he was positioned behind the grate centered over the unnamed exit, just as the stack of crates started to move. He held his breath and silently prayed to the Makers that he'd chosen the right place to be.

Across the landing bay he finally saw the weasel and rat that had been talking about him. They seemed to be on the verge of coming to blows. The ground vehicle pivoted until the stack of crates was farther from him, and he started to whimper, certain that he was about to lose his last chance to escape. Then it started to move. A beeping sound began at the same time as the vehicle moved toward him. He let out a breath he hadn't realized he'd been holding and carefully pushed the grate open, turning it so that he could pull it into the conduit.

His trembling fingers almost dropped it, making his heart skip a beat, but he managed to get the grate in without too much noise. It was a tight fit to scramble over the grate so he was positioned at the edge of the conduit, but he managed it a few mils before the vehicle passed under him. The weasel across the bay let out a vicious sounding snarl and launched himself at the rat. Tony took advantage of the distraction to propel himself onto the moving pile of crates.

He'd timed his jump well. Not only did he land where he wanted but he managed to avoid notice. Curling into a ball he tried not to move any of the precariously stacked, oddly shaped packages that surrounded him. The vehicle moved at a pretty good clip through the corridor and out a double set of outer doors into the sunlight of the planet. Tony dared a peek over one of the lower packages and saw so much greenery that he was overwhelmed.

On the *Dark Matter* he'd been to the hydroponics bay several times and always loved the sight and smell of green growing things, but this was a million times more growth than he had ever seen before. He knew that the cities had green things growing along the streets, but the realization that it grew so wild and untamed was staggering. They moved from the bright sun into a darker more shaded space which made Tony look up. He was awed to see that the greenery actually spread over the road creating a feeling like he was in some sacred place. It made him realize how small he was in comparison to the life around him. Suddenly he understood why the planet looked blue and green from space. It was the vegetation making its presence known.

While he had been staring at the plant life, the vehicle had come to a halt. He was jolted from his rapt contemplation by the sound of voices.

"Hey N'Dachi!" the driver of the vehicle called out.

A few mil later, a pretty giraffe walked out of the building in front of them. "What is it now, Eamon? Did you get lost on your way home again?" She put her balled paw on her right hip and cocked her head to the side.

Eamon chuckled. "No lass not this time. I have a delivery for you. Seems a bunch of pirates used an ident from a ship that was decommissioned six cycles ago and got found out. They did a runner, but they'd paid galactic credits for their cargo and left it in the bay."

N'Dachi's ears perked up, and her paw dropped to hang loosely at her side. "You don't say? And you just happened to volunteer to bring it all the way out here did you?" She came toward the vehicle as the driver, a sheep of some sort if Tony was right, got out of it.

"I brought you the preliminary inventory. But we haven't opened the crates up to see if the codes are correct yet. He passed her a small data pad, one that Tony, now that he had more time to think, recalled being used to scan the barcodes on the crates as they were stacked.

"You know where to park it." She took the pad back through the door she'd come out of, and Eamon directed the land rover through the larger door that slid open for him.

Even with the lights, the shed was darker than the sunlight, making Tony blink a few times to let his eyes get used to it. The room they were in was surprisingly small, leaving only about a meter on either side of the vehicle. Since there was no lift mechanism, Tony was a little startled when the floor gave a lurch before smoothly starting down. They went down several meters to a cavernous room that held dozens of stacks of crates and oddly shaped packages similar to the ones on his stack. The driver headed down the center aisle until he reached an empty spot on the left. Some sort of feet came out of the vehicle to touch the floor. Tony almost tipped over when the stack of crates rose slowly, lifting up and over the cab to settle in the empty spot. The driver disconnected the arms and moved off back the way he'd come. Leaving Tony alone, trapped inside a warehouse, on a planet that he had no hope of leaving, surrounded by people who thought he was the worst scum in the Galaxy.

Just when he thought things couldn't possibly get any worse, the lights went off.

There was enough ambient light around him, coming from various sources, that his eyes quickly adjusted to the gloom. His ears swiveled this way and that, but he didn't hear any more sounds from the direction that the vehicle had gone. There was a soft buzzing coming from a few stacks down on the other side of the aisle. When he investigated, he discovered a collection of very sophisticated electronics, some of them better than those issued to most Peacekeeper forces. His shipmates would kill to get their paws on some of these. But right now, he had to find out if there was another way out of this place. It wouldn't do to escape from the Peacekeepers and be trapped in here for the rest of his life.

He unboxed one of the pads and was pleased to see it had about a half charge on it. He opened an interface and set it up to automatically map his course. Then he found a wall and started walking toward the lift.

The interior wall looked familiar to him, made of metal and covered in a poly fiber that was hard to damage. He'd seen the same walls all his life. The ship and the Independent Colony were both built of the same substances. If he was right, then the storage bunker he was confined in should have an opening about...

Yes, there it was. He was in one of the old shipping containers that the Makers had used to transport the hybrids to their new homes. He manually input the dimensions of one of the old shipping containers on his map, using the opening as a reference point. Forty meters long and twenty meters wide with a twenty meter ceiling. He looked up. The ceiling was more like ten meters overhead, the standard height for storehouses that accommodated all the known species. That meant modifications had been made to the container. Not surprising, they'd done the same on the Independent Colony, turning the old containers into habitation pods and various other useful things.

Now that he had a better idea of what this place was, he turned his attention to the opening. An air lock—again no surprise there. A lot of old ship parts were reused in the construction of the colonies. This one was open on the inner side but sealed off on the outer. It had a hole in the floor with a ladder that led deeper into the ground and one in the ceiling that led up toward the surface.

When he stepped onto the floor, emergency lighting flickered on, giving the whole place a gentle reddish-orange glow that didn't disturb his night sight but rather enhanced it. He looked up as light bloomed above him, illuminating another pod. They were stacked vertically with a darker expanse between them that indicated a ladder. Below he saw another pod light up under him.

Since he was underground on a planet, he figured if he climbed up to the highest point, it should have a door to the surface and freedom. With that in mind, he started climbing. The ladders were on alternating sides of the shaft. That was standard safety protocol, so that if you slipped, you wouldn't find yourself falling the entire length of the shaft, just down to the level underneath.

As he climbed, pods above him lit up, while the ones falling away under him went dark. He lost count of the number of pods he'd gone through when he finally reached the last lighted pod.

It was rather disappointing.

The outer door on this level had been sealed as well. He could go through the inner door to another level of storage, but there wasn't a way out. It didn't make sense. There should be an exit somewhere, if only for emergency use.

He considered for a mil. If he was on a ship, then each of the levels would have had a functioning air lock. Of course if he was on a ship, he wouldn't have assumed the exit was at the top. He looked down. Was it possible?

He along with all the rest of the Independent Colony had been taught that planet dwellers lived on the surface. Curious now he started back down the ladders. As he continued down, his belly rumbled letting him know that he needed to put something into it soon. Another few levels down and the scent of something sweet tickled his nose. Pausing in his climb, he went through the inner door to explore this level of the storage facility. His nose was right. It contained foodstuffs. Dried fruits and vegetables mostly, but he caught the scent of honey, and it made him start to salivate.

The first few stacks he found were mostly dried insects, fine for snacking on and as a protein supplement. He grabbed a few of the smaller containers to stash in the pockets of his ship suit, but he needed something more substantial to fill his empty belly. Further in he found honeycomb, the beeswax still sealed meaning there was honey in the little compartments, several kilotons of it, all sorted in individual little boxes. Beyond that, honeyed dates—each in its own little wrapping—and next to that, nectar in small beeswax sealed tubes. Further down the row of stacks, he came across carrots and potatoes packed in dirt. When he brushed a carrot off, he found it was starting to grow roots. so it had been there a while, but when he bit into the carrot he found it was still fresh and good.

Now with his nutritional needs taken care of, what he needed was a good source of water. That turned out to be trickier than he expected. Apparently on a planet, water was free and abundant so hybrids didn't see a need to keep containers of it on hand. He found bales of nip, containers of fermented mash, and beetles soaked in maple syrup. All of which, along with the honey, nectar, and other sweets, were illegal on most planets. Too much of it would permanently damage an individual's brain, something that was considered grounds for termination. Anything that altered a hybrid's brain chemistry as drastically as too much sugar had been outlawed on the Galactic Alliance worlds. Another reason Tony was glad he grew up on the Independent Colony.

The only water he found was in the tanks of impounded vehicles. He didn't want to chance drinking that just from the scent. It had to have been in there quite a while as it gave off a musty scent that made the raccoon's stomach churn. That left him only one option.

He continued his climb down through the airlock pods. He was beginning to think his internal spatial awareness was off, so he glanced at his mapping program. The read out said he'd climbed down nearly 150 meters vertically. This storage facility seemed to go on forever.

Finally he came to the lowest airlock and adjacent storage container. The outer door had the correct opening mechanism and wasn't sealed in any way that he could see. Of course he didn't have the access code, but that was easily dealt with.

It took him about ten cens to crack the code that opened the door using the new data pad and connectors. A space walk compared to the programs he'd learned to crack in the crèche. He left a tracer in the system so that he could get any new codes faster, then cautiously opened the door.

He looked out on an empty corridor. It was made of the same material that he was used to on the ship, with overhead reddish-orange lighting that came on as you walked and turned off behind you. Tucking the data pad and connectors into his pockets, he started down the corridor. It branched several times, but his nose told him the branching corridors were all as disused as the one he was walking down. So he picked a direction that had a slightly fresher scent to it and continued forward.

Ahead he saw a brighter light, more yellow in hue, and slowed his pace. He crept forward to find himself on a wide roadway that continued to either side of him. Across from the corridor's opening, he saw guardrailing, the same kind that was used on the ship to keep hybrids from falling off high walkways. Beyond the roadway was empty space with lighting all over the ceiling. He crossed the road and looked down, leaning on the guardrailing.

What he saw below him was wondrous. Pillars fully forty meters in diameter reached from the ceiling down so far that it was dizzying. The pillars were so numerous that Tony couldn't count them all. Arching between them were bridges that supported roadways ten meters wide, though the ones farther down looked smaller due to distance.

Each of the bridges came together with the surrounding bridges in centralized hubs that were overgrown with vegetation—tall trees, smaller bushes lining the edges of the platforms, even vines and roots spilling over the sides. In the center of the platforms what looked like water was contained in large basins—something that would never have occurred on the Independent Colony. There was too much danger of losing the precious liquid if the outer hull were to breach.

The major levels each had two roadways that spiraled down around opposite sides of the pillars to the next level. There were smaller walkways around the pillars, about every five meters horizontally, each with its own railing. These walkways were lined with doors of various sizes, some that had ladders leading up to them. He assumed these were individual nests that were sized for the inhabitants.

Long vehicles, that Tony could only describe as smaller transport pods connected together, zoomed through tunnels in the pillars and along the larger roadways seemingly at random.

All this was just background though. What amazed Tony the most was the hybrids.

The roadways and walkways were teeming with them. So many species that he couldn't name them all. Bustling about, moving from one pillar to the next. Riding in the transport pods. Driving ground vehicles, even carrying other hybrids. Groups of kits being ushered here and there by worried looking adults. Hybrids selling small items of interest and various foodstuffs. Hybrids just sitting along the sides of the roadways talking with each other. The sights, scents, and sounds of that many hybrids in one location were staggering.

Tony and everyone he knew had always assumed that the spaceports and their connected above-ground cities were the main habitations for planet dwellers. That they actually lived underground like this was a revelation Tony couldn't wait to share with his friends.

That thought brought him back to the reality of his situation.

If he could reach one of those platforms, he could bring some water back. Of course he'd have to find some containers first. He felt inside his inner pocket for the rest of his personal credits, and his fingers found the galactic card he'd been given to buy things for the ship and crew. Pulling it out he considered the dangers involved in using it. If he acted quickly he might be able to make a large withdrawal before the card was flagged by the Port Authorities. Each of the pillars seemed to have a grouping of commerce outlets around the mouth of the tunnels. The nearest bridge to him was about twenty meters to his left. The thought was the deed; before he could change his mind he hurried toward the bridge.

When he reached the platform in the center of the bridges, he looked down over the edge. There was a pattern to these platforms. They were set up so that there was one for every four of the major roadways directly under him. But two major roadways down to either side, there were others that connected to different pillars. That meant about twenty meters between platforms. He could see, several deseci below, platforms under the ones closest to him. Tony's eyes widened as he realized how many meters down these pillars went. This city ran deeper than the central core of the *Black Hole*.

As he got closer to the pool in the center of this platform, he noticed several hybrids watching him curiously. Looking at himself he realized why. His ship suit, while practical on the ship, seemed out of place when he compared it to what the average hybrid here was wearing.

His red ship suit had short legs and sleeves but covered most of his torso, while the majority of those around him wore clothing that nearly covered their whole bodies—shirts in bright colors with ruffles down the front of the chest and long sleeves that trailed on the ground when they held their arms at their sides; skirts and pants of more subdued hues that clung to the legs like sheaths but also had an over skirt of diaphanous billowing fabric that was translucent and swirled about them when they walked. Even the kits where fully clothed. They wore tunics that came down to their ankles covered in bright patches of color that approximated some of the floral patterns in the greenery he could see.

He would have to find suitable clothing along with containers if he was going to be forced to venture out for water. Well, first things first, find a credit machine. Tony slowly circled the pool, checking down each of the bridges until he found a commerce center. Showing more confidence than he felt, he moved purposefully in that direction.

He was looking for a credit machine when he realized that he was going to need something to carry the credit chits. Some of the kits closer to his age had satchels over one shoulder that seemed to be meant for carrying large objects.

When he found the machine, there were two hybrids ahead of him, so he looked around while he waited. There was a boy about his age watching him. He was a cougar or a mountain lion. He had tawny fur and the bluest eyes Tony had ever seen. He too was dressed differently than the other hybrids on this level. He had on a simple modesty cloth and carried one of the satchels over his right shoulder so the bag rested against his left hip. He wasn't wearing much jewelry, as a kit on the ship would, but he was wearing what looked like a chrono on his right wrist. The more Tony compared him to those about him, the more he noticed what was different about him. He walked like he carried the weight of the planet on his shoulders, stooped over slightly. Honestly he looked as out of place as Tony felt.

Tony looked away so as not to appear rude and realized it was his turn at the machine. Taking a deep breath, he slid his card into the reader, bracing himself for some kind of alarm that would alert the authorities to his whereabouts.

All that happened was a blue screen that asked him to verify he was authorized to use the card. It was rather anticlimactic. He input the correct code and withdrew five hundred credits. Five bright yellow chits fell in the small cup on the machine, and it bid him a good day.

Tony hastily collected his chits, tucking them and the card into an inner pocket of his ship suit. There was a clothier a few meters from his current position, so he headed there first. A few cens later, he was the proud owner of a modesty cloth and a satchel; however he was also some three hundred credits poorer. Things were expensive here.

His next stop was a general merchandise shop where he found two clear containers with lids, suitable for holding water. Another fifty credits lighter, he decided to try his luck at the credit machine again. This time when he put the card into the reader, the screen flashed red and a loud siren went off nearly deafening him. It startled him so much that he just stood there staring at the machine.

Someone grabbed his left arm and pulled on it. He reacted by trying to shake free of the unwanted touch, assuming it was someone trying to take him back to the surface and Port Authority.

"Come on! The Peacekeepers will be here any cen now! If we don't get moving they are going to catch us!" The voice was deep and rich like golden honey to Tony's ears, even under the blaring siren. He twisted around to come muzzle to muzzle with the tawny furred boy who had been watching him before.

He stopped resisting the pull on his arm, allowing the other boy to lead him through the gathering crowd into the center of the pillar. He expected them to run, but they didn't. The cougar, definitely a cougar now that Tony had a chance to smell him up close, dropped his arm as they hurried toward one of those transport pod things. They got in, the boy dropping some credit chits into a slot, and found seats together amid the press of bodies.

It was impossible to talk without being overheard with hybrids pressed around them, so Tony held his questions for now. The pod moved at quite a clip, passing through several of the pillars in just cens. A mechanical voice announced, "Level two, New'ork tower." A few mil later, they stopped, and a bunch of hybrids left only to be replaced by a few more. This happened several times before Tony realized they were heading down lower into the city. The level number kept changing, but the same six towers kept repeating, meaning they were going down in a spiral pattern.

Fewer and fewer hybrids were getting on, so the pod they were in started to empty out. By the time they reached level seven, they were the only hybrids left in the pod. Once the pod door slid closed on the platform where the last rider left, Tony turned to his rescuer. "Why are you helping me?"

"Shhhhh!" The cougar lifted his paw vaguely gesturing over his right shoulder. Tony was confused at first, but then his eyes spotted the small recording device in the upper corner of the pod. A quick, yet careful, glance around showed three more recorders in the other upper corners. Tony frowned, his ears folding back against his head, but decided to wait until they got wherever they were going to ask his questions. A few levels lower the cougar got up and moved toward the doors. Tony followed his lead since the only other option was to stay in the pod.

They walked out of the pillar into another commerce center, but this one was very different than the one on the upper level. It was darker here and much warmer, but the real difference was in the hybrids. They were all dressed like the cougar, wearing little more than modesty cloths and carrying the same satchels, though theirs were not as well cared for. They walked like they were tired, shoulders slumped, heads hanging down slightly. All the little things that made the cougar look out of place above made him fit in perfectly here. There were markedly fewer hybrids on this level, at least fewer visible hybrids. Those few that Tony could see all had the same disheveled look of the fighter pilots and gunners on his ship the *Dark Matter*. In that way his silent companion was different; his fur and clothing were neat and clean.

Tony was lead through the commerce area out onto a central platform. The greenery here was less vibrant, the water looked sort of murky, and he could see small shapes moving below the surface. The whole place felt grimy, like it hadn't been clean in a long time.

The cougar's tail was loosely hanging, the black tip curled up so it didn't drag on the floor, showing he was as comfortable here as he had been when Tony first glimpsed him on the upper level. Tony had to force his tail to relax out of the bristled brush that showed his agitation. They passed over the central platform and went to the right, down a connecting bridge heading toward another of the pillars that his guide called towers. Tony expected to enter the main opening on this pillar, but his companion led him around the pillar about a quarter of the way, then ducked through a small opening. When Tony hesitated, the cougar's face and paw appeared in the gloomy opening, beckoning him to enter. Looking around Tony realized that if he stood where he was, the denizens of this place would find him interesting, and he didn't like that idea in the least. He swallowed hard and followed the helpful stranger into the small opening.

Tony was pleasantly surprised when the gloomy entryway opened up into a more comfortably sized den area. Once they were both inside the den, the cougar turned and punched a code into a small data pad that closed a door Tony hadn't noticed on the way in; it blended perfectly into the building material that surrounded it.

"Okay, we can talk now." That deep liquid voice purred, sending shivers down Tony's back and making his tail quiver. "I'm Andrew, but everyone calls me Andy. What were you doing on level one with a stolen card?"

Tony blinked in confusion, then shook his head in denial. "It's not stolen. I have the code for it. It's just.." He hesitated to tell the cougar, Andy, about being wanted by the Port Authority.

"You're in trouble with one of the branches of the Peacekeepers, right?"

Tony's striped tail lashed nervously. "How do you know that?"

"I saw your image on the news feed while we were coming down here." Andy flashed a grin. "Besides that's not a very good fake Galactic Ident. It looks like an ordinary wrist unit, and it's on the wrong wrist." He pointed at the chrono on Tony's left wrist.

The smile made Tony's stomach flutter and his muscles tighten. He'd never had this kind of reaction to anyone before. It was distracting. "Galactic Ident?" He glanced at what he'd assumed was just another form of chrono on the Cougar's right wrist and realized it had a different kind of interface.

Andy nodded. "Every citizen of the Galactic Alliance has one. Since you don't, I'm assuming you're a cull like me." He said it so blandly that Tony almost didn't believe his ears.

"Did you just say you're a cull?" The thought that someone who'd been culled could be standing there talking to him was so horrifying to Tony that he took an involuntary step backward.

A frown settled over Andy's face, and he hissed the next words. "You got something against that?" The fur on the back of his neck lifted, and his tail puffed out to twice its normal size.

Tony lifted his paws, palms out, and backed up a few more steps until the back of his lower legs came up against something hard. "I.. I've just never met anyone who's been culled." He tried to get his ears to lift from his head so he didn't look so submissive. "I mean where I come from, it's an honor to give yourself for the good of the Colony."

"Honor!" Andy sneered. "Don't make me laugh. The government must have really brainwashed you good." His fur relaxed a little, but his tail kept lashing in agitation.

Tony frowned. "The council doesn't brainwash any of us. They are very straightforward with the needs of the Colony and how the average person can best benefit the Colony as a whole." When Andy looked skeptical, Tony went on. "The only dealings we have with the Galactic Government are when we make supply runs like the one I was on before I got stranded here."

Now it was Andy's turn to frown thoughtfully. "You don't deal with the Galactic Government? Everyone deals with the GG; that's why it's called the Galactic Government and not the Planetary Government. The only way you could avoid that is if you came from somewhere outside the settled planets." The cougar's eyes widened. "Wait are you from the stolen Colony ship?"

Tony hissed, "It wasn't stolen, it was liberated." Now his tail was lashing, and his eyes narrowed in anger.

"Woah, calm down. I didn't mean anything by that. It's just what we've been taught." Now Andy's paws were held out, palms toward Tony.

The turn about was too much for Tony. His anger melted away, and he started to laugh. Andy's ears folded to the sides ruefully. When Tony finally managed to stop laughing he said, "I know, let's start over. I'm Anthony, but everyone calls me Tony. Thank you for helping me get away from the Peacekeepers." He folded his right arm over his stomach and tucked his left behind his back, then bent at the waist while keeping his eyes on Andy in a traditional first meeting gesture.

Andy tilted his head to the side, a curious look on his face. "We shake paws." He held out his right paw waiting expectantly.

Tony hesitantly put his paw in the cougar's. When Andy's paw closed around his, warmth suffused his body. Confused, he lowered his eyes trying to hide his reaction to the other boy.

"Ah, yeah." Andy broke the silence. "Why are you running from the Peacekeepers?" He moved to sit on one of the cushions that littered the floor. He made a broad gesture that indicated a few more of the cushions.

Tony took that to mean he could also sit down, but he didn't see a chair in the whole room. A little awkwardly he settled himself onto one of the cushions. "They were after my ship, but since it got away, they want me. I am guessing they think that I will give up the coordinates of the Independent Colony." He shrugged. "Doesn't matter what they want. I don't have the coords and I wouldn't give them away if I did." Tony stifled a sudden yawn. It had been a long and tiring day for him. He'd lost not only his job but his home, friends, and family all in a flash. Found himself hunted by the Peacekeepers and Port Authority alike. Discovered that there were a lot more planet-bound hybrids than he'd ever thought possible and been found and rescued by this strange cougar boy. It was almost more than he could process.

Andy noticed the raccoon's flagging attention. "I'm an idiot! Here I've been picking your brain when you must be exhausted. Have you eaten at all today?" He turned to rummage around on a shelf behind the cushion he was sitting on. "I have some protein substitute, but not much in the way of vegetation, I'm afraid. I don't know what raccoons eat." When he turned back Tony was blinking as if he were fighting sleep. "Here you can curl up in my nest." He stood up and helped the sleepy boy to his feet, then got him settled for the night.

***

Tony woke slowly. He'd been having a terrible dream where he was separated from the ship and stranded on a planet. He checked his chrono in the darkened room and sighed. It was almost time to get up and start his day. He listened for the comforting sound of Justin's snoring, but it wasn't there. That was odd. He always had to shake the badger boy awake. He started his usual stretches, pushing his paws up out of the blankets, only to hit a wall that shouldn't be there. With a yelp of surprise he sat bolt upright, trying to make out details in the dark room.

"S'wrong?" a sleepy voice asked as the warmth beside him, what he had assumed was part of the blankets, stretched out into the cougar boy, Andy. Despair washed over him as he realized it hadn't been a dream after all. He fell back into the nest trying not to let the tears that were welling up in his eyes fall. "Tony?" The concern in Andy's voice was the raccoon's undoing. He turned his face into the blankets, starting to sob uncontrollably.

"Tony, it's alright. I promise it's going to be alright." Andy pulled Tony into his arms. Tony struggled, not used to the physical contact, but Andy was stronger and he wouldn't let go. Tony finally settled his face against the cougar's shoulder and gave into the despair. Andy started purring soothingly, petting the back of Tony's head as he remembered his mother doing when he was a kitten.

It took a while for Tony's well of tears to run dry, but Andy never let him go, providing the reassurance he needed. When his tears were drying in his facial fur and Andy's shoulder fur, he stayed in the warmth of Andy's arms not sure why he felt so safe there. "Sorry. I'm usually not this emotional."

Andy nodded slightly. "Your world just fell apart. You're allowed to breakdown. What matters is what you decide to do now."

Tony shifted so he could see Andy's face. "What do you mean?"

"When I found out I was culled, I had a similar reaction. But when I was finished crying, I made up my mind that I wasn't going to let that be the end. I decided to fight the system and live my own way." He shrugged.

"I figure you have the same choice. You can either give into the despair you are feeling, or you can decide to fight for what you want."

Tony pulled away from Andy and sat up. "You're right. I still have the pieces of my long range comm unit. I bet I can find some way to fix it and get in touch with the ship."

"That's the spirit!" Andy stretched languidly as only a cat could, each and every muscle getting the same attention. When he was finished, he rolled over Tony to get out of the nest. "First course of action is food. I don't know about you, but I am starving." Tony realized the cougar was naked. This wasn't unheard of; after all they were covered in fur. Still there was a feeling of intimacy that he hadn't experienced since he was a kit sharing a nest with his litter mates.

"I don't know what raccoons eat, but I have some protein substitute on hand. If that doesn't work, we'll have to go out to find something."

Tony grinned. "Chef would have your hide for eating that junk, but it'll work for now." He accepted the piece that Andy handed him. It looked like dried out meat but was actually a combination of beans, fungus, and a binding agent. It was mostly used as emergency rations for the predators on the Independent Colony's ships.

"Chef?" Andy's ears perked as he settled onto one of the cushions.

Tony settled onto one opposite him. "Chef was the head of the Galley. He always took care of us young ones, made sure we ate properly, kept us from getting into too much trouble."

"Sounds like a nice fellow." They fell into silence while they ate what Tony knew as First Meal. Protein substitute was tough and dry, but it did meet the minimum dietary requirements. "Do you have anything to drink?" Tony finally broke the silence to ask.

"Oh, sorry, I should have offered sooner." Andy turned and pulled a container from one of the shelves behind him, offering it to Tony. "Here, it's nutribev. Tastes better warm, but it's not half bad cold like this." Tony took a hesitant sip and let the liquid rest on his tongue for a few mil. It had a nutty flavor that tasted bitter to Tony, but then he was used to stimbev which had a sweeter more fruity flavor. He wrinkled his nose but took a longer drink allowing the liquid to moisten his mouth and throat.

"Don't you have nutribev where you come from?"

Tony made another face. "Not to my knowledge. I'm used to stimbev." He passed the container back to Andy.

Andy changed the subject. "I've been thinking, the only thing that really identifies you as different from raccoons here is the things in your fur." He indicated the beads and small bits of metal braided into Tony's head and tail fur. "If you took those out, you could pass as a native."

Tony's first reaction was shock that Andy would suggest such a thing, but then he realized the cougar didn't know what all his items meant. "If I did that, no one would be able to recognize who I am and where I'm from." He wasn't sure someone not raised in the Independent Colony could understand how important that was.

"That's kind of the point. As long as you wear that stuff, the Peacekeepers are going to be able to pick you out of a crowd."

"You don't understand. The things in my fur, they all have personal significance. Like this little circle, it was given to me by my mother. It represents my family's crest. This one shows which crèche I came from. This is my ship affiliation. I could go on and on. Every piece is a part of my experience, part of my past." He fondly rubbed the last green bead Chef had given him. "They remind me of the hybrids who care for me."

Andy held his paws up, palms toward Tony. "Hold on, I'm not saying you get rid of them. I'm just saying you should take them out of your fur. I think I have a keepsake box around here some place that you can use to put them in." He paused tilting his head slightly. "If you want to go out without getting caught that is."

Tony weighed his options then nodded. "You have a good point." He fingered one of his oldest pendants and frowned. "I might need some help though. Some of these aren't going to come out without a fight."

As they worked to take the beads, pendants, and other baubles out of Tony's fur, Andy laid out their current situation. "I have about enough food for another day. I will have a few more credits after I do my delivery runs for midday meal and later at day's end. But I don't think it'll be enough to support the two of us. I can barely manage to support myself most tendays."

"If you don't mind mostly dry-stored or frozen stuff, I know where we can get more food. Also electronic parts for my comm unit." Tony winced as Andy worked a particularly stubborn bead loose from his head fur.

"How is that possible? You've only been here a day." Andy took a mil to pull a clump of gray fur off the bead then dropped it into the keepsake box.

Tony shrugged. "In order to get away, I hitched a ride on the goods they seized from the ship. They took the whole lot to a storehouse. I found a way out, but I left a tracer program buried in the circuitry, so I can get back in if I want to."

Andy stared down at the back of Tony's head for a mil. "You know how to get around the locking codes?" There was a touch of awe in his voice.

Tony shrugged once more. "Every kit in the Independent Colony can do that. It's one of the basic skills we are taught in the crèche." Tony's fingers ran over the bead that Justin had braided into his tail, a bright red one, his first trainer bead.

Andy pulled the last of the beads out of Tony's head fur and set it into the box, which was rather full now. "You have the right clothing to pass for a messenger or a delivery kit. Do you think you could show me where this storehouse is?" He picked up a small metal mirror from one of the numerous shelves that lined the walls of his little den and passed it to Tony.

"Yeah, sure." Tony paused as he looked into the mirror. "I look so different, like I'm someone else altogether."

"That's the point." Andy picked up his modesty cloth and started getting ready to go out. "You'll want to empty your satchel out, so we have more room for foodstuff on the way back."

Tony hesitated. He didn't like leaving his things behind. After all he'd only met Andy the day before. As he watched the cougar feed his tail through the hole in the back of his cloth, he made up his mind that he'd trust Andy, at least for now.

***

They started where they first met, back on level one. As they got off the train, Tony inwardly cringed, afraid that someone would recognize him from the vid feed. His fears were unfounded. Without his beads, he looked just like any of the other older kits rushing about here and there on this level. This time he took the lead. He headed up the bridge toward the central platform with Andy close behind him. The bridge he remembered didn't seem to have any traffic on it which was a little odd since all the other bridges were buzzing with activity.

"Tony, are you sure this is the way you came in?" Andy sounded a little concerned, his tail tip flicking rapidly back and forth.

Tony paused to look around then nodded firmly. "Yes. There is a kind of road on the other side, and about twenty meters to the right from the bridge, there is the corridor I came out of."

Andy still seemed a little nervous, but he followed Tony onto the bridge. When no one challenged them, Andy seemed to relax a little. They crossed with no trouble, found the corridor Tony remembered, and started into the tower.

"Only your tracks in the dust, that's good. Means no one else has been in here since you left." They followed Tony's tracks past the side corridors, all the way to the airlock door. Andy ran a paw over the frame while Tony input the code to open the door. "I haven't seen a piece of the old Maker Colony ship in person before, only on training vids used in the crèche."

"I lived in one of the colonization ships, so this is all familiar to me." The door opened, and Tony motioned for Andy to enter first.

"You're sure you can get us out again?" Andy asked in a hushed almost reverent tone as he peered into the airlock pod.

"Of course, I wouldn't go back in if I couldn't get out." With this reassurance Andy stepped onto the ancient floor, staring around himself with wonder. Tony followed and locked the door behind them. The raccoon started up the ladders, heading for the level where he remembered the dry food was stored.

Andy had his nose pressed against the glass that looked into the cold and frozen storage. "Wow that's a lot of food in there."

"I think it's all stuff that was confiscated, like the things they took from my ship," Tony called back down the ladder. Andy took one last look through the window, then followed Tony up the ladder.

When they entered the level that held the dry storage, Andy's nose twitched and his eyes widened. "Honey? Nectar? Creators' blessing, even maple syrup. This stuff must be worth a fortune!"

Tony canted his head, looking at Andy thoughtfully. "I don't suppose you'd know anyone who'd be willing to buy it would you?" His nose twitched as he scented a possible credit making venture. "It wouldn't be too hard to carry some of this stuff back down to your level."

Andy looked dubious, his eyes narrowing and his ears flattening against his head. "I don't know about that. Right now the only reason that I am avoiding the Peacekeepers is because of some stupid arbitrary garbage about my parentage. I don't want to get into something that's so blatantly destructive."

"Andy, what do you know about the effects of sugar?" Tony kept his voice calm and level, patterning it after the teaching programs that were used in primary crèches.

Andy reacted as the raccoon expected with an almost programmed response. "Sugar is in all nutrients. It's a part of our normal dietary requirements. However, sugar in it's raw unfiltered form is dangerous, especially in large doses. It causes the neurons in the brain to fire faster than normal which can lead to a stroke. It makes the heart pump faster which can lead to failure over a prolonged period of time. It causes an overabundance of energy storage in the body as a whole which translates into excess fat that has several detrimental health effects."

Tony nodded slowly. "That sounds like the official line directly from the GG if you ask me. Have you ever seen any of these so-called detrimental health effects? Do you know what they look like?" He canted his head slightly as he waited to see if Andy would use his brain or just keep holding onto his preprogrammed response.

For a moment Andy stood there with his mouth open, his eyes confused, and his ears folding back against his head. When he finally spoke it was in a sheepishly soft voice. "Okay, I don't really know what the effects are, just what I've been told." He sighed softly then asked, "I am guessing that you have a better school environment than we do, don't you?"

Tony shrugged. "It's different is all. We're taught at a young age to enjoy learning for the sake of learning, then encouraged to follow our curiosity."

"I looked into the effects of sugar on the average hybrid. It affects each species differently: Carns are hit the hardest; they can become addicted to the rush it gives them, but unless they are consuming large quantities every day those effects you mentioned are negligible."

Andy's ears perked up. "You mean it isn't deadly?"

"I didn't say that, but in order to have the kind of lasting effect that your government is suggesting, you'd have to consume more than 25 grams of sugar daily for cycles at a time." He picked up one of the honeyed dates. "These contain less than one gram of sugar each. The honey comb is portioned to a single gram in each container. Same for the nectar and the maple syrup. Can you really see any one hybrid finishing twenty-five or more of these individually wrapped sweets a day?"

Andy shook his head. "No, I suppose not."

Tony canted his head, perking his ears inquisitively and waited.

Andy sighed, nodding slowly. "You make a good point. I guess if that's the case, it wont bother me if we sell some of this stuff." He held up a paw with one finger pointing toward the raccoon. "But you have to promise me, we don't sell more than a few pieces to each individual."

Tony nodded, his whiskers splaying and arching forward. "Agreed!" He extended his paw in the traditional gesture to conclude a bargain. For a moment Andy just looked at his paw as if he was considering a deal with a CEO. But it only took a few mil before he grudgingly shook paws, sealing their agreement.

"Okay then as I see it the only problem left is how to get it down to the lower levels." Tony glanced around the stacks of illegal sweets, considering how much of each he and the cougar boy could manage to carry down without being obvious about it.

"Oh, that's easy." Andy chuckled. "This tower has a lift that runs from level one all the way down to level ten."

"How do you know that? You didn't seem to want to come here." Tony went to the crates of carrots and pulled one out to nibble on while they talked.

"I keep forgetting you aren't from here." Now it was Andy's turn to teach the raccoon something, "Every crèche kit knows that this is the Power

Tower. It leads to the surface where they collect wind and solar power, which is transferred to the surrounding five towers by conduits on the underside of the bridges." Andy ran his fingertips over a line of individually packaged honeyed dates. "Sorry, I probably sound like a training vid."

Tony shook his head. "Nope, I could listen to you all day." He blushed. "I mean, you sound good to me." Tony realized that didn't sound much better and hastily changed the subject. "So this lift, it runs down the core of the tower?"

Andy didn't seem to notice Tony's awkwardness. "Yep, the one in this tower is likely inside the storage complex. If you could bypass the security vid recorder, we could just move the stuff from this level all the way down to nine.

"Let's go see if your genius brain can get us past the security so we can take the lift down."

Tony rolled his eyes and shook his head. "I told you it's nothing. All the kits in the Independent Colony can do it." They found the lift that Tony was originally brought down on, where Andy thought he remembered the one that lead to the bottom should be.

The outside had a data pad that looked like it used paw print recognition. "Well, that will be a little harder, but I can still crack it." Tony pulled the cover off and hooked a cable from his pad into the port that was revealed. "While I'm working on this, you could move a crate of each of the individually wrapped sweets. Those will be easiest to sell." He settled into a cross-legged position on the floor and started sorting through the security protocols, looking for a way in. Andy followed Tony's suggestion and pile up crates against the wall in anticipation of having access to the lift.

A quarter chron later, Tony looked up as the door to the lift slid open. "There, the recorder is off, so we should be safe enough using it." They loaded the collection of merchandise onto the lift and pressed the button to take them down to the ninth level.

They were a little surprised to find that level nine seemed to be in use by some of the denizens of the depths. There were signs of habitation along the corridors: blankets, other assorted pieces of cloth, and packing crates filled with miscellaneous personal items.

Both of their heads whipped around as they heard a piercing scream down the corridor further into the tower. Tony's ears swiveled toward the sound, and his body followed. "Wait!" Andy put his arm out to block the shorter boy's attempt to seek out the source of the scream. "It's not a good idea to go looking for trouble down here." His tail tip flicked in agitation, and his ears folded tight against his head.

"How can you say that, Andy?" Tony looked at the cougar in confusion. "It sounds like a child. How can you just leave them to whatever is tormenting them? Maybe all they need is someone to stand up for them?" He remembered the kits on the ship and how by working together they managed to rescue another kit who needed their help. "I won't try to make you come with me, but I am going to find out what's going on and see if I can't find a way to help them." He moved around Andy's outstretched arm, purposefully walking down the corridor toward the sound.

Tony had just rounded a corner to see two adult males, one of them an elephant, the other a hyena, closing in on a group of three kittens. The felines looked to be from the same litter; all three had the same medium length gray fur with white markings around the eyes. They were terrified, huddling together and hissing at their tormentors. Every time one of the adults tried to reach for them, the kittens hissed and spit, claws raking over the extended appendages and teeth sinking into exposed flesh. Which explained where the screams were coming from.

Tony was about to charge toward the scene when he felt a paw on his shoulder. "We need a plan," Andy whispered. "Those are Dionysus' guys. I know the elephant. He has a soft spot for kits. Maybe if we talk to him, he'll let them go."

"What about the hyena?" Tony peeked around the corner to see the hyena advancing on the kittens with his arms spread wide.

"We'll have to chance that he'll go along with Jandar," Andy said as one of the kittens hissed again. "We're as ready as we're going to get." The two boys stepped around the corner and walked purposefully toward the disruption.

"Hey guys." Andy called out, "What's going on?"

"Andy!" the elephant called back. "What are you doing here?" He was keeping the kittens from leaving, while the hyena tried to catch them by the scruff of the neck.

"I saw you come down this way and thought I'd say hello." He glanced at the cornered kittens. "What's going on?"

"Dionysus says he has a buyer waiting on some young ones." Jandar indicated the kittens with his left paw. "Just wish there was some easier way to catch them."

Andy nodded. "Maybe you need to get into a different line of work." He wandered closer, pretending to examine the kittens. "Not sure these ones are worth the effort. Too scrawny and way to much fight still in them."

"Jandar, what are you doing talking to this kit? You know Dionysus will have your hide if you don't bring these little snots in." The hyena spoke up for the first time.

Jandar glanced at his associate then shrugged. "Kit has a point. I don't like catching little ones for Dionysus."

"What kind of hold does Dionysus have over you anyway Jandar?" Andy's ears perked up, and he canted his head slightly to the left.

Jandar shrugged his broad shoulders. "Nothing much. It's just hard for a guy like me to find good paying work down this far. You know how that is."

Andy nodded slowly. "Oh I understand. Most tendays I just barely manage to feed myself." He paused to consider for a mil then added, "It'd be kind of cool if you could set up a more efficient delivery service. You could pay the runners more than just crumbs. That way everyone would win."

"And you could hire more runners," Tony put in, indicating the kittens.

"Yeah?" Jandar seemed to consider the problem for a few mil. "Alright, I think it's time I switched jobs anyway." He backed away from the confused kittens.

"You fool! Dionysus is not going to like this when I tell him." The hyena started past Jandar, obviously planning to head right to his boss. The elephant shook his head sadly, reached out, and with a closed paw, delivered a heavy blow to the top of the hyena's head. He dropped like a stone.

Jandar frowned down at his erstwhile coworker. "He's going to be a problem." He scratched behind his left ear with the end of his trunk.

Andy walked over to examine the hyena. "Sure is. We're going to have to figure out something to do with him."

Tony followed the cougar and quietly told the kittens, "We're going to get you out of here, alright?" They nodded solemnly, their identical green eyes wide and frightened, but one took his outstretched paw while the other two wrapped their paws in his tail fur.

Jandar leaned down and picked up the unfortunate hyena. "Don't worry, he won't make it back to Dionysus, I'll see to that. Thanks for the talk, Andy. See you around sometime." He shifted the hyena's weight on his shoulder and headed out of the tower without a backward glance.

The kittens were about to run when Tony sat down on the floor and pulled out some of the dried meat he and Andy had brought down with them. "Are you hungry?" They nodded nearly in unison. "Well you can have some of our food. But while you eat, I'd like to hear why you are alone down here."

Andy rolled his eyes but took a seat beside Tony. The kittens put their heads together and whispered, one of them looking over to see if Tony or Andy had moved. After a few mil they seemed to come to some agreement. Cautiously they settled on the floor close, but not too close.

Tony gave them each a piece of the meat, which they snatched out of his paw and proceeded to gobble up faster than was safe. "Hey, slow down, you're going to make yourselves sick." Now that they weren't in a desperate situation, Tony could tell that one was a male while the other two were females. They were covered in grime, and their fur was dull and oily, a sure sign of malnutrition.

The kittens were silent, even when they had finished the meat. "Can you at least tell us your names?" the raccoons coaxed, reaching into his satchel for more of the dried meat.

The one on the right, one of the females, looked at the other two and then said in the softest of whispers, "I'm Nessa, that's Nechtan, and she's Niobe."

Tony passed them another piece of meat each. "Litter mates?" Nessa nodded. "What are you doing down here away from the safety of your crèche?"

They were all silent, slowly chewing their food while watching Tony. It was Andy who answered him. "Saw them on the news feed, they were culled. But on the way to the facility, their transport pod broke down. When the Peacekeepers got there, the kittens were missing." He leaned in and whispered in Tony's ear, "There is a big reward for turning them in."

"No!" was Tony's firm answer. "We didn't save them just to see them killed."

"So why did we save them at all?" Andy seemed confused.

"Do they look like they have physical abnormalities? If they don't have mental deficiencies or psychological issues, they could be just like you." Tony made a point of meeting Andy's eyes. "Culled for nothing more than having the wrong parents."

"Sure, but how is that our problem?"

"Andy, are you telling me you could really leave these kittens to the mercy of the system?" Tony was aghast that Andy could possibly have that little compassion. "We have to do something; if we don't who will?"

***

The alert Tony had set up on their network to let them know when they had a new buyer dinged. "Looks like we have a new customer. Feel like a little jaunt?"

Andy frowned slightly, his tail tip flicking quickly. "I don't like these clandestine meetings, Tony. You said we were just going to do this until we had a nest egg. Haven't we got enough credits now to stop?" He folded his arms across his slender chest, his right footpad tapping the floor.

Tony sighed and turned the motorized bucket seat he was reclined in to face Andy. "We still have a half kilogram of the honeyed dates to offload. Once we get rid of those, we can quit if you like."

"I like," Andy declaimed. "I never wanted to get into this business in the first place."

Tony turned back to his vid screen, "This guy just asked for a kilo of stock. We haven't got that much, but I think we can offload the last of our stock if that makes you happy." He glanced over his shoulder with a slight smile on his lips.

Andy's eyes widened, and his ears perked forward. "Y-you mean it? We can really get out of this? Today?" He took a step toward the raccoon, his tail doing happy loops behind his back. "If you're serious, I'm in!" The cougar leaned in toward Tony, his eyes only millimeters from the raccoon's. For a mil Tony thought he was going to... going to... Andy pointed to something on the vid. "Is this the location? Seems alright, it's on the concourse of level nine between the Power Tower and New'ork Tower." The observation jerked Tony's attention back to the screen.

"Ah." It took a mil for his brain to switch gears. "Yeah, that's what I thought." He zoomed in on the location and pointed out several possible escape routes. "I figure if it goes out the airlock, we can always slip down one of these side roads and lose ourselves in the service tunnels under the bridge."

***

"Do you boys have any idea how much trouble you're in?" the white mouse asked as he drummed his fingers under his chin. "You've been encroaching on my territory for the last week. Did you think I wouldn't notice?" Dionysus asked in a deceptively calm voice.

Tony stole a glance at Andy, but the cougar boy seemed as nervous as he was. "No, I just thought it'd take you longer to catch on," the raccoon stated brazenly.

This got him a disapproving flick of the ears from the mouse. "I don't know where you're from boy, but in this city there is a system through which all... transactions of a sensitive nature pass. You've gone outside that system. There are consequences for going outside the system." The two female lions framing the mouse showed their teeth in an unmistakable threat.

Tony held up a single paw. "Hold on a mil. What if we cut you in on the profits?"

"Tony!" Andy hissed, shaking his head vehemently.

The mouse's ears perked up and swiveled forward. "It seems you partner doesn't think that's a good idea, little raccoon."

Tony scowled at the mouse. "Well if you *don't* want part of our take, what *do* you want?" His tail lashed in agitation, brushing against Andy's.

The mouse smiled, showing his teeth. "To make an example of you." His ears flickered to the sides and back, as he licked his teeth. "Get 'em ladies!" The two goons on either side of the mouse exchanged a nasty looking grin that showed all of their very pointed teeth.

As one the two boys turned and bolted for the side road closest to their current position. "After them!" Dionysus yelled as he put the scooter he was sitting on into forward motion. "Don't let them get away!" Hissing something nasty, the two goons gave chase.

Without having to talk about it, Tony followed Andy down over the side of the roadway into the dingy service tunnels. Once inside Tony took the lead, his familiarity with the tight spaces on the *Dark Matter* giving him an advantage in the tight spaces of the lower city. Without having to think much about it, Tony led them back toward the Power Tower.

Once they were inside, they went through one of the access hatches into the maze of corridors. Andy took over the lead once more since he knew the inside of the Tower better than his smaller companion. "This way! I figure if we take the lift up to level five or so, we can shake the goons and come back down on either the mag-train or one of the other tower lifts." It sounded like a good plan to Tony, so he concentrated on following Andy's black tail tip through the maze.

"I don't see why we have to search this far down. I mean if they were going to hide the stuff in this tower, they'd have used one of the more accessible levels, wouldn't they?" a gruff voice said as Tony and Andy made their way down the last side corridor before the lift in the center of the tower. The boys paused, exchanged a telling look, then crept forward slowly to where the corridors met.

"I will rip the whole city apart until I find the miscreant who used *my* security access code to steal illegal goods from *my own* storage facility!" Tony recognized the white mink in the Port Authority uniform and her two attending canines, but not the brown bear in the Peacekeeper uniform.

Andy stepped back, pulling Tony with him, and whispered, "This doesn't look good!" His ears swiveled to point back the way they had come, where the sounds of pursuit were starting to become noticeable. Tony's brain was working overtime, trying to find a way out of this mess. Behind them was a crime boss bent on their termination, and in front of them were the combined forces of the Port Authority and the Peacekeepers, also bent on destroying all traces of both of them. They were caught between a rock and a hard place with no obvious way out!

Tony forced himself to take a deep calming breath and let it out slowly. There *had* to be a way out. They were too far into the maze to access any of the service tunnels. The only exit in sight was a door just behind them that led into a dead end room. Tony's eyes followed Andy's movement as the cougar glanced back around the corner. His paw was carefully holding the satchel he wore closed so that none of the small packets of honeyed dates fell out.

Tony's eyes widened! "Andy?" he whispered as he gently tugged on the taller boy's arm. "Drop the satchel," he added when Andy's eyes met his. He followed his own advice and lowered the satchel he was carrying gently down onto the floor. As he expected the loosely packed dates spilled from the top to make a tempting pile. Andy, not sure what was going on but trusting his friend, dropped his satchel beside Tony's.

Tony nodded then pulled Andy after him toward the door. Andy's eyes widened once more, and he shook his head not wanting to get caught in the room with no way out. Tony leaned in close and whispered, "Trust me?" He entered the code into the reader that opened the door. The two boys slipped inside with barely a mil to lose. Just as the door closed behind them, Dionysus and his two lionesses came around the last corner.

"Hey, boss," one of the females called out, unaware of the authorities lurking just around the corner. "Looks like the kits gave us the slip." She stooped to scoop up the discarded satchels. "But they dropped the goods." She turned back to face the mouse holding out the pair of overloaded bags. It took her a mil to process the look of horror on Dionysus' face and the way her partner was holding her paws out, palms toward her. Slowly she turned once more, her eyes widening and her ears wilting back against her head, as she came face to face with the large brown bear.

"Well, well, what do we have here?" the gruff voice asked as he lifted one of the satchels from her unresisting paw. "Looks like you've been a very bad kitty." He pulled a pawful of the individually wrapped honeyed dates that were clearly marked with the Port Authority sigil from the bag. "I guess searching level nine was worth it after all. Don't you think, Commander Jessup?" He grinned down at the white mink showing his teeth.

She stepped closer to examine the items in his paw. "I told you! My nose never lies, Chief Kovalev." She lifted one of the small fruits from his paw and waved it under the lioness's nose. "You are in a lot of trouble."

While two of the most powerful individuals in the city had been speaking, their respective underlings swarmed the adjacent tunnels, cutting off any chance of escape for their quarry.

"I'll have you know, you've tangled with the wrong mouse!" Dionysus yelled as his arms were caught by two of the Peacekeepers. He struggled feebly, but it didn't make a difference as he and his two lionesses were rounded up and herded toward the lift. "I have friends in powerful places!" He continued to spout curses at his captors until the lift doors closed on the entire party.

***

Five cycles had passed since Tony and Andy had met. During that time they had moved into the base of the Power Tower. Level ten had been completely deserted without even the power converters installed. They had their pick of the rooms and settled on two close together. The smaller room they turned into a command center with some of the electronic equipment from the storehouse above. It was also used as a storage room for the foodstuffs that they needed to support their growing family.

In addition to the original three kittens they'd rescued, they had over a dozen more kits that had been scheduled for cull for no other reason than their parentage.

Andy had a contact network that spanned the city and included hybrids in the medical units. Many of them were disgusted by the criteria that made them mark perfectly healthy kits for cull and had begun reaching out to Andy in order to save some of them.

Tony walked into the tower from the New'ork bridge with a confused young filly. "But if there isn't anything wrong with me, why was I scheduled for cull?"

"The government doesn't want species mixing," Tony explained.

She tossed her mane. "We were taught that isn't even possible."

Tony nodded. "And in order to keep that from being discovered as a lie, the government has ordered any child who has mixed genes to be culled. With the increase in multi-species pairings lately, it's increased the number of kits born with mixed parentage."

"That's... horrible!"

"Which is why we've been saving kits in your situation." Tony led her down the corridor toward their base of operations. "Your mother, the mayor, found out when you were an infant. She's been paying the medical facility to ignore your issue since then. But the medic that was taking her bribes was moved to another facility, so you were in danger of being found out. That's why she contacted us." He opened the door to the den room and ushered the filly inside. "As you can see, we've amassed quite a few."

The room had been turned into a maze of individual dens, created out of packing materials and other things that the younglings found or traded for. There was power and running water but only at a communal pool where several kits had gathered. A sonic had been installed against one wall along with a pair of reclamation facilities.

"Hey Nechtan." Tony waived a young kitten over. "Can you show Lyssa around? She's just come down and might have a few questions."

Nechtan nodded and grinned up at the taller filly. "Hi, I'm Nechtan. I was one of the first kittens that Tony and Andy saved." The boy had come a long way from the withdrawn frightened kitten he had been. He and his sisters had taken over orienting the new kits into the family. They did a really good job of it. Nechtan would make sure to get a video of Nyssa to let her mother know she was safe. Tony left the filly in Nechtan's capable paws and went to find Andy.

The cougar was where Tony expected to find him, muzzle deep in a list of culls scheduled for the next day. "Hey," Tony said as he entered the small space that had been walled off from the storage shelves.

"Hey, yourself. How'd it go? Any trouble from the Peacekeepers?" Andy's eyes never left his screen.

"Went smooth, not like last time." Tony still cursed the luck that had Peacekeepers on hand when he had tried to get to the last kit they had identified. He hadn't had a chance to get close to him, let alone get him out before he was ushered into the termination facility. It had been a big blow to the soft hearted raccoon.

"Good. Once we send confirmation to her mother that we have her, she'll leave the other half of the credits at the drop point. Jandar is already in position to make the pickup." Tony's ears twitched, and he leaned in closer to the vid as one of the names scrolling past lit up in red followed by another one right below. Then the feed paused.

"Another one?" Tony leaned over Andy's shoulder to get a better look at the information on the feed.

"Two more on level eight. Won't be able to get much for helping that family."

"No, but that's not the reason we're doing this." Tony slid into his own seat and pulled up the vid. "The facility on that level is in Osten. We haven't used the D and D in a while. Jandar will be happy to stretch his trunk out again."

"True, but we need to be careful. Last time he was put on the watch list for unacceptable behavior. We can't afford to lose him." He frowned at the files of the two kits he had pulled up on his vid. "Tony, these ones are young. They got flagged when they did their crèche entry eval. We've never pulled anyone this young before." He turned worried eyes on Tony.

Tony peered at Andy's vid for a few mil, his ears folding out flat to either side of his head. "Family must be on basic government pension. No extra credits to bribe the medics." This was a difficult situation. He wanted to help the kits. At only two cycles the kits were ready to enter the crèche system, but they didn't have the facilities to take care of infants. "Lyssa is almost of age, but I can't in good conscience ask her to take on two kits when she's only barely arrived. I just don't see how we can take care of them." Tony felt a sinking feeling as he admitted that. "We're going to have to let them go."

Andy placed a consoling paw on Tony's shoulder and squeezed gently. "If we weren't helping the ones we are, they'd all be culled. In a half a year we have saved over a dozen kits that would have been termed without us. You shouldn't beat yourself up over the ones we can't save."

Warmth filled him, the same warmth that came every time Andy touched him. The same warmth that he was too afraid to do anything about. He cleared his throat to hide his conflicted desire. "Jandar's delivery business has a new client. There is a new merchant on level four that wants his goods brought up from a storage facility on level eight as needed. That means we need to station someone at the storage facility during business chrons who can coordinate with the storefront."

"Sounds like a pretty important position. Any idea who's up to the job?" Andy asked.

Tony, who had a better head for business than their elephant partner, had been handling all the scheduling for that part of their operation. "I was thinking possibly Niobe. She's got a head for organization and the respect of the other kits, so it wouldn't be too hard for her to step into a leadership position." Andy slipped out as Tony focused on his screen and the problem at paw.

A buzzing startled him; the comm was trying to get his attention. Figuring it was one of their customers, he toggled the Jandar construct on and accepted the communicae. "Jandar here."

The face that looked back at him was that of a stranger, but the mouse was wearing beads Tony immediately recognized. "I need to speak to Anthony."

Tony flicked the construct off, his heart beating so fast he was afraid it would explode. "This is Tony." Tony could tell by the pendants in the mouse's fur that he was from the *Supernova*, a sister ship to the *Dark Matter*. He also knew that the mouse was related to Brady, one of his previous shipmates.

The mouse frowned at him for a few mil. "I'm assuming that your lack of identifying markers is some sort of disguise? However, your facial features match up. But we need to make sure you are who you say you are." He waited until Tony nodded then began a barrage of questions. "Who is the Captain of the *Dark Matter*?"

Tony answered without hesitation, "Nathan Heart."

"And the kits you served with most recently, their names?"

"I don't know their last names, but there were four of them: Marissa, Justin, Brady, and Illandra, though she'd only just joined the crew."

"One more, what's the name and designation of our leader?"

"Last I knew it was Queen Mireya."

"Good good, I'm satisfied you are the Anthony we're looking for."

"I never expected to hear from home again," Tony said, his emotions making his voice unsteady.

"Why ever not? We've been getting your tenday updates for cycles now." Tony had left a few details out of those updates, like what they were doing to help the kits and why. "The Queen was just trying to figure out how best to make use of your unique situation. I'm still having trouble believing that there are so many hybrids underground."

Someone off vid said, "Captain Ganbold, we're clear for landing."

The mouse nodded in acknowledgment before addressing Tony once more. "We're here to offer you a choice. You can come home, resume your place aboard the *Dark Matter*, and finish out your contract with no penalties for being gone so long. Or you can choose to stay on the planet and become part of our network there. The contacts you have made are a valuable commodity which the Queen would like to make use of. However, the choice is yours." He leaned in toward the vid, his voice softening to a more personal tone. "I mean that Tony. No one will blame you if you just want to come home."

"That's a very generous offer, Captain. I can't say I'm not tempted." Tony glanced at Andy's vid where the two names were still lit up in red. "If you'd asked me a few cycles ago, I might have taken you up on the offer. As it stands, I believe I'll stay right where I am."

"Good lad. Right, then I have some instructions for you—"

"Hold on. I didn't say I was going to be a part of your network. If you want my access to this planet's underworld, then you have to be willing to give me something in exchange."

Ganbold started laughing. "Nathan told me to watch out for you. Said you were one of his best bargainers. Right then—" He slapped his paw down on his knee. "—what are your terms?"

Tony grinned. "You first, what is it the Queen would like me to do for her?"

"You're a shrewd one, aren't you?" The mouse chuckled again. "All right, since you are the first Independent to infiltrate one of the Government planets, she'd like you to gather as much information on them as possible. The more we know about them, the better we can trade with them. We need to know what we have that they don't and what they have that we need."

"That sounds reasonable. What form of compensation am I to get for this information?" Tony's nose was twitching as he fell into the old familiarity of bargaining for his services.

"I was authorized to give you access to the contacts we already have set up, access codes and locations." He arched a brow. "Though from what I've heard, you already have a better network than we've managed to build."

Tony inclined his head slightly in silent acceptance of the compliment. "True, however we've come across a problem that we can't find a solution to."

Andy pushed past the curtain into the command center. "Who are you talking to?" His eyes widened as he took in the mouse's appearance.

"Andy, this is Captain Ganbold of the *Supernova*. Captain, this is my partner Andrew. I've included him in my updates, so I'm sure you're aware of his importance to my endeavors."

"Indeed I am. Pleased to meet you, youngling. Tony and I were just working out the details of the contract we'd like to enter with your group," Ganbold explained.

"Are you? What have you got so far?" Andy sank into his seat pulling up a second file on his vid. As Tony and the captain filled him in, he typed out a basic contract.

"Okay," Tony said. "I have an additional proposition for you, Captain."

"Oh, what might that be?"

"Fresh blood." Tony grinned. "The Colony has been seeing a lot more culls in recent years due partially to inbreeding. I propose that in exchange for traditional apprenticeship contracts, we send you individuals from this world that for one reason or another need to escape."

Andy hissed in a breath, turning wide eyes on the raccoon.

"Well now, that's something I wasn't expecting." Captain Ganbold's ears perked forward, and he leaned into the vid on his end. "Standard contracts? With you the receiver of the initial payment?"

"That's the idea." Tony nodded. "It would give us a better financial footing to help more hybrids who are in danger."

"What kind of danger?" Ganbold's eyes narrowed in consternation. "Are they likely to be a danger to the Colony? You know the Queen won't go for that."

"No, the trouble is mostly political in nature. Kits who would be considered contributing members of the Independent Colony are being culled here simply for having mixed parentage."

"WHAT!" Ganbold nearly jumped out of his chair. "What could possess them to do something so stupid?"

Andy broke in: "The Government has the population convinced that it isn't possible to mix species. Any time a kit is born that counters that belief, they have the kit culled before anyone finds out. I'm a prime example of that situation.

"My mother discovered I was on the cull list when I was an infant. She bribed the medical facility to tell her why, and then she kept bribing them to cover it up. Eventually her contact moved to another facility, and she could no longer pay to keep my mixed heritage a secret. I managed to escape, obviously, but I no longer exist as far as the government is concerned."

The more Andy spoke, the more incredulous the mouse looked. "You can't be serious. Why would a population stick its head in a vacuum like that? Some of our brightest and best have mixed parentage." He looked at Tony as if to confirm that Andy was messing with him.

"It's all true unfortunately." Tony stated gravely, "We have contacts in most of the medical facilities in this city who are feeding us the names and reasons that kits are on the cull lists. We've been saving as many as we can, but we can't help the infants. We just don't have the facilities to take care of them."

"Makers save us. That's a situation I'm sure that, while she doesn't yet know, the Queen would be more than happy to help with," Captain Ganbold decided.

"I was hoping you'd say that Captain." Tony glanced at Andy, who shook his head in disbelief. "We have two such kits on our screen right this mil. The only question is how do we get them to you?"

Ganbold paused a mil, his nose twitching as he considered the possibility of having to immediately make good on his claim of assistance. Finally he nodded slowly. "In for a gram, in for a kilo. I'll contact one of our suppliers and see if he can't find a way to get the kits past Port Security, but I've no idea how to get them to the surface."

"You leave that to us." Tony grinned from eartip to tailtip. "We have hybrids in key positions to get them out of the city. We were just trying to find a way to get them off planet."

"It sounds like you have been busier than you have been telling us, youngling." There was a note of justifiable pride in the captain's voice.

"I didn't want to risk being intercepted by the Peacekeepers. How soon do you think your contact can be ready? I'd like to speak with the parents so we can move the kits before they end up heading to the termination facility."

"I'll contact you on this channel as soon as we have things set up." Ganbold leaned in toward the vid once more. "And Tony, good work. I'm sure Nathan will be proud when he finds out what you've accomplished here." Before Tony could respond, the link went dead.

"Wow!" Andy sagged into his seat. "I never would have believed it, if I hadn't heard it with my own ears. Talk about a happy ending."

"Ending?" Tony shook his head smiling slightly. "This is just the beginning."

The Stacy Bark books bring two puppies together. When we share our stories, fiction can break down walls.

No Dogs

KC Alpinus

"Come on, Taissa. We don't wanna be late for your first day!"

The small Staffordshire Terrier shouldered her bright, pink bookbag and hurried to catch up to the brindle terrier. Why did her mom have to walk so fast? Stubby, puppy legs weren't made for chasing down adult terriers!

As Taissa looked over her shoulder, she saw the other neighborhood pups just getting up: a diminutive Doberman feeding the hens, a plucky Rottweiler blinking sleep-laden eyes and fetching the milk, and a Mastiff lumbering towards the outhouse. Taissa wished that she could be going to their school, but her mother's stubborn determination had ensured that she wouldn't be going to the school around the corner this morning, or any other morning, for that matter.

"If you're early, you're on time, and if you're on time, you're—"

"—late." Yes Momma, I know," Taissa said, rolling her hazel eyes and brushing a floppy, gray ear out of her face.

"Good. I want you to make a good impression for these dogs. Okay, baby?" Dominique looked down at her daughter, who yawned and scratched behind an ear.

"Yes, Momma," Taissa repeated, hopping over a puddle, taking care to keep her dainty paws dry. As she followed her mother, she noticed how there was more grass and less concrete the farther they walked. She wanted to go over and give it a good sniff, maybe roll around in it, but she knew her mother would nip her for the offense.

"I just want you to know that today might be a little rough," Dominique said, placing a paw on her daughter's shoulder as they stopped in front of the schoolhouse, "but remember that you're here to make a difference, okay? I want you on your best behavior. Make your Momma proud."

"I will, Momma." Taissa buried her square muzzle into her mother's blouse, the smell of this morning's breakfast biscuits enveloping her. As she looked over her mother's shoulder, she saw the other dogs whisper behind their paws at her, their faces accusatory, but Taissa just took it as a sign that she should be getting to class.

She broke away from her mother, wagged her tail once, and walked into the building. As Dominique watched her daughter pad off, she shivered, the staring and whispers beginning to get to her. Looking down at her watch, she noticed that she had less than an hour to get to work. Shaking herself, she began walking in the direction of the office buildings, before she felt the sharp jab of a baton in her back.

"What you doin' on this side of town, girl?"

Dominique wheeled around to see a police shepherd, his pointed ears as rigid and unyielding on top of his head as his demeanor. He seemed young, about as old as her son Frederick, but like all his kind, he stuck his chest out and seemed to want to assert himself over the older terrier.

"I was on my way to work," Dominique replied, her ears pressed against her head and her eyes downcast.

"You got some ID?" he spat, the edges of his muzzle wrinkling in disgust.

"Yes sir, right here in my purse." Dominique fumbled with the clasp of her bag, but despite her shaking paws, she managed to grab the thin piece of laminated paper and held it out to the officer. He snatched it away from her and read it, his eyes narrowing as they glanced over each line.

"Well you best go on then," he said, shoving the piece of plastic back at her. "Don't let me catch you wandering around here with no business, you hear?"

"Yes, sir" Dominique mumbled, but the cop had already begun his stroll back down the street. Once he was out of earshot, she snorted in his direction and then hurried off towards the bus, not wanting to be late to work.

***

"Haha, stupid puppy!"

"Give it back, Robbie!"

"No way, curly hair! You're not even a real dog 'cause dogs have fur and you've got stupid, curly hair!"

Taissa lifted a floppy ear, listening to the goings on of the playground while keeping her muzzle buried between the pages of a book. With her free paw, she gnawed on a massive hambone, a prize she'd won off her older brother the night before in a game. Taissa wanted to share it with the other pups, but like most of her day, it was refused and derided.

"Small, weak poodle!"

This made Taissa look up, a soft growl on her lips. She hated when dogs teased her, so a flash of anger coursed through her when she saw a chubby, Golden Retriever and a Dalmatian shoving a smaller, curly-furred poodle. Without a second thought, Taissa tossed her book to the side (something she'd whine about later) and charged at the two larger puppies. "Hey! Back off!"

The boys turned, the Dalmatian growling at her, while the retriever wrinkled his muzzle and snapped. "What are you doing? This is none of your business, terrier!"

"You're being a bully and my momma always told me to stand up to bullies, so that's what I'm doing!"

Taissa stood in front of the poodle and squared her paws, her smaller, agile body poised and ready. The retriever smirked and crossed his arms across his chest, his eyes narrowed.

"What would you know about bullying, you pibble? You and your kind aren't even worthy of being known as dogs. My father says that you're savages, almost wolves!"

From behind her, Taissa heard the poodle gasp and even the Dalmatian recoiled from his words.

"You're the dog that's pushing other pups around and being a fat bully. Seems like you're closer to being a wolf than I am!"

Two things happened at once: the retriever clenched his fists and swung, and the science teacher stepped into the middle to find out what happened. The blow of the retriever pup didn't do much by way of hurting the science teacher, but he wasn't pleased about being hit.

"Robert Duckfetch, did you just hit me?"

"I-uh well, she started it!" Robbie pointed to Taissa, who recoiled and wrinkled her muzzle in her own defense.

"I didn't do nothing!"

"I'm all for this integration and mingling of pups, but if this is how your kind acts, I think we may be mistaken!"

The science teacher reached for Taissa's scruff, but suddenly the poodle girl was there, her eyes wide as she came to Taissa's defense.

"She didn't do anything, Mr. Barker! It was Robbie who pushed me and started this. She saved me!"

The teacher looked from one pup to the other, but then he sighed and folded his arms. "Well Alice, I know that you would never involve yourself in a fight, and judging from the dirt on your dress, I'm inclined to believe you. Robbie and Arthur, you two will meet me after school for detention. We're training you both to be good dogs, not bullies."

Both boys groaned and kicked at the dust, but Alice brightened, giving Taissa a hug around her middle. The teacher, however, wasn't finished. He rounded on Taissa, his ears erect on his head and his tail straight behind him.

"Now, I know you're new here and I don't know what they allow at that school of yours across the tracks, but we don't tolerate that here. If you're going to be around well-bred dogs, you will act as such, you hear?"

Taissa whimpered a 'yes' and shrank in on herself. Satisfied that all parties had been thoroughly chastised, the teacher grabbed both boys by their scruffs and dragged them inside, leaving the terrier tilting her head, ears wilting. She hadn't started the fight, but why did it feel like she was chastised as well?

A snuffling sound made her turn and look down. It was the poodle, Alice, her jacket returned and a smile on her face.

"Nobody has ever stood up for me. Thanks for that. My name's Alice."

"I'm Taissa and uh yeah, no problem," she said, padding back towards her reading spot with Alice in tow. The poodle seemed unsure around her, but the moment Taissa pulled out her book, she brightened and started chatting incessantly.

"Is that a Stacy Bark book?"

Taissa looked at the front of the floppy-eared book and raised an eyebrow. "Um, yeah. My old school gave me this before summer break."

"That's nice of them, but that's one of the old ones. My momma and papa buy me one every time we go to the market 'cause I get good grades in school. I'm waiting for the new one to come out."

Taissa stared at the poodle, her muzzle agape. Books for simply getting good grades? Momma and Poppa were proud of her grades in school, but books were far too expensive for her family to splurge on every week. Who were these people that they could afford books every week?

"That's one of the old ones," Alice said, matter-of-factly, touching at the folded-over corners of the book.

"It's new to me," Taissa said, jerking the book away, feeling the fur along her spine rise.

"I'm sorry, I meant-uh, well, would you like to read some of the ones that I've finished? I've got loads of them!"

"Um-I—"

"I'm sure my mom won't mind!"

"No, I'm—"

BBBRING!!

Both pups perked their ears at the klaxon-like wailing of the bell. There were groans and scuffling as the other pups scurried towards the doors, their tails wagging behind them. Alice looked as if she wanted to say more, but the barks of the science teacher made her wince.

"See you after school?" she asked, bounding off before Taissa could respond. Shoving her book into her bag, the sanctity of her lunch broken, she trudged into the school. She received a quip from the teacher about being the last one inside of the classroom. Her ears burning, Taissa slid down into her seat, grateful to be seated at the back of the classroom so she didn't have to have more of her classmates' eyes boring into her. Why'd Momma have to put her in a school with such mean-spirited teachers and students, where everyone else looked different?

**

"It's gonna be rough and we might get tired, but we just have to press towards the mark. We're fighting against something that's greater than me, you, and even you, Sister."

The terrier had been pointing a blunted claw at the other dogs that had gathered in the small, homey church until it landed on Dominique. She'd been stewing on the day's events, especially with that rude poodle at work and her stereotyping, but when James elbowed her in the ribs, she huffed and looked up to see the entire congregation staring at her. Before she could stammer out a reply, the congregation murmured and nodded their heads, agreeing with his words.

Feeling the warmth flood her cheeks, Dominique buried her muzzle in the center of her bible and tried to remain unnoticed for the rest of the service.

"You shoulda been paying attention to him," James said, shoving his bible into his briefcase. "I know he's on the young side, but the man can move people with his words. I think this boycott of his will work."

"I know," Dominique huffed, shoving her arms into her woolen jacket, "and I shoulda been listening, but I had a lot on my mind today."

"Like what?"

"Just work and sending Taissa off to that school. I'm wondering if we did the right thing sending her and not JR or Marcus."

James eyed their two eldest children, a pair of rambunctious boys and then stared at his wife. "You mean the same JR or Marcus who aren't even five seconds away from me sending them to sleep outside? Boy, don't you put that in your muzzle!"

James stormed away to separate his sons and give the elder JR a thorough shaking of his scruff before returning to Dominique, who smiled despite herself.

"Sorry baby, but I swear that we can't leave them alone for a minute before they're chewing on everything. But what was I saying?"

"You were talking about my job and sending Taissa to that school."

"What? Oh yeah, yeah. Well, it's all for a good cause, 'Nique. We chose Taissa to be the one to go 'cause of her good grades and being smart as a whip. If anyone can get through to them, it'll be baby girl. 'Scuse me, baby, I gotta get them."

Dominique lifted an eyebrow and sighed while watching her mate corner their two boys once more and threaten to make them sleep outside for the evening before she turned back to gather her hymnal and her purse. While she packed up, she felt a presence near her and, thinking it was James, began rattling off her feelings.

"I know you said Taissa would be the one to get through to them, but I just don't know. I mean, she's just one girl and they don't want her there anyways. Are we setting her up to be picked on by them, James? Are we doing the right thing?"

"Change ain't easy, Sister, but it's gotta come sometime."

Dominique jumped and turned, making the young reverend laugh and toss his floppy ears.

"I-uh-I'm sorry, Reverend. I thought you were my husband, James. My apologies."

"I get that a lot. You sound a lot like my wife when she's telling me about our pups." He laughed. His voice was mild and soothing, like a cup of tea with a dollop of sweet molasses, just as smooth and easy to take. His dark, chocolate fur seemed to add a regal air to him, despite his young age, but the look in his eyes sent a jolt through Dominique. This terrier seemed like one to not be deterred from his mission once he set his mind on it.

"Thank you, Reverend. I just-I just want to be doing the right thing and I don't want my baby girl to get hurt because of a few, angry people."

The Reverend nodded, brushing a paw against the thickened fur of his muzzle. "Yeah, we all feel that way. I understand that we're asking a lot of ourselves and our children, and sometimes we wonder if the cost is worth it."

When Dominique nodded, he continued. "But during times like these, we have to ask ourselves: do we want our pups to be safe or to be respected as full citizens? What's a good, safe life if it's a life spent groveling, begging for scraps from dogs whose only difference from us is the texture of their fur? They bleed just like we do."

The Reverend laughed, the light growing in his eyes before he grew somber again. "We have to ask ourselves, 'is that the life we want our pups to live'?"

Dominique looked away, feeling abashed from having this question asked of her. All her life, she had watched her parents, her grandparents, and other family members bow and scrape in the houses of the nearby poodles and retrievers and for what? To be kicked whenever they felt like it? To have to cower before them, lest they be deemed too uppity and summon the Catchers, who left only ashes and despair in their wake?

"I hear you, Reverend, but who am I to change this? Why my baby Taissa too?"

"We are all called to a higher purpose, and fight it as we might, we cannot deny it. It's hard now, my sister, and it may seem like an uphill battle, but I know we're doing the right thing. I know that if I can give my pups, and your pups, and all of our pups the ability to stand, not just before the poodles and the retrievers, but to be counted as an equal among them, then I know that all of our labor will not be in vain."

Dominique wanted to speak with the Reverend more, but his attendants and confidants came forward, citing urgent matters for him to attend to as they ushered him off. Dominique was left standing there, mulling over his words until a soft whine spilled into her ears.

"Momma, are you okay?"

Dominique blinked and then looked down, jerked out of her thoughts by her daughter. Shaking herself, she took Taissa's paw and squeezed it, nodding.

"Yes baby, Momma's okay."

***

"Momma!"

Taissa stood in the middle of the sidewalk, her bookbag slung haphazardly over her shoulder with her arms crossed over her little chest. A tiny fang peeked from underneath her jaws as she stared down her mother. Dominique crossed her arms across her chest too and tapped her paw, her ears pressed against her head.

"I'm not telling you again, pup. We've gotta run before it rains."

"But I wanna ride the bus!"

"I said 'no,' Taissa! We're not riding the bus anymore."

"Whyyy?" Taissa dragged the last syllable out, the tone grating on Dominique's already brittle nerves.

"Because we have to prove a point. No one is riding the bus until they start treating us better. Now come on 'fore it starts raining!"

Dominique grabbed her daughter by the paw, but the pup resisted. Growling, she snapped at the stubborn girl's shoulder, forcing her to move with a whine. Why today, of all days, Taissa decided to show her stubborn side, Dominique would never know, but if they were late in getting home, she would be late cooking James' dinner and Lord help her if she had to hear that dog whine about a late dinner.

Just as she was getting her daughter to move, she felt a drop land on her muzzle. As she looked up, a massive thunderclap sounded, making Taissa yelp and clutch Dominique around her waist. Dominique opened her muzzle to chide her daughter, and the sky opened, catching the pair in a characteristic thunderstorm.

Grabbing each other's paws, they ran, Dominique praying that she wouldn't slip in her pumps and Taissa squealing behind her, until they came to rest under the roots of a massive oak tree. As she stood there, she noticed her pup shivering while she tried to lick the water off her fur.

"See what happens when you want to be a stubborn cur? And I don't have my umbrella, so we'll have to wait under this tree until this passes," Dominique chided, stripping off her sweater and wrapping it around Taissa's thin shoulders. Heaving a sigh, she stared up, hoping that they could go into the nearby store, until she saw the sign.

NO VICIOUS DOGS

Dominique choked off a growl and felt her paw clench around her purse. *Damn them*, she thought, her eyes glistening when she looked upon that sign. As a pup, she'd never questioned the signs that barred her and dogs of her breed from entering certain establishments. It had always been that way for the Rotties, the Bulldogs, and her kind, the Terriers.

Why were they judged based on their appearance and breeding, despite their intelligence and personalities? Why were she and dogs like her, judged and mistreated based on stereotypes that weren't true?

HONK! HONK!

Dominique lifted her muzzle to see a small car in front of her, with the annoying poodle woman, Betty from work, and her daughter inside, well she was. Her daughter had her head out of the window, barking enthusiastically.

"Mom! Mom, that's her! That's the girl that helped me with Robbie and got my jacket back!"

"Taissa..."

Her daughter tucked her tail between her legs when her mother looked down at her, but the dog interrupted them.

"Wow, small world! Dominique, right?"

Dominique nodded, wrapping an arm around Taissa's shoulders and moving in front of her. These were poodles, and this Betty had already insulted her a couple of days ago, but still, they had at least stopped to speak once they spotted her and Taissa huddled underneath the tree.

"Yes'm. This is my daughter Taissa. I'm guessing our girls have already met."

"I'm glad they did. That Duckfetch has been a right tick in our ears, but thanks for standing up for her. By the way, what are you doing in the rain? You want a ride?"

"Please Momma, can we?" Taissa's furiously wagging tail threatened to knock the puppy off her feet.

Dominique stiffened, her tail stiff behind her. She'd never ridden in a car with a poodle before, and she still felt mistrustful of the poodle because of her words the day before, but Taissa's whining got the better of her.

"Alright, alright," she sighed, watching her daughter bounce up and down before darting into the newly opened car door. Grabbing her things, she hopped into the passenger seat and was surprised to see how nice the car was. Besides riding on the area bus, Dominique didn't get to ride in vehicles much.

Betty seemed to take note of this and grinned as she put the car into gear and began speeding towards the area where Dominique lived. The quiet settled between them while Taissa and Alice chatted in the background about the newest Stacy Bark book, but as the rain splashed down on the windows, the silence began to weigh the adults down. Moment by moment, it grew, like water being held back by a damn, until Dominique sneezed, bursting the damn.

"Ah, so any reason why you two aren't taking the bus? It's thunderstormin' and I could never just see myself walking into the rain like that with my pup."

Betty turned to look at Dominique, who was looking out the window, but turned one of her ears in acknowledgement.

"Perfectly good buses out there and I'm not going to tell you how to spend your money because I wouldn't let anyone tell me how to spend mine, but catching a bus would have been much better than—"

"Sometimes, it's better to walk in the pure, sweet rain, than to be treated like scum on an old, rickety bus."

Betty recoiled as if she'd been hit. "I'll have you know that the buses are always in pristine condition, though some dogs just don't know how to appreciate the nicer things. My husband says that it's like they don't know how to act—"

"Why wouldn't they know how to appreciate the nicer things? And what 'nicer things'? The buses that they send across the tracks have holes big enough to fall through and our own Dog Park has more concrete than grass," Dominique shot back, now turning to look at Betty.

"But who put those holes there?" Betty said, her eyes darting to the pit bull that was seated next to her. "I'm not trying to be mean, but some of you dogs can be very aggressive and ill-trained. I know it's your breeding and you don't know any better but—"

"Stop the car! Taissa, get your things." Dominique pawed at the door, preparing to dart out as soon as the car stopped.

"Hey now! What are you doing? I'm not saying that you're like that, just some dogs—"

"Just some dogs that look like me!" Dominique snapped. "It's the same thing with all of you poodles, retrievers, and collies. You don't even know us, but you'd rather keep your paws on our bellies just to make yourself seem better. Y'all bleed the same blood as the rest of us dogs 'cross the tracks, but still act like you're better than us."

Dominique opened the door and hopped out, grabbing Taissa by her paw. Before storming away, she looked Betty in the eyes and growled.

"Before this boycott, dogs like you would have never seen dogs like me if it didn't directly benefit you. Funny how you see us now 'cause it directly affects your pockets."

***

Taissa and Alice sat back-to-back, both of their muzzles buried within their books. They had avoided each other for the next couple of days after their respective mothers had their argument, but like two best friends, they found their way back to each other, laughing and giggling, despite the disapproving stares of their teachers.

"Did you read the part where she found the rat hiding in the wall?"

"I did! I would have been so afraid to have it just burst out on me!"

"Me too! I would have run."

"I wouldn't run. I would face it."

"How are you always this brave?" Alice asked, her eyes wide underneath her mop of curly hair. Taissa looked at her, one ear flopped backwards as she tilted her head to the side.

"Huh? Brave? I'm not brave."

"Yes, you are. I mean, you stood up to Robbie and his stupid friends, but you also always know all the answers in class, even though teacher calls you a 'know-it-all.'"

Alice heard Taissa sigh and looked at her friend who, for the first time that semester, looked worried. "Did I say something wrong?"

For a few tense moments, Taissa didn't respond. She sat there, her tail no longer wagging in the dirt as she looked towards the schoolyard.

"No, it's not that, it's just- well, I'm tired of the teachers and everyone else treating me differently because I'm from across the tracks. I-I sometimes hate being a terrier. Everything I've read or seen, besides Stacy of course, showed dogs like me as monsters, and poodles, collies, and everyone else havin' all sorts of fun. I'm-I'm not a monster. I'm just a puppy, and I want to have fun too."

Alice whined and reached out with a shaky but determined paw and put it on Taissa's shoulder. "Why-why would you want to not be a terrier? You're not like me, but-but you're not a monster either, you're my friend! Anyone who says differently will have to face me!" Alice folded her arms across her chest and snorted, causing Taissa to wag her tail in glee. Alice was weird and wasn't one of the friends she knew from growing up across the tracks, but she was a friend, despite her odd looks.

"I've gotta say, I never knew that a poodle or anyone that wasn't from across the tracks could be so cool. Momma always said it was hard to trust ya'll because you sniff and bite tails at the same time."

Alice tilted her head and looked at her friend, clearly puzzled. Taissa laughed, clutching her book to her chest at her friend's bewilderment.

"She says it means that it's hard to trust ya'll because ya'll turn your backs on folks 'soon as it suits you."

"I would never do that. Mama says that only bad dogs bite everyone like that."

"You're right. I don't want dogs to treat me differently because they don't know me, and now that I think about it, I shouldn't treat you any differently either. Let's treat each other the same Alice. I'll be your best friend if you'll be mine."

Taissa had extended her paw for a firm handshake, but Alice jumped into her friend's outstretched paws and they tumbled to the ground, laughing and giggling in the pale winter sunlight.

***

The shove in the center of her back caught Taissa completely off-guard. Her paws splayed on the tile while her books and papers scattered in front of her. As she tried to figure out what had happened to her, she heard the sound of snickering, interlaced with low growling. Turning around, she saw the retriever, Robbie, from earlier, with Arthur and another young dog behind him. His face was twisted in a cruel smile, despite the wagging tail behind him.

"Looks like you got in my way, terrier."

In a flash, Taissa was on her paws, ears pressed against her skull and teeth bared. "What'd you do that for, Robbie?"

"Because you're a stupid terrier and 'cause I could," he sneered, gathering more chuckles from his friends. "Why don't you go back across the tracks and be with your own kind? We don't want you here, stinking up the place, thinking you're better than anybody."

Taissa clenched and unclenched her paws into fists, feeling the anger surge inside of her. "You don't tell me what to do."

"Yeah, I can," Robbie said, nibbling at a patch on his shoulder. "My father owns the factory where your daddy works, and I could get him fired if I wanted to, so you'd better watch yourself."

"You're not the boss of me or my daddy!" Taissa barked at him, her voice shrill with emotion. There was a crowd gathering around them now, but Taissa didn't mind them, her focus was on the retriever and his taunting words.

"With your daddy working for mine, it means I am." He laughed, pushing her again. The anger welled up in Taissa once more, so she stuck one of her paws out, just as Robbie tried to walk past her. His resulting collapse brought a grin to her face. As Robbie shrugged off his friends, his pale flesh coloring underneath his golden fur, his face twisted into a snarl.

"How dare you disrespect me, you-you filthy pibble!"

There was an audible gasp from the crowd as he rushed towards her, pushing past his two, opened-muzzle friends to shove Taissa again, hard. She yelped and did the first thing that came to her mind: bite. She sank her teeth into Robbie's shoulder and held on, despite the nips and bites that attacked her little body. Just when she thought her strength would give out, she felt Robbie being pulled off her and pushed back. It was the science teacher again, his eyes blazing.

"Fighting? In this school?"

"She-she started it!" Robbie whimpered, holding up his arm that, for all his whining, only had a few hairs missing.

"Nu uh!" Taissa cried, before a growl silenced her.

"But Mr. Barker, he-he called her a p—"

The teacher rounded on Alice, eyes blazing, before returning to the pair. "Robert, go to your mother's classroom and let her know what you've done. As for you, Little Miss Biter, we'll be having a chat with your mother. This is the second time I've had to deal with you in as many weeks, and I'm sick of it. I knew this entire experiment was wrong."

He grabbed Taissa by her shoulder and dragged her along, leaving a slew of bewildered dogs standing in a crowd behind them.

***

It had been a couple days since the car ride and work had been irritating to say the least, but Dominique managed to stay away from the poodle and other dogs. Despite their whispers and stiffened postures when she passed by, they tended to give her a wide berth. That was for the better, as dealing with their bigotry and ignorance daily kept the fur along her spine raised, and that didn't include the treatment they'd been receiving at the dog park and bus protests. How James managed to tolerate it six days a week was a mystery to her. *Brrring!*

Dominique flicked an ear towards the front door before she got up to investigate. She didn't have to travel far before her youngest pup nearly knocked her over barreling toward her room where she slammed the door. Bewildered, Dominique stormed back after her, ready to read her daughter the riot act, until she heard whimpering coming through the door.

"Taissa?" Dominique said, scratching gently against the door before turning the knob and walking into the room. Taissa's room was as immaculate as ever, a clear deviation from her two older brothers. Dominique found her curled up in a corner, her paws grasping at her floppy ears.

"Baby, what's wrong?"

"GO AWAY!"

Dominique jumped, not expecting this from her usually bright and bubbly daughter. Frowning, she opened her muzzle to reprimand Taissa, but when she caught a glimpse of those red-rimmed hazel eyes with tears streaming from them, she dropped to her knees, her ears touching her head as her tone softened.

"Taissa, talk to me, sweetie. Who hurt you?"

Dominique didn't receive a verbal response, but a slip of paper eased from the clenched paws of her daughter and landed at her paws. Dominique grabbed the sheet of paper and as her eyes scanned the slip, she felt a snarl building in her throat.

> *Dear Parent,*
>
> *Your puppy was involved in a fight today at school. As a reminder, violence of any kind will not be tolerated and as such, your puppy has been suspended for the following days: 2. After such time, we expect to see you for a Parent/Teacher conference to discuss your puppy's future at our school.*
>
> *Regards.*

"Fighting? Taissa, now I know your father and I raised you better than this, but fighting?" Dominique said, swallowing the spittle that was collecting at the back of her throat.

"It wasn't my fault, Momma. Robbie Duckfetch started it!" Taissa curled in deeper on herself, the tears freely flowing. Dominique choked off a growl at the mention of that name. Among the old families that lived in town, the Duckfetches were the ones she and her family wanted the least to do with. From owning the kibble packing plant to being the Assistant Mayor, the Duckfetches had that town within their jaws for the past two hundred years, with no intention of disrupting the status quo.

"Come here, baby." Dominique wrapped her paws around her daughter and clasped the little head to her chest, scratching between the ears. "You shouldn't be fighting in school, but no one should put their paws on you, regardless of whether they're upper-crusty mutts or regular dogs like you and me."

"Th-that's not even the worst of it, Momma." Taissa whined, nuzzling into her mother's soft fur, the scent of fresh soap, cooking dinner, and vanilla enveloping her as Dominique ran her soft tongue over her daughter's face.

"Oh? What else happened?"

"He-he called me a p-pibble."

The word hitting her ears had the effect of someone slapping her. The slur, a misnomer for all Staffordshire and American Terriers with defined muscles and a tenacious countenance, was used to classify them as vicious and controlled every aspect of their lives. Though they were long removed from the stockyards and open plains, they were often denigrated for their ancestors' courageous fighting spirit.

"He what?"

"He called me a p—"

"You don't need to repeat it. I heard you the first time," Dominique said, her words short as she felt anger course through her. "So, was he suspended too?"

"No," came the angry reply, "they just sent him to his mom's classroom."

"Is that right?"

Taissa looked up to her mother, who pulled her close, the anger vibrating off her short coat. "Momma, why wasn't he punished and I was? Why do they hate us?"

"Because they're afraid of change, of new things happening to them, of losing their lot in life because new ones are made."

"But I'm scared going to this school and I-I miss my friends," Taissa whimpered, burrowing deeper into her mother's arms.

"I know, pup. I'm scared too."

Dominique's face was hard, the single tear rolling down the corner of her blazed muzzle her only movement. Taissa reached out with a shaky paw to wipe it away, to which her mother gently grabbed the paw and rubbed it against her head.

"You're scared?"

Dominique nodded, her heart heavy as she prepared to watch the last vestiges of her daughter's innocence fade from her. "I'm scared for you, for how they'll treat me, and how they'll treat you 'cause I'm protesting. I worry that this boycott will be for nothing, and I might lose my job."

"I didn't know you got scared, Momma," Taissa said, cuddling closer to her mother, her eyes drying.

"I do, like all parents, but I want you to have a better life than I had, without being shunned for being who you are, like I was. I resist their ugly, hateful ways because someone must show them how to be better."

When Taissa didn't reply, Dominique looked down into her daughter's eyes and it almost broke her heart to see the change there, a certain hardness of character that had grown there. It pained the older dog to see that change come upon her daughter, and for a moment, she felt helpless until an idea came into her head.

"I'm not happy about your suspension, and as I've said before, I don't condone fighting because they'll look for any reason to make you into an animal and I refuse to let you give it to them. But I'm not going to let a bully get the best of you. I refuse to fight bullies for a seat on a bus or life within the dog park, while you have to fight them in school."

Taissa looked at her mother, the determination gleaming in her eyes, and hugged her harder. She felt a little sickness in her stomach for what might be coming, but she was glad that her momma wouldn't let her be treated unfairly by adults who were afraid of a puppy.

***

"I really don't understand why we're here. I'm a very busy woman and have better things to attend to," a Golden Retriever female said, her tail rigid behind her and jewel-laced collar gleaming with every movement.

Taissa sat on the chair beside her mother, fidgeting with the buckle on her dress. Beside her, Dominique sat stock still, her keen eyes trained on the muzzle of the corgi seated in front of her. His glasses had inched their way down his long muzzle, which he currently rubbed his paws along as the retriever's snobbish voice snapped at them.

"My son Robert would never be seen fighting and degrading himself like a vicious dog from across the tracks. To think that you, Principal Trotter, would accuse him of this!"

"Mrs. Duckfetch, please," the corgi sighed, now rubbing his temples, "if you would please sit so we can allow the children to discuss what's happened."

Mrs. Duckfetch huffed, the air blowing out roughly through her clenched muzzle, while muttering about 'uppity mongrels' and crossing her arms in front of her. The corgi turned a sympathetic eye towards Taissa and Dominique, waving for Taissa to speak.

"I-I was just tryin' to go to class when R-Robbie pushed me from behind—"

"Nu uh, that's not true!" Robbie interrupted, his brown eyes flashing. "She just charged up to me, growling and snapping for no reason. You can ask Arthur and Tommy Lee and they can tell you exactly what happened."

"I think my daughter was trying to tell her side of the story first, son—"

"Excuse you, but Principal Trotter wanted the children to explain, not you. I'm not sure of how you dogs handle issues on the other side of the tracks, but we civilized dogs let others finish speaking before rudely interrupting them," Mrs. Duckfetch snapped, her soft, wavy coat whipping around her as she pressed her ears back. "Honestly Kevin, I don't know how you deal with the likes of them."

"I-I don't, that's-that is to say that I want to hear the entire story, irrespective of where any one dog comes from and I'd prefer no more over-talking from either side," Principal Trotter said, his eyes darting between parents. "Now, continue on, Taissa."

Taissa splayed her ears, hunkering down in her seat underneath the withering gaze of Dorthea Duckfetch, but with a gentle nudge from her mother, she found her words again.

"Robbie shoved me, making me drop my books, and then he called me a really nasty name," Taissa said, her ears lifted atop her head. "And he shoved me again, which is when I tripped him. I-I didn't mean it but—"

"But you still put your paws on my son, you filthy—"

"There's no need for name calling, ma'am," Dominique said, her words coming out evenly, though her body was still and alert.

Dorthea narrowed her eyes at the older terrier and when she spoke, her words were clipped, as if she were holding something back. "Still, sticks and stones never hurt anyone and if she has such a rabid temper, perhaps this social experiment of those loose-collar dogs in Congress was a failure after all."

"No, but it wasn't just a name that your son called my daughter. My daughter has a tougher hide than that and speaking of social experiments and manners, what kind of mother of refined breeding would allow her son to just bully on a younger dog like he has?"

The retriever's ears shot up, and she was on her feet, growling once more. "To think that you, a common dog from across the tracks and of disreputable breeding, would accuse my son of such abhorrent manners is nothing short of an affront to me and my family! I'll have you know—"

"Dorthea, please! Calm yourself!" Principal Trotter said, standing to his paws and barking. "I would expect better of you!"

"Oh please, Kevin! You've always been soft on these types of dogs, and it's downright dishonorable for a dog of your pedigree to take the barking of an ill-bred terrier over the words of a Duckfetch! Besides, it's her word against his and my Robbie would never do anything like this unprovoked."

Principal Trotter looked imploringly at Dominique and Taissa. It was true, it was Taissa's words against his and they had nothing to refute his claims.

"I'm sorry, Mrs. Hunter, but it is just her word against Robbie's and we don't have any proof of his doing this before, while we've had a report from Mr. Barker that said that your child did provoke Robbie previously. I'd hate to say this, but it might be better if Taissa went back to her old school, where she would be accustomed to learning with dogs of her own kind and temperament."

Taissa's whines filled the room while Dominique's muzzle lifted, revealing a single canine in defiance of what he said.

"Principal Trotter, with all due respect, I think this is a tad unfair, and I'm not just saying this from a parent's view, but as an adult. You're making it seem as if my daughter is singling this one pup out to fight right in front of his two friends and only this pup. It sounds as if you're falling for the same prejudiced notions that have me and dogs like me protesting in the streets and boycotting the buses and Dog Parks. You haven't even given her a chance to defend herself, yet you're ready to expel her?"

"I-well—"

"That's where I knew you from! You're a part of those rowdy hooligans who've put so many hard-working dogs out of work with your ways. Why can't you dogs accept that we're separated for a reason? You and your kind can't help but be savages, starting from puppyhood!"

This time, Dominique was on her paws, her snort making the retriever take a few steps back and the corgi shrink down in his seat. For a moment, Dominique felt like tearing the place apart, but then she paused, choked the growl off and shaking her coat. Taissa was better than this, she was better than this, and she wouldn't allow this bigotry to bring out the worst in her, especially when that was exactly what this retriever was looking for to discredit them both.

She stood, motioning for her pup to follow her out the door. Pausing, she turned and look back at them, the smug look on Dorthea's muzzle making her want to growl again, but she swallowed it because when they decided to be craven and low, she, her pup, and dogs like her would go high. Fighting them in their own doghouses would bring her down to their level, where she would surely lose.

"You can call us savages all you like, but we're not the ones making pups out to be vicious or judging a dog's breed against their character. C'mon Taissa."

Dominique snatched open the door to see Alice and Betty, standing there in front of them. The younger poodle yelped and hopped back, her little ears pressed against her head. Betty whined at her daughter and nosed her forward, along with taking a step forward herself.

"I hope we're not too late, but I think my daughter has something to say. Go on, Alice. Tell them what you told me."

The pup clutched at her mother's dress and looked around, her eyes wide and twitchy. When they landed on the worried face of her friend, she swallowed hard but stepped away from her mother's skirts.

"Taissa didn't start the fight. Robbie did. He took my bag and without Taissa's help, I wouldn't have gotten it back. He also pushed her first in the hall while we were walking and laughed at her."

Dorthea took a step back, her face contorted with fury, as she stammered out a retort. "B-Betty Waterhound! To think that you would force your daughter to lie against an upstanding pup like Robbie, in defense of these dogs? The nerve!"

"What nerve, Dorthea?" Betty asked calmly, her curly, white fur shaking lightly. "The nerve to stand up to your son's bullying and even yours? I'm tired of being afraid of your family's influence and strong-arming of the local dogs to stay on top. It may not be much, standing up for this sweet girl and others like her, but it's a start!"

Dorthea's muzzle opened and closed rapidly, before she snorted and grabbed her son by the shoulder, yanking him out the door with her.

"My husband will hear of this, Betty! I won't stand for this, and neither will he!"

The door slammed in their wake, causing Principal Trotter and the pups to shudder. When he recovered, he peered from around his desk and came to stand next to Betty and Dominique.

"I'm sorry for all of this as well, ladies. The Duckfetchs are a powerful bunch and I-well, I shouldn't have cowered to Dorthea. But Taissa," he said, peering over his rimmed glasses at the terrier pup, "I'm sorry for this. I hate to admit it, but I too let some of my preconceived notions get the better of me. Will you accept my apology?"

He held out a paw, which Taissa shyly took, nodding as she shook it. Above the trio, Betty smiled at Dominique and lowered her voice.

"I wanted to apologize for the way that I spoke to you when I offered you the ride home. I was speaking from a place of ignorance, and I ought not have said the things I said."

Dominique tilted her head. She'd never had a poodle apologize to her before.

"Are you sure you want to do that? Won't it offend the other 'ladies' seein' you apologize to me?"

"I couldn't care less what they thought," Betty said. "The other day while my husband was driving me home, I saw some of you all protesting and asking for better treatment. At first, I thought everybody got the same treatment, if they put in the hard work and kept their paws clean, but after talking to you and seeing pups out there, fighting to just be regular pups, well, that got me to thinkin'."

Dominique was frozen, stunned that she would ever hear something like this come from the muzzle of a show dog. "I-I, yeah, we are fighting for what we believe in. We're tired of being treated like second-class dogs."

"After thinking it over," Betty began, "I figured that I should do something—"

"But you have no dogs in this fight. It's not—"

"Yes," Betty replied firmly, "it is necessary. I've been given a better lot in life than some others, and to see dogs fighting to just be able to work like I work and be respected as a regular dog, without being judged for things they'd never do. So, I've decided to help you in your boycott. It ain't much, and I don't 'spect my husband to like it, but I can't keep sitting around and ignoring suffering and injustice. I want to do my part to make it right."

Betty considered Dominique's eyes and those amber pools softened and a slow smile dawned on Dominique's face, as pure and as bright as the first rays of sunshine after a long winter.

"Well, I expect now's as good a time as any, but glad you came on 'round to it."

"Ahem," Principal Trotter coughed, looking up at the pair. "I'm glad that I could help facilitate a meeting of the minds, but I do believe these two young girls need to get back to class. Ladies?"

Dominique and Betty shared a chuckle and waved the pups out of the office. The two poodles padded out of the office, their tails wagging, leaving Dominique and Taissa to follow. Dominique had taken two steps when she felt a gentle tug on her skirt.

"Yes, baby?"

"Thank you for standing up for me today," Taissa said, her tail wagging behind her. "I didn't know that you could be so brave."

Dominique kneeled and hugged her pup tightly, the corners of her eyes glistening. "No, thank you for being so brave. You showed your momma how to stand up for herself and what she believed in, which is more than I could ask for in a daughter."

Taissa didn't respond, just lifted her tail a little higher and hugged her mother before scurrying off to catch up with Alice, ready to discuss the next Stacy Bark book.

About the Authors

Watts Martin lives in Silicon Valley, and can frequently be found writing (and drinking) at microbreweries around Northern California. Watts's works include the science fiction novel *Kismet*, the Cóyotl Award-winning novella *Indigo Rain*, and short stories that have appeared in anthologies including *Inhuman Acts*, *The Furry Future*, and *Five Fortunes*.

Searska GreyRaven has been writing stories since someone was foolish enough to leave her alone with a crayon. When she isn't chasing down some shiny new idea, she can be found herding bees, hoarding books, or attempting to eat her weight in mangos. (Which isn't hard to do, as she is a very smol noodle of a dragon.) She's been previously published in the anthologies *ROAR 8*, *Arcana: A Tarot Anthology*, and *Bleak Horizons*. You can follow her on Twitter @SearskaGreyRvn. *Nevertheless, she persisted.*

A. Humphrey Lanham is a fantasy, social science-fiction, and YA writer. She lives along the Willamette Valley in Oregon. She reads and writes a wide range of fiction, but prefers strong female characters who refuse to cater to patriarchal social structures, expectations of romance, or cultural gender norms and stereotypes.

A. Humphrey is chair of Wordos, an internationally renowned writers' group based in Eugene.

Her interests outside of the literary realm involve kombucha kitcheneering, cat herding, and language learning. She speaks English, German, and French; is learning Spanish and Chinese; and plans on tackling Klingon soon.

She lives with her cat, Ru. He is an anthropologist studying humans and their strange proclivities. She speculates that Ru is actually an alien xenobiologist, but everyone keeps telling her that he is just a common Earth cat. While he is an avid only child, Ru permits his human to pet sit for a variety of stinky dogs.

You can follow the adventures of A. Humphrey (@ahumphreylanham) and Ru (@thecupcakebeast) on Twitter.

Ellis Aen is the nom de plume of a genderqueer author who pretends to be a cross-dressing skunk-fox on the internet.

Back before he had any of that figured out, he was just a guy growing up with his nose lost in the pages of science fiction (*Hyperion*, Dan Simmons) and amazing animal stories (*Tailchaser's Song*, Tad Williams). Despite a passion for reading, it wasn't until stumbling upon the online furry community (FuzzyLogic, FurryMUCK) that he discovered a passion for writing.

After years of struggling with his own sense of identity, the expressive, welcoming (and sometimes a little weird) people there offered him an environment in which to explore himself and his boundaries. In creating worlds, characters, and ideas of his own, he would ultimately find the confidence to become the person he is, today (who is, consequently, also a little weird).

With interests that include the strange, the furry, the occult, the future, and the complexities of the self, Ellis enjoys bucking tradition and subverting expectations, and he is a strong opponent of the demonization of sex, sexuality, and fetishism.

He can be found on Twitter as @skonqfocks.

David M. Sula grew up in Herscher, IL where he and his family raised rabbits out in the country. His love of animals has always been an inspiration for his writing both inside and outside of the furry fandom. He currently lives in Chicago with his pet rabbit Reagan where he is an instructor of first-year undergraduate writing at Columbia College Chicago. David is currently a graduate student here working towards his MFA in fiction writing. He has had other short stories published in *The Lighter* and *The Lab Review*. Beyond teaching, David works as a freelance writer and video editor. In his free time he enjoys creating visual effects and editing short films.

Valli (**Val E Ford**) lives in Oregon and has done so her whole life, with several excursions into the outside world. She almost immediately becomes disenchanted when she is away and returns to her homeland, where she practices as an LMT and is training as a Jedi healer. Her children are old enough to buy this book with their own earnings. She didn't replace the pets who went with the kids to their grown-up homes, but after Jedi school is finished, who knows. She loves West Coast Swing dancing, singing karaoke and standing on top of snowy mountains, but hasn't done them much, lately. She has read a few awesome books by the fireplace, though. She prefers great genre fiction to the classics and just finished watching all twelve seasons of *Criminal Minds* with her favorite guy.

Ryan Campbell has been involved in the furry fandom for 20 years as both a fan and a writer. He has contributed to *ROAR, X, New Fables*, and *Abandoned Places*, and is the author of *The Fire Bearers* trilogy. Other published books include *Koa of the Drowned Kingdom* and *Smiley and the Hero*.

Currently, he is working on multiple projects, including the conclusion to *The Fire Bearers*, a sequel to *Koa of the Drowned Kingdom*, and the RAWR workshop for furry writers.

As a wildlife biologist, **Amy Fontaine** has studied all kinds of creatures, from wolves and hyenas to honey bees. She has collected raccoon tracks and followed whales and sea lions in a Zodiac boat. The wonders of nature never fail to inspire her. Amy's writings tend to be on the fantastical side, and she enjoys dreaming about what the world could be. You can find more of her published work, including short stories, poems, and a novel or two, through her website, https://amyfontaine.wordpress.com.

John Giezentanner finally went to a doctor and was a little surprised by the agoraphobia diagnosis, but medicine really does help and he highly recommends talking to a doctor if you find yourself stuck outside a wall of fear whenever you need to speak or go somewhere unfamiliar. He still ought to get himself into therapy, though. Maybe this year. John lives in Denver, Colorado with Peregrin Underwood, Adam, and Walter (a tabby, a human friend, and a Great Dane, respectively) and commutes to

Boulder to remove invasive plants from natural areas. He writes genre fiction and his stories can be found in *ROAR 7*, *ROAR 8*, and *ROAR 9* and online at fantasyscrollmag.com and, recently, allthatwillburn.com. Check out his twitter @Latrosaurus.

Al Song is a Laotian-American red kangaroo living near the caffeine-fueled city of Seattle. He has majored in German Studies and Comparative Literature, and plans to one day use his degrees to go back in time and interview Franz Kafka. He admires John Green, and his great works of literature have deeply influenced the kangaroo's own writing. Al has also been published in *FANG Volume 8* and *Tales from the Guild 2: World Tour*. When the roo isn't writing or working, his guilty pleasures include watching competition reality shows, wasting time on viral videos, figuring his way out of escape rooms, thinking up how to parody top 40 music on his guitar, and playing flirty bards in tabletop role-playing games.

You can find more of his scribbles at www.furaffinity.net/user/ alsong/ and alsong.sofurry.com/

Bill Kieffer has only one admitted vice -- being himself on the internet (where he is a 6 foot tall – which Bill is convinced makes him very tall – anthropomorphic draft horse that types as Greyflank). He is ever-so grateful to his wife of over 25 years for putting up with him and his unadmitted vices. His coworkers at a virtual reality company totally grok that he's a furry... but are still a little confused by the concept of a married, monogamous bisexual. Humans are funny.

He is a member of the Furry Writers' Guild, a social media volunteer for the NJ LGBT Chamber of Commerce, and a columnist for *Underground Book Reviews*. Past fiction credits include the Cóyotl Award winning *The Goat: Building The Perfect Victim* from Red Ferret Press. More recent publications include short stories in *ROAR 8*, *Bleak Horizons*, *Seven Deadly Sins: Furry Confessions*, and *In Flux*.

"Qibla," the story in this book, is set on Aesop's World, a furry version of Earth that first appeared in "Brooklyn Blackie and The Unappetizing Menu" (see *Inhuman Acts* from FurPlanet). More stories from Aesop's World are collected in *COLD BLOOD: Fatal Fables*, a collection of furry noir stories from Jaffa Books.

Matt Doyle lives in the UK and has been a member of the furry fandom since the 90s. When not writing speculative fiction, Matt can be found blogging about pop culture, working on cosplay, and experimenting with art. Want to know more? Stop by Matt's website, www.mattdoylemedia.com.

Blake Hutchins lives in the green hills of Eugene, Oregon with two very responsible cats who help him raise two free-spirited teenage girls. A member of the Wordos writing group, he has a modest publication history that includes *ROAR 6*, *Writers of the Future Vol. XXII*, *Polyphony*, *Shimmer*, and a variety of lead writer videogame credits such as *Tribes*, *Starsiege*, *Night at the Museum 2*, and *Enigma: Rising Tide*. When not writing or single-parenting, he practices yoga, medieval European swordfighting, and bodyweight training. He is a politically active member of the Resistance.

At six years of age, Kittara Foxworthy first saw Disney's *Robin Hood*; from that point on she was always pretending to be a Fox. At Halloween, she wanted to have a red tail and ears, but her mother talked her into being a cat instead since fox ears and tail were harder to find and more expensive. She found the furry fandom in 1998 through a friend and realized for the first time that she wasn't alone. In late 2010-early 2011, writing became her favorite hobby. Friends who read her stories encouraged her to try to get published. So far she has had some small success in having her scribblings published.

Kirisis "KC" Alpinus is a graduate student of Florida State University and a happy-go-lucky dholf who likes to spend her weekdays reading, writing, and providing social commentary on her Twitter. Her weekends are usually spent playing Magic the Gathering, playing board games, or hunting Pokémon in Pokémon GO. Her favorite foods include fresh-picked peaches, barrel pickles, kimchi, and sushi, the latter being something she'd eat three times a week if able. KC prefers to spend most of her time reading philosophy and zoning out with world mythology and urban legends, but she's always open for enlightening conversation.

Her furry works can be found in the Cóyotl Award winning anthology *Inhuman Acts*, the sci-fi horror anthology *Bleak Horizons*, *Dogs of War II: Aftermath*, *Infurno*, and the upcoming *A Sword Master's*

Tale. When she's not sleeping, she can be found getting into various forms of trouble with a certain purple-striped tiger creature or splurging on Kickstarter games. She'd like to dedicate this story to her niece, mother, and grandmother, who were largely the inspiration for her story.

About the Artist

Kadath is a furry artist who runs on coffee and giraffes.
http://www.furaffinity.net/user/kadath

About the Editor

Your fearless editor, **Mary E. Lowd**, is a science-fiction and furry author in Oregon. She's had more than one hundred short stories published, as well as several novels, including the *Otters In Space* trilogy and *The Snake's Song: A Labyrinth of Souls Novel.* This is the fourth volume of *ROAR* she has edited.

www.ingramcontent.com/pod-product-compliance
Lightning Source LLC
Chambersburg PA
CBHW071903020726
47502CB00003B/871